Andrea Goldsmith originally trained as a speech pathologist and was a pioneer in the development of communication aids for people unable to speak.

Her first novel, *Gracious Living*, was published in 1989. This was followed by *Modern Interiors*, then *Facing the Music*, *Under the Knife* and *The Prosperous Thief*, which was shortlisted for the 2003 Miles Franklin Award.

Her literary essays have appeared in *Heat*, *Meanjin*, *Australian Book Review*, *Best Australian Essays* and numerous anthologies. She has taught creative writing throughout Australia, and has mentored several new writers. She edited an anthology written by The Burnt Fingers Collective, a group of people with gambling problems.

She lives in inner Melbourne.

REUNION

Andrea Goldsmith

FOURTH ESTATE • *London, New York, Sydney* and *Auckland*

Fourth Estate
An imprint of HarperCollins*Publishers*

First published in Australia in 2009
by HarperCollins*Publishers* Australia Pty Limited
ABN 36 009 913 517
www.harpercollins.com.au

HarperCollins*Publishers*
25 Ryde Road, Pymble, Sydney NSW 2073, Australia
31 View Road, Glenfield, Auckland 0627, New Zealand
1–A, Hamilton House, Connaught Place, New Delhi – 110 001, India
77–85 Fulham Palace Road, London W6 8JB, United Kingdom
2 Bloor Street East, 20th floor, Toronto, Ontario M4W 1A8, Canada
10 East 53rd Street, New York, NY 10022, USA

National Library of Australia Cataloguing-in-Publication data:

Goldsmith, Andrea, 1950 – .
  Reunion/Andrea Goldsmith
  ISBN 978 0 7322 8783 2 (pbk.)
A823.3

Cover design by Nada Backovic Designs
Cover images: woman by esthalto/Matthieu Spohn; group of friends by Supernova/Getty
    Images; frame by Adam Radosavljevic/iStockphoto
Photograph of Andrea Goldsmith © Alden Ford
Typeset in 11/16.5 Baskerville BE by Kirby Jones
Epigraph on p vii from *Open Closed Open* by Yehuda Amichai © Harcourt Inc, Florida;
quote on p 166 from 'This Be the Verse' from *High Windows* by Philip Larkin © Faber and
Faber, London; quote on p 167 from 'Lazarus Not Raised' in *Selected Poems*, 1950–1975 by
Thom Gunn © Faber and Faber, London; quote on p 167 from 'Heptonstall' in *Three Books:
Remains of Elmet, Cave Birds, River* by Ted Hughes © Faber and Faber, London; quote on
p 167 from 'Letters to Live Poets, XXI' in *New and Selected Poems, 1960–1990* by Bruce
Beaver © UQP; quote on p 167 from 'Dust to Dust' in *Selected Poems* by Gwen Harwood ©
Collins/Angus & Robertson; quote on p 180 from 'Musée des Beaux Arts' in *The Penguin
Poets. Selected by the Author* © W.H. Auden; quote on p 201 from *Errata: an examined life* by
George Steiner © Weidenfeld & Nicolson, London.
Printed and bound in Australia by Griffin Press
70gsm Bulky Book Ivory used by HarperCollins*Publishers* is a natural, recyclable product
made from wood grown in sustainable forests. The manufacturing processes conform to the
environmental regulations in the country of origin, New Zealand.

5 4 3 2 1   09 10 11 12

To Jenny,
Roger and Jan

The good want power, but to weep barren tears.
The powerful goodness want: worse need for them.
The wise want love, and those who love want wisdom;
And all best things are thus confused to ill.

Shelley, *Prometheus Unbound*

All my life I have loved in vain
the things I didn't learn.

Yehuda Amichai, *Open Closed Open*

REUNION

CHAPTER ONE: The Reunion

1.

On a chill Melbourne evening early in the new millennium, Jack Adelson was driving across town. The city roads were clogged with six o'clock traffic, rap music blared through the open window of a hotted-up Holden. Jack idled closer to the van in front.

The music thumped, the traffic dribbled forward, exhaust smoke hovered in the glare of headlights. Jack was about to realise a dream as familiar as his own skin, a reunion with the friends of his youth. It had been twenty years since they were last together and he should have been excited, he should have been prepared to dump the car and complete the last kilometres on foot. Instead he wanted to whip the car around, ram the accelerator and bolt into the night.

It was Ava he dreaded seeing. Ava Bryant, the woman he had loved throughout their undergraduate years in Melbourne, their postgraduate study in Oxford, and all through her long marriage to Harry. It was the sort of love as futile loves always are, that flourishes best in the absence of the beloved, sustained by dreams and memories and the reliable satisfactions of pure invention. Jack was about to see Ava again, in the flesh and with her husband alongside, and he felt like a man driving to his own execution.

Jack was too honest to blame anyone else for his disappointments, but he was prepared to admit that if not for Harry Guerin his life would have unfolded very differently. When Harry first appeared in Oxford a quarter of a century ago, Jack had already acquired a reputation in the history and culture of Islam, an arcane but, at the time, seemingly secure corner of comparative religion. If his career had followed the trajectory everyone had predicted, he would have taken up a position at one of Europe's universities and on regular visits back to Oxford witnessed first-hand the life Ava shared with Harry. More real contact with her and her husband and his long-suffering love may have dwindled.

Jack was in Oxford and working on his first book when Ava and Harry had returned from Paris with their news.

'We're married.' Ava put her arm around Harry and pulled him close. 'We were married in Paris.' Jack was too horrified to speak. 'Show him Harry.' And the two of them held up their left hands to display identical gold wedding bands. Even in the shock of the moment, Jack noticed how Harry's finger bulged above the ring. Harry Guerin had never been an attractive man.

Jack thought he would manage living just a short walk from Ava and her husband, but as reality gripped him in its practised jaws, the situation quickly became untenable. Jack put his head down, he avoided Ava and Harry, he finished his book and he returned to Australia. From half a world away, it was easy to shift Harry to the shadows while placing Ava, once again, in the high beam of his imaginings.

The letters were partly responsible. Within days of arriving back in Melbourne Jack had written to Ava, a long humorous account of the potholes of homecoming that disguised the misery he actually felt. And she had quickly responded. The pleasure of that letter was astonishing. This written communication, Jack realised, involved the two of them in the sort of intense and intimate conversation he had always longed to have with her. Soon they were exchanging weekly letters in what would eventually become a twenty-year correspondence – not that he could have predicted this when first he began writing to her, for he had intended only a temporary move back to Australia. But by the time he had the stamina to face Ava and her husband again, universities had moved out of the ivory tower and on to the bourse, and comparative religion had either been struck off university registers or absorbed into other more serviceable disciplines.

The contemporary reshaping of universities may have had less of an impact on his career if not for his failure to publish. He had completed a second book not long after his first; but for the past ten years, with the exception of his letters to Ava, he had written nothing new. The prestigious university that had employed him on his return to Australia did not renew his contract, and neither had the less prestigious university where he was next employed. His most recent position had been at a regional university on the South Island of New Zealand, teaching a hotchpotch of ancient history, philosophy and a postmodernist piece of fluff called Religion, the Establishment and *The Sopranos*. It had been a lonely time, during which he had tended his dreams and memories of Ava more diligently than ever. So bloated had they become, there had been neither time nor inclination for his own work. Jack's scholarship had stalled long ago, but in New Zealand it stopped altogether.

With the rise of Islamic fundamentalism and terrorist attacks across the globe, his career's backward slide had recently reversed. And while he was not the only scholar of Islam whose work was suddenly receiving attention, he was one of the few who spoke English without an accent, making him a favourite with the press. The renewed interest in his early work had done little to dispel his own intellectual doubts, but it had swept him out of New Zealand and back to Australia and he was grateful for that. Conrad and Helen had come home too, lured, as he had been, by the Network of Global Australians.

The Network of Global Australians – NOGA – was Harry Guerin's domain, and unsettling to Jack that the person responsible for his present resurrection had been the one to kill off his prospects in the first place. Jack had never associated Harry with serious work. Harry collected corkscrews and barbed wire, he considered himself an aficionado of cheese and an expert in the evolution of the computer. Harry's interests were diverse, obscure and, from Jack's perspective, useless, although on a number of occasions he had actually managed to turn them into paying jobs. His knowledge of French artisanal cheeses, for example, had earned him money over the years, and his passion for computers had helped secure him the NOGA job. The hobbyist had become a planner and organiser. Hard to credit in such a man. Hard to credit that Harry Guerin would ever be in demand for anything.

In the intellectual world there are two types of people, so Jack believed. The first are those who leave their mark, scientists or artists, the true originals. And there are those who make it possible: the housekeepers and trench-diggers. Jack would not hesitate in assigning to the first group Ava Bryant, novelist; Helen Rankin, molecular biologist; and Conrad

Lyall, philosopher and contemporary soothsayer; while he, Jack, might at a pinch scrape into the second – along with the newly fashioned Harry Guerin. It was not a congenial thought.

There was nothing about this reunion Jack would have chosen – except the night. Thursday had been their Laconics night back in their student days, but instead of gathering at a pub as they had when members of the Laconics Society, Ava and Harry had offered their home. Jack would have preferred anywhere else. In a rash of emails he had appealed to tradition, he had resorted to nostalgia, but his friends had opted for comfort and he had been overruled.

The internet had allowed Jack to keep track of the public Ava; she was his screensaver and he kept updating her. But whenever he imagined her, he knew it was a two-dimensional Ava he saw, carefully positioned against a range of self-serving backdrops. He tried to prepare for the real encounter by rehearsing various possibilities and practising potential conversations, but in the end he settled for delay, returning from New Zealand while Ava was away in Kyoto as a writer-in-residence. She had arrived back in Melbourne just the previous week and within hours she had telephoned him, eager that they get together. But still he delayed, for while he might have settled himself sufficiently to talk with her on the phone, he did not trust himself to be alone with her. However, he knew he needed to see her before the reunion, to cushion that first face-to-face shock. So every morning since her arrival home, and despite his flat being on the opposite side of the city, he had visited the street where she and Harry lived, across from the cemetery, in order to catch a glimpse of her, in order to prepare.

Jack had taken up running as a serious preoccupation around the time of Ava's marriage, attracted to that hard pain that manages so effectively to evacuate the mind. Each morning, camouflaged by the crowd of early walkers and joggers, he would coast around the cemetery circuit, slowing his pace as he passed Ava and Harry's house.

It was a large, free-standing Victorian dwelling, which loomed even larger in the vague pre-dawn light. Built of bluestone and hawthorn brick, it had an ornate tessellated tile verandah and a small cottage garden. Like most Victorian dwellings, there was a fence of wrought-iron railings more in service to aesthetics than privacy. Jack would pass the house puffed up with expectation; a glimpse, just a glimpse of her was all he needed. But the curtains were always drawn, the newspaper lay in its plastic wrap on the porch, and the occupants were nowhere to be seen.

In one of her letters, Ava had described how the house had materialised, *fallen to us*, she wrote, as things so often did with her and Harry. On their return to Melbourne two years earlier, they had been introduced to a man at an arts function, a well-read fellow who was also well-endowed with real estate. He rather fancied having a renowned novelist living in one of his properties and had offered the house to them for as long as they liked.

The four friends are atheists. Conrad, Helen and Ava arrived at atheism via Christianity, Jack from Judaism. Yet over the years, as fortune has shone ever more brightly on Ava and Harry, it has occurred to Jack that only a God could be behind such consistent good luck. A large house on a peppercorn rent, a non-teaching university fellowship for Ava, the NOGA position for Harry, financial security and excellent health for both, marital commitment with extra-marital side trips for Ava, it was not surprising that Jack was tempted by the long arm of the Almighty. From his increasingly barren existence, Ava and Harry had it all. And maybe that's why he never bothered to inquire too deeply into Harry's role at NOGA – none of the friends did. Not that Jack had ever been interested in Harry's work. When you loved another man's wife as he had loved Harry's for close on a quarter of a century, it was preferable not to think about him at all.

In one of those sad ironies, or perhaps, again, the mysterious hand of God, Jack had introduced Harry to Ava. It would never have occurred to him that Ava, who could have had any man she wanted, would be attracted to so innocuous a fellow. Harry was reading geography at Oxford but was no scholar, he was Australian but came from Adelaide, he was their age but Victorian in manner, and, unlike the rest of them, he came from money. Indeed, there was so much Guerin money that apparently Harry could have passed his entire life in a leisurely tinkering with his collections. But for some years now, according to Ava, he had been earning a substantial amount on his own account, and for the past two years there had been his work with NOGA.

Throughout their correspondence, Ava had provided regular reports about Harry, and while Jack would prefer that she didn't, neither did he complain. For he loved receiving her letters and he loved writing to her. If words were the only presence, then he and Ava had never been separated – or so he would like to think. No matter where in the world they were, no matter how their other passions were taking flight, they had shared ideas and private confidences, news and gossip, with the intimacy and romance unique to an epistolary relationship. Ava believed they had the best of each other, a friendship without limits. But there were limits: she was the love of Jack's life, while Jack was her beloved friend. And he knew it was better they had lived apart; face to face his love would incinerate the friendship.

2.

The Network of Global Australians truly was Harry Guerin's kingdom. He had conceived it, defined its role, and lobbied the right people for funds and influence. Two years ago, with the planning phase finished, he and Ava had returned to Australia so he could set up the organisation. NOGA's primary objective was to tap into the skills and knowledge of Australians working abroad. Or, in Harry's special vernacular: 'NOGA will ensure that information is effectively sourced from the wealth of Australian talent working overseas.' Into the NOGA offices flowed news from Australians working across the globe, fewer than one hundred members to begin with, but by the time of the reunion, numbering in the thousands. The information was studied, sorted, stored or disseminated as Harry thought best, particularly in light of the organisation's second objective: 'By making extensive use of state-of-the-art technology, NOGA will provide the means to connect people and nations in a way political strategies cannot.'

There was a daily online Australian newspaper, as well as a weekly online journal containing news and articles from business people, politicians, senior bureaucrats, diplomats and NOGA members themselves. NOGA also funded a fellowship program that brought selected specialists home to Australia for periods of up to two years. The fellows would work on their own research, but at the same time, through occasional lectures and consultancies, were expected to provide the public face of the organisation. Jack Adelson, Helen Rankin and Conrad Lyall were the inaugural NOGA fellows.

Harry was NOGA's chief executive officer, a position Jack had confined to the organisation's factotum until a few weeks ago when he saw him on the evening news, a fatter, balder version of the younger Harry, sporting the sort of moustache that had made David Niven appear elegant but looked vaguely sinister on other men, a suited figure in a suited cluster coming out of a highfalutin meeting. It struck Jack as extraordinary that Harry could belong in the corridors of power. The rest of them had their particular talents: Ava her fiction, Connie his philosophy, Helen her microbes, and his own once-noteworthy history of religion, while Harry was a fellow of shallow currents who always seemed out of his depth with the likes of them.

When first they met him at Oxford, they tolerated him with the sort of good humour that comes easily when a person is of little consequence. Harry was so unprepossessing, a squat chest-of-drawers sort of man, with thinning hair, pasty skin and red parallel lips reminiscent of a ventriloquist's doll. Glasses would have improved him but his vision was excellent. Even when his passion for Ava became obvious, Jack, Helen and Connie would, without malice, refer to him as her homunculus, a description that nailed him firmly to the lower rungs of their world. But any goodwill dissipated when a year later Ava married him.

Overnight, Harry went from benign presence to grand usurper. His many odd interests, formerly considered quaint, now condemned him. No well-rounded person collected barbed wire and corkscrews; no well-rounded, well-occupied person would have the time or inclination to collect anything. Harry was, they decided, stupid, insensitive and vain, and that Ava Bryant, loved and revered by them all, had chosen him was incomprehensible.

Nothing Jack had learned about Harry in the years since the marriage had led him to change his mind. But as time passed and with little choice if he wanted to maintain contact with Ava, he, like Connie and Helen, had become less hostile. Harry, Jack decided, was like the edible paper covering traditional nougat: if you wanted the sweets, you tolerated the tasteless accompaniment. Yet as he drove to Ava and Harry's place ✦ that Thursday night, he felt the threat of impending disaster. Nothing to do with what eventually did happen, rather a far more personal trial. All his memories warped by constant reworkings, all his dreams of meeting Ava in far-flung places with Harry out of the picture, all those happy-ever-after scenes worn smooth through over-rehearsal were about to be thrust into the real world. And now, when it was too late to turn back, he knew he did not need to see her – not tonight, not ever again, and, curiosity aside, he did not want to see her. Dreams brook no compromise, and in his dreams she was always his.

3.

A few weeks earlier, Helen Rankin and her sixteen-year-old son Luke had flown in from America. Jack was at the airport to meet them. It had been six years since he had last seen Helen and in that time her career had soared. Not that her work had ever been ignored, but food-borne disease, her area of molecular biology, once so unfashionable was now attracting attention from a broad spectrum of powerful interests. These days Helen spent a good deal of her time away from the laboratory advising policy-makers across the globe.

Despite her new-found eminence it was the Helen of old who exited customs, clad in her usual clash of colours, a pair of iridescent green glasses low on her nose, a laptop tucked under one arm, her passport gripped between her teeth. With her reedy figure and bob of dark hair she had always reminded Jack of Olive Oyl in the Popeye comics. She still did.

For the first few days back in Melbourne, Helen and Luke squeezed into his flat. Jack turned a blind eye to the disorder, he even managed to tolerate the grit and chaos of a teenage boy. Much to Jack's disappointment, Luke was no rare exception in this age of horrible adolescents. His conversation was largely confined to grunts or abuse, all interaction seemed to be mediated through electronic extensions, he was allergic to clean clothes, his skin was an ooze of hormones, and he left a trail of mess. Helen, however, was well satisfied: that he talked to his mother at all and was a passably good student made him an excellent son, she said. Not for the first time, Jack noted how parenthood takes a heavy toll on personal standards.

So much mess and disruption yet Jack relished the company. Such a pleasure to come home to a flat that wasn't empty, so satisfying to cook for more than one person. Flush with an energy he had not felt for years, he flirted with spontaneity, then he plunged: why didn't he and Helen set up house together?

'It would be an unorthodox household, of course,' he said. 'Like Strachey and Carrington.'

'And my son?' she asked.

Jack was triumphant. 'They had cats, we'd have Luke.'

She paused long enough for him to think she might accept.

'It wouldn't work,' she said finally. 'You and I would both want the Strachey role.'

Always the most organised of their group, within a week Helen had rented a house not far from Jack's flat, and Luke had started at his new high school. A few days more and she had acquired some bench space at a laboratory connected with the university. She wanted to return to grass roots, she said, and planned to include the laboratory work as part of her NOGA fellowship.

Then Ava returned from Kyoto. Hearing her voice, hearing her live as it were, had not been as nerve-racking as Jack had feared. In fact he wished – too late – he had not avoided the phone for all the years they'd been apart, for there was something of the same intimacy that characterised their correspondence as he sat alone in his living room with the phone jammed to his ear. But being in her presence was a different matter, so despite her eagerness to see him, he had put her off until the reunion when he hoped the others would provide insulation.

It was important then not to be the first to arrive. But despite doing a load of washing at five o'clock, despite a trip to the supermarket for goods he did not need, despite stopping at an automated car wash and despite the heavy traffic, he turned up at Ava and Harry's exactly on time. The others were nowhere to be seen. Helen was coming from a World Health Organization tele-conference which, she said, could run over time, and Connie, who had arrived in Melbourne just the previous day via the Japan, Asia, east-coast-of-Australia lecture circuit, preferred a grand entrance and was usually late.

Jack parked in the darkened street a block up from Ava's

house and waited. A moment later, with the waiting intolerable, he started the car again. He changed into gear and moved forward a few metres. Suddenly faint, he jerked to a stop, yanked on the gear stick, extinguished lights and engine, wrenched on the door handle and found himself leaning over the bonnet gulping in air. His heart was punching inside his chest, acid punished his stomach; he had not yet set eyes on Ava and he was already falling apart.

He allowed himself only a brief collapse before straightening up and marching along the footpath. He trod with deliberate care, he synchronised his breathing with the movement. He heard the twitter of birds, a jet flew overhead, a door slammed; outdoor sensor lights were activated as he passed. He paced himself out of the panic and, by the time Connie drove up, he was as calm as could be expected in a time of trial.

Back in the late 1970s, when Jack, Helen and Ava were undergraduates, Conrad Lyall had been their philosophy lecturer. In those days it was neither unusual nor frowned upon for academic staff and students to become friends; as for sexual liaisons, they were a common enough rite of passage and wisely ignored. Connie had left Melbourne and his first marriage and moved to Oxford when they did, although in his case it was via a post-doctoral fellowship. And when he took up a position in the US he continued to make regular trips back to Oxford, thereby remaining an integral part of the group. Now, as he unravelled his lankiness from a low sporty vehicle and ran his hand through the cloud of white hair, Jack was aware of an unmistakable joy: Ava might be the passionate centre of his existence but this reunion was not simply about her. Helen and Connie had helped form him; they were cemented into the happiest years of his life.

Twelve years older than the rest of them, Conrad was now in his late fifties. He had never been a conventionally handsome man, his lips were too thin and his nose too angular; but with his ice-blue eyes and the wild white hair he was a man with presence. He had something of the appearance of Bertrand Russell, a likeness, Jack had long suspected, Connie deliberately cultivated.

Jack pulled his hands from his pockets and set off down the street. Connie was walking round the front of the car towards the kerb. Suddenly the passenger door opened and a woman emerged. Jack immediately stopped. Still the same old Connie. He had been back in Australia only a couple of weeks and on a book tour for most of that time, his wife and sons were still to join him from the States, and already he had installed a girlfriend. And because Connie had never been the object of his desire, Jack could look on his foibles and misdemeanours with fondness. Conrad Lyall would never change and there was a good deal of comfort to be derived from that.

Connie swung the woman into his arms. They exchanged quiet words, kissed long and deeply, then she hopped into the driver's seat and, with a hand waving through the open window, accelerated down the street. At the same time, Helen pulled up in her ancient orange Volvo station wagon – oddly hearse-like for a family car, Jack had said when she purchased it a few weeks earlier, although he expected Volvo would be wiser to public taste than he. She and Connie fell upon each other with whoops of delight, and quite a performance given these two saw each other regularly in the States. But then there had always been a larger-than-life quality about both of them; in fact, all three of his old friends were centre-stage people.

As Helen and Connie passed through the gateway into Ava

and Harry's front garden, Jack sprinted down the street to join them. He threw his arms around Connie, he really had missed the old charmer.

'You look bloody great,' Connie said, holding Jack at arm's length. 'A pact with the devil? Plastic surgery?'

'Too much time spent on the outskirts of life,' Helen said quickly, and linking arms with both of them, marched them up the garden path. At the front door Jack slipped behind the others. Connie pressed the bell.

After years of yearning for her, imagining her, taking her through the stations of his days, Jack could be accused of a distorted view, but many would confirm it: Ava Bryant was beautiful. She was poised in the doorway, her mass of golden hair was caught loosely in a clasp, stray curls glistened in the light from the hallway. With the lush hair, the thick dark eyebrows, the heavy-lidded charcoal eyes, the lightly polished skin and the full symmetrical mouth, Ava was a Pre-Raphaelite's dream.

She wore no make-up in the old days and none that Jack could see now. She was coloured naturally, the light and shade just right. And still the same full-bodied figure beneath the filmy flowing clothes she had always favoured. She was utterly familiar to him, yet the curve and shine of her, the ripples and gestures, the ever-changing perspective of her, this presence, this Ava was of an entirely different order to his Ava. Jack jammed his feet together and shoved his hands in his pockets, silently taking her in.

Harry was standing alongside, his arm draped over her shoulder. He was dripping with smiles and importance as he welcomed his wife's friends to his home. The homunculus had done well for himself and he knew it. Sweat bubbled on his shiny scalp, the hand offered to Jack was damp and warm, the moustache was definitely a mistake.

And then Ava was embracing him. Was she holding him longer, closer, than she had the others? Jack could feel her body beneath the gauzy clothes, he inhaled her lily-of-the-valley scent, he heard her murmur something, couldn't catch it, wanted her to repeat it, but she was pulling back, letting him go and leading them all down the hallway into a large living area. Jack moved forward with the others, but his perceptions were latched only on to her. The swirl of voices, the revving figures, the room itself – everything that was not Ava was a blur.

Soon they were seated on couches with glasses of wine and snacks to nibble, and talking their customary accelerated talk as if the years apart had never occurred.

'So, how long has it been?' Helen asked.

'Since Jack left Oxford,' Ava said, smiling at him.

The conversation shifted back and forward, cutting a swathe through personal news, work, travel and, to Jack's mind, containing a surprising amount of gossip.

'Remember Adam, the political theorist from Balliol?' Helen said. 'I bumped into him in Washington of all places. He's come a long way.'

'His work has merely kept pace with his vanity,' said Connie. 'On that alone he could well end up prime minister.'

'And Nicola seems entrenched in Manchester,' Ava said, referring to another Oxford friend. 'She says that if ever she receives a gong from posterity, her mistakes – including Manchester – will be forgiven.' Her great brown gaze swept across the group. 'Do you know Manchester?'

'Of course we know Manchester,' Helen said. 'But when it comes to Manchester, what extent of knowing is necessary?'

They then moved on to someone called Ivan, of whom Jack had absolutely no recollection.

'You must remember him, Jack,' Ava said. 'He was a Laconic for a while, during the time he and Helen had their grand affair.'

Helen laughed. 'Ivan the all-rounder. Such a dab hand he was with a tool kit. Blocked sinks, dripping taps, squeaky beds, rickety shelves, broken clasps on handbags. Any mishap and Ivan would produce his tools.'

Harry raised his eyebrows.

'Oh yes,' Helen was still laughing, 'he was a sexual giant too.'

Jack had no memory of the man.

'I expect I have a photo of him somewhere,' Ava said vaguely.

Soon afterwards, she rose from the couch and slipped into the kitchen. Harry too stood up, topped up their drinks and went to help her.

Connie turned to Jack. 'So how's your work coming along?'

There was no work and there hadn't been for years, but Jack hoped this was about to change. He mentioned a new book – 'Early days at the moment' – and mumbled some generalities about history and Islam.

'You'll need to make it sexier than that,' Connie said. He ran his hand through his hair and down the back of his neck. Languid, smooth, he seemed to lean into his own touch. 'I've got it!' he said. '*Islam the musical.*'

Both Helen and Connie laughed, but not Jack.

'Any longer across the Tasman,' Helen looked at Jack with mock grimness, 'and the loss of humour might have been terminal.'

Jack managed a smile, but in truth he was still grappling with the mysterious Ivan. Why would Ava have a photo of him? What was her relationship with this sexual giant whom he could not remember?

A few minutes later, Ava returned to the living room with a platter of food and no photo. Jack didn't want to eat, he didn't want to talk. The same sick feeling that had walloped him outside came rushing back; he gulped down his wine in an attempt to shift it.

A heated discussion about the best bars in Melbourne started up; even Connie, home for less than twenty-four hours, joined in. Jack left them to their wine lists and tapas and gazed through the glass doors across the lighted courtyard to the old stables that had so captivated Ava when first she looked over the place. There was nothing special about the house, she had written at the time, but the stables were a writer's dream. Her study was on the upper storey, while below, and according to Ava, bursting with his computer equipment and his various collections, was Harry's home office. Even at work they were only metres apart. And no one to blame but himself. Yet all those years ago when he introduced Harry to Ava, he had thought only to please her.

It had happened about twelve months after they arrived in Oxford. Helen and Ava had moved out of college into a flat. In an attempt to rescue home-cooked food and lively conversation from extinction, they decided to revive the Oxford tradition of Sunday brunch. Good conversation required virtuoso conversationalists and many hours passed before the four of them – Connie had not yet left Oxford – settled on the guests. Then they turned their attention to the food. Their attachment to home-cooking owed more to Sebastian's luncheons in

Brideshead Revisited than anything from direct experience, so it was not surprising they nominated originality as the key to success. With a double gas ring, a mini-fridge, neither oven nor grill, limited crockery and cutlery and extremely limited funds, originality was in greater abundance than anything else. It was Helen who finally arrived at the solution: a cheese fondue. It would meet the budget, it would be unique in the experience of their guests, and it was an ideal meal for conversation.

Fondues had been out of fashion for quite some time. Jack eventually found a fondue set tossed in with a herd of crock-pots in one of Oxford's second-hand shops; only the recipe book was missing. He should have left it to Ava and Helen to consult the cookery books at Blackwell's; instead he produced Harry.

He had met Harry in the Eastern Art and Archaeology section at the Ashmolean Museum. The two had got to talking over the Islamic utensils where Harry said he was looking for early forms of the corkscrew. He told Jack that he collected corkscrews and barbed wire, and it might have finished there, except he also mentioned his interest in cheese. Jack, already attuned to supplying as many of Ava's needs as possible, immediately suggested he and Harry leave Byzantium and adjourn for coffee. Within ten minutes, Jack was convinced that this odd, guileless man was the answer to Ava and Helen's fondue problems. So he made the introductions.

Harry provided an excellent recipe as well as the gruyère and emmental for the first fondue brunch. And that's where it should have ended. But he also turned up to the event unin-vited, and once arrived he never left – apparently his plan all along. Years after Jack left Oxford, Ava revealed that the meet-ing at the Ashmolean had been no accident. Harry had long wanted to meet her, and having devised, considered and ultimately abandoned several strategies to bring about an introduction, he had seized on her friendship with Jack. As for the earliest forms of the corkscrew, they dated to the nineteenth century: no corkscrews in Byzantium and Harry knew it. Harry was never the guileless innocent Jack had taken him to be. Then as now, Jack reluctantly conceded, Harry was a man with a profound self-interest and a will of iron to service it.

There comes a time in a life of intense and enduring emotion that it secretes a sort of chloroform. To break the pattern is to wake up under the anaesthetic and it is terrifying. Jack's love was under threat as he sat in Harry and Ava's home watching their perfect duet. She passed food, he poured wine; she went for another bottle, he uncorked it; he called her 'Davey', she called him 'Oak'. And all those fond nudges and casual caresses as they went about their hostly duties. And a shorthand communication of gestures and eye movements, with words used so sparingly they might be grains of caviar.

What about me? Jack was thinking. What about me? as he watched the two of them so easy together.

Sex was partly to blame. Never had he been able to imagine Ava and Harry in bed together – not simply because he didn't want to put Harry where he himself had so briefly been, rather he could not imagine the pale and flaccid Harry Guerin pumping his seed into anyone. Yet within weeks of the fondue brunch, Helen had reported that Harry was an overnight fixture at the flat.

Jack had been incredulous. 'Surely not for sex.'

'The walls are thin, Jack, paper thin. And believe me, they're not discussing Shakespeare.'

Jack refused to accept that aspect of their relationship lasted very long, and when in her letters Ava clearly referred to her bedroom as a separate space from Harry's, Jack found the proof he needed to relegate Harry to a marital twilight zone, a sexual no-man's land. But when he eliminated sex from the marriage, he tossed out all other intimacy as well.

There was no avoiding it now.

He tried to screen Harry out, to focus only on Ava, but she was strange to him. He did not doubt the truth of his Ava, the Ava of his thoughts and imaginings, nor did he doubt the reality of the woman who sat so close he could reach out and touch her. It was more that the two realities were fundamentally different, like the United States is different from Tanzania. As he tried to scramble out of his confusion, he found himself wondering how it might be to live without this love. He felt the possibility like a man losing his footing high above an abyss, a moment of doubt, a moment of falling, a mere flicker and then it was gone.

So make an effort, he told himself. There was a pause in the conversation while Ava passed around a platter of food.

'I was reading an article the other day,' he began, 'in which metaphor was described as the wild child of language.'

'These are delicious,' Connie said, indicating some pastries. 'What's in them?'

While Harry provided the recipe, Jack prepared his comments about metaphor, but he had no opportunity to speak. After the first recipe came another, then another; even Helen who never cooked was listening. And after recipes came a discussion of cars.

'I can recommend a 1980 Volvo,' Helen said to Connie.

From cars they moved on to television, specifically a television series on contemporary philosophy and social life to be hosted by Connie, a multinational production that after years of planning was finally looking as if it might receive the go-ahead.

'There's every reason now to be optimistic,' Harry said, slapping Connie on the back. 'After all, who better than you to make sense of these times?' – as if Harry would know anything about it. Although Connie, Jack noticed, didn't object.

The focus switched to Helen. She said the NOGA fellowship had come at just the right time for her. She needed a break from her usual schedule to take stock of recent trends. 'Scientists don't control the applications of their work any more.'

'They never did,' Connie said quickly.

Helen looked annoyed. She was, she said, enough of an idealist to believe he was wrong.

Jack, who already knew something of her predicament, reached out and put a hand on her arm. 'Not much room for idealism in today's scientific world.'

She shook him off. 'I think you're both wrong. Times have changed and we scientists need to change too. For a start, we need to ask more questions of the funding bodies.'

'So what's the problem?' Ava asked.

Helen removed her glasses and dangled them between her fingers. She took a moment to collect her thoughts, then settled her gaze on Ava.

'In research you put your mind to a task,' she began. 'Your vision is narrowed by the particular problem you're exploring. The way ahead is clear.' Her hand rocked the glasses in a gentle pendulum. 'While you're working on your problem it becomes the whole picture, and your goals, as against the goals others might see in your work, are the only ones that matter.

But they're not.' Her hand stilled, the glasses wilted. 'It's not a simple matter of me and my bugs any more. It's not just about me and my science.'

Food-borne diseases, formerly the domain of scientists, epidemiologists and hygienists, were now of serious interest to politicians and the military.

'Bioterrorism.' Helen shook her head slowly. 'My work is being used for bioterrorism. It's unbelievable.' And she really looked as if she could not believe it.

'What happened about eliminating shigella infections from refugee camps?' Ava asked.

'For some years now, a good deal of scientific research has been funded through military-related companies or the military itself.' Helen sounded defeated. 'Even research into vaccines is funded by the military.'

'Including shigella?' Jack knew a shigella vaccine was the end-point of Helen's work.

'Yes, including shigella.' Helen replaced her glasses, she looked to be on the verge of tears. 'These funding bodies have insisted on complex ownership practices regarding any new science produced. Scientists rarely predict all the applications of their research,' and now her face relaxed into a smile, 'which has led to some amazing and unexpected discoveries. But under the present funding arrangements, my research could easily be channelled into work on biological weapons.' She shrugged, 'I'm faced with some difficult decisions.'

Harry said her NOGA fellowship was ideal for just this purpose. 'And don't forget, there's plenty of help around. Just let me know if there's anything or anyone you need.'

Harry then turned to Jack, cocking his head in such a way that the light bounced off his baldness.

'These troubled times have brought you back into the swim,' he said.

There are bald heads that are classical domes which concentrate the thoughts, others are globes of worldliness. Harry's baldness, Jack decided, was not of either kind. His head lacked hair and the skull thus bared lacked those interesting mounds that suggest wisdom and experience. Harry's head was big. His skull was naked. A numbskull, Jack thought, and stifled a laugh.

'Well, Jack, what do you say about your new popularity?' Harry's voice was raised.

And Jack's humour evaporated. It was as if Harry were conducting the evening, conducting them all. Jack looked across at Ava. She was watching her husband with a smile on her face, gazing at him with unambiguous pride. This new Harry had an unnerving confidence entirely lacking in his younger self. This new Harry, it seemed to Jack, was accustomed to running the show.

4.

Jack was home by eleven. His flat was empty, the evening was empty, his life, if not yet empty, was draining fast. He poured himself a glass of wine and stood at the window, staring into the blackness. From the road outside came the swish of cars speeding people home to families and conversation and someone to sleep with. He stared at the glass until his own image forced itself into consciousness, then abruptly he turned away.

He had chosen the permanent glitter of the remembered past over an increasingly parsimonious present, but now he was wondering if it was nothing more than the comfortable familiarity of the past that made it so attractive. Like nostalgia, that B-grade emotion. For everything about tonight had disappointed: the conversation, the humour, his best and oldest friends.

He refilled his glass and wandered into his study. This room, little changed from his university days, used to be his bedroom; this place where he now lived, was where he grew up; this flat used to be his parents' flat. Around the time he had left for New Zealand, his parents had moved down to Tasmania. Unsure whether they wanted to start again in a new place, they had rented out the flat. But several years later, drawn by what they described as the only truly radical community in Australia and the only location with a civilised climate, they decided to move to Tasmania permanently. In the same week that they put the flat on the market, the NOGA fellowship was offered to Jack. The flat was withdrawn from sale and Jack moved in. He bought some furniture, he stocked the kitchen drawers and cupboards, otherwise everything remained much as it was when he was growing up.

There was a flyer on his study wall advertising an anti-apartheid demonstration and next to it a 'Sisterhood is Powerful' poster; above his desk was a picture of a blood-coloured mushroom cloud and the caption 'One Nuclear Bomb Can Ruin Your Whole Day'. An old school tie hanging from the door handle was pinned with badges: 'When this button melts we are in a nuclear accident'; 'Seen one nuclear war you've seen them all'; 'Who killed Karen Silkwood?'. If he were to flip through his notebooks and diaries of his university days, he would find references to debates, lectures, seminars, radical theatre, late-night readings, seasons of European films, and discussions with an astonishing array of people. There was something intrinsically wonderful about those days when he and the others first met. Such a contrast with the bullish ordinariness of tonight.

Whenever Jack looked back to his university experience and compared it with today's student life, so much seemed to have changed – even friendship itself. Without computers and mobile phones, face-to-face communication ruled the day. He, Ava and Helen had started talking before their first classes, they talked between classes, they talked over lunch in the cafeteria. They talked at the pub in the evening, they talked as they ate supper, they talked long into the night. They trawled through hundreds of ideas across a multitude of subjects. He learned very quickly he would need to get over his shyness if he was to belong to this group; and similarly, a scientist like Helen had to read energetically outside her discipline to be a fully-fledged member.

And there was so much to read. Books were constantly passing between them: Sartre, de Beauvoir, Adorno and Barthes, Ginsberg, Rilke, Rimbeau, Plath, Orwell, Woolf. Lawrence Durrell's *Alexandria Quartet* assumed iconic status, as did Canetti's *Auto da Fé*. In the early hours of the morning alone in his room, Jack would find himself reading not only for his classes and assignments but for conversations in the days ahead.

To attend university in the late 1970s was to enter a promised land where anything seemed possible. There was a church-going, private-school girl in his philosophy class who metamorphosed into a radical lesbian separatist before the end of the first semester; and a classical pianist and first-class dork from his high school discovered basement jazz clubs and reconfigured himself as an avant-garde musician. As for his own guitar-playing, a few weeks after the start of the university year he was regularly performing at an inner-city folk club. Such things just happened: someone suggested it, someone else made the introductions, and suddenly he had a regular paying gig.

Fortified by free education and feminism, mature-age students flocked to the university. Together with Ava and Helen, he met nuns in civilian clothes and housewives fairly bursting out of their narrow lives. They mixed with Greeks, Italians, Indians, Chinese and Vietnamese, throngs of people from Melbourne's multicultural heart. Ava from the white and uniform outer suburbs and Helen from provincial Geelong met people the likes of whom had never before crossed their paths. Even with his own left-wing, Jewish background, Jack's circle of friends was soon more colourful than that of his parents.

For students fresh out of school, university supplied a brilliant sojourn between the restrictions of childhood and the responsibilities of maturity. And it was surprisingly easy. With free education and living allowances, no one needed to work more than a few hours a week, and although money was always in short supply, particularly for Helen, he and Ava were happy to cover for her. Ava, with no family to call on, never seemed to run short. She said she had savings; once she mentioned a bequest from an aunt. Neither he nor Helen pursued it. The personal was far less intrusive back then and a great deal more private.

Theirs was the post-Vietnam generation, wise to authority but not stymied by cynicism. Pre-Thatcher and pre-Reagan the world was more than a collection of GNPs. The iron curtain was still in place although the cries from behind had become disturbingly shrill. No one was denying the repressive culture of Soviet politics any more, but the loss of ideals was palpable in many quarters, and his own parents, who had quit the Party in 1959, were not alone in their political griefs. The Cold War was arctic, and with nuclear stockpiles increasing at a terrifying rate the world was sandwiched between two righteous Goliaths, neither of which was about to fall. In the aftermath of Vietnam and Watergate there was a pervasive anti-Americanism among their generation, but also a loss of confidence in the power and promise of the left. Spin was confined to tops and planets, backroom boys were illegal gamblers, and globalisation and the global economy were yet to enter the lexicon. The marriage between science and the military was still in its honeymoon phase with both parties on their best behaviour, and business donations to political bodies were made with a sturdy veneer of social responsibility. Broadsheet seriousness dominated tabloid trash; CNN was yet to be born and the BBC lived up to its accent. Australia was poised to make its way in the Asia–Pacific region, but in the real world of Europe, the only world that mattered to those like them with scholarly interests, Australia was not on the map. In the post-Nixon era in America and the post-Whitlam era in Australia, politicians in the West had lost much of the respect they had formerly engendered, although were far from being the sweet-talking, poll-driven shysters of recent times. In fact, the cavalier attitude of the self-righteous liar so common to contemporary democratic leaders was thought back then to be the exclusive province of despots and criminals. When they entered university there was a sense of the future, and the future was positive.

It was also young. Far from parents being your best friends, in those days of free will and self-expression, the family, rotting deep in the reservoir of determinism, was definitely on the nose. People moved out of home as soon as possible, and many of them, including Ava, returned rarely, if at all. Both Helen and Ava were the first members of their family to attend university. Helen's parents were proud of their daughter but, according to her, bewildered. Ava marched into the future as if her family did not exist.

Jack was willing to give up sleep for his new friends, he was willing to share his music, he would dress down, read up, he would march for the liberation of women, but when it came to family he was stymied. Family was his connective tissue: to turn away from his mother and father would be to walk away from himself. He, too, was the first of his family to attend university, but unlike the Bryants and Rankins, his parents, forced by circumstances to leave school early themselves, had always touted tertiary study as a basic essential of life, along with food, drink, shelter, warmth, a sense of history and left-wing politics. He would observe Ava and Helen as they shaped themselves according to the times and their ambitions, and even if he had wanted to follow suit it would have been impossible. It was as if he were grafted onto his parents and their past, saddled with all the hopes and opportunities denied by Polish anti-Semitism, by Hitler, by the brutal deaths of aunts, uncles, cousins and neighbours who had remained in Poland long after his own grandparents had migrated to Australia. Then there was communism and the years of loyalty, visionary years followed by confusion and distress and disbelief and finally his parents quitting the Party not long before he was born. Jack doubted he would ever be a child of his times although he tried to make light of it. 'I am a cyst on history,' he wrote at the top of a blank page. But despite his efforts, neither the essay nor his levity progressed.

He knew that Ava and Helen envied him his background; more families like his, they said, and the institution might be worth saving. And he accepted their compliments, although in truth what they admired he had experienced primarily as discomfort. He was convinced that 1960 was a most inauspicious time to be born. All the excitements of the sixties, the new politics, protest music, students determined to strip the world of their parents' mistakes, all of this was happening while he was still in primary school. Too young to have a personal stake in the movement for change, as the child of activists he nonetheless found himself at its centre.

He had marched with his parents in Vietnam moratoriums and anti-apartheid demonstrations; he had accompanied them on each new campaign championed by the left. But he wasn't of draft age and he wasn't under threat; he was just a child, a child, moreover, who hated crowds. The crush of people so much bigger than he was, the shouting, the huge banners with their precarious lurchings, how he envied the babies and toddlers protected by prams and strollers. And he couldn't rely on his parents to look after him as they were seasoned banner carriers and loudhailer users. He might well have attended some of the defining moments of the sixties and seventies but his childish fears and failings were inflamed to a far greater extent than any political passions. For all that Helen and Ava admired his background, all too often he had felt a fake.

Family aside, in most other respects he, Helen and Ava inhabited the same made-to-order, one-size-fits-three utopia, and a queer business how oddballs and outsiders managed to find one another. Not that it was always a happy liaison. Lawrence and Loeb, for example, gravitated together only to commit what turned out to be the not-so-perfect murder, and

Parker and Hulme, those two imaginative creatures from New Zealand, suffered a similar fate. And there were some outsiders like Orwell and Wittgenstein who abhorred other outsiders. But not so for the three of them. After years of finding sanctuary in the solitary protectorates of their own minds – the same solution for all three despite their different backgrounds and sensibilities – they arrived at university and found one another.

Most conversations would find them in an impassioned state of wonder, most days an exhilaration which never ceased to amaze. Serenity was on the dark side, serenity looked across the river to death; together they experienced so much that was new, and change itself seemed to add to the intensity. They fell in love with ideas, they fell in love with books, they fell in love with films and songs, they fell in love with their tutors who fell in love with them, and they fell in love with each other – although only Jack would make it an enduring devotion. Restraint was practised very occasionally and only when issues of safety were involved. Like most students at the time, they believed all ages of consent should be lowered, marijuana should be decriminalised, judges and lawyers should stay out of the bedroom, that the law was an ass.

They regarded their friendship as special, and wondered, or rather hoped, they were perpetuating the tradition of the Bloomsbury group or the Cambridge Apostles or the luminaries who gathered at Sylvia Beach's Shakespeare and Co in Paris. They assumed they would always be friends.

'Early friendships are cemented with the hardest glue,' Ava had proclaimed one evening, about a month after they all met.

As for the wider world of the 1970s, it came via films and music, books and periodicals, all reinforcing how very seriously Australians had missed out. Australia had neither Jimi nor Janis nor Woodstock nor Black Panthers. There were no Beats on or off the road. Critics like Foucault and Barthes would starve in the wilderness that was Australian culture where intellectuals were regarded as less desirable than dole bludgers. There were no Australian Buñuels or Wertmüllers or Herzogs, and the only thriving political groups were feminism and the anti-nuclear movement and these were nourished by their overseas counter-parts. The brain drain of the fifties and sixties that had eased during the Whitlam years was again a stream and they planned to add to it. They wanted to make a difference, they wanted to contribute to the future, and there was no point in staying where they were not appreciated. Indeed, the major reason for being at university in Melbourne was to acquire the credentials to be transported to a university elsewhere.

And yet despite its apparent shortcomings, there was a sense in which Melbourne, located in a country from which they all felt estranged, provided well for them. Together they discov-ered an underground city, a secret intellectual city of art-house cinemas and makeshift theatres where entry was by donation and included a tumbler of wine. They patronised bookshops without street frontages and attended public lectures in dusty back rooms. They read alternative journals and newspapers and a welter of broadsheets. And in pubs and cafés and clut-tered student houses at all hours of the day and night they argued about love, death, betrayal, responsibility, progress, goodness, evil, marriage, as if these concepts had never before been properly considered.

One night at the pub in the middle of a particularly volatile argument on the origins of evil, Helen suddenly pitched forward, held up her hands and silenced the lot of them.

'We should start a club,' she said, 'a club for discussion – like the Cambridge Apostles. We could invite others to join, choose an evening, a venue, present papers, make a few rules.' Helen was now on her feet. 'It would have to be secret of course, for the mystique factor. And members would need to pledge eternal loyalty to one another and the life of the mind.'

And so the Laconics Society was born. They settled on Thursday evenings for their meetings and the pub in which the proposal was first advanced became the first location. They used a room off the main bar – formerly the ladies' lounge, according to the publican, 'Back in the days before women's lib, when there were sensitive female souls who could only swallow alcohol separately from men.'

Helen and Ava were quick to remind him that away from the environs of an inner-city university, ladies' lounges were still essential to Australian life. And in an aside to Jack, Helen had added, 'My mother would prefer to be seen in her under-wear than in a public bar.'

The former ladies' lounge suited them well. The walls were a pale khaki and adorned with cigarette posters: Kent, Lark, Camel, Marlboro, Kool, Craven A 'they never vary', Turf cork tips, and 'fresh as a mountain stream' Alpine. The floor of ancient pine boards was heavily gouged and stained with cigarette burns and booze; over in a corner they dubbed Pollock was an interesting splash of blue and orange paint. There was a table of murky green laminex roughened with food and spills which Jack attacked with steel wool and cleanser the afternoon before the inaugural meeting. The chairs with slatted backs and wooden seats were so uncomfortable they could only have been designed by a misanthropist and purchased by a publican who never sat with his customers.

The Laconics Society endured throughout their under-graduate years and reconvened when they moved to Oxford.

Every Thursday they would meet to hear a paper presented by one of the members, followed by raucous discussion fuelled by house wine and hot chips. Membership was by invitation, and once admitted members were bound to secrecy.

Ava, Helen and Jack formed the core group, to be joined at the end of the first year by Conrad Lyall – Connie. Other members were drawn from classmates, from Connie's best students, and from their own lovers, many lasting only as long as their affair with one of the founding members. The weekly meetings rarely garnered more than six people, but no matter how tired they were or at war with the world, no matter how severe the headache or chest-cold, no matter how hostile the weather, Jack, Ava, Helen and Connie when he was in town, would attend.

Other interests simply could not compete. Apart from Ava and Helen's feminist groups and the Campaign for Nuclear Disarmament they joined no clubs. Although Jack had long been partial to sport, specifically middle-distance running, a predilection he kept to himself, not because he was unable to defend an interest in sport, but he worried he might be a middle-distance man.

Unlike the others, he lived in constant discomfort. He didn't like it this way, but it was how he understood living in good faith to be.

'Like Hell,' Ava had commented after listening to a paper he had presented to the Laconics on the nature of perfection.

'But always in sight of the sublime,' he had replied, looking pointedly at her. He paused a moment before adding, 'I suppose I could apply for a transfer to purgatory.'

'I don't think that would be much of a promotion,' she had said.

Ava, in contrast, was happy and she made others happy.

Even at eighteen she was possessed of great intellectual sympathy, an almost tangible effect she had of being in step with you, of knowing you in a way no one else did. When she listened, she seized you with her great hooded eyes and in you went as if she were permeable, and you never wanted to leave. What Ava recognised in others and what needed to be protected was passion itself. People without passion are wasting themselves, she would say. She lit up the skies, and not only for herself.

One day during their second term at university, when she and Jack were hurrying across campus to meet Helen, suddenly she stopped. It was dusk, a light rain was falling, her face was pale with cold and the mass of caramel curls glittered wetly. She raised her arms to the sky, he had to hold himself back, hold his own arms tight to his sides.

'This is exactly how I hoped university would be,' she said.

They discovered the world together, the three of them and, by their second year, Conrad Lyall too. Every day was marked with wonder. None of them demonstrated temperance when it came to reason. The brain, the mind, was an instrument of excess. They were contemptuous of sleep: it was high tide every hour of every day.

You know what it is like. You hear a piece of music from long ago, you pick up an old book, you find a scrap of faded photocopying or catch a vaguely familiar scent and you are whisked back to a time that was – truly – perfect. And nothing, neither years nor experience can harm it. Memory is a stalwart protector and the sturdiest of time capsules.

So how to explain tonight? Jack wondered. Either his memories had failed him or his friends had changed in ways he could never have predicted. And what was he now to do? With his friends? With his stalled work? And most of all with Ava? After a single evening of her real presence, he had a strange sense of himself in the third person, no longer the narrator of his own life.

He closed his eyes, as if that would silence the questions, and set about re-creating one of his Ava dreams. Venice, he decided, they would meet in Venice at the end of winter for the Festival of the Masks. He creates Venice's narrow passages, the canals and bridges, he selects for himself a magnificent mask of gold and black leather with glossy feathers fanning wide to each side of his head, he sashays out into the streets. It's a cold, white day, the air so crisp and clear it dries the throat. The crowds, the laughter, the men in flowing cloaks, the women in lavish costumes, he creates them all. And now, coming towards him, the familiar shape, the familiar walk. But he can't make it right. And the clothes, he can't find the right Ava clothes. And there's no mask, just a white porcelain oval where her face should be. Something is happening, his dream is not working, the familiar scenes are dissolving. He opens his eyes, he can't make the dream work. What has always been so easy is suddenly impossible.

He goes to his desk and takes out some notepaper: he will write himself back into a familiar world, he will write to Ava. But a half-hour later he gives up. After thousands of letters to her, his words have jammed.

5.

Ava lay propped against her pillows, gazing through the bedroom window. The sky was a uniform whitish-grey, the trees wallowed in the wind. She heard the rattle of the window in the bathroom, and from the kitchen the clatter of crockery as Harry prepared his breakfast. She tightened the quilt around her and nested into its softness. The wind blustered, the trees pitched, while inside the house a stillness fell as Harry settled to his food and newspaper.

A scattering of books lay next to her on the bed. Ava opened a volume of poetry then put it down again; still caught in the mood of last night, her reading could wait. The familiarity of them all, the familiarity of herself with these her oldest friends. The same ease and spontaneity they had always enjoyed, the same blunt candour, the unparalleled pleasures of a social occasion stripped of the usual protective devices, she had felt her brain springing into action. She had, in short, felt miraculously restored.

These past two years it was as if she had slipped off the tracks of her life. Trapped in the same drab wasteland day after day, her brain might have been dust; as the months stacked up, not only did she no longer recognise herself, she became less and less sure who her usual self was. But after last night, Ava felt again the swirl of possibility, that familiar sense she could achieve whatever she set her mind to. Last night she had discussed and gossiped and questioned and listened with a lightness and ease she feared had deserted her forever. Last night she had not given Fleur a single thought. Last night, far from thinking she was finished as a novelist, she felt again the urgency that had propelled her through six novels. She was now sure there would be several more.

Her poor lagging brain, she had wondered if she were losing her mind. Yet there were obvious reasons for her functioning below par. Not simply the long aftermath of Fleur, nor her current novel dragging its feet, but the return to Australia after a twenty-year absence posed many more difficulties than the exciting perils of a youthful leaving. And there had been concerns about Harry too.

Her husband was a careful, meticulous man with talents that had never been fully tested. And while she and Harry had made a point of not interfering with the other's work, she had nonetheless been worried that NOGA was a rather large challenge and the ramifications far-reaching should he fail. Then there was his involvement with her old friends, not actually directing their work, but certainly overseeing it and managing the funds. Knowing her friends and knowing what they thought of her husband, this situation was so potentially fraught she had hardly dared consider it. But last night her friends had treated him as one of their own; for the first time ever Harry had been part of the group.

From the beginning, she and Harry had observed that unwritten marital geography whereby husbands and wives skirt around fractious topics. Jack, Helen and Connie could easily have driven a wedge between them, but Harry, preferring better than evens chances when embarking on an argument, had left the issue of her friends well alone. Despite what her friends might think, her husband was not stupid.

Although during those early years in Oxford they had often treated him as if he were. All those evenings of exuberant argument – Ignorance and Pragmatism, The Novel as Truth, The Death of Metaphysics, Science and the Murder of Morals, The Death of the Family (death always figured prominently among their interests), accompanied by makeshift food and flagons of Spanish gut-rot, the group of them squeezed into a beery alcove leaving caution behind at the pub door as they throttled that week's Laconics topic. And hours later, still fired up, they would tumble into the streets, all spark and histrionics among the Oxford stone, as they each tried to out-quote the others from Eliot, Shakespeare, Yeats and the main herd of Romantic poets, advertising their Dionysian spirits as much for themselves as for any nocturnal passers-by. Helen, Jack, herself, Connie too when he was in England, and Harry always as fifth wheel. Night after night of their own essential ecstasies with Harry by turns aggrieved and silent, defensive and monosyllabic, or aggressive and opinionated as he trawled through one of his pet topics indifferent to the disinterest of the others.

These discussions with her friends were not only fun, they formed an essential part of her life. But Harry was essential too. Many were the times she had interrupted her own pleasure in order to rescue him, which made the others resent him all the more. With or without her help, it seemed her husband would always be shunted to the margins of their group.

That Harry seemed unfazed by her friends impressed her from the outset, revealing as it did a sense of self and purpose immune to the generally partisan judgments of others. Harry was always reliably Harry and she derived a great comfort from that. Fortunately she had never been the type to want the people she loved to love one another; indeed, in service to her own freedom, she had struggled to keep her loves separate. But in the case of her husband and her best friends it had not been easy, and a little less rancour between them would have cut some slack in a life already pushed to the limits.

During the past several years with the others living in different parts of the world, the high-pitched strain they had placed on her marriage had been absent. She had seen each of them when they had come to England or she had travelled abroad, but singly they were easier to square with her marriage than ever they had been as a group. And there had been Fleur too; balancing her with the friends as well as Harry would have required planning and endurance well beyond her capabilities. Of course she had missed them, they were after all her only true friends, but in many respects it had been easier with them at a distance. And there was no escaping Harry's pleasure they no longer trespassed on the daily terrain of his life.

What a relief, then, last night had been. Harry had joined the various conversations, he had cracked jokes and aimed pot-shots at some shared and deserving targets. As for the discussion about NOGA, Harry had guided it with an authority never before seen by her friends. And while Ava suspected they would accuse him of attempting to shore up kudos in their own circle, many people across the world kowtowed to her old friends, but her husband did not. What Harry had done, she knew, was for the benefit of the Network.

She could hear him rummaging about in the kitchen again, filling the kettle, the scrape of the coffee pot on the sink, the door of the fridge opening and closing, the familiar movements of a long marriage. And a short time later there he was in the doorway of her room, a mug of coffee in each hand. He bent down to kiss her, then propped himself on the edge of her bed. They launched into a post-mortem of the previous night.

'Entirely successful,' Harry concluded. 'Although I can't say any of your old mates has changed.'

'Helen struck me as rather subdued.'

'If she's sensible she might well be the next Australian to win a Nobel.'

Ava grabbed his hand. 'You really have that much faith in her?'

'I have faith in her need to do science and I don't think she'd let anything stand in her way.' He paused, 'I intend to remind her of that.'

'You wouldn't want her to do anything morally questionable.'

Harry raised his eyebrows. 'You know her better than I do. Would she be capable of that?'

They moved on to their plans for the day: Harry had several meetings and Ava was heading to the university library; they would meet up later at the NOGA cocktail party. There followed a summary of the news – Harry was a dedicated reader of newspapers, Ava was not – some gossip about distant acquaintances, their usual morning rout, and how they never ran out of conversation Ava did not know. When she had finished her coffee, Harry took her mug to the kitchen, washed it and put it away as he always did. He collected his things for the office and returned to her bedroom to kiss her goodbye. Then his heavy tread down the hallway, the opening and closing of the front door, the clink of the gate and he was gone.

An hour later, wrapped in coat and hat, Ava strode through the parkland on the western side of the cemetery, powered by an energy largely absent these past couple of years. She passed joggers and walkers on the path and students muffled in coats; she inhaled deeply as a smoker drifted by. There was a line of nuns' graves on this boundary of the cemetery, all of them plain grey stone and each identified with the nun's religious name and her dates. The earliest deaths had occurred in the 1950s when the order, the Carmelites, had clearly made a large investment; the latest had died only recently and there were many unmarked plots for nuns to come. After a life cloistered together, all the sisters were buried together, and why it should be such a moving thought today – Ava actually felt a prickling of tears – she did not know. But if the gate on this boundary had been open, despite her eagerness to start work she would have entered the cemetery and sat for a while in silent contemplation with the sisters.

Instead she pushed on towards the university. The day was cold, with one of those saw-blade winds unique to Melbourne and a sky murky with cloud; it looked as if it would rain. Ava picked up her pace. She could see the towers of the residential colleges, and beyond them, out of view but lodged firmly in the topography of her mind, Melbourne's town centre of shops and churches and Victorian buildings and the lovely jumble of bluestone lanes. This was the city she had discovered as a university student and how quickly it had become familiar, as familiar as family – an ideal of family and certainly not the Bryants. Familiarity. Family. Most people have forgotten the connection. Ava had been back in Melbourne for two years, but only now did she realise how very pleased she was to be home.

'I think I have a greater need for place than you,' she had once said to Helen. It was a moment of rare confession and she had quickly pulled back. But the fact remained: a city was easier to love than people, you could love it unself-consciously, without performance and it demanded nothing of you in return. Ava had known this ever since her eighteen-year-old self had left her mother and brother in the outer suburbs, shed her failed past, and moved the thirty kilometres to inner Melbourne and the university. And there, surrounded by books and conversations, in the shadows of huge trees and lofty buildings, in cafés and streets crowded late into the night, she met the people who would become her lifelong friends: Helen Rankin, Jack Adelson and Conrad Lyall.

You must change your life, Rilke, one of her favourite poets had written, and Ava had taken him at his word. In steady and sometimes reluctant increments she had transformed herself from an hereditary shopgirl with a confined future to a university student and woman of the world. Everything she had hoped for had eventuated: university in Melbourne and then Oxford, a long, loving marriage, friends, travel, excitements and the only career she had ever wanted. And it had all started here.

'My university,' she thought, as she entered the campus and made her way towards the union building. 'My university,' she had thought all those years ago when first she entered here as a student.

It was early March and very hot her first day of university. She had entered by the same gate she had used today, and had lingered at the edge of the quadrangle in front of the union building. She remembered so clearly the moment with its surprising realisation: home was familiar and yet she had been burdened with self-consciousness, while here, where everything was new, she was brimming with comfortable anonymity. As she stood in the swelling heat on her first day of university, she realised that this levity, this ravishment, was happiness.

She had walked to the campus alone, better to stamp the experience on herself. The heat for once had not bothered her, softened as it was by the old European trees. The air, she remembered, was juiced with fresh-mown grass. She had strolled towards the union building, past the university bookshop packed with students, all the buildings so massive and solid, weighted by age and accumulated knowledge, or so she liked to think, and such a contrast to the squalid portable class-rooms of her high school. She passed from the heat of the day into the cool of the law faculty cloisters and there found herself in as foreign a place as any of Europe's ancient universities. Overhead were Gothic spines, the slabs of stone beneath her feet were worn smoothly concave, her sandals slapped with an other-worldly echo. Yet foreign as it was, she knew she belonged here, in these cloisters, at this university, surrounded by people she wanted to know, and all of them intellectuals – how she loved the subversive curl of that word. This university would truly be her Alma Mater, and a far more bounteous mother than the one biology had allocated to her.

You must change your life.

Some people pull themselves up by the bootstraps, Ava had used her brains. Every step of the way the emerging Ava had been forced to hack away at the life she had inherited. By the time she began university, she had shed everything from her background except her name.

Ava. After Ava Gardner, whom Meryl Bryant had glimpsed during the filming of *On the Beach,* an event that had marked a high point in an otherwise flaccid life. When Meryl found she was pregnant, it was ordained that if the baby were a girl she would be called Ava. The choice of name was Meryl's single attempt to love her daughter. But while language can deceive, cajole, distort, convince, disguise, seduce, a single word, a single name cannot produce miracles.

Hollywood Ava might easily have overshadowed Australian Ava, but instead, the circumstances of young Ava's naming persuaded her that deep down her mother really did love her, and it fuelled the driving passion of her childhood: to extract that love. Later, when she realised there was no love and no effort of hers could conjure it up, the circumstances of her naming shaped Ava's desire to escape. Ava Gardner had famously described Melbourne as an ideal place to make a film about the end of the world. She had been desperate to leave, so too was her Australian namesake.

During the stiff pallid years of childhood, Ava had no conception of her future and this frightened her, but she was drawn to the idea of destiny and allowed her imagination to play through a range of attractive futures. What remained indisputable was that like the ugly duckling she had been plopped into the wrong pool. As for the right pool, the right family, it was not so easy to define; indeed, as the years passed and her mother's indifference became evermore entrenched, Ava had a sense she was not made for any family. Or perhaps it was more fundamental: she simply was not suited to childhood.

It took Ava most of her youth to learn that no matter how well behaved you are and no matter how helpful, if your mother has decided she doesn't want you it is well-nigh impossible to change her mind. Meryl Bryant never actually said Ava had wrecked her life but she made it clear she believed this to be the case. She insisted she would have managed with only one child, particularly as Timmy was such a love. But this second child, this Ava, who would never have been conceived if not for an alcohol-soaked mistake after a party when she and Bob had tumbled into bed together, this child she was carrying when Bob walked out never to return, this child made life an impossible burden.

Ava's childhood was a shabby affair for both mother and daughter. When the mother was too cold or the home too hostile, Ava would escape to the streets. But there's nowhere to take your confusions and disappointments in the suburbs, no hiding places where you can dream of a better life, no crowded streets in which to lose yourself, no warm nooks in which to read without disturbance. A civic centre that included a library was built when Ava was ten and this supplied a welcome bolt hole, but the suburban streets always condemned her just as much as her family. She did not dare complain, after all, she was fed and clothed, she had a roof over her head, she received gifts for her birthday and at Christmas. But her mother and brother resented her, and despite her efforts to be useful to them, they were not interested in her help, they were not interested in her.

Ava knew that come sixteen her mother expected her to leave school and start work. Other bright girls opted for nursing with its learning on the job and accommodation in the nurses' home. But just as Ava could not see herself as the shop-girl her mother had been, neither could she see herself as a nurse, not even as a means to an end. And the end? To live overseas and be a writer. She needed to finish school and she needed to find a way of paying her mother rent and board while she did. The way she chose would have led many people to condemn her if they'd ever found out, although she always knew they would have condemned Stephen a great deal more.

She kept Stephen secret and she kept her ambitions secret, for to reveal them, she believed, would spoil them. But even with a major ambition finally realised, the start of university and the happiest day of her life, she was aware of a drag on her heart as natural and permanent as the heartbeat itself: that she would grab her mother's affection without a moment's hesitation should it ever be offered. She would observe mothers smoothing their child's hair or wiping a smudge from a young cheek. She would see them rolling up their child's sleeves before play or reaching for a small hand before crossing a street. She would notice all these small motherly gestures that no one notices because they are so small and normal, and could not ever remember her own mother doing such things for her. But she missed them, and she wanted her mother still. She nursed this irrational desire like a punch-drunk fighter who still believes the title will be his; it was her burden and it refused to be wished away.

That first day of university she had arrived early, and with ample time to enrol she had wandered through the campus before returning to the quad outside the union building and a grassy patch in the shade of one of the old trees. The heat was filtered by a light breeze; she shuffled against the bark until she found a smooth hollow, then rummaged in her bag for her copy of Rilke – this was a day deserving of ritual – and opened the book to 'Archaic Torso of Apollo'. She lit a cigarette, and hidden behind her sunglasses she recited the poem silently by heart.

You must change your life.

And so she had. With a hefty swag of unrequited longing and sufficient knock-backs for a lifetime, she intended to pack up her past and shove it out of sight. Don't be a masochist, reason insisted in her sweet firm voice, just turn your back and walk away; that R.D. Laing and David Cooper had announced the death of the family reinforced her decision. Life with her family had been like an interminable stay at a railway station, waiting for that special train to whisk her home. It would never come, it was never going to come. And should she ever be tempted to linger a little longer, there was the final evidence: Meryl had gone shopping the day her daughter left home, she had not even said a proper goodbye.

Nostalgia and love fertilise childhood's attractions, Ava reminded herself, and she had recourse to neither. She would leave childhood behind and stream into the future without the sting of disapproval to slow her down.

She leafed through to Rilke's *First Duino Elegy* and read the familiar words. Every angel *is* terrifying – Rilke hit the jackpot there. Hide, reveal, do whatever seems best but always take the plunge. Ava longed for angels, though she was quite prepared to take the devils as well. And at that moment, right on cue, Stephen appeared from the union building. She watched him stroll towards her, watched his deliberate slowness, his careful nonchalance, the delicate stretch of his own pleasure. Stephen, her own angel–devil. As he drew closer, his greying hair lifting in the breeze, his large frame slightly stooped and, yes, endearing, it occurred to her that freedom, like ambition, always requires some degree of secrecy. Stephen had spelled freedom to her, he still did, and while there was a price to pay it had always struck her as a bargain.

And here he is, smiling and greeting her – and uneasy; she senses his nervousness as he meets her in this public place. He refuses the invitation to join her on the grass: forty-something university staff are wary of grass-sitting with students fresh out of school. Yet still he lingers.

He indicates her Rilke. 'One of the first books I gave you.'

She opens to the dedication: Stephen's name crossed through with a single stroke and written beneath in his neat familiar script: *For Ava, from my library to yours.* It was an early gift; later he would never have been so careless as to leave his full name. But then later there was more to be careful about.

In the unaccustomed awkwardness between them, Ava finds herself searching for words. Usually there's so much to talk about: books, politics, theatre – he has taken her to the theatre many times – films, people in the news; she can discuss anything with this man who might have stepped out of a book he is so different from other adults she has known. And he looks after her, properly cares for her, not like her mother, and certainly not like her terminally absent father.

He is talking, his voice is low, and instead of his usual eloquence punctured with sharp questions he plies her with platitudes about her first day at university – he actually refers to 'the first day of the rest of your life'. And she knows he is wanting reassurance, but he won't ask; Stephen is strong but the nature of their relationship makes her stronger. So his questions remain unspoken while they make idle chat about enrolment procedures and signing up for the best tutorials. The wind picks up; he bends down and brushes a stray wisp of hair from her cheek. Quickly he retracts his hand. And a short time later, with nothing left to say, he walks away. He looks old, she thinks, as she watches him enter the crowd. He *is* old.

During the past three years with Stephen, she has delved into literature and history and philosophy. During the next four years at university she will amass experience and acquire wisdom. Already she has written several stories, enough to know that in fiction she can be most of all herself, a fluid self, a restless and knowing self, a self cloaked in magnificent disguise. She will find her own way as she always has done. She will go where the hard flame burns. She will be fearless, and she will write.

Twenty-five years later, her Alma Mater was still proving to be bountiful, with a non-teaching fellowship, library privileges, and a well-equipped office. Very little had changed at this end of campus – some landscaping, more places to sit, a bank and post office in the approach to the quadrangle, but it was very different inside the union building. No longer the messy cafeterias smelling of chips and boiled peas, no longer the trestle tables packed with students shouting to be heard over the general clamour, the union had been taken over by commercial food outlets and resembled a miniature food hall. Formerly the hub of the university, this place with its efficient renovations was now almost deserted, and hovering in the sedate space an echo of something lost. Ava found the nearest exit and hurried outside.

She walked past mostly familiar buildings and soon her face was prickling with warmth. There was a gorgeous pull on her thighs, she sprang from stride to stride in her cushiony shoes, she removed her hat and shoved it in her pocket and pushed herself forward in one of those floating moments when all which makes a responsible, civilised human being is legitimately switched off – like in meditation, or listening to music, or playing pinball, or the third drink alone. Harry had at last found a job he loved, her best friends were just a phone call away, and the weight of Fleur was finally shifting. Now she would start working again.

Ever since she and Harry had returned to Australia, she had struggled to hold Fleur locked in memory, but despite her efforts there had been a steady oozing through the cracks. She knew that the end of the affair had been a good thing, but it was good in an abstract moral sense, just as the affair itself had been bad in the same abstract moral sense; but neither the affair nor its ending had settled calmly in the far-from-abstract beat of her heart. She had tried to be disciplined – she truly wanted to forget. The early years of passion and pleasure could not be revisited, the cards and letters could not be reread, the box filled with all those silly treasures lovers keep could not be opened. Because of the pain, all of the good – and there had been so much good – had been put in storage along with the rest. Throw it all out, Ava had told herself when she was packing up the house in Oxford, throw this stuff out. But she couldn't. Not the letters nor mementoes, and not her own diaries with their predilection for misery, pages of detailed yet incredulous accounts of Fleur's neglect, pages more of her own pathetic crawlings – no humiliation was too much to keep Fleur in her life. All these welts and wails were as impossible to read now as the love letters which had preceded them.

But the work had been marvellous. In the six years before meeting Fleur there had been two novels; then came the extraordinary rush of four novels in seven years. 'I'm your muse,' Fleur said after the first of the four was finished. 'You're my muse,' Ava said again and again during the writing of the next three. And so Fleur had been; how else to interpret the drone of the past two years? Ava had turned in desperation to the two novels written before she met Fleur, searching for evidence that she could write without her. And while she had read the novels with both pleasure and relief – if she could do it then, she could do it again – it was only now, after last night's reunion, that she knew she actually would.

For the first time since the end of the relationship she felt no need to steer clear of her Fleur tokens, no need to cover the page in her diary when Harry came into the room, no need to visit surreptitiously the file of Fleur's old emails. No need to avoid the huge store of inflammable memories and keepsakes, no need to lie.

And yet secrets formed the fabric of a life like hers. Not simply the failed childhood shoved into a crate and welded shut, not simply Fleur, a parallel marriage if ever there was one, but a cache of secrets added to throughout her forty-five years, hidden in memory, in diaries, in a bale of documents. Secrets enrich a life, she truly believed this, and without them life becomes a thin bedraggled affair. But secrets require unwavering vigilance, to be loyal to them can be exhausting.

She wondered how many of her secrets had leaked out. Who, for example, other than the players themselves knew about her month with Jack or her affair with Connie? As for Fleur, Jack knew, and of course Harry, who believed that as long as Ava remained with him she was choosing him above Fleur. And while she would never leave Harry, sometimes you choose but are not chosen in return.

Old secrets gradually lose their radioactivity, acquiring instead a certain nostalgia. Secrets left behind after your life has moved forward become safe. Fleur, so recently full of hard heat, was finally cooling.

As for the often squalid side to secrets, Ava had never regarded hers in this way. What both Stephen and Fleur had given her was valuable, and so much of what you value is never put on show. As she walked the grounds of her old university, this place that filled a special part of her past, it occurred to her that memories can become secrets too, sometimes so deeply buried that barely a whisper remains. But at the most unexpected of times they emerge, lovely and lively, returning you to times no longer lost.

The wind had dropped and as she left the arts building and made her way to the library she felt the first spatter of rain. And what, she wondered, might she not know about her old friends? Helen's ambitions, for example, and this predicament of hers with science, her longest love. And Jack's achievements, surely there were more than he had revealed to her. And Connie, how did he square his moral philosopher's stance with three marriages, a swathe of children and numerous lovers? Only Harry was in the clear, Harry who slept with his bedroom door ajar, who worked always with the door to his office open, her Harry had no secrets.

CHAPTER 2: The Buried Life

1.

It was the evening after the reunion and in a building by the river, in a huge white space with soaring ceilings and a colossal wall of glass, Harry Guerin was working through his final check-list. He had selected this venue for the NOGA cocktail party confident that the three to four hundred people required to fill the area would make the effort to attend. A few guests had already arrived and were idling self-consciously in the no-man's-land of a room before a party. Harry glanced at his watch, not yet six, and certainly too soon to worry his hopes might have muddied his expectations. He rustled up a waiter to give the early arrivals a drink, then slipped into the kitchen for last-minute instructions to the catering staff. Back in the bar area, he inspected the waiters; he insisted one fellow restrain his dreadlocks and another remove a line of eyebrow studs, and, to quell the murmurings, promised a ten per cent cash bonus for the lot of them. Money, he had learned long ago, was a reliable pacifier.

He was about to do a final check with the sound and light people when he saw Helen arrive. She might well be in line for a Nobel, but it didn't take much nous to realise that if improving the lot of the starving multitudes was a widespread priority, the starving would not amount to multitudes. Unlike Helen he was a realist, and his job would be a great deal easier if she were too.

He shoved his list in his pocket and followed her out to the terrace where she had already lit up. Too busy to be anything but blunt, he told her this was not the time for a crisis of conscience; she knew exactly where her expertise lay, and so, for that matter, did NOGA.

'Many people have invested in you and your science,' he said. 'You owe it to them, yourself as well, to be sensible.'

The smile she had raised to greet him slid from her face, but before she could find an answer he had turned and headed back inside. And while he would have preferred a more diplomatic approach, given the pressures on him tonight, pussyfooting around the issue was not an option, nor, he suspected, would it produce results.

A few more people had wandered in but not nearly enough for reassurance. Assuming a confidence he did not feel, he marched across the room to the adjacent auditorium where the formal proceedings would take place. In this area was seating for three hundred and ninety, and should his estimates be wrong, too many spaces here would condemn him far more strenuously than a thinnish crowd chatting over drinks and savouries next door. He paused inside the auditorium, took a few deep breaths, then gathered himself up and marched down the aisle to the stage. He mounted the steps two at a time, gazed at the rows of empty seats, just a moment's hesitation before returning to business. Here the main work of the evening would occur: his own welcome, followed by

Sir Richard Treat's speech and Conrad's keynote address. He waylaid the lighting technician to discuss the stage lighting, he cornered the sound technician and was assured yet again that the body microphones were highly effective, he checked the podium height and the reading light, and with everything in place he returned to the main reception area.

Just ten minutes had passed but now the room was crowded. Conversation surged, hands waved, mouths worked hard around words, while waiters glided through the throng dispensing drinks and hors d'oeuvres. Harry's anxieties vanished as he stood in the doorway savouring the scene. He would present the Network's mission statement and strategy plan; Jack, Conrad and Helen, the inaugural NOGA fellows would be on show; there was Conrad's speech – whatever Harry might think of his appalling morals, Conrad was an excellent speaker; and among the guests were some of the more beneficent members of the community. If the evening went well, and as he surveyed the crowd he was now convinced it would, NOGA would net millions of dollars and incalculable prestige.

Harry helped himself to a drink from a passing waiter and walked into the throng. He made his way towards Lady Stiller, whom, he noticed, like so many wealthy women did not carry a handbag.

2.

Jack dawdled along the path by the river. Night had already fallen but the area was well lit; in fact, all of the city was lit up these days. The temperature had plummeted and his hands ached with cold, but he was in no hurry: a large cocktail party, much less one in which he was on display, was simply not his scene. He checked his watch and continued on his way.

Renovated to the far more respectable 'precinct', this area on the north side of the river had been the domain of derelicts when he was a student, a rat-infested corridor of the city reeking of menace and bad reputation. The contemporary upgrade was now busy with suited pedestrians wearing trainers, and home-bound joggers with their work life crammed into backpacks. There was a vigour and prosperity about both the people and the area, and a youthfulness too, which by the very fact he noticed it made him uncomfortable: he had not realised he had reached that stage of maturation when youth is viewed as other, as not yourself.

He wandered a little further, stopped and checked the time again. The cocktail party venue was perched at the top of the slope; it was glowing hugely against the night sky, and the terrace out the front was already thick with smokers. He lingered a moment longer, then left the path and made his way slowly up the hill.

There was a jostle of people at the entrance to the building. He stood aside allowing others to pass ahead of him, amused that his reluctance to go in might be misconstrued as politeness. While he was waiting, a commotion started up at the door, someone struggling against the new arrivals, a woman wanting to leave and making no bones about it. Hats were dislodged, a bag fell to the ground, and amid a chorus of aggrieved protests Helen emerged from the crowd.

She was furious.

Jack caught her by the arm. 'Where are you going?'

'As far from that insufferable shit as possible.'

'Harry?'

'Of course Harry. Who else but Harry?'

She dragged Jack away from the entrance, pulled out a cigarette and lit up. 'I made an effort for Ava's sake. We all did. I won't say I became a Harry convert, but he was growing on me. But this NOGA business, this power, has made him a monster.' Small puffs of smoke accompanied each word. 'He thinks he can tell me what work I should do. He actually threatened me.'

Jack asked her to explain.

'Not here, not now,' she said. 'I have to leave before I do something I'll regret.' She rummaged in her bag for her hat. 'I'll ring you,' she said, pulling on a green cloche. And with her scarf flapping in one hand and the cigarette glowing in the other, she bolted down the steps and into the night.

Inside the venue Jack's body temperature soared to tropical discomfort. He helped himself to a glass of wine and made his way through the crush to a small raised area at the far end of the room. There he cooled off while his gaze traversed the crowd. There was no sign of Ava, but he could see Connie and was about to join him, when Connie slipped from the party into the adjacent auditorium.

Jack remained on his perch at the edge of the throng. He took in the array of hairstyles, the shaved domes, the mobile mouths, groups of people in twos and threes and fours. He noticed Harry weaving through the crowd, working the room. The Harry Guerin he knew was an entirely different creature from this host of the party, this expansive and attentive man laughing with this guest, talking closely with that, a slap to a finely clad back and kisses to the cheeks of elegant women.

Whatever had transpired with Helen just a short time ago had left no detectable impression on him.

Power, it's in a class of its own, Jack found himself thinking. The beautiful know they're beautiful, the successful know they're successful, but people with power tend to exercise it as their right, without reflection, as if power confers its own moral authority. NOGA was not a big player even by Australian standards, but within the context of this party Jack could see that Harry was powerful – even more powerful than the position he occupied, more powerful than NOGA itself. How human power inflates itself. And not for the first time he wondered what he and Connie and Helen had got themselves into. So much information flowed into NOGA. How was it being used? How might it be used? And who would have access to it? He had raised these concerns with Harry, but Harry had an answer for every question, an explanation for every doubt. That in itself was troubling.

Jack slipped back into the crush. He stopped to allow a passing waiter to fill his glass, then went in search of Ava. While he sifted through the crowd, he told himself that now was neither the time nor place for doubts about NOGA; he, Helen and Connie had signed up as the inaugural NOGA fellows and they were integral to tonight's show. Harry had nominated Connie to speak on their behalf, and Jack and Helen had agreed, not simply because Connie had a new book to promote and a TV series in the offing, but of the three, Connie seemed a better fit among Harry's guests, his 'knights of industry' and 'people who make things happen'. Although as a NOGA fellow, Jack assumed that he, too, must be one of those 'people who make things happen', but more in the way of primary producer, he decided, than the value-added people who made up this party. He stifled a smile. He had known for a good long time that it was easier to parody Harry than envy him, although as he caught a glimpse of the homunculus bobbing through the crowd, a blur of glistening head and a permanent smile beneath the ridiculous moustache, Jack was forced to concede that no amount of parody or ridicule would alter their situations.

The air was heavy with perfume and food and too many people speaking at once; Jack moved through the pack to the wall of glass with its view to the riverside promenade. The stream of home-bound workers had been replaced by groups of sauntering youths. Some of the boys sported bare arms, yet it must be only seven or eight degrees out there. Tough and cool was their message, but the fact Jack was thinking cold and stupid just made him feel old again. So much made him feel old these days.

He swapped his empty glass for a full one – his third, he reminded himself – and helped himself to a savoury from one of the mobile waiters. The food fell apart before it reached his mouth. He hated finger food and he hated standing around pretending to have a good time. The evening had hardly begun, he was hungry, he was drinking too quickly and there was no escape.

He made his way across the room to the entrance and the book display he had noticed there. With his gaze hard ahead and sheltering his glass from the crush, he made it through the worst and into the lighter air of the foyer. And there she was, Ava, standing in front of the bookstand, oblivious to all around her. Ava, with his own *The Reinvention of Islam* in her hands, the new edition with the buy-me cover and Connie's read-me preface.

It is an extraordinary experience to chance on someone reading one of your books. It has the same sort of adrenalin-charged impact as when you come face to face with a long-lost friend. But to see your book in the hands of your beloved, she might be touching you, touching your bare skin. Jack felt the blood flushing through him, and inside his own shuddering self he was joined to her. It was a perfect stilled moment, then she looked up and saw him.

There was a single month long ago when they were lovers, four glorious weeks when Jack knew perfection. As Ava beckoned to him, it was as if she were calling him to her side just as she had for that one perfect month when they were eighteen. And then the present muscled in.

'I've been reading you,' she said, holding up his book. 'You really were very good.'

Such are the inadvertent condemnations of the past tense.

There were a few hundred people only metres away but it felt to Jack as if he and Ava were alone. He stood close to her, close enough to feel proprietorial while she spoke about the reunion last night, the four of them together again and, gesturing towards the display, their books and achievements. As she talked, Jack was seized by the play of words and emotions across her face. Beauty shocks, beauty surprises, it is uncommon, exceptional. For him, beauty was, and would forever be, Ava Bryant.

He had loved her first. And he knew she had loved him too. Why then had she chosen Harry? And why Fleur rather than him? Although the very fact of Fleur had always given him hope: if Ava could admit a lover there was still a chance for him. But as the affair dragged on year after year, seven long years with a husband and what seemed like a permanent lover,

Jack's own chances grew very thin indeed. Fleur, who had inspired him with hope, eventually added to his failure.

It was Jack who had introduced Fleur to Ava, just as years earlier he had introduced Harry to her. He had often wondered if others would have recognised such self-defeating acts before it was too late. He only wanted to help, to be useful to her.

He had accrued several months of study leave and Ava had persuaded him to spend it in Oxford, his first visit back since gaining his doctorate. He had arrived to find her stranded in the holding pen between novels, and immediately took it upon himself to provide her with the stimulation to free up her imagination and start working again. One outing he planned was to a public lecture given by Fleur Macleish, a specialist in Indian antiquities. Three months later, with the affair in full heat, Jack had returned to Australia determined to keep half a world between him and Ava Bryant.

Through her letters he had kept abreast of the affair's numerous flare-ups and its equally numerous burn-outs. Whenever Ava wrote about Fleur, Jack could feel the compulsion that joined her to this woman. It was a type of love he recognised – explosive, unrestrained, addictive, irresistible, and totally unlike her love for Harry, which was useful like an electric kettle is useful, and ordinary. Yet as the affair with Fleur continued, it was impossible not to feel sorry for Harry; the poor man must have been mad with pain.

Throughout the seven years of their affair, Ava and Fleur loved in cycles. It was all fire and fury for a time, a wild burn that consumed work, thought, body, health, each other – like Icarus flying towards the sun, Ava once wrote to Jack, and nothing to equal it. Two or three months were as long as they could tolerate, then they would break away and Ava would lodge Fleur somewhere safe while she returned to the rest of her life. Such a relief to settle, Ava would write in her letters to Jack. And her work would flow.

Love is astonishingly immune to learning from experience. As Jack appeared unable to extricate himself from Ava, so it seemed Ava could not extricate herself from Fleur. Months might pass when the two women had nothing to do with each other. Ava would be hard at work in Oxford or travelling the world's literary circuit, and Fleur would be hard at work in London and, as Ava would eventually discover, conducting a string of affairs. Then, inexplicably, a shift would occur, sometimes in Fleur, sometimes in Ava, a switch turned on, a tautness, an awareness, and one of them would seek the other out. They would always meet on the neutral ground of a café, where wrapped in eagerness and good intentions they would swap stories of their time apart. But even before the coffee was finished and the neglected food whisked away, the sizzling would have started again. And from there it was just a brief span before they were clawing at each other in a fume of emotions turned up to the level of pain.

It was a love impossible to reject and impossible to maintain. As a means of protection, Ava would retract the boundaries of her relationship with Fleur, inadvertently concentrating the emotions and raising the intensity. Obsessive loves are never cool and neither are they open to cool reason. Just like Jack's love for Ava. So many similarities but with two crucial differences. Despite the tumult with Fleur, despite the frequent bruisings and the sharp cut of the separations, Ava produced four new novels in seven years; far from Fleur hindering her work,

Ava believed she was essential to it. In contrast, Jack's writing and research dwindled and then stopped altogether as Ava came to occupy more of his time. In fact, all his other passions waned. There used to be other women, many other women, but there was little beyond sex with them and after a while he rearranged his sexual needs to minimise potential complications. By the time he returned to Melbourne to take up the NOGA fellowship, what intimate ties Jack had outside his relationship with Ava occurred mostly in cyberspace.

And the other crucial difference? Ava had Harry. Rather than focus on the affair with Fleur, Jack would have done better to study her marriage. But he preferred not to look.

Husbands and wives make pacts with each other, shared commitments about how they will conduct their relationship. They also make pacts with themselves as to what they will tolerate in their partner's behaviour. The shared pacts and the private ones can be the same, but in the rocky terrain of most marriages there are disparities. So it happens that in a marriage in which both partners have committed to fidelity but one embarks on affairs, the marriage does not break down during the first affair, nor the second. But the third spells the end for the faithful partner, even if it was nothing more than a drunken fuck with someone never to be seen again. The personal limit has been crossed. If Fleur had lasted another year, another two, would Harry have stuck by Ava? Would his personal limit have been crossed?

The important issue, and Jack was well aware of this, was not whether Harry would have tolerated another year of Fleur but the fact there was not another year to tolerate. It was Harry who made sure of it with the move back to Australia.

There had been yet another separation from Fleur, but different this time, for Fleur had put a stop to the affair. She had met someone else, she said, and while this had happened many times during her relationship with Ava, she intended to be faithful this time. *Faithful in a way she never was with me*, Ava wrote to Jack in one of her many sad, aggrieved letters. Harry had been toying with the idea that would become NOGA, and with Ava shredding in distress he decided it was time to act. It took a surprisingly short three months to finalise NOGA on paper and bring it to the attention of the right funding bodies; a further two months and Harry and Ava were on their way home to Australia. Harry had acted to ensure his limits were not stretched any further.

It would be easy to conclude that Harry loved Ava sufficiently to withstand any amount of humiliation, or even that he lacked the usual complement of pride. But Harry was equipped with pride in abundance, that much was perfectly clear even to Jack. Just seeing him here at this function, strutting around with his 'captains of industry' and his 'people who make things happen', Harry was king and no one could doubt it. And this was not simply a quality acquired in his middle years: the very fact he set his sights on Ava in the first place, a prize by anyone's reckoning and the only prize as far as Jack was concerned, showed how highly he had always regarded himself.

Harry's voice sounded over the clamour. He had mounted a podium, and with a microphone in hand he was calling for attention. The hush was immediate, the people waited for direction. He asked them to make their way into the auditorium and instantly they began to move. Harry Guerin was in control – as he had always been.

Ava too was watching Harry even while Jack's own book was in her hands. She watched her husband at the centre of his own creation and, as much as Jack might wish it otherwise, the absolute centre of her life.

Conrad Lyall was churning in the wings of the auditorium. He was accustomed to nerves before a lecture, the extra adrenalin charged up his performance and he had learned to capitalise on it, but tonight he was more jittery than usual. Melbourne might be located well off the world stage but home always demands more of you. There was family out there, his mother in particular, his ever-supportive mother who from the moment of his birth had set out to make something of her son. Even now, an old woman in her eighties, she would remind him he had been named after the great Joseph Conrad – more a reflection of her own youthful desires to be a novelist, Connie had long believed, than anything she might have observed in her infant son. His sweet, hungry mother who had channelled all her passions into her only child, so that in the patchy night hours when work and mothering were finished, it was a sour whine which dribbled from her pen. She had always been burdened with more aspiration than talent when it concerned her own ambitions, but in the case of her son she had long been convinced he had lived up to his name.

His mother was in the audience, together with old friends and acquaintances. Over drinks he had mingled with former colleagues – they'd certainly be watching his performance tonight – as well as two former students who had done rather well for themselves. There were snipers out there too, Connie knew exactly who they were, academics who had been quick to target him as all charm and artifice twenty years ago and had used the time since to practise their punches. Connie had long been aware that reputation was considerably less sturdy than he would like, but with his career now well established surely it would take more than a lecture to a home crowd and a few bitter philosophers to topple the cumulative effects of twenty years' work.

And Sara was out there too. He peered around the wings. Sara, 'it rhymes with tiara', was in the fifth row on the aisle and already on friendly terms with her neighbour. All glossy brown skin in her skimpy black dress, he definitely wanted to impress her.

It was a part of Australian folklore that expatriates only returned home when they were on the wane in the wider more important world. But his star had never been brighter. He had been attracting huge crowds both here and in the States; even the Europeans now acknowledged him. Such suspicion attached to popularity, yet in his own case there was no reason for popularity to condemn him as a lightweight. If there was a problem, and he was unsure whether there was, it lay with the well-known collegiate capacity for envy. For the fact remained that while he might be tired and unduly anxious, and yes, he was very popular, irrespective of what some of his dryer colleagues might think, popularity did not rule out a serious and significant contribution. Dickens had been popular, Russell too, and Einstein had been a celebrity. Not to mention the de Bottons and Shamas of his own age – although he harboured the same doubts about them as he did about himself.

He moved deeper backstage; if he hadn't already had more than enough to drink he would have nipped back into the hall for another glass. He found a small room with table and chairs and settled himself down with his notes. Logic insisted there was no reason to worry: his work was rigorous, it was relevant to these volatile times and it reached a substantial number of people. Moreover, it armed them for the challenges of a fractured uncertain world far more effectively than turgid papers cobbled together in neglected corridors of academe. And his reception since he had arrived back in Australia could not have been better. His lectures had been well attended, the radio interviews deferential, and talk-back sessions had presented him as revered seer on all matters contemporary; there had been TV spots usually reserved for celebrities, and, to top it all off, there had been exotic Sara – her background was Chilean – to remind him of the man he still was. Of course he wasn't finished yet.

His own expectations had always been the hardest to satisfy – a quality he shared with his friends, although his situation was different from theirs in that no one would ever question the seriousness of their work. Helen was stamped with the imprimatur of serious science; Jack's choice of a corner of comparative religion so obscure that he had been forced to work in universities equally remote was of little consequence now he had been resurrected as the background expert of choice on Islam and the new terrorism, and Ava had been treated seriously from the publication of her first novel. Only Connie's work was questioned. His last two books, both exploring communication, power and the fall of knowledge, had received what was, even in the desperately hopeful view of the author, a muted reception. No one had actually criticised him, no one had labelled him lightweight, but the reviews were without muscle and the reviewers themselves seemed lightweight. He suspected that among his more serious colleagues he was thought to have sold out, while others believed he had peaked with *God and the Webmaster*. Yet by his own reckoning he had plenty of good years left. And even if *God and the Webmaster* remained his best-known book, he wouldn't be the first writer of renown with a long career and high output in which one book dominated. He recalled Joseph Heller's response when asked whether he was disappointed he had never written a novel to surpass *Catch-22*. With such a book, Heller had replied, is there any need to better it?

Was *God and the Webmaster* Conrad Lyall's *Catch-22*? The barb in the question did not escape him. He truly believed there would be other books, better books, but with expectation such a powerful shaper of opinion he needed other people to think the best was in front of him too – all other people: his friends and family, the strangers who came to listen to him, the readers of his books, even envious back-stabbing philosophers. He wondered whether Ava with her stellar career was still vulnerable to public opinion and decided to ask her. A moment later he knew he would not: there was something unpalatable about a man who desired the good opinion of everyone, including those he neither liked nor admired himself.

Connie collected his notes and made his way back to the wings. The auditorium was vibrant with hundreds of voices. Harry came up behind him. 'Ready?' he asked. And before Connie could reply, 'You know this is a crucial part of our campaign,' – it wasn't a question – 'and we're relying on you.' With a nod in the direction of the audience, he added, 'There's a lot of money out there.' And after a matey pat on Connie's back, he walked out on stage.

The silence was immediate.

Harry began by welcoming the guests 'to this auspicious occasion', then he provided a brief history of NOGA and an account of 'its already substantial achievements'. He singled out the NOGA Energy Forum – 'the most up-to-date information bank on energy research and development across the globe', and also the leading role taken by NOGA in monitoring new developments in bioweapons, mentioning Helen by name. Connie was listening in spite of himself. Far from rambling as used to be his way, Harry showed himself to be a succinct and witty speaker who knew exactly how to hold an audience and exactly when to stop. After some remarks about the Network's plans for the next triennium, he introduced the chairperson of a steel corporation that was one of NOGA's main backers. Sir Richard Treat, with thick greying hair and pin-stripes over a softening girth was, Connie decided, a perfect fit for his knighthood. As his voice boomed through the hall, Connie made a final check of his notes, while a technician grubby with stubble attached a body microphone and repeated his instructions from the earlier sound check. When he was finished he patted Connie on the backside and wished him luck.

What on earth was that? Connie wondered. A come-on? An over-the-line familiarity? An accident? An insult? He might well be the contemporary soothsayer, but he simply could not read the gesture.

He shuffled his weight to ease the ache in his knees and tightened his stomach muscles to reduce the press of his belt. Before he had left America he had been sufficiently concerned about his health to have a medical check-up, but whatever was infecting his spirits wasn't revealed in medical tests. A temporary malaise was the most likely explanation. After all, as Oscar Wilde once said – or was it Somerset Maugham? – only the mediocre man is always at his best. Exercise might help, and he made a note in his organiser to investigate the sports centre at the university. And he needed to deal with the Linda problem.

A decade with the same woman was a record for him, and for the first five years he had been almost monogamous. He should never have married again. Two failed marriages were proof enough that for a man like him only short-term relationships were advisable, two or three years at most, with insufficient time for the issue of children to arise. Not that he didn't love Laurie and Oscar, nor for that matter Hugh, now twenty-five, and the twins almost sixteen – another note not to forget their birthday – but at five and four Laurie and Oscar were exhausting. It was impossible to work when they were home, and none of the nannies was as effective as their mother in maintaining discipline. The situation would be much improved if Linda had not insisted on returning to her practice. But as she was quick to remind him, anaesthetists earned considerably more than philosophers, so if either of them were to give up work to look after the children it should be him.

You can't turn yourself into someone else, particularly not at his age, and surely better to acknowledge his limitations and cater for them rather than allow them to run roughshod over those he cared about. Linda said that everyone had to compromise in relationships, but he had reached his limit. He needed to make some hard decisions, and he needed to make them now, otherwise he would be faced with ending his marriage after Linda and the boys arrived in Melbourne.

And he needed time to explore this thing with Sara. Just thinking about her caused a gripping in his abdomen. He had met her only three weeks ago in Brisbane. A Melbourne girl, she was researching her PhD in an archive up there, not philosophy but a topic located in some arcane outpost of post-colonial studies. When he was ready to leave on his lecture tour, to his delight so was she. 'On the road with Connie' was how she described it. Twenty-four-year-old Sara, who twenty-four hours after they met was groping him under the table as they sat in a restaurant with a group from the university discussing the widening communications gap between the first and third worlds. Yes, there was definitely more of Sara to explore.

And for the first time in decades his closest friends were in the same city. Ava, Jack and Helen, the three he had always relied upon for wise counsel, how he wanted them to be impressed, how he needed them to tell him how good he was. He stepped forward again and looked around the wings. Ava and Jack were in the front; Helen, as usual, must be running late.

Jack was leaning towards Ava, but then Jack had been blindly leaning towards Ava ever since they first met. How much he had missed of life, the only one whom they had designated a genius, a man who had produced no new work for years, who lived in the same flat in which he had grown up, who had stripped his life back to the white clatter of bones. Even the revival of his career would not by itself loosen his fixation on Ava.

And Ava herself. It occurred to Connie that as a young woman she had revealed many of the same qualities which now attracted him to Sara. He had not made the connection before. Ava at eighteen stretched across the rug in his office, the lush hair in a lovely tangle about her face, the unbuttoned blouse, the perfect white breasts, her jeans knotted around her ankles. Nearly thirty years ago but still so clear. The shabby maroon rug, the floor hard against his elbows and knees, and while a large age difference and student status had never stopped him before, with Ava – he did not know why – it seemed courteous, responsible too, to express a certain caution.

'We can't take it back once it's done,' he remembered saying.

Her knowing look, the half-smile and her reply, he had

forgotten none of it: 'Enough with the pre-coital clichés,' she had said, hooking her hand around his neck and pulling him down.

Sara had done much the same three weeks ago.

It was all too simple to suggest he was using Sara to hold on to his own youth; Sara would be viewed as a catch by most men. Something more fundamental was happening. If anyone had asked him as a twenty-year-old whether there would be a time when he was not reliant on other people's good opinion, he would have responded with a confident, 'Of course.' From the stand-point of youth, maturity always seemed so secure, so worry free. And yet here he was in sight of sixty and requiring approbation as much as ever. Even as he drew his last breaths he would probably be wanting reassurance that he was dying in the best possible way, the most intellectually rigorous way, dying with humour rather than cynicism, with grace rather than fear, with dignity not resentment.

There was a burst of applause. The steel magnate had finished and Harry assumed the podium again. Jack was still hard up against Ava. If anyone was holding on to youth it was Jack. Nothing was simple any more, Connie was thinking as he stepped out on stage, but unlike Jack, he, at least, had plenty to show for his years.

4.

Connie strolled across the stage to the podium. He arranged his notes on the lectern, he raised his head slowly, he looked out at the auditorium and he smiled. Ava glanced along the row and saw people smiling back. Connie had not said a word yet already he had captured the audience. For the next thirty minutes he would give his usual compelling performance, the crowd would remain transfixed, and Jack would lean heavily against her and probably not hear a word.

Poor Jack, what a waste he had made of his life, although Ava no longer blamed herself. For years she had felt responsible, not simply for that night on the beach which began their month-long affair, but for his having fallen in love with her in the first place. And blaming herself she had tried to dissuade him. She had sent him books about the Bloomsburies and the Beats – *Friends like us, minus the hot-housing and the drugs.* She made sure he knew about her lovers, about Fleur above all; she shielded him from none of her faults. And Harry, she tried to make Jack understand why she loved her husband and why he was *beyond any doubt* the right man for her. Ava did everything she could to persuade Jack out of his love until the week she received not one but two thick letters from him – interesting and entertaining as were all his letters but each more than four thousand words long. Two letters in a week which added up to ten per cent of an average novel. And finally it dawned on her that not only did Jack want to keep his love for her, his grip on it was welded tight. As for that night on the beach, he was already in love with her; the consummation, she came to realise, made no difference. Jack was proof that memory is a safer country than any other.

Yet she knew why she had succumbed. Jack was all attraction in those first days, and what flaws were apparent, like his shyness and his fastidiousness, she ascribed to sensitivity. He loved poetry, all her own favourites – Rilke, Baudelaire, Mandelstam, Akhmatova, Auden, as well as Yeats, Coleridge and Keats – and history, they shared his ancient and her

European and a swag of other worlds in between. And his parents were unlike any parents she had ever met, not just their foreignness and their activism, but the way they loved their son – they called him darling – and that they welcomed his friends to their home. And he was so good-looking, the lapis blue eyes, the thick black curls, the slight, well-proportioned body, and he was her own age. And he talked like other people wrote, in beautiful sequences of cut and polished words, the first person she had ever known to do this. Soon after they met she asked if English was his first language. It was, he said, before adding that he had read rather a lot, and indeed there were the occasional mispronunciations common to people whose greatest exposure to words was on the page. And he played the guitar, not the numbed strumming over a handful of chords typical of most eighteen-year-olds, but like a proper musician.

The night on the beach that had begun their month together, he had played his guitar especially for her. It was three o'clock in the morning and the beach was deserted. A group of them had spent the evening at a folk club where Jack had been performing, and how it happened that she had ended up alone with him on the sand she could no longer recall. But his music she would never forget. He had played the blues, swaying with the music and humming along in an odd rumbling beneath the melody. And she who knew nothing of music was gathered up by those broken rhythms in an experience that went beyond words (she would come to know the same sort of brimming emotion with Rothko's paintings). Jack played his guitar, the waves shuffled to and fro on the shore, there was the gentle rush of late-night cars on the road behind, and it seemed absolutely right to move into his arms. By the time the sun rose and the traffic had begun in earnest, the moment of perfect harmony had passed. But never for Jack.

Connie stopped for applause. Jack did not move and, not wanting to embarrass him, Ava, too, remained still. The applause subsided and Connie began again. Knowledge used to command authority, he was saying. But in our era, it's been overtaken by information. Connie leaned in towards the audience, his face overwritten with excitement, his hands beating the emphasis. And it was not simply his being a compelling speaker, he was passionate about these ideas and wanted to share his passion. But then Connie exuded passion in most things. Ava would never forget her first philosophy class when he appeared in the doorway of the lecture theatre, his hair wild with heat, face tanned, brown sinewy arms shown off by the sleeveless T-shirt, walked to the lectern, laid out his papers, looked out at the students and told them that the only life worth living was the examined one (she had assumed he was the author of the aphorism until Stephen set her straight) and it was his intention to introduce them to the tools for such an examination.

For a first-year student in 1978, Dr Conrad Lyall, with talent to match his ambition and already well on his way, was exactly the right man to sleep with. Jack, who neither then nor now knew how to look after himself, was not. So six months into her first year of university Ava made a choice. She would always regret starting the affair with Jack, and regretted even more the way she finished it, but without an act both incontrovertible and reprehensible she believed Jack would not stop wanting her. As it happened, the attempt proved futile. Your infatuation was a god-finder, Ted Hughes wrote about Sylvia Plath. Perhaps all infatuations are.

A murmur ran through the audience. Ava had not heard what Connie said and neither it seemed had Jack. They continued to sit motionless, their arms hard up against each other while the people around them again broke into applause. Jack had utterly stilled. He had heard none of Connie's lecture. He was back on that beach with Ava, he was in her arms, he was making love, and afterwards the gift of his history stones, a dozen stones collected from different locations across Europe, fragments of the old world brought to the new by his grandparents, who had passed them on to his father, who had passed them on to him. After the night on the beach he had wanted to give her something special and enduring. His history stones were his most precious possession.

He had placed them in a Petri dish lined with cotton wool. 'A history of the world in the palm of your hand,' he had said.

Then followed those four weeks of whitely flying, as if all of him, and not just his earthly feelings, had sprouted wings.

I am, O Anxious One. Don't you hear my voice
surging forth with all my earthly feelings?
They yearn so high that they have sprouted wings
and whitely fly in circles around your face.

He read Rilke constantly during that time because Rilke knew love. But pragmatist that Rilke was, there was always part of him responsive to gravity. Not so Jack. He was in love with Ava Bryant and she was in love with him. Through twenty-nine days of bliss they read, they talked, and he played his music for her. Twenty-nine days of conversation and laughter, of guarding their secret, of special meals and special remembrances. Twenty-nine days of her beautiful face, that bulwark against boredom. Twenty-nine days against drawing the short straw in life's lottery. Twenty-nine days in which to rewrite metaphor.

This was a time when even his usual anxiety was ringed with bliss. He was anxious something might happen to her, anxious she might decide she didn't love him, anxious that sex be the rapture he knew it was meant to be. He had turned to Baudelaire for guidance, but while the erotic tone and texture were just right, what he really needed was practical direction. He read *The Story of O*, but the men were monsters and the women couldn't possibly enjoy what they were made to do. He read *Lady Chatterley's Lover*, which was thick with words but thin on technique. He even read *Portnoy's Complaint*, but masturbation and Jewish families were familiar territory, while proper sex the Portnoy way was as romantic as a crawl through the gutter.

Such moments aside, he was happy – happier than he had ever been after twenty-nine mornings like that last one, lying in Ava's bed while she slept, her head resting on his shoulder, his hand gliding over the fine corrugation of her ribs, the plunge to her waist, the surge to the full smooth buttocks. Her skin so fine, hardly a blemish, the soft down cushiony under his fingers, her quivering with his light touch. And only later when he realises they will never lie together again does it occur to him that far from love or pleasure or innocuous tickling, she was probably wanting to shake his hand off, peel it – and him – from her body.

She shuffles against him and snuffles in her sleep. (A thousand times has he revisited that morning.) He needs to use the toilet but instructs his body to wait, curls his hand tighter to the lovely hollow of her waist, his fingers acutely sensitive as they stamp her skin into the memory of his skin. And beyond the glass the sky lightens and the sun enters the room, stencilling the plane tree in the street on to the wall near the bed and moving quickly, too quickly, past the wardrobe to her desk. The sun strikes the Petri dish and throws off a spark. Another ten minutes and it has passed to the pile of paper which he knows to be her philosophy essay.

His gaze shifts back to the Petri dish; out of the sun's glare it is clearly visible. And – he cannot make sense of it – the stones have gone. He can see the dish but his history stones are missing. He raises himself a little higher and searches the surface of her desk. They are nowhere to be seen.

She wakes with his movement. He can't stop himself, he asks about the stones, careful not to say *his* stones. She won't meet his gaze. He wishes he could remain silent, but he can't. He asks again: Where are the history stones? She wrenches herself from his arms, turns to face him, is about to speak, then changes her mind, bolts from the bed, drags on a coat, shoves her bare feet into boots, and clomps out to the small verandah at the rear of the house. He follows naked, not a thought given to the others in the house, only Ava and those stones from history which he gave her.

There is a scattering of pot-plants on the back verandah and some hanging baskets. This is Ava's garden, target of her lavish attention. Portable yet enduring, she had once said, 'Like family is supposed to be.' He is shivering from fear more than cold. She looks at him, presses her lips into a shrug, then picks up a poinsettia, loosens the plant from the sides of the pot and pulls it free. There are stones for drainage in the bottom, she tips these out, sifts through them, shakes her head, replaces the stones, slides the plant back on top. She reaches for the next pot, an azalea in flower; again she loosens the plant, eases it out, examines the stones, carefully replaces the plant.

He knows what is coming, he knows he should protect himself. And now, more than a quarter of a century later, with the thrill of her against his arm, he realises he missed his chance that day so long ago, perhaps his only chance of breaking his love for her. But the fact that he didn't walk away proves he has always wanted to hold on to his love more than he has wanted anything else, perhaps more than he really wanted her.

He does not turn away, he does not leave. He makes himself watch as she picks up a third pot. It is terracotta and heavy, it contains a tall glossy-leafed plant. The pot is wet, it slips from her hands and crashes to the concrete below. Soil and leaf, root and stones litter the cracked cement. He steps down into the mess. The shards of terracotta are sharp on his feet, the gritty earth is nasty between his toes; he feels the stretch of his exposed buttocks as he squats down and sorts through the mess. He finds nine of his stones. He straightens up, the stones are clasped in his fist, and it is then he might have chosen not to love her. The opportunity lasts no longer than a second as he stands naked in the grey air in front of the woman who has treated him and his gift so brutally. And then she moves towards him, opening her coat and pulling him against her. She folds the coat around them both.

'We have to move on,' she says. 'We have to move on.'

Ava would always regret what she had done with the history stones, but she thought it would save him, that it would drive his love away. That Jack was never a suitable candidate as a lover she should have seen from the beginning. His beliefs would always condemn real experience as second-rate. No one could ever live up to his standards of perfection. And no matter how many his disappointments or how painful they were, he would cling to his standards like a miser with his stash. If Jack had been any less interesting, any less well read, if that morning on the beach he had not played music which beat so deeply into herself, she would not have so misjudged. For all the reasons she valued him, she should never have made him her lover.

Over the four weeks they were together she was to acquire other more pragmatic reasons. Clean would never be clean enough for Jack, tidy would never be tidy enough, well groomed would never be well groomed enough. Initially she interpreted his peccadillos as a manifestation of an entrenched hostility towards others: setting such high standards that people were bound to fall short. But soon she realised that aspiring to perfection was Jack's clumsy attempt to control an uncontrollable world and that his behaviour was directed entirely at himself. His socks were lined up on a shelf with military precision; his pens and pencils were arranged according to size, colour and type; his filing cabinet was as neat and accessible as a library. And making love – well, there were simply too many variables to accommodate, so, with the exception of that first time on the beach when she had taken him by surprise, their love-making was a disaster.

What Jack lacked, Ava realised later, was that quality of being sexually ardent. For despite his grand passion for her, he skirted the edges of love in much the same way as he would skirt the edges of life. Loving sex would never be his strong suit, but sex without love would see him as something of a maestro. His letters would often include a short polite paragraph, like a biography note, of the latest woman to share his bed. By the time Ava had received the next letter, the woman had usually been replaced.

In the presence of love, however, Jack was a stickler for getting it right, and his idea of right was drawn from Donne, Rilke, Keats and a large part of Greek mythology. This notion of sex, Ava told him one night during their month together, was as likely as Byron coming back from the dead to grade his performance.

'Orpheus. If anyone were to judge me, I'd prefer Orpheus.'

She and Jack were sitting in her bed sharing a pre-coital cigarette. It was a night like several others when there would only be pre-coital connection.

'Orpheus was the perfect lover with music in his soul and love in his heart –'

'And impatience in his bones.'

Jack shook his head: by looking back, Orpheus might have put an end to life with Eurydice, but his terrible grief hastened his own death. 'Everlasting love in everlasting afterlife. Looks like the jackpot to me.'

Ava had laughed. 'Only you could draw such a conclusion from so self-defeating an act.'

Jack was writing his own Orpheus sequence, and an anxious project it was, particularly after Ovid and Shakespeare and, of course, their revered Rilke.

'I have a draft.' There was a hint of a question in his voice.

At this messy point in their relations, Ava was in no doubt of her preference for the scholar and musician over the lover. She tasted the familiar excitement she associated with his work and asked to hear his Orpheus. And in the years to come, when the only writing Jack seemed to be doing was his letters to her, she would recall the night of his Orpheus. He was the brightest of them all.

Yet she would not have wanted to give up his letters. He wrote about the books he was reading, each of them analysed, interrogated, quoted from and evaluated within the relevant canon. He reported interesting conversations, he wrote vignettes of students and humorous accounts of his colleagues, he told tales of his travels. He sent her drafts of scholarly articles which were never finished to his satisfaction, and idiosyncratic personal essays styled like Roland Barthes's *Mythologies*, again never sent out for publication. In his letters, Ava liked to think he exposed the real Jack, the Jack released from the constrictions of his own exacting standards.

She had always loved him, different from how she loved Harry, different from her exhausting love for Fleur. Although during the worst Fleur times, when it was all whip and torture and no good coming of it, Ava would recall what she had done with Jack's gift of stones, an act so brutal that it should have slaughtered his love. Perhaps someone cannot kill off your love, perhaps only you can finish it off. And perhaps it requires an assault so prolonged that your love simply cannot recover. Like the bare-knuckle boxing match Harry had taken her to – for the spectacle, he had said, and data for the novels to come. It was ghastly; the spectators were out for blood and the referee did nothing to earn his money. For ten, twenty, thirty minutes the two men bashed each other until they were both on their knees still fighting, their faces and bodies bloodied. The crowd was shouting and egging them on, and only when both men were sprawled on the mat in their mingled blood and sweat did the fight finally stop. Perhaps this was what she needed to break from Fleur, and what Jack needed to break from her, some sort of intense and continuous assault.

Then again, perhaps nothing would change Jack's mind about her, like nothing changed hers about Fleur. Love seems to have an innate resilience to reason – at least for people like her and Jack.

The audience was clapping, Connie had finished and Jack was now sitting up straight. Her arm was a mass of painful pricklings as the blood seeped back. Connie was looking down at her and Jack. She raised her arms and applauded more vigorously; so, too, did Jack. And then Harry stood up to thank Connie and to take the opportunity to announce the forthcoming TV series *Travels in Cyberspace*, featuring Conrad Lyall and his work, an ABC–Channel 4 joint production to be shot here and in Europe.

As the audience broke into fresh applause, Ava saw how surprised Connie was, as indeed was she – the previous evening Connie had made it clear there were several more hurdles before the series went ahead. Harry had clearly passed a very fruitful day. Her Harry, and never any danger of losing herself in him, for as much as she loved him, he would always be the more loving one. She disagreed with Auden; she far preferred her position.

CHAPTER 3: A Type of God Search

1.

Throughout her youth and particularly at the Laconics meetings, Helen had championed science's humanitarian charter. Hers had been a lone voice against the bumper opposition to the scientific enterprise that prevailed at the time. With bulging nuclear stockpiles in East and West, with Three Mile Island in 1979, the Bhopal disaster of 1984 and Chernobyl two years later, with the thalidomide catastrophe and cities choking in asbestos, there were many who wanted to bring the whole enterprise down. And Helen would argue that scientific research and discovery were fundamentally good, that when science turned bad it was driven by people with bad intent. She would vow never to be co-opted, never to put money or might ahead of scientific purity and the benefit of humankind. She would use these terms, romantic as they were, but in those days ideals were not simply accepted, they were expected.

On the day after the NOGA cocktail party, she and Jack met for brunch at a St Kilda café. While waiting for their food, Helen described her recent research. She was shining with her work.

'All I've ever wanted is to do good science.'

'Ever the idealist,' Jack said, with a smile.

As she talked about her ambitions – 'The end of diarrhoeal disease, that's the goal' – Jack was thinking how easily ideals and delusions can stretch across a narrow divide to become one. Or perhaps there is a tainted core to all idealism. He thought of Edward Teller, father of the H-bomb and fierce anti-communist, who conflated his ideals of science and his ideals of democracy not only to justify horrendous weapons but also to bring down a number of his friends. Deluded? An idealist? Both?

'Do you think Edward Teller was justified in what he did?' Jack asked.

Helen was slathering sour cream on her potato latkes. 'In a purely scientific sense, of course he was,' as if 'a purely scientific sense' were ever possible, 'but taking his politics into account, the man was dangerously deluded.'

And you? Jack wanted to ask. Have you been deluded too? After all, any molecular biologist working today could not fail to be aware of the use of bacteria, including her own shigella, in biological weapons. But Helen would be horrified to be lumped in with Teller, so he kept his thoughts to himself and settled to his cheesecake.

He ate slowly, drawing out each mouthful. Savouring the pleasure, he realised, of this food from the past. It was the taste of childhood, of security. And this café, too, so comfortably familiar it might have been an extension of the Adelson living room when he was growing up. Every Sunday would see him and his parents seated here, Jack at one table eating cake and ice-cream with the children of his parents' friends, while nearby the adults argued how best to change the world.

Helen put her fork down. 'The last time I was here was with your parents. Years ago.' And she smiled. 'Our farewell dinner before we left for Oxford.'

During their undergraduate years, Helen and Ava had often visited the Adelson home. Jack's mother was an atrocious cook – not that it mattered, they said, for they came for the family, not the food. It was a compliment of such lofty proportions that Jack kept silent about any difficulties associated with ex-communist Jewish parents from Central Europe with little money and loads of social conscience who believed that action was the best policy no matter what the circumstances. On the night of the farewell dinner they had been prepared for one of his mother's meals; instead she proposed her favourite restaurant.

'I ordered latkes then,' Helen said.

'You always ordered latkes when we came here.' Jack was laughing. 'And you still do. I'm convinced there's only a small number of meals you can hold in your anti-epicurean brain.'

She laughed too. 'It simplifies the business of staying alive.'

Just like ideals, Jack was thinking. You could aspire to be like Einstein or Arendt or Segovia, you could aspire to be an honourable person. But you would never know if you had attained the ultimate in being honourable or indeed the quintessence of Einstein, Arendt or Segovia. Ideals are like mirages, Jack decided, they provide direction and they keep you moving; but if the light changes and your ideals are revealed as delusions you would be literally stopped in your tracks. No wonder Helen was floundering now.

A flock of noisy newcomers entered the café, the boys with long hair and drooping jeans, the girls with plunging necklines and bulging breasts, all of them talking with exaggerated emphasis as they made their way to the tables at the back.

'They sound so banal,' Jack said, nodding towards the group.

Helen was watching them too. They were a little older than Luke and to her mind just a normal bunch of kids. 'You need to spend more time around young people.'

Helen was probably right. These days kids struck him as being from a different species, and as if to guard his own values and beliefs he sensed a certain hostility towards them. He would eavesdrop on their conversations, everyone talking breathlessly in an American-infected sing-song, so excited over a new personal trainer, a website for free music downloads, the knock-out cocktails at Club G, the best strategy to use on eBay.

'I'm a dinosaur,' he said, sinking a fork into his cheesecake. And then added, 'I never thought anything this side of eighty would feel so old.'

The young people had dragged two tables together in the back section of the restaurant. One of the girls was standing on a chair displaying a pair of multi-coloured boots, the others were admiring them as if they were the Sistine Chapel ceiling. Everything seemed pushed to an extreme these days, Jack was thinking, either turned up very high or mere background murmur. And nothing was relative any more: getting a new job was in the same category as getting new shoes, and losing an iPod much the same as losing a friend.

'They seem to be managing the unexamined life extremely well,' Jack said, indicating the young people.

Helen smiled. 'You sound envious.'

Not knowing whether he was, he gave a noncommittal grunt and changed the subject. 'So what happened with Harry last night?'

Helen took her time to answer. 'Unlike you,' she began, 'I made an effort with Harry. With his corkscrews and computers, all his bizarre collections, he struck me as an eccentric and I've always made allowances for eccentrics.' She paused for a mouthful. 'And then there was Ava – I was prepared to like him because of her.'

'You're wrong about Harry.' Jack spoke more loudly than he intended. 'Eccentrics are imaginative, but Harry's the sort of person who can listen to Shakespeare and hear only rhyme and metre. Whole pools of meaning dry up in the glare of his type of appreciation. Harry has the mind, the soul, the ear of an engineer. His heart exists solely to pump the blood around his body.'

Helen stopped him with a hand on his arm. 'Ava's been married to Harry for decades. He's her anchor, Jack, and whether you like it or not, he's permanent.' She gave his arm a squeeze before pulling away. 'Ava might well choose the dance steps but Harry chooses the ballroom and he always has. Ava needs him, from the beginning she needed him, but I –' and a smile flickered over her face as if the idea had only just occurred to her, 'but I don't.

'In fact,' she continued, 'it's people like Harry I'm desperate to escape. Men in suits who dole out money to scientists like me for projects that they, the suits, deem important.' She stabbed at a piece of latke. 'I've no intention of staying the term of the fellowship with Harry's precious NOGA. But I'll leave in my own good time.' She waved the impaled food through the air as if to ward off any opposition. 'Meanwhile I'll do the work I choose and Harry be damned.' With that, she popped the food in her mouth.

Across the table Jack was thinking how wonderful it would be to possess her confidence. Just this morning he'd taken a phone interview, an early current affairs program on commercial radio before the weekend sport took hold. He had been questioned about Indonesia and Islam, just a skimming of the surface and well within his competence, but because Islam in the Asia–Pacific was not his primary specialty he felt as if he were speaking under false pretences. Even when he was treated as an acknowledged expert, even when he experienced that comforting buffer between himself and others which admiration and expertise construct, he could never know the confidence which Helen applied so naturally.

'So what happened with Harry last night?' he asked again in a deliberate shift to safer ground. 'Why's he so concerned about your work?' And, as a private afterthought: how does he know so much about your work?

Helen put her fork down and pushed her plate aside. 'Have you heard of dual-use research?'

Jack shook his head. 'But I expect it refers to the same piece of research having two different applications.'

'Exactly. What I'm working towards, as against what other people might want me to do, is to bring about immunity to shigella, all the shigellas.' And anticipating his question: 'There are four major types. In the course of my research, quite a complicated process I should add, I need to create a new organism.'

'So you're playing God?'

'But doing a far better job,' she said, smiling. 'If God were a scientist I'd find him a great deal more credible.'

She took a pen from her bag and drew a few snake-like marks on a serviette – 'The shigella chromosomes,' she said, pointing to them. 'And they don't occur in pairs as they do in human cells so every gene counts.' She looked up at Jack. 'I like that about bacteria. In fact, I like everything about bacteria. And I like shigella most of all.' She returned to her squiggles. 'The deeper we travel into the molecular structure of shigella the more likely we are to find its virulence mechanism, or rather mechanisms – the same, I'm convinced, for all the shigellas.'

She continued to explain her work, and Jack marvelled as he listened, he marvelled at *her*. You associate major scientific advances with the likes of Macfarlane Burnet, with Fleming and Florey, or Helen's own idol, Barbara McClintock, people of almost mythological status known the world over. And here was Helen convinced she would eventually have the solution to one of the major causes of diarrhoeal disease. His old friend Helen who had got stoned with him, swum naked with him, who now sat across a table in a restaurant she knew only because of him. Hard to equate the worldly scientist with the far more domestic friend.

'Now over here,' Helen drew another squiggle, 'we have a harmless *E. coli*.'

Jack pulled his attention into line. 'I'm surprised there are harmless *E-coli*.'

'There are lots of them, a good many we know about and others we're bound to discover. All told, there are hundreds of strains of *E. coli* and they've been the target of extensive study. This means their genetic make-up is largely known and it makes them ideal for my type of research. My aim is to find shigella's virulence genes, separate them from the rest of the organism, then splice them into a harmless *E. coli* and if all goes according to plan, cause a specific antibody response. And from there,' she smiled wryly, 'it's only about forty more steps before we have an effective vaccine.'

'So what's the problem? Where's the dual research?'

'When I splice the shigella genetic material into a harmless *E. coli*, I could create a nasty new *E. coli*.' She shrugged. 'I already have.'

'And people want to make use of these new bugs?'

'At this very moment, an organism I've created is being tested for toxicity and durability. And the testing's happening in my own lab. My own lab where I'm supposed to be in charge.'

'And this dual research spinning off from your own, has it got much muscle?'

'Of the steroid-enhanced variety,' she said grimly. 'Of course, this sort of work isn't new. We know that during the Cold War the Soviets tampered with anthrax and created a much more virulent form.' (Jack couldn't help but wonder about this 'we'.) 'And we know there are stockpiles of bacteria lying around in the former USSR. What we don't know is where they are and the exact organisms involved. But I guarantee there's enough to kill the entire population of the planet several times over and all of it could fit in an area the size of your kitchen.'

She leaned forward, her eyes bright behind her glasses. 'We humans are cream puffs when compared with bacteria.'

Power, politics, weapon stockpiles. 'Are you very important?' Jack asked.

She nodded and shrugged. 'I suppose so, but not primarily for the work that matters to me.'

'And Harry?'

'Harry, like a lot of powerful people, is far more interested in the bioweapons applications of my research than the shigella vaccine. A new organism for which there's no treatment, produced for targeted delivery to recalcitrant populations,' she raised her eyebrows. 'For certain groups, it's like winning the lottery.'

This powerful Harry whom Helen was talking about and he, himself, had observed at the NOGA cocktail party, when exactly had he emerged? Jack simply could not get a grip on the new Harry Guerin.

He looked across the table at Helen. 'So who funds your current research?'

'The US military – but it's not as you might think. Bioweapons aside, a shigella vaccine is in the military's interest. Soldiers in the field, even those on the side of right and might, are susceptible to shigella infections.'

'Although surely less so these days with food security so tight.'

Helen let out a derisive snort. 'Food supply to the military is now contracted out to private suppliers,' she said. 'Political favours are not unknown. And even if the company is competent, its main purpose is to turn a decent-sized profit. Cut some of the invisible corners – like food sourcing, like quality control – and the profits go up.'

Jack was immediately put in mind of private prisons and private water supplies: some functions should never be put in the hands of the free market. He was about to raise this with Helen but for the thought of Harry and his power. Why was Harry so interested in her research? And who or what gave him the right to be so interested?

'Harry's risen in the world,' he said.

Helen shook her head slowly. 'I think Harry is exactly where he always intended to be.'

2.

Helen should have seen it coming. She was not one of those grown-up innocents who populate some of science's most revered haunts; she knew about the promises and disappointments of scientific research, she knew about research's unforeseen yields and applications, and she knew about dual-use research. She may well have been working to eliminate shigella infections from the third world, but it didn't take a genius to realise that her work was equally useful to those deliberately wanting to infect a group of healthy people – not to kill, not with shigella or any of the common food bugs, but to create social disruption and widespread alarm. Even the relatively small 1984 Oregon salmonella outbreak, when a group of Rajneeshees deliberately infected salad bars, had resulted in severe strain on the local hospitals and unprecedented levels of fear and anger in the populace.

She should have known.

After leaving Jack, Helen pushed her way through the weekend crowds of Acland Street and headed for home. At Luna Park the big dipper was rising and falling on its scaffolding and the shrieks of the revellers soared over the traffic noise. She had never ridden the big dipper, she had never been to Luna Park; when she was young there had been too little money and when she was older too little time. Even the trip to Disneyland with Luke had been made to coincide with a scientific meeting in Los Angeles. As for Luke himself, if not for a conference in Toronto and a Dutch geneticist on the look-out for some extra-marital fun, if not for too much alcohol and too little attention to contraception, her son would never have been conceived.

Science is like that. You put your head down, you do your work and you are not distracted – not even to have a baby. But surely any scientist with a skerrick of social conscience would have been aware of the wider ramifications of her work? And surely any responsible scientist would not have ignored the unpalatable but obvious fact that when powerful interests foot the bill it is those interests that will decide how research will be applied.

When the early nuclear physicists realised that tampering with the nucleus of matter could lead to weapons the likes of which had never before been imagined, some of the central figures, including Einstein, agitated for social and political restrictions on scientific work. They agitated for what they believed to be right for humankind even though their own science might be curtailed. These were, she had always believed, good scientists, responsible scientists, the sort of scientist she wanted to be, the sort of scientist she assumed she was.

It had been easy to take the high moral ground when the way ahead was unambiguous and all ethical considerations remained theoretical. But now when she was faced with a choice of doing the science of her desire and ignoring some of the possible applications of her work, or giving up her work because it might well be used for immoral ends, what she most wanted was for politics to stay out of the laboratory. To put it bluntly: she wanted to do her science and have all questions of ethics disappear.

She crossed Marine Parade and set off along the beach path at a brisk pace. There was a stiff southerly blowing off the water and whipping up the sand; she pulled her hat lower and shoved her hands in her pockets. To what extent would she compromise her ideals in order to do her science? The scientist who would pose such a question was not the sort of scientist she ever thought she would be. You think you know yourself, you think you understand the passions of your work, and perhaps you do as long as there is a calm and temperate air. But it is the storms that matter, the storms that test you. Yet would Ava ever be forced to give up writing novels for the greater good? Would Connie have to stop doing philosophy?

Politics and science were an old coupling, as old as biological warfare itself. Nearly two thousand years ago the Scythians dipped their arrowheads into rotting material for a more lethal effect, and back in the fourteenth century Tatars tossed dead bodies infected with plague over the walls of enemy cities. During the Second World War Jews suffered agonising deaths when they were deliberately infected with malaria, typhus, yellow fever, smallpox, cholera, diphtheria. Hitler's scientists emptied the entire bacterial pantry into those poor doomed souls in service to science and the Third Reich. And then there was the German physical chemist Fritz Haber, master of modern dual-use research and the true progenitor of the present-day alliance between science, politics and the military.

Helen had always been fascinated by Haber. Such a brilliant, flawed man, his life in science was a warning to all scientists. He rose to prominence in the years before the Great War, when he devised the process of fixing nitrogen from the air for the commercial production of fertiliser. The same process led to the manufacture of explosives. Both discoveries contributed to Germany's success early in the war – more plentiful food on the one hand, more efficient killing on the other. In those years Haber was a hero in his beloved Germany.

Haber and Einstein met as relatively young men and maintained an unlikely and often strained friendship until Haber's death a year after Hitler assumed power. They shared a few similarities – both were scientists, both were German Jews – but Haber was a great German patriot while Einstein was profoundly suspicious of what he called 'the blond beast'.

Einstein, with his commitment to humanitarian causes and his advocacy of world government, wanted to keep science independent of national, political and commercial interests.

Haber's science always served the cause of Germany's greatness. After fertiliser and explosives, he went on to spearhead the development, production and delivery of the chlorine gas used by the Germans during the Great War. This cruelly efficient, silent killer shocked the allies, and quite a few Germans too. But for Haber anything was justified if it helped Germany assume its rightful place in the world. Einstein was critical of Haber's bullish patriotism: it compromised the moral obligations of the scientist, he believed. But of the two men, and despite the contemporary reverence accorded to Einstein, Helen was in no doubt Haber would settle more comfortably with today's pragmatic and politicised science.

Helen had never experienced a moment's patriotism – loyalty to an idea of place simply made no sense to her – and she had always admired Einstein, yet now she was being expected to act like Haber. And not for the first time she wondered what choices she would have made if she had been a scientist in Hitler's Germany. What criminal acts might she have committed in order to keep working with her bacteria?

When she had decided to specialise in food-borne diseases, it was a patch of science so unfashionable that her professors had tried to dissuade her. But she was already smitten. Salmonella, campylobacter, cholera, shigella – the names were flamboyantly lyrical – how she admired these bugs with their truculent vanity, their stubbornness to survive. Bacteria, the first of life and so deceptively simple, would outlive all other creatures. But with molecular biology now the new physics, and the military people mad for new 'biological strategies' (defensive rather than offensive, according to them, but Helen didn't believe anything they said any more), where she had started and where she now found herself were very different places indeed.

Science is a calling and the scientist compelled to find order, sense and truth in a type of God search, whether Kepler seeking the geometrical underpinnings to the earth or Einstein and his doomed unified field theory. And it is a jealous calling, an all-consuming calling: when you are grappling with a scientific problem it will not let you go. Science had given her a life and given generously, her work had mattered – her own voice of reason argued her case; but now she felt caught, not because science had betrayed her but because of the particular circumstances that currently shaped the practice of science.

It was this notion of a calling that she, the scientist, and Ava, the would-be writer, had recognised in each other when they first met.

'Fiction found me. Fiction found *me*,' Ava had once called out across the water of Sydney Harbour. And science had found Helen. But now she wondered if original work were possible any more. The teams of scientists like her own in Maryland were brought together to work on specific projects, and their discoveries, it seemed to her, were pre-ordained. These days fear, myopia and a sturdy line of command tethered scientists far from the anarchic fringes of surprising originality.

She stopped on the path and turned to face the bay. The sea was dark and rough, the foam was muted in the leaden light. She leapt over the low wall and walked down to the shoreline. The waves scrambled up the beach heaping one over another. The sand whipped and swirled. The heaving waves, the choppy seas, the shallows murky with sand, all was chaos.

She stood motionless at the water's edge. The noise slammed into her, the wind rocketed through her; she lingered until her thoughts were still. Then slowly she wandered back up the beach and made her way home.

3.

Helen settled at the kitchen table to read what she hoped was the finished version of a paper she'd been working on since her arrival back in Australia. Work was her solution to most problems – even work problems. Luke was still asleep, and how anyone could sleep for twelve hours straight she would never understand. She had always resented sleeping as so much time wasted. She would hear people say how much they loved it, but to love sleeping was, as far as she was concerned, as ludicrous as loving breathing or defecation or any essential bodily function.

She was nearing the end of the paper when she heard stirrings from Luke's bedroom. Then followed some half-hearted coughing and some full-bodied groaning, the squeak of the bathroom door, the toilet flushing, and there he was in the doorway, already connected to his iPod, his head faintly nodding to the music. He had pulled on a football jumper – blue and white, she noticed, the colours of his grandparents' team; his sweat pants could do with a wash. As he leaned down and pecked her cheek she felt the startling brush of bristles and a whiff of something stale and sleepy. The whole feel of her son had changed; all angles and bones, Luke was now taller than she was. His voice, a flattened bass for more than a year, still sounded strange.

He pulled out one of his earplugs and nodded at her paper. 'So you're going ahead with it?'

'I'm told it's not up to me, that I do not own the laboratory nor do I pay to use it.' She assumed a blank-faced authority and an American accent. 'I've been further reminded that while the research was made possible by money awarded to me in my capacity as leader of the team, the team itself is not employed by me, nor do I pay for the materials, nor any of the equipment or the lab utilities.' Now she allowed herself to smile, although it was more in the way of a grimace.

Luke mumbled something that she interpreted as sympathy before attending to his breakfast. He filled a mixing bowl with cereal, added the better part of a litre of milk and joined her at the table. With his head bent over the bowl and his hand in a steady spooning, he smoothed the edges of his hunger. A couple of minutes later he lowered his spoon and pulled out the other earplug – totally disconnected, Helen found herself thinking.

'Stop beating up on yourself, Mom. You need to chill a bit. And you're far too hung up on ideals. Get rid of them or upgrade.' He replaced his earplugs and returned to his cereal.

As if it were so simple. And while the scientist and citizen in her wanted to argue with him, the mother would not; there was time enough for him to oscillate, to lose his footing on the uncertainties of life. She wanted him to be happy, she wanted him to be successful, she wanted to ease his passage into maturity, guard him from hurt, from disappointment, from suffering – all those experiences that would help prepare him to tackle life's uncertainties. And yes, she was aware of the contradictions, but she would do anything to protect him from unhappiness.

Fritz Haber had been a neglectful father to his three children and a failure as a husband. His first wife, the brilliant chemist

Clara Immerwahr, became a housewife when she married; she shot herself with her husband's service revolver in 1915 soon after she learned of his work with chlorine gas. And after a decade of marriage, Haber's second wife, Charlotte, chose to be divorced rather than ignored.

Haber's two loves had been science and Germany; Helen's were science and her son, with science the less complicated until recently. Luke at sixteen cared nothing for science, he preferred virtual friendships to real ones, there were a few essentials – computer, cell phone, iPod and a few other electronic excrescences – and most other things he could take or leave. She had tried to interest him in science, but he was easily bored – boredom, she decided, was the defining trait of his generation. In so many ways Luke was different from her, yet bound so close that the love and the anxieties pulled tight enough for pain.

She was in her late twenties when she discovered she was pregnant. At that stage she had not given any thought to motherhood, yet when it became a possibility she realised she wanted a child and the chance might never come again. The decision was clear, spontaneous and immune to argument. The Dutch geneticist, with a wife and children in Rotterdam, wanted nothing to do with a baby, indeed Roeland wanted there to be no baby. And if it had concerned only Helen, there would have been no identifiable father; but she believed her unborn child had a right to two parents. Roeland fought her throughout the pregnancy and for the first year of Luke's life. And then – reluctantly – he agreed that if in the future the boy wanted to contact him he would comply. He demanded discretion, he stipulated conditions, a document was drawn up and duly signed.

As it happened, Roeland and Luke were now in regular contact. Roeland's wife had left him years ago, his other children were parents themselves. Roeland had visited Luke in the US several times, Luke had visited his father in Rotterdam. These days, the son born of a conference fling was one of the most important people in his father's life.

'I'll be sleeping over at Edith and Barry's tonight,' Luke now said. And in response to the blank expression on her face: 'I told you, Mom. I'm taking the train to Geelong. Barry's giving me a golf lesson, and tonight we're having a *Lord of the Rings* marathon.'

Twenty minutes later and still looking grubby despite a shower, Luke left for the train station. She thought she heard him whistling as he closed the front door. Her all-American son had never been happier. He liked Melbourne, he liked his new school, his classmates were friendly and he was a natural at Australian Rules Football. But most of all he liked having a family – aunts, uncles, cousins and most especially grandparents.

Far from being the rigid, conservative people of Helen's accounts, Barry and Edith Rankin were, according to Luke, 'quite cool for oldies'. And while Helen was prepared to acknowledge her parents had changed, her mother in particular who 'loved the internet', and confessed to googling Helen on a regular basis, the long confined years of childhood were not so easily erased.

The Barry and Edith Rankin of her youth were solid conforming people who had venerated the status quo. And from Helen's perspective – far more critical than Luke's – they still did. They liked established facts, and they liked the elements of their life – friends, children, grandchildren, politics, home decoration – to make sense. Doubt brought more than discomfort, it gave rise to questions, and questions led to unknown destinations. Then, as now, Barry and Edith liked their life exactly as it was.

Only Helen among the Rankins had ever sought to question, and this from early childhood. Does the grass hurt when we tread on it? Why do all Chinese people have black hair? How do you know that dogs don't have a special dog language? What makes the sky blue?

'You'll have to watch that one,' several Rankin friends had remarked when Helen was growing up.

Edith, with three other children to watch, strenuously ignored their advice. All she and Barry wanted was a nice manageable life in a nice family-focused area, Edith's priority the home and children, Barry in a steady job with the post office, and when the Postmaster General was privatised, success with his post-shop franchise. And while at a superficial level there had been changes, as far as Helen was concerned, her parents were fundamentally as they had always been.

Their second child was an enigma from the beginning. Helen was walking at nine months and talking in sentences by her first birthday. And there was an exuberance about her that was, frankly, embarrassing. A child of incessant questions, she refused to accept anything at face value.

'Why do you want to make everything so difficult for yourself?' Edith said to the three-year-old, the six-year-old, and the nine-year-old Helen. But in truth, Helen's questions made life difficult for her and Barry.

On the TV news Helen would see black-skinned children, little more than babies themselves, caring for a baby brother or sister, she would see children sifting through rubbish tips in Colombia, and boys and girls with brittle limbs and distended stomachs working barren African fields. None of these children had a chance of childhood; they were born, they learned to walk and talk, and if they survived disease and starvation they assumed adult responsibilities. All quite different from Helen. She had a childhood at her fingertips: school, the town pool, Brownies, Girl Guides, shops, pets, other children thrilling in their childhoods. The childhood on offer was not so much a cloak of nettles but the emperor's new clothes, and Helen saw through to the bone.

She created her own entertainment much to her parents' embarrassment, schemes like the great lavender heist of 1970 when she and her friends appropriated their mothers' stockings and pantyhose, stripped the neighbourhood of lavender and went door to door selling lavender sachets made of 15 denier nylon. She established a local, and lucrative, poker school for sixth-graders; and a substantial number of her year-seven class turned blond when she demonstrated the chemical properties of peroxide. With all her madcap projects, her parents would cut off her pocket money and withdraw any privileges. But boredom was far more powerful than parental anger or personal deprivations and within a day or a week or a month she would be up to something else.

Once all the children were of school age, Edith joined Barry in the post office – not that home and children had become less important, but work was 'the right thing to do'. There was a quality Edith referred to as 'backbone' and work was its marrow.

'No matter what you do,' Edith and Barry would say to their children, 'it's important you do it well. Whether driving a bus, cooking in a canteen, or running a post office.'

Or doing science. In some fundamental ways it seemed Helen had turned out to be more of a Rankin than she could ever have predicted. But back in childhood, apart from her father's features stamped on her own, she might have been a Martian. It was a book that finally solved the enigma, a cloth-covered volume about the childhoods of famous scientists. The vast majority of these scientists were odd, unconventional, impatient children, some of whom played for laughs, others who passed their growing years in solitude with their nature collections and books, and a few like Helen who swung both ways. It occurred to her that she might well be heading for a brilliant future, although far more significant was the discovery that in places far from Geelong she would be considered normal. The problem, she decided, was her parents subscribed to a different brand of normal.

Many years later when Jack showed her Robert Frost's poem 'The Road not Taken', Helen said it should be compulsory reading for all children. Childhood was less innocence than ignorance, she believed, and no child should ever be locked in a solitary confinement of his or her own peculiarities. She was of the opinion that bright children would make a far better fist of childhood if many of the rewards of maturity arrived early. But given they didn't and given she loved her parents, she tried to protect them from her more excessive excesses.

Helen's resolve may have weakened if she had not won a residential scholarship to a private girls' college in Melbourne. A teacher at her primary school had been the prime mover, a man who had taken a special interest in her and to whom she would always be grateful. He had coached her after school and on weekends, he had lent her his own books, he treated her as special, not odd. Both were rewarded when she won the schol-arship. Her parents, however, were opposed: the local high school was good enough for everyone else, and surely good enough for a clever child who ought to be able to learn anywhere. When Helen refused to be dissuaded, they said she was not to expect extra from them, not for books, nor travel, nor any out-of-the-ordinary expenses. They had three other children to consider, they said, and they were determined to be fair. Fair treatment in her parents' scheme of things was exactly the same treatment for all four children.

For the next several years Helen made the passage between two different universes. She lived at school during the week and went home most weekends; she rarely talked about school at home, nor did she talk about home at school. And she continued to love her parents as they did her with their watchful, nervy love. And of course they relented, providing for extra books and extra travel, and funding outings and excursions – often to theatre productions and art exhibitions that would have horrified them. But despite their visiting the school for the occasional drama performance and annual speech night, it remained well outside their comfort zone.

When the final exam results were published and Helen was among the top students in the state, her parents were still bewildered by their daughter but proud. They presented her with a hard-cover book about Madame Curie to mark her success. She took it to Oxford, she took it to America, it was now in her study down the hall.

Her parents' pride countenanced her full residential scholarship at one of the university colleges with its living-away-from-home allowance. But her choice of a science degree alarmed them. She needed a proper job, they said. Why not medicine or pharmacy? Girls were doing all sorts of things these days, they said. But Helen remained firm.

Throughout the years of her undergraduate degree she

telephoned her parents each week and attended all family functions. She kept her new life to herself – her studies, her new friends, and most particularly her decision to relinquish her residential scholarship to join Ava in a communal student house. Although whenever a food-poisoning outbreak was reported in the news, she would tell her parents she'd solve problems like that one day. But it was hard for them. They simply could not understand how someone who might have become a doctor would prefer bacteria.

When Helen was notified about her postgraduate travelling scholarship she knew better than to interrupt her parents' bridge night. She waited until the following Sunday when the family was gathered for lunch and there she announced she would be going to Oxford. No one knew what to say.

It was Edith, her face pressed with concern, who finally broke the silence. 'I worry about you Helen, I really do. When are you going to get a job, settle down? When do you plan to get on with your life?'

They worried when she went to Oxford, their worries increased when she didn't come home. They were shocked and worried when she was unmarried and pregnant, and horrified and worried to discover the baby's father was married to someone else. But now, decades later, they seemed to have embraced the son born out of wedlock; even the daughter they once found so perplexing seemed less strange to them.

The past – childhood – takes the best cut of memory. Whenever Helen saw her parents behaving differently from how she remembered, it emphasised not what they had become but what they once had been. Luke, however, saw his grandparents as they were and he loved them as he seemed to love everything about Australia. Helen assumed he was responding to what she saw as the Americanisation of Australia, but he assured her it was the differences which attracted.

'I can be myself here,' he said.

Helen was surprised. Australia was so changed from the place she remembered, so much more American, and not just in terms of entertainment and food and retail franchises, but politically too. Whenever there was a natural disaster or a sporting tragedy, the prime minister could be heard on the evening news offering up prayers for the families. Prayers from the mouth of an Australian politician would have been unthinkable when she was growing up. And she had arrived home to a background debate on abortion – less on the boil than in America but nonetheless creating some heat. She'd marched for a woman's right to choose back in the 1970s. What was happening here? And military personnel were being raised to the status of heroes. It didn't matter who they were or what personal qualities they possessed, if they were soldiers they were worthy of respect. Australians, with their experience of fighting other people's wars, used to have a healthy suspicion of the military.

Then there was Gallipoli, an historical landmark shunted to the shadows when she was at school. At her Melbourne laboratory the two youngest scientists, both in their early twenties, were planning to visit Gallipoli next ANZAC Day. Gallipoli, they said, defined all that was best in the Australian character. 'But we lost,' Helen wanted to say. 'It was a bloody slaughter. We were cannon fodder for the Brits.'

Having lived so long in America, where patriotism was imbibed with first words, Helen was understandably cynical. Patriotism: such an effective form of persuasion, no better way of getting large numbers of people to think and act together.

Patriotism: membership open to all, thugs particularly welcome. Patriotism: the great equaliser, the great mobiliser. Patriotism, and farewell to Australia's larrikins, farewell the iconoclasts.

Haber's life was a cautionary tale to all patriots. As a Jew he could never be properly German, so at the age of twenty-four, with an ambition common to young men of his time and class, he had himself baptised. He lived a German lifestyle, his houses were run on German lines, he believed in the superiority of German culture. Photographs depict him as the stereotypical German with a large bald crown, wire-framed pince-nez and a penchant for military uniform.

He rose through the ranks, people honoured and obeyed him, but no one forgot his Jewishness. Einstein tried to warn him, but Haber did not want to hear. When Hitler assumed power in 1933, Haber lost first his job, then his science and ultimately his country. But despite his sufferings he still remained a staunch German patriot. Not long before his death in exile in Switzerland, he wrote to his son that if it were appropriate to inscribe an epitaph on his grave he would like it to be: 'In war and peace, as long as it was granted him, a servant of his homeland.'

Fritz Haber's headstone in Basel bears no epitaph.

One of Ava's early novels tells the story of a composer who entered into a Faustian pact in order to write the music of his dreams. This composer was willing to trade his beliefs and betray his values in order to produce his art. Helen went into her study and found the novel, but even before she opened to the first chapter she knew she was too agitated to read. What she really wanted was to talk to Ava. She hovered over the phone, she dialled and then she disconnected. She was not prepared to deal with Harry.

There was no food in the house and she decided to go to the market. She picked up her research paper and there lying on the table was one of Luke's pictorial notes – clearly the Dutch geneticist had artistic talent as she certainly did not. Luke had drawn a scientist working at a bench with a sparkling halo tipped at a jaunty angle. The caption read: GO MOMMA.

Impossible to predict this boy of hers. Mostly he had the sensitivity of a slab of concrete, then there were times when he knew exactly where to lay the hand. Helen texted a thankyou to him before adding this latest note to her cache of his notes. She rarely threw out anything of Luke's. Poor boy would be mortified if he knew.

Not just her son, but all her old friends were adept at reading people and situations. Helen returned to the study and picked up the telephone. Her desire to speak to Ava was, she realised, more powerful than her antipathy towards Harry. She lit a cigarette, she dialled, she prepared herself for Harry, and such disappointment to hear the answering machine. Helen left a message for Ava suggesting they meet over the weekend.

'I need to talk to you,' she said.

4.

I have found my lifelong friend, Helen had written in her note-book on the day she met Ava. For other people and other friends, lifelong might require the perspective from the end of life, but Helen knew at the beginning, she truly knew. Long before she started at university she had been aware of the creases in her life – everyone has them, those dark spaces you would prefer not to exist. For Helen, as long as she had Ava, her creases mattered less.

Ava was proof that if one is too much in thrall to everyday demands the imagination, for want of quiet and unfettered energy, becomes dormant. Her clothes were unpressed, her room was a shambles, her desk was a mess. Almost daily she would riffle the layers for a lost page, a lost pen, a phone number, and with mounting impatience would pledge to keep a tidy desk, a tidier life, but she never did.

'If I found myself in the same situation, the same state of knowledge this year as last, then I might as well be dead,' she said to Helen over their very first cup of coffee in the university cafeteria.

Ava insisted on being a non-believer but at the same time she acted as if there were purpose to life, the main tenet being not to waste it. She was already writing fiction when she started university and her presentations to the Laconics were often drawn from her stories. Far from the usual autobiographically infused fictions of most new writers, Ava's stories roved far and wide. Why confine yourself to the tiny arena of your own life? she would say. Why shun all those marvellous excursions of the imagination? Young men, old women, dogs, gods, monsters, castles, caves, starvation, snow, all found a place in her fiction.

It did not take long for Helen to realise that Ava Bryant was unlike anyone she had ever met, and what struck her as so remarkable was that Ava had chosen her.

'Ours is a romantic friendship,' Helen said when she moved out of college to join Ava in her communal house. 'Like Virginia Woolf and Vita Sackville-West.'

'You don't think they slept together then?' Ava asked.

'No, I can't imagine Virginia would be in it.'

There was a long silence before Ava spoke. 'I think people can sleep with practically anyone if there's a good enough reason.'

They had known each other a year at this time. They were best friends and best friends shared their deepest secrets. Now Helen wondered if this really had been the case, particularly given Ava's embargo on her family.

'Some actions and events have their own place and their own reason,' Ava continued in a rush. 'Nothing would be served by making them public.'

And despite her curiosity Helen left it at that.

There are snapshots in memory that never fade. Ava playing both Romeo and Juliet using the sculpture of a severe-faced university benefactor as a prop; Ava giving a spontaneous recitation of *Howl* at Tiamo café in Lygon Street; Ava with a loudhailer outside the Swanston Street sex shop during a Reclaim the Night march; the two of them sitting by Sydney Harbour eating mango for the first time.

The invitation had arrived in the mail, even though Ava's bedroom was the next one down the hall.

AVA BRYANT INVITES HELEN RANKIN

TO AN ALL-EXPENSES PAID TRIP TO SYDNEY

TO LEAVE THE DAY AFTER HER LAST EXAM

Helen had never travelled outside Victoria and she assumed Ava's experience was the same. The Opera House, the harbour, the bridge, Sydney! She and Ava could not wait a moment longer. Or at least that was how Helen understood it. But just as she did not press Ava on how she managed to fund two return train tickets and pay for everything during the trip, neither did she question her obvious familiarity with Sydney. Ava was always so generous that to question, to ask for more, seemed ungrateful.

Such an adventure, Helen knew nothing to compare. The train was not crowded and the two of them had a second-class compartment all to themselves. They placed their bags in the overhead rack and spread themselves, their books, a cache of sweets and cigarettes, and coats for warmth across the two long seats. The compartment was an assortment of browns, from the cracked leather of the seats to the wood panelling from which all polish had disappeared, to the ooze of cigarettes and other journeys that hit them as soon as they entered. But it might have been the *Orient Express* as far as Helen was concerned.

It was still light when the train pulled out of Spencer Street Station. They passed quickly through central Melbourne into the inner industrial suburbs, rendered strange from the raised perspective of the train. Within an hour they were in the country. It was dusk and the sky was radiant with pink and maroon strokes between long grey ribbons of cloud. When it was completely dark they pulled down the blind, and in the mustardy light, their feet propped on the opposite seat and their bodies rocking with the train's rhythm, they talked through the night.

The train pulled into Sydney at eight o'clock the next morning. They washed in the station bathroom and bought bacon-and-egg sandwiches at a kiosk. Everything ordinary was extraordinary. The station at peak hour was dizzy with people and that particular fuel-and-grime smell of large train stations. Ava dragged Helen out of the main bustle to a space near a wall.

'Close your eyes,' she said. 'Close your eyes.'

And the two of them stood at Central Station in a swarm of noise and smells, their eyes closed and arms linked as the foreign crowd of Sydney streamed past.

'Where are you?' Ava asked, raising her voice above the din.

'London. No, Cambridge,' Helen said. 'And you?'

'St Petersburg,' Ava said, 'in the summer before the revolution. And in Cambridge with you. And London, and Paris, and –' she raised her arms and opened her eyes, 'Sydney. I'm in Sydney now!'

They spent the day around the harbour. They tramped all through the Opera House, the steps and paths that were open to the public and a good many corridors and performance rooms which were not. They ate their lunch perched on a low wall, the harbour on one side and the marvellous sails of the Opera House shimmering above them.

'Imagine being up there,' Ava said, nodding at the sails. 'Your body spread-eagled on those gorgeous curves.'

For dessert, Ava bought a large, exorbitantly priced mango and the two of them sat on a parapet overlooking the water while Ava sliced off pulpy cheeks and cubed them with her pocket knife, introducing Helen to the wonder of mangoes. The taste was paradisaical, the taste of Eden, Helen said. And she would never change her mind, not even when mangoes became common fare and she could eat them every day. But her first mango, like so many firsts, she experienced with Ava. They asked a tourist to take a photo of them. And when the tourist moved on they took turns in capturing the other on black and white film in every stage of eating mango.

'Black and white is more artistic than colour,' Ava said.

They made a frieze of the photos above the fireplace in the house they shared. The same photos, now limp and faded, stretched in a vertical line down the side of Helen's study window. Wherever she had lived she had put up the mango pictures. It was a way of establishing home.

Before Thursday's reunion she had not seen Ava for nearly three years. But three years or three days would make no difference. The best connections do not require support material from time. She would fix the NOGA fellowship, but she was not in a hurry to return to America. To be living in the same city with Ava, to see her as often as she liked, was exactly what she needed to sort through her work problems. As for Harry, her friendship with Ava had survived twenty-plus years of him, and it would now survive his new-found power.

5.

At seven-thirty on Monday morning Helen punched in the security code and entered the laboratory. She left her coat and laptop in the office and headed out to the bench. She had passed the weekend battling her career dilemmas and struggling to hold Harry's threats at bay. Ava had not returned her call.

Well-functioning laboratories are bigger or smaller, better or lesser equipped, older or newer, but fundamentally the same the world over – like churches have a sameness whether an open-sided thatched structure in New Guinea or a cathedral in Bruges. There's the familiar prickling of chemicals, the particular coolness of the air, the crisp green-white of the lights, the hum of the refrigerators. Helen had arrived at the lab early in order to see if the gene had taken. She set up the gel bath, checked everything was in order, the sample properly in place, the electrolyte level, and turned on the current. Such a lovely process – the electric current separating and arranging the genetic components so they can be seen in vertical arrangements of bands. Life's mysteries made visible.

While the current sorted out the DNA, she returned to the office to deal with her email. There were the usual queries from Maryland, invitations to meetings, greetings from friends, all routine until the email with the subject line FLYER FOR YOUR FORTHCOMING LECTURE, at which point the calm of the morning, the pleasure in her work, her sense that she could do her science and let everything else be damned, crashed.

This lecture had been arranged months ago while she was still in the US. It was to focus on new frontiers in molecular biology, but according to the flyer she was to speak on 'Bacteria and the New Bioterrorism'. She was described as 'the renowned expert on bioterrorism'. How typically Australian to call a spade a bloody shovel; in America the lecture would be couched in optimistic euphemism, something along the lines of 'Securing our World: Safe Food, Safer Future'. But that was beside the point: her area was not bioterrorism, a bioterrorism expert was not who she was.

She knew who was to blame. She printed off the flyer, grabbed her things, locked the lab and set off for the NOGA offices. Bloody Harry whose 'Be sensible', 'You know the right thing to do', 'Many people have invested in you', whose unsmiling face in fish-eye lens close-up was hounding her through the days and nights. Harry was as lethal as any bacteria, but there was something spoiling in him, something not playing by the rules.

∽

His door was open, he was seated at his desk, his polished head bent close to a newspaper. He started as she entered.

Helen slapped the flyer on top of his paper. 'What's this?'

Harry read it slowly. He seemed to be considering every word. He picked the page up, he took it in at a distance, he drew it in close. 'It reads well,' he said at last, looking up at her. 'I'm pleased with it. Yes,' he said, nodding his big head, 'very pleased.'

'So you are behind this?'

Harry's features settled into ostentatious concern. 'I wanted to spare you,' he said. 'You've far more important things to do than write an advertisement for a public lecture.'

He was being deliberately evasive. She grabbed the flyer and waved it in his face. 'This is not my research.'

'But it is,' Harry said quietly, settling back in his chair. 'And a good deal more interesting than diarrhoea in Somalia or contaminated oysters in Japan.'

'This is not my research,' she said again. She spoke slowly, emphasising each word. 'I do not work in bioterrorism.'

He smiled, how she hated that smarmy smile. 'But you do,' he said. 'A glance at the last half-dozen international meetings you've attended testifies to that.'

She was standing over him, glaring down. 'It's an off-shoot of my work, not its main thrust. And it's certainly not my primary interest.'

'Are you equipped to address this topic –' he twisted his head so as to read the title from the flyer, as if he didn't know it already, 'Bacteria and the New Bioterrorism?'

'You know I am.'

'And would you like a good-sized crowd?'

'Of course I would.'

Again he smiled. 'You have to admit it's a catchy title.'

'It's terrible and I want it changed. And that appalling bio-line as well.'

He gazed up at her from his big shiny desk. 'Too late I'm afraid. Notice of the lecture has already been emailed out.' He cocked his head to one side, he frowned with concern. 'I'm sorry to have upset you. But don't you think you might be over-reacting to what is essentially just a difference in emphasis?'

She took in the frown, the fake concern, his aggressive courtesy. She took in Harry Guerin.

'You really are a bastard, Harry.'

Chapter 4: Vanity of Vanities

1.

'You'll be stars for a day,' Connie said.

'At last,' Jack said with a laugh, 'our fifteen minutes of fame.'

But Connie wasn't in the mood for jokes. He cuffed a hand at the back of Jack's neck and pulled him close. 'Just agree,' he said. 'Please.'

Almost three months had passed since the NOGA cocktail party and contrary to reputation, the massive machinery that was TV programming and production had been working flat out. Gathered now in the round reading room of the State Library were Jack, Helen and Ava, together with Luke for the youth appeal, recruited as extras for the pilot of Connie's TV series, *Travels in Cyberspace*.

It was only the third time since the reunion the friends had met as a group. Jack had tried on numerous occasions to get them together but with Ava and Connie living north of the city and he and Helen in the south, plus Helen's inability to apply temperance to her work and Connie's lack of temperance when it came to Sara, to settle on a time and place that suited them all had been well-nigh impossible. With Helen just a short walk away Jack saw her often, and he managed to catch up with Connie about once a week; Ava he could see every day she had so much time to spare but he preferred not to be alone with her. What he longed for was their old Laconics nights, all of them in that heated togetherness uniquely theirs, and being involved in the pilot, he believed, was a move in the right direction. The fact that Connie had called on his old friends rather than Sara's crowd, and that the friends had so readily responded, gave Jack confidence they would find their rhythm again.

The director, a woman much their own age, was calling for silence, and Connie, so anxious in the lead-up to filming, now seemed entirely at ease. He was standing under the lights at the head of a bank of computers – Connie, the computers and the shelves of old books captured together in the one frame. He looked prophet-like, Jack thought, not simply the thick halo of white hair and loose pale jumper, but his appearing simultaneously flamboyant and ascetic in this Olympian space. Andy Warhol's dictum aside, Connie's fame required a measure far more solid than minutes. Mountains would be ideal. Four or five prominent piles large enough to bend the horizons of culture. And if Connie's fame could be measured in mountains then Jack's own was a matter of teaspoons. A teaspoon of talent, a teaspoon of fame.

Jack found the notion surprisingly irksome. Fame in any quantity should not matter to him for he never had the same ambition as the others. Perhaps what was different now was his desire to work, a new book, just simmering at the moment, but his first inclination for years. Being asked his opinion on matters Muslim from the Koran to the alienation of Islamic youth, Jack felt the pleasures of an active brain again. And the proximity of his friends helped too; through the get-togethers with Helen and Connie, along with regular email and telephone contact with all three, he was connected to the dailiness of their work, which seemed to provide fuel for his own.

A phalanx of black-clad people conveyed Connie from one end of the bank of computers to the other while lights were adjusted and sound was tested. So much care was taken with him, everyone so deferential, and Jack found himself wondering at the connection between people treating you as brilliant, your belief in your own brilliance, and most important of all, your ability to come up with the goods. What person who believed himself to be ordinary ever produced remarkable and original work? And while there were legions of people who over-estimated their talent, might it be possible, Jack wondered, to miss your own talent, actually fail to see it?

He gazed around the great domed space, at the shelves of books lining the walls and the spokes of desks radiating out from the keeper's desk at the centre. The State Library had recently been spruced up and the thick sepia cloud he remembered from his high school years had disappeared in fresh paint and polish. But the old-book smell had seeped back, and the original desks had been retained, and still the green lamps, although greener and brighter than they used to be, and still the familiar safety and solitude common to all libraries. Some people count their travels in churches, others in galleries and museums, Jack could count his travels in libraries. Wherever he was in the world, a library was home.

How many of the authors lodged in this place had been convinced of their own gifts, Jack now wondered. His major obstacle was that the more he learned, the more ignorant he knew himself to be. And while this was typical of most writers, rather than energise him as it did Connie, Ava and Helen and probably most of the authors represented here, he could never be satisfied with anything he produced. Always falling short of his own desires, he hadn't finished anything for years. And yet if he was to be asked if his friends' work was always perfect, he would not hesitate to say that of course it wasn't, although with Helen's he was probably not competent to judge. But he would also add it was different for them: their solid reputations could buoy them through an occasional lapse, but with no reputation to speak of, the smallest fault would sink him.

One of the black-clad film crew shifted him and Helen to one side (Ava had been given a more prominent position by the wall of books), there was a volley of last-minute orders, a stretch of silence, then filming began. Connie strolled along the bank of computers, pausing a moment in front of each screen to press a key and change the display – such a variety, and Connie speaking with ease and eloquence about each. At the end of the line of computers he stops at the wall of books, takes from a shelf Russell's *A History of Western Philosophy* – Jack recognises Connie's own copy with the distinctive woven-cloth cover – and retires to an armchair to read. He looks so pale and graceful against the dark red leather. Ethereal, Jack finds himself thinking, and entirely in keeping with his prophet-like status.

Slowly Connie lifts his gaze. His tight intelligent face stares into the eye of the camera. 'Come back in an hour or two,' he says, and returns to his book.

The camera waits and watches, the people wait and watch. A couple of seconds more and Connie looks up from his book, his angular features softening to a smile.

'Watching someone read lacks something in the way of entertainment,' he says, and closes his book. 'So stay a while and let's try to understand what's happening here, between this world of knowledge,' he waves at the computers, 'and this other world of knowledge,' he holds up his book.

The filming stops and the director takes him through his paces again. Connie resumes his position at the line of computers, he pulls down menus, he alters screens, his hands wave in emphasis, he laughs, he frowns, he cocks his head in enquiry, he's feverish with excitement. Jack watches enthralled. Connie looks like a man in love.

They begin rehearsing a new scene. Connie is indicating the array of computers, there's a smorgasbord of information here, he is saying. 'On this computer there's the world news, on the next the program schedule at the local cinema complex. And here's the Glenn Gould website including,' Connie presses a key, 'a sample of his playing,' – the first couple of bars of Bach's 15th Goldberg are heard – 'and how we would like to stay and listen, but with so much on offer there's no time to stop.' He moves to the next screen, a blog from a sixteen-year-old Japanese snow-boarder, the next computer is downloading music, the one after that is playing a DVD of Fritz Lang's *Metropolis*, the last displays a page from Connie's current work in progress. 'Actually a whole chapter,' Connie says. He scrolls to the end of the document and laughs. 'A regrettably short chapter.'

'All this,' and he waves his hand at the computers, 'all this for my edification, entertainment and livelihood. And I want to take it in. And I want to do it now.'

He sits at one computer then the next then a third. He swivels around to face the camera. 'Imagine that I spend an entire day at the computer. How quickly will time pass, how filled – saturated – I'll feel when finally I rise from my chair.

But when I peruse the contents of the day, how much do I retain? I pour myself a glass of red,' – 'The booze will have to go,' Jack hears one of the crew whisper – 'and I settle in my armchair and try to recall. Not only do I fail to retrieve all but a handful of sites I've enjoyed these past eight hours, but I find I can't sit and think. The chair is comfortable, the room is nicely heated, the wine is excellent, but something has punctured my ability to be still and reflect.'

Connie now leaps to his feet. 'We are at an extraordinary moment in human evolution. The very nature of thought and memory is changing. This has a profound effect on who we are, but even more importantly it will affect who we can be.' He flits from one computer to the next. 'We can condemn the new technology for making us lazy and superficial, or we can exploit it in order to make us newly and brilliantly smart.'

Connie leans into the camera. 'How,' he asks, 'can we preserve memory in all its tangled richness, memory whose very existence requires prolonged reflection, when the conditions for prolonged reflection have radically altered?'

His voice is raised, he is speaking quickly, too quickly, and he is twitching with his Connie twitches, those odd shrugs of the shoulders and the prickling at the left side of his mouth, peculiarities that originally Jack thought might indicate neuro-muscular dysfunction but turned out to be nothing other than Connie gripped by excitement.

'There's not one but two generation gaps opening up in the technologically advanced world,' Connie continues. 'Two generation gaps creating three distinct populations. Each of these populations is defined by the means it employs to acquire knowledge. The first group consists of mainly older people who turn to books, newspapers, radio and mainstream

TV to learn about the world. They read, they listen, they reflect, they discuss. Their knowledge acquisition tends to be focused – no multi-tasking when this group wants to learn; it's also language-based and, to the modern sensibility, quaintly leisurely. Then there's the baby-boomer population. The members of this group have a choice of how they learn. They grew up in a world of books and libraries, they listened to the radio and watched TV. As children, their play tended to be improvised and imaginative with no group leader to guide the proceedings. While still young they learned how to think and developed the patience to think things through. But as well they're familiar with the online world of immediate information. They log on to the web for instant knowledge – the date East Timor gained its nationhood, the name of the current president of France, the Nobel Prize winner for physics in 1934, the four-day weather forecast for New York, and wider searches as well: the signs, symptoms and prognosis of a rare blood disorder, the life and recordings of Bob Dylan. When they want knowledge they can choose between printed material or the web, or use a combination of both. Often they'll start with the convenience of the web but soon realise that Wikipedia alone will not satisfy. This group understands,' Connie's excited twitches have shifted into high gear, 'that there are different ways of accessing knowledge and that knowledge is not the same as understanding. This group can choose which way is likely to have the best yield in any particular situation.'

Luke has moved away from the set. He is clearly not impressed. In fact Luke, who used to be so close to Connie he would refer to him as his Boston dad, is not interested in anything Connie has to say these days. The producer is not

impressed either. He is trying to get the attention of the director, but she is fixed on Connie and looks to be entirely satisfied.

'Now to the third generation,' Connie says, 'the online,
hooked-up generation who likes its knowledge fast and changing, the generation unlikely to include books as a knowledge
source. This is today's youth for whom free time has always
been organised time, from baby playgroups and toddler
gymnastics to after-school ballet, piano, tennis, karate, to
weekend sports and vacation camps. After days, months, years
of timetabled activity, this group has little experience of idle
time or time spent alone in thought. This is the communication
generation, who will fill every vacant moment by connecting
with real friends or cyber friends or indeed technology itself.
The members of this group negotiate the web imaginatively
but have little experience of wandering their own imagination.
As for memory, with information on tap and an array of electronic notepads, memory is exercised far less than it used to
be. To lodge something in the depths of memory requires stillness, it requires that other noise is silenced, but this is not a
quality of these times, nor of the third population.'

Connie peers into the camera, his brow is creased, he is
grappling with difficult issues. 'If you believe as I do that
memory is essential to identity, and if you further believe that
memory and imagination contribute to the ability to abstract,
then you will be concerned that the very cognitive sensibility
that has taken us from the cave to the skyscraper, which has
given us art, literature, music and technology itself, may now
be under threat.'

Luke looks disgusted. He retrieves his backpack and, brush-
ing past Jack, he quits the reading room. The director,

however, has no complaint. She indicates that Connie is to return to the red armchair. He settles into the leather and crosses one leg over the other. He is frowning, his lips are pressed firmly together, he is concerned.

'We are faced with an ever-changing present,' he says. 'We live in the ever-new. To exploit the new technology, to exploit the world past and present always at our fingertips we need to withdraw, *you* need to withdraw, to separate for a time from your computer, your cell phone, your PDA, your iPod. Otherwise you run the risk of becoming a person without memory, the quintessential person without qualities who flies fast and ceaselessly on a stream of changing images. You could even become,' and he is now speaking in such a rush that even the director looks bemused, 'you could become like an old person lost in dementia who lives in the moment and a minute later has forgotten and moved on to the next moment and the next moment and the next.'

Connie was hard to stop so thrilled was he with his idea. And so, too, was the director, although it would benefit from some scripting, she said with a laugh. When a few minutes later Connie joined Jack and the others for a short break, he told them the notion had only just occurred to him. They moved into the foyer of the library, but with a clear sky and a bright sun outside they continued through the doors to the colonnade, and there amid the bluestone and columns and the newly washed air of early spring they found an alcove out of the wind. Helen lit up and Connie regaled them with his new thought.

'How bizarre,' he said, 'that the modern sensibility with all its tools and information and its unabashed adoration of all things youthful might lock us into a world that resembles the evanescent, unconnected experiences of dementia.'

Connie was fascinated by his idea, although how it would stand up to scrutiny he did not know. But for now, the wonder he felt was written across his face; just watching him, Jack felt inspired.

Luke, who had gathered with a group of people to watch two galahs pecking the grass in front of the building – galahs in the city! – now broke away from them and made his way towards the colonnade. As he approached, Connie put aside his new idea and returned to the issue of access to knowledge.

'So, what do you think of my three populations, Luke?'

'You haven't convinced me. In fact, I can't imagine anyone under twenty agreeing with you.' He raised a hand against Connie's interruption. 'Let someone toss us a question, doesn't matter what, and I bet I have the answer before you.'

'But what if there is no single answer?' Connie said. 'What if the answer is more in the way of analysis?'

Luke shrugged. 'Whatever it is, I'll find it before you do.' And he wandered back to the galahs.

His mother watched him, a smile on her face. Connie, almost as if the exchange with Luke had not occurred, turned to Ava. 'All of your novels play around with memory. So what do you think? Can events, ideas, can thoughts of any sort lodge into retrievable memory without conscious deliberation or reflection or just a moment of acknowledgment that something has happened. If, for example, you pass a fancy building and do not notice it, if you do nothing to register it, can it later be recalled?'

Jack wanted to suggest hypnosis but had no opportunity as Connie linked his arm with Ava's and led her down the colonnade. Just before they were out of earshot he heard Connie refer to a character from Ava's fourth novel, a girl with a prodigious memory. 'Now where did she come from?'

'They're so alike,' Helen said to Jack, a smile lingering faintly as she watched them striding up and down the colonnade. 'Easy to see why we love them.'

Jack, too, was watching them, tall white-haired Connie and lush golden-haired Ava streaming through the electric air. At other times Jack would have seen only Ava, but now he was gripped by them both.

2.

The metaphors which attached to Connie and Ava were of a set. They were the sun around which revolved the planets; the star which exerted the strongest magnetic force; they were the strelitzia and anthurium of flowers, the leopard and whale of animals. Exotic and mythic, powerful and essential that's what they were, and while Helen and Jack were aware of frailties in both, they were equally aware their frailties would never hold them back.

In every aspect of life Connie moved into the future; through his work, Connie actually forged the future. And similarly with Ava. Every one of her achievements had taken her further from the shopgirl of her birthright. Even during her most tempestuous times, both Helen and Jack believed Ava had it all.

True empathy is a rare thing; most people are unable to imagine what it is to be someone else and many would actually prefer not to know. Jack and Helen expected to see Ava at the centre of every group, and so they did. They expected to see her working well and effectively, and so she was. She might appear a little tired, she might be quieter than usual, but this was no reason to worry because Ava Bryant always knew what she needed and where she was going.

So it could happen that when they moved to Oxford, Jack and Helen met with Ava every day and did not notice she was falling apart. But falling apart she was. Ava did not recognise the person she had become and had no notion of how to right herself. For years, she had imagined Oxford as a student paradise, an essential stopover on her way to the future. And yet here she was, arrived at last, and the place was incomprehensibly hostile. She had to force herself out of bed, down to breakfast, force herself to meet Helen and Jack, force herself to carry on as if nothing was wrong. And while she was a better performer than most, as the weeks passed into months she found herself with less and less energy for any sort of pretence. Yet through it all, the others failed to notice because they would not allow the possibility that Ava Bryant might ever be foundering.

Their inability to see what was happening was intensified by Oxford itself. Helen and Jack saturated themselves in Oxford and it in turn saturated them. Life seemed looser, more elastic when released from the demands and scrutiny of home. Jack said it was like being immersed in a grand symphony. Postgraduate study was less demanding than any of them had expected, with a manageable volume of work and very few people to please. Ava, searching for explanations for her mood could not find them in the pressures of work. In fact, she would have coped better if she were busier. It took more than a month before she managed to meet her supervisor, a well-known scholar with a specialty in the Romantic poets, a moon-faced, chinless man with inflamed gums and pungent body odour, a man hard to equate with the swashbuckling fervour of his publications. Ava made increasingly desperate efforts to set up a regular meeting with him. In the end his rejection – for that's how she interpreted it – seemed to add to Oxford's condemnation of her. She told the others she had the best of him in his books, and while she would entertain them with mimicry of him, she would observe herself in these perform-ances with a black and sinking horror.

She had expected Oxford to inspire that same marvellous exhilaration she had felt when she started university in Melbourne. Yet as her misery thickened she began to question not only her earlier experience but her very capacity for exhila-ration. She'd always had to plan so carefully for her rewards and pay upfront for most of them too, she wondered if what she had previously interpreted as exhilaration might simply be relief that, having planned and paid, the reward had duly appeared. Although in those early days at Oxford she would have settled for something considerably less lavish than exhilaration.

Everyone in Oxford was intelligent, or rather everyone she was likely to meet, so being bright could not protect her as it had in the past. As for the sons and daughters of the ruling class who went up to Oxford on the steel tracks of family tradition rather than intellectual capacity, they were unlikely to pursue friendships with Australians, who, Ava quickly discovered, registered rather poorly on the colonial scale. Although most colonials, no matter what their other credentials, were not highly regarded, so the scholarships which she, Jack and Helen had assumed would be their tickets to Oxford acceptance had little effect other than locating them in the colonial underclass.

Whether he was accepted or not was of little concern to Jack. His self-consciousness slithered away as he soused himself in life away from home. He worked at the library, he met with

Ava and Helen, he was adopted by a group of Zimbabweans (he joked he was their token white), he had a regular spot at a popular folk club. And for hours at a time he would walk the streets of Oxford, a bristly figure hunched in his jacket, nodding and chortling to himself. So unmonitored was he, he would find himself lost, a curiously liberating experience for a man accustomed to following maps in practically every aspect of his life.

Jack fell under Oxford's well-documented spell. The romance of the cobbled lanes and walkways, the towers and spires, the massive blocks of Oxford stone, the pubs spiced with ancient spillages, high street shops from the Middle Ages spruiking the latest in modern trinkets, the ornate wedding cake of the Radcliffe Camera, Magdalen's gargoyles, the quarterjacks on Carfax Tower striking the quarter-hours: he loved all of Oxford's wonders and oddities.

'I feel a different person here,' he said to Ava. 'I feel new.'

He took his long walks even during the brittle, truly frigid cold that is Oxford's special province in winter and would return to his room hours later where his musings would collect into short bitey nuggets of a thousand words or so on topics as diverse as 'Hair Dye and Ronald Reagan's Foreign Policy', 'Deceptive Sentimentality: the Demonising of Lindy Chamberlain', 'The Lunacy of Humane Murder: Death Sentence by Lethal Injection'. Helen and Ava said he should try to have them published. But despite the plethora of Oxford periodicals, none wanted his articles, so he proposed instead that they start their own magazine, a monthly publication known as *AA*, its full title, *Antipodeans Abroad*, being as alluring as hemlock for most Oxonians. The magazine would feature his essays, Ava's stories, a Modern Alchemy column with scientific news and anecdotes from Helen, together with poetry and fiction drawn from the broader student body – a quota not difficult to fill, Jack said, given that nearly everyone at Oxford seemed to be writing poetry or a novel.

The inaugural issue of *AA* came out at the end of their first year, long after Ava had returned to her old self. They managed to produce three more issues, more quarterly than monthly, and what meagre sales they made barely covered the cost of the Spanish plonk which nourished the magazine's production. *AA* was pronounced by Jack a magnificent failure.

Notwithstanding their being Australians, Helen and Jack believed that Oxford would judge them on their merits. And besides, Oxford slotted so neatly into the continuing narratives of their lives that they experienced almost from the beginning a strong sense of belonging. Helen had long planned to study and work overseas. Her ties with home were neatly sustained by a weekly aerogramme to her parents, and what loyalties she valued were to the friends who had left home with her. She had found in Oxford the science of her dreams. She would walk around town as if on hallowed turf, citing what discoveries had been made in which buildings, and what discoveries were happening now. Just by being there, she said, she was a part of history.

Jack's situation left him just as happy, although more than a little surprised. If not for Helen and Ava, he would have remained in Australia close to his family for his postgraduate work. As it was, his parents were intending to visit at the end of the Michaelmas term and he was already planning their itinerary. He wanted them to see his Oxford life: the Bodleian with its six million volumes, including some of the oldest books and manuscripts in existence; the desk where he worked in overcoat and hat, and no, he didn't mind the cold.

He would show them the fakes in the Ashmolean – they'd be amused by those – and give them a tour of Oxford's chapels and churches to fire them up about conflicts between church wealth and Christian charity. And together they would travel up to London to visit Highgate and the buxom bust of Karl Marx, and Panizzi's round reading room at the British Library where he would point out Marx's favourite seat and show them some of his papers, although he had recently discovered, to his surprise, that most were held in the Netherlands. He was thrilled about their visit – as was Ava. Anyone from the familiar past was welcome, she only wished someone would make the journey especially to see her. But the only person she had was Stephen and she didn't want to ask him.

Throughout those early months, Ava felt constrained by the triple stigma of being Australian, being an Australian from the wrong background, and being an Australian without ties to home. It was like being stranded on a sheet of clear glass with nothing but blackness beneath. The college rules made no sense; privacy was impossible; the other students had already formed cliques, and while she joked about her supervisor, in truth she was desperate to see him, desperate to know whether the books she was reading were the right books and the papers she was writing had any merit. The food was appalling, the weather inhospitable, and the price of escape, whether a cinema ticket or the return train fare to London, exorbitant.

In despair she wrote to Stephen, a long letter rather than the postcard platitudes she had sent him on her arrival. She filled page after page, confiding in him as she would no one else, and at the letter's end she asked him to ring her. She didn't care that there was only one very public phone on her floor at the college, she was so desperate to speak to him she would have taken his call anywhere. And such luck, the first since her arrival, the day he rang the college had emptied out for a bank holiday long weekend. She blurted out her woes; pressing the phone against her ear and herself into a corner, she told him everything. He soothed and reassured; she was not to worry about money, he said, she was not to worry about anything, and of course he would ring her again, he would ring as often as she wanted.

Every Monday morning thereafter would see her by the phone waiting for his familiar voice, his reassurances that she was not alone, that he loved her and would always care for her, that he was not so far away, nor was she so far away, and most important of all, that no one would make her stay in Oxford. 'You can come home whenever you want. But give it a little longer,' he said at the end of the first month. Give it a little longer, he said during the second month. Give it a little longer, he was still saying at the beginning of the third.

The turning point came unexpectedly as turning points often do. It was a Friday towards the end of the Michaelmas term. Helen and Jack, together with a couple of Jack's new friends, had gone up to London for yet another farewell party for two more Zimbabweans returning home. Ava had invented a pressing paper, but in truth their high spirits just made her feel more inadequate. She did, in fact, dabble at her desk in order to consume some time, and then might have gone to a film but there was nothing she could bear to see. The only free lunchtime concert featured a contemporary concerto for tuba and glockenspiel, suggesting the program director was in as desperate straits as was she, so she walked down to Magdalen Chapel on the off-chance that one of the organists was practising. It was quiet within, nonetheless she settled into a pew hoping the churchy tranquillity would soothe her, but the stillness scratched her raddled nerves, the cold too, so she returned to the street and made her way back towards college. With nothing better to do, she would sleep the afternoon away.

She slowed up as she approached Blackwell's, glanced in through the glass, hesitated, and then entered the main book-shop – no heart to explore, just a place to warm up, to expend thirty minutes of a day of painfully sluggish minutes. She walked downstairs, she walked back up again. She touched covers and spines, she flicked through pages, she watched the shoppers. Some were alone, others were in pairs, all had purpose. She browsed through an out-sized book on the Sahara – better that inhospitable landscape, she found herself thinking, than inhospitable Oxford. She lingered until the lingering itself was an added irritation and headed for the door. As she left the shop she checked her watch: only twenty-three minutes had passed. Twenty-three measly minutes.

There were at least three hours before nightfall. And after that? Two years of counting off each malnourished minute. The prospect was unbearable. For so long, this place, this Oxford, had been the apotheosis of desire; how could she have so miscalculated? In the past she had not always known where her choices would lead, but she had trusted herself to make them. Now she was doubting all the decisions, some going back to childhood, which had led inexorably to this moment, this situation, this Oxford.

The wind had gathered strength, it was freezing outside. People were hurrying between warm places, only Ava was loitering. She glanced at the posters on doorways and in shop windows, an overlapping jumble of advertisements for sports, talks, clubs, concerts – Oxford's rich lode on display yet out of reach of her pathetic grasp – and was about to head back to college when her attention was caught by a small roneoed flyer, not particularly distinctive but for a slightly skewed, grainy image of a fat laughing woman's face in the lower right corner. Ava stood in the chill and gazed at it, acknowledging a flutter of interest. The pamphlet was advertising an exhibition of self-portraits and she took down the details. Back in her room, a map showed the gallery to be located in a village a good hour's ride away. With little reason to view the exhibition, but every reason to escape Oxford, she collected her bike and set off.

Ten minutes later and the Oxford of the university was behind her. The streets were wider here and lined with proper houses, at first in rows, then free-standing; another ten minutes and she was in the country. She followed the road as it curved through meadows and pastures, past clumps of rickety trees and the huddled buildings of farms. She clung to the shoulder of the road to avoid the black ice, and swerved back onto the bitumen to miss the boggy patches. The sky was thickly white, her eyes bleary with cold and concentration; at one point she dismounted to stamp the sensation back into her feet.

If there was any sense remaining to her, she would cancel this mad adventure and return to Oxford. But to what? Her solitary room? A dingy café? An under-heated library populated by strangers? Better to remain in the freezing wind, riding treacherous roads, heading towards an exhibition that under normal conditions she would not venture a block out of her way to see.

She reached the village in just under an hour. It was an English storybook place with a few shops, a cluster of cottages, and, at the far end, an old house set in a straggle of garden. This was the gallery. She chained her bike against the fence and entered the building, helping herself to a pamphlet from a pile near the door. She appeared to be the only visitor, and the first time in months she had felt her solitary state as anything other than punishing. The rooms were small, and with the low lighting and deep shadows they might have been soaked in varnish. A good backdrop for old masters, she found herself thinking, not that there were any here.

The self-portraits were the work of local amateurs. Each was displayed alongside a photograph of the artist, a layout which seemed unnecessarily cruel to an aspiring talent. The artists had attempted to reproduce the figure in the photograph accurately, photographically in fact, and in all of them were failures of scale, perspective or both. The one exception was the fat laughing face used on the exhibition poster – not a painting but a drawing in oil pastels and by far the best of the exhibits. The accompanying photograph depicted the artist as a dour, forbidding figure clad in grey. It was a full-length, front-on photograph while the pastel was head and shoulders only. Such discrepancy between the two depictions could only be deliberate, Ava decided, given the evident skill of the artist. And in the nature of the discrepancy she saw mystery, possibility, conflicting desires, and in that knowing, laughing face, trickery too. Ava checked the details of the artist in the pamphlet: 'Anonymous'.

'Touché,' she said aloud.

Apart from the fat woman there was little of interest; Ava moved quickly through the exhibition until she reached a larger room at the back of the cottage. Here were prints and photo-graphs of self-portraits by well-known nineteenth- and twentieth-century artists, all men incidentally, unlike the exhibits in the other rooms, which were mostly women. There was Matisse depicted very much as the painter squire, and a childlike pencil drawing of Paul Klee as an oriental thinker. Edward Hopper had produced a figure out of an Edward Hopper painting, Picasso had painted a cubist Picasso, and Modigliani was long and slen-der like one of his women. Dali presented himself in liquid surre-alism and Escher was seen through a play of optics. Hung closely together in a blatant display of either irony or ignorance were Francis Bacon depicted as a swirling, distorted Bacon, and Andrew Wyeth palely poised within a pale Wyeth interior. Kokoschka, one of Ava's favourite artists, had been incompre-hensibly cruel in his 'Portrait of a "Degenerate Artist"'.

We keep our true selves closed, Ava found herself thinking. And in the absurdity of some of these images, the very act of self-presentation seemed to be mocked. How many of the painters were laughing as they worked? And it occurred to her that these artists might have deliberately chosen self-portraiture in order to retreat from the public eye in simultaneous acts of self-conjuring and disguise. Like writers use fiction. Like Ava, herself, had chosen fiction.

How, she wondered, might her friends depict themselves? Rather than the brilliant scholar whom most people saw, Jack, with his gropings for perfection and his major talent for disappointment, might opt for a quixotic man on a mule – and claim the mule as being truer to his character. And Helen would probably choose an absurdist image, a grasshopper perhaps, propped before saucepan-shaped test tubes and Petri dishes heaped with oranges, all six limbs busy at once. As for herself, all spark and passion as far as everyone else was concerned, she would settle for a set of brightly painted *matryoshka* dolls, diminishing to ever-smaller figures, the very last one tinier than a thimble and painted a featureless white.

She peered at the sadness in the Francis Bacon, the doubt in a rare Ruskin, and the startled, illuminated face of Munch. No matter what the emotional resonance, there was a swagger to these works, as if the artist were saying: *This is how I choose to present myself. And whether you want to believe it or not won't make a scrap of difference to me.*

And wasn't this the way she had always lived?

When she rode back into Oxford, it was as if layers of hardened mud had been washed away. Suddenly her mind was back in top gear. She must check out the self-portraits at the National Portrait Gallery; at last she could see how to structure her paper on Coleridge; she would write on Jane Austen's feminism for her thesis. And she would unpack her novel so assiduously avoided since arriving in Oxford. She had left Melbourne behind, Stephen too, and while she had not left her friends, it was in the writing of this novel where her creative and always portable self found a home. How foolish she had been to neglect it.

It was after four and the street lights were coming on. Oxford looked old and golden. She was ravenous, but first to the post office and a card to Stephen to let him know she was on the mend. Then to a café where she ordered a toasted sandwich and a hot chocolate. The sandwich arrived oozing butter and cheese, and the hot chocolate came with bobbing marshmallows. She pushed up her sleeves in the fuggy air and settled hungrily to the food. Her future was back.

~

Six months later, *Rock Father* was accepted for publication. Another four months and Ava had met Harry; with him at her side the way ahead looked clear and calm.

The others never knew how close she had come to falling.

Friendships become swaddled in invisible protective layers and nothing short of a cataclysmic blow can break through to the inevitable stress points beneath. If Ava, or indeed any of the friends were to lose their footing now, would the others notice?

As Jack stood in the colonnade of the State Library alongside Helen watching Connie and Ava tossing ideas between them, far from thinking any of them was in trouble, he felt something of the same excitement as when first they met, that same sense of a future opening up. Connie would get his TV series, Ava would publish another brilliant novel, he would write a new book, and Helen would find her shigella vaccine – all of them with careers on the rise and all of them together again. Their friendship was as strong as ever. They just needed to make more of an effort.

He turned to Helen to float the idea of reinstating the Laconics Society when one of the TV crew appeared and herded them back inside. They crowded through the library entrance, a jostle of elbows and shoulders, the four of them laughing and talking all at once.

The production assistant was smiling at them. 'If ever we do a program on friendship,' she said, 'would you be the stars?'

CHAPTER 5: The Sea Is Not Full

NOGA's first location was a single office in a nondescript university building equipped with an administrative officer, a computer, a photocopier and telephone conferencing facilities. Two and a half years later it occupied an entire upper floor of a new glass and metal tower on the edge of the city. Jack's office, one of three Visiting Member's Studies (or, in the NOGA predilection for prescriptive acronyms, a ViMS), was marginally smaller than his entire flat. Another of the offices had been allocated to Helen but she spent most of her time at the laboratory, while Connie's area, even larger than Jack's and with a corner location, adjoined Harry's suite. Such grand premises had only become possible, Harry told Jack, when the building's owner-developer had been invited on to the NOGA board. This had paved the way, Harry had lowered his voice, 'for special commercial arrangements'.

The walls were hung with contemporary paintings, all by up-and-coming artists according to Harry, and highly rated on investment scales; the floor was carpeted in a velvety blue plush, the furniture was an elegance of timber and pale leather,

Jack's desk was solid Tasmanian blackwood. An entire wall of his office comprised floor-to-ceiling glass with a panoramic view of the southern half of the city. Jack would stand by these windows twenty-seven storeys in the sky, the fingertips of his left hand in a steadying pose against the glass, relishing the vaguely thrilling vertigo.

He had moved into this office the week following the reunion, and on the very first day had dragged one of the armchairs across to the wall of windows. In the intervening months he had spent hours – accumulated days – staring through the glass. Sometimes he saw only shapes and colours, as if the city were a huge abstract mosaic; other times he would latch on to familiar sites like the Botanic Gardens, the Shrine, and the neo-classical piles of town halls from Collingwood to Caulfield. He would trace the major thoroughfares to the bay, to the eastern hills, to the docks and loading yards in the west. And the slender spine of the Westgate Bridge, where one blustery night long ago, he and Ava had walked hand in hand across one side and back down the other, oblivious to the lumbering traffic, the fumes, the plain ordinariness of life outside their spectacular selves.

He was expected to work in this room and he had made an effort. The NOGA fellowship had brought him a rush of consultancies, mainly to business groups, although people from the media regularly contacted him for comment and background material, and increasingly there had been inquiries from political figures as well. But the work he most wanted was to write a new book. He was convinced that the best way of explaining the complex persuasions of contemporary Islam was by returning to the Islam of its golden age. You can't understand Islam's trajectory, in particular its response to the post-Enlightenment world, he would say in interviews and focus sessions, without a thorough knowledge of its history. And most particularly, you can't ignore Islam's own perspective of this history. This was not what people wanted to hear, nor was it what publishers wanted to publish. They preferred instead the frisson of their own fear, the safety of clear-cut blame, and the sensational explosions of boys and girls giving up their young lives to defeat the infidels. With today's spectaculars, the past did not stand a chance.

Ever alert to modernity's special deals, Luke was critical of Jack's attachment to the past. 'And it's not just your work,' he said. 'You act as if everything important has already happened.'

In the past few months, Jack had come to know Luke well. While he seemed to be a typical teenager in many respects, he also demonstrated a sensitivity to others and an acuteness of understanding rare in his generation. 'It's being the only son of a single mother,' Luke said with a smile. 'I don't have much choice.'

Luke often had dinner at Jack's place when Helen worked late, and the previous week, while Helen attended a meeting in Jakarta, he had stayed with Jack for a few days. They were taking a stroll along the Esplanade after dinner one night when Luke spoke up. 'This place for example,' and he waved at the beach, 'you remember it as it was early one spring morning – twenty-five? thirty years ago? Why not look at it now? Clean sand and lots of it, hardly a syringe to be found, and far better for outdoor sex than ever it used to be.'

Luke's point was valid, but what Luke and everyone else failed to see was Jack preferred it his way. The beach was precisely significant because it was where he made love to Ava, yes, in the past, but still of far greater interest than today's cleaned-up, syringe-free stretch of sand. Yet now as he sat in his office high above the city he was aware of a strange unease. What sort of man is always oriented towards the past, towards what is already known? And what sort of life does it produce? No surprises, no originality, just treading the same old familiar groove. And so conservative – the thought shocked him. Perhaps it was not surprising he had written nothing new for so long.

Yet he wanted to write and he had tried these past months but the discipline had perished, maybe the ideas too, although that was harder to accept. And his mood was at odds. The pleasures he had felt at Connie's pilot the previous day had disappeared even before he had left the library; in fact, all pleasures these days were short-lived. After the filming, instead of bundling into a bar for a spirited wrap-up, Helen had dashed back to the laboratory to check on an experiment, Connie had dashed back to Sara who was expecting him, and Ava, who looked uncharacteristically tired, went home. They gave their excuses, leaving Jack alone on the lawn in front of the State Library. He watched Ava board the tram heading north, then he walked to the corner to wait for a tram to carry him in the other direction.

Today he had arrived at the office just before ten o'clock. He had browsed the newspaper, more out of habit than interest, and an hour later he could not have named the main stories. His email was similarly uninspiring, consisting of petitions, advertisements and an annoying message from Harry, highly critical of an old friend of the Adelsons. This woman, a fearless and very public campaigner for human rights, had recently sought Jack's help in applying for refugee status for an Iraqi family. A series of emails had passed between them. The woman was a well-known figure, she was often in the press, nonetheless, Harry's timing was uncanny – suspiciously so. But the possibility that Harry might be shadowing him in cyberspace – and if him, perhaps anyone associated with NOGA – was so unpalatable, so beyond the realm of acceptable behaviour, Jack preferred to ascribe the interference to coincidence. He trashed the email without acknowledging it.

He paid a couple of bills and checked out the *Guardian* online with much the same attention he had given to the morning paper. He cruised some of his favourite websites, but even these failed to stir. He read through the letter he had written to Ava the previous night; it would, he realised, be added to the never-sent file, which was now so large it occupied an entire drawer. He went to the window and gazed out, but was savaged by an irritation so intense that if he could have cracked open his body and leapt out of his skin he would have. At quarter past twelve he heard the squawk of Harry's voice along the corridor, and knowing he could not face him, not even a short polite greeting to the man long married to Ava, he grabbed his things and left the building for an early lunch.

He crossed to the other side of the river via the footbridge and went directly to a café in one of the lanes off Flinders Street. He had become a regular here – not just the good coffee and Mediterranean food, but with the parade through the lane and the coppery old shops he might be in London, Paris, Amsterdam or Florence. Everywhere and nowhere. There should have been freedom in the geographical slipperiness, but he experienced only the slipperiness,

Soon he was settled at his usual table, dipping into a plate of antipasto and drinking the first of two espressos. He propped his novel against the sugar bowl and began to read. It was Bellow's last, not because Bellow had spoken to him in recent novels, but long ago *Herzog* and *Humboldt's Gift* had set his world on fire and he longed for the same again. He turned pages while he ate, cleared the plate, had no idea what he had read, turned to the previous page, no recognition, and the one before that, still nothing, and with a surge of frustration closed the book. So much din in his brain and he couldn't even attend to a novel any more. He ordered his second coffee; it arrived too quickly. He wasn't ready to return to the office, he would prefer never to return, and why from this cerebral wasteland should rear up one of Archimedes' maxims he did not know, but it did stop the bluster.

Give me a foothold and I shall move the earth.

He was fifteen when first he read this and had been in no doubt Archimedes was speaking to him. He had loving parents, his country was safe and prosperous, he was a successful student and a talented musician; his foothold was excellent, the rest would be up to him. Later he found a different translation: *Give me somewhere to stand, and I will move the earth,* and realised he may have misinterpreted. There followed days of doubt and frantic research until he remembered something he had once read: that the first translation of a favourite work is like a first love – it may not be the most reliable, but by being first it receives special consideration.

Give me a foothold and I shall move the earth.

His foothold had indeed been excellent, yet here he was in his mid-forties and might as well be on life support for all the effect he'd had on the world. He wasn't writing, he wasn't researching, he had produced neither children nor brilliant students, and his only significant scholarship had occurred decades ago. He was dishing out simplified information to anyone who asked, which was then distorted into simpler sound-bites. His group of friends hardly comprised a group any more, and while he clung to his thoughts of Ava like a doomed man clings to life, with her in the same city it was as if these thoughts were cut adrift from their *raison d'être*, thereby setting him adrift. He could no longer indulge in fantasies of their meeting in romantic corners of the world, nor could he use such imaginings as a distraction from the disappointments of his own ordinary days. Not only did he not have Ava in the sense Harry had Ava, but his own Ava was fast slipping away.

He knew that Connie and Helen had long viewed his love for Ava as a disability, but he felt disabled now, as if he had contracted one of those muscle-wasting diseases where each new day is a reminder of a dwindling future. What Connie and Helen had never understood was that the way he conducted his relationship with Ava had worked for him. He had been happy.

'If you'd lived the first twenty years of your life in a brick cell, happiness would be a bedsit with a tiny window looking out to a garbage dump,' Helen had said recently.

It was a couple of days before she left for Jakarta, and Jack had invited her round to the flat for an early dinner to sample one of his experiments: a basil and slow-roasted tomato soufflé served with a salad of blanched green beans and toasted almond slivers drizzled with a thyme-infused olive oil. It was entirely wasted on her of course, food being no more than a bodily requirement as far as she was concerned, but Connie, who would have been more appreciative, seemed unable to separate from Sara even for a quick meal, and Ava was out of the question. They had just begun the meal, but given the turn of conversation Jack wished it were already over. For Helen was wrong: he had reliable standards of comparison, he knew what happiness was.

'You don't, Jack. You've never had a real relationship with anyone.'

He poured himself more wine and sipped slowly, as if that could quell the seething. Helen had no idea what she was talking about. He had been with many women; the problem was they failed to make the grade.

'Your standards have been carved out of a long-standing, non-existent relationship with an idealised woman. No real woman could ever measure up. And as far as I can see you've stopped bothering.' Helen helped herself to another spoonful of soufflé and dumped a pile of salad on top. 'You don't need to step out your front door any more. It's very tidy, very safe in here.'

He defended himself vigorously and with growing peevishness. But no matter how much he insisted his relationship with Ava was real, no matter how apposite his arguments, Helen refused to shift. As for his long correspondence with Ava, Helen believed this had nothing to do with real love.

'The written word is a powerful aphrodisiac. Or as Luke would say,' and she smiled at the reference to her son, 'the written word is hot. Look no further than the countless people who have been caught up in cyberspace romances only to discover that their partner is a fourteen-year-old boy with bad acne, raging libido and excellent written expression.'

He was about to protest: his correspondence with Ava had nothing in common with chatroom sleaze, but Helen was not finished. 'Whether cyberspace or old-fashioned mail, written communications make you feel very good. And the pleasures are always solitary, they're always intense, and –' she paused for emphasis, 'they are always self-serving.'

Helen had always been blunt. You welcomed it when she was agreeing with you, you welcomed it when you were head to head in intellectual argument, and you certainly welcomed it in the days of the Laconics. But with his relationship with Ava already struggling, Helen might just as well have plunged the blade in and left him to bleed. They had planned a quick dinner before Helen collected Luke from football practice. Jack cut it even shorter. Helen was wrong, she didn't understand. And who was she to judge? With the exception of Luke, her most enduring attachment was to bacteria.

He had been determined to dismiss her opinions out of hand, but not only had he found himself dwelling on what she had said, he had dipped into some well-known correspondences – Virginia Woolf's with Vita Sackville-West, de Beauvoir's baggy tender letters to Nelson Algren, even John Evelyn's correspondence with Margaret Blagge, these last such chaste letters yet emitting such heat.

Anyone who has enjoyed an intense written relationship is well acquainted with the impact of words that are read rather than spoken. In the silence of a room, with all stops pulled out on imagination, emotions swirl like magma below a charged earth. You feel the fire and the erotic plumes, you spark with possibilities, and it begins even before you open the latest instalment, when you collect the mail and recognise her letter. You know her handwriting, the way she prints your name and address, the way she underscores the area code, you know her scrawl of sender details on the back, you can see her fingerprints, her signature as it were, all over the envelope. You feel the quickening of your heart, the thump of anticipation as you take the mail inside. You sort through the letters, you leave hers till last. Then you make yourself a fresh cup of coffee, sit in a favourite chair, open her letter and read, once, twice, three times, the burn of just you and Ava together and nothing to intrude on your secret and highly charged tryst. And during the writing and the reading and the re-readings, and all the times in between as you shop and cook and clean, as you sit out the tedium of dried-out colleagues and plodding students, you not only relive your love, you make it and remake it and embed it in a world that seems both miraculous and tangible. There is nothing to compare with the clandestine enclave of letters.

But now that Jack could see her whenever he wanted, the enclave had broken its borders. It was not that he loved her any less, he doubted that were possible, but the dynamic of his love baulked at its usual functions. The disorientation was at times unbearable, as if he had lost the coordinates to his very existence – much like his parents must have felt when they quit the Party. They had been quick to find other causes, other groups, but Jack didn't want to leave his Ava; he was hanging on for dear life.

A new book would help, but he couldn't write. Good causes would help, but he lacked his parents' commitment. He told himself the situation would pass, that in time his love would find its season again. But despite these assurances he knew something fundamental was changing. Something that had for so long been thoroughly known, thoroughly secure and unquestionably reliable, was losing its form and its footing.

Ava was not similarly disturbed. She rang him often, proposing lunches, drinks, walks, gallery visits – 'Not Harry's thing at all' – but after two of these occasions Jack was determined to find excuses. Indeed, the very first time alone with her was sufficient to reveal how things really were.

She had invited him to her place for lunch. He was nervous, excited, it was as if his whole past had been rolling forward to this moment. He had dressed with care, mindful of colours and styles she had always liked. He selected two books to lend her, he copied out a poem by Yehuda Amichai – they often included poems in their letters – and after a short search he had triumphed with a giant-sized version of her favourite chocolate bar.

The failure of the chocolate bar turned out to be emblematic of the occasion. She had taken it with a vague 'Why on earth are you giving me this?' expression, and when he reminded her, she had smiled and said it was very thoughtful of him but she hadn't eaten chocolate in years. Why didn't you tell me? he had blurted out. And when she replied that it didn't seem important in the scheme of things, he wondered what else she had kept from him.

The meeting was stiff with unfamiliarity. Ava drank green tea and not the strong black coffee she had introduced him to. Espresso was *de rigueur* among the existentialists, the eighteen-year-old Ava had told him, implying that no other considera-tion, including that of taste, was relevant. So Jack had persevered until he could drink his coffee no other way. But now she had swapped to green tea. What intellectual ever drank green tea? he wanted to ask. And the books he had chosen missed the mark too. One of them was a biography of the Strachey family. 'It looks interesting,' she said as she flipped through, 'but I haven't read the Bloomsburies for years.' She handed the book back to him. 'Perhaps another time,' she said vaguely. She loved the poem, but it's not diffi-cult to keep track of poetry tastes in letters.

There were numerous other changes, her slower speech and the careful pauses – suitable for a public interview but not at home with an old friend. Although worst of all was her refusal to ignore the phone. While she was speaking with someone called Barbara, he found himself wondering how she wrote her letters to him, how much attention she gave to a task that for him was sacred. He would write only at night, a glass of wine beside him, consulting his notebook where he had made jottings during the previous week. He would spend the better part of an evening writing to her, then the following morning he would give the letter a final reading and make last-minute changes, print it off, seal it in the same airmail blue envelopes he had always used, and send it at a post office rather than a kerbside letterbox as there would be less chance of its going astray. A whole ritual. But after enduring ten minutes of incon-sequential banter between Ava and Barbara, during which he waited, ignored, on her couch in her living room, he wondered whether Ava had treated their correspondence with the same indifference he was now receiving.

By the time Jack left the café he was feeling worse than when he arrived. If not for the lingering disappointment following Connie's pilot he might have passed an hour at the public library, instead he took a stroll through the city lanes and arcades. After thirty minutes, aware that all this time-wasting felt uncomfortably incriminating, he decided to return to the office. He looked around to take his bearings and saw a shop he had never noticed before. In the window was a display of hand-made journals. He stepped closer. Such intricate covers, scenes from old Venice, Japanese pen-and-ink drawings, colourful abstract patterns like the Bargello tapestries his mother used to stitch. And the old-fashioned rough-cut, creamy pages. These books were so elegant, so beautiful, he was tempted to buy one for himself – as if quality tools alone ever produced anything of worth. Then he thought of Ava; she was never without a notebook.

The woman behind the counter looked up as he entered. She invited him to browse and then returned to a page of figures. Mid-twenties, dark, slender and stylish, Jack would have thought her more suited to a fashion house than a business dedicated to handwriting and hand-crafted paper.

The shop was tiny, 'delicate' was the word that occurred to him, just a few steps across and a dozen steps deep. There was a free-standing table with a display of paper and cards, and around the walls, arranged on wooden shelving, were the journals. Perhaps it was the lighting, but what might have been musty and oppressive was polished and warm.

With no other customers in the shop, Jack was free to make a systematic search for Ava's notebook. He wrapped himself in the task, so much so that when the phone rang a few minutes later he started at the noise. The girl at the desk answered, and after an initial greeting she switched to Italian. Perhaps she was in the right job after all.

A few minutes more and Jack had selected nine journals of varying size, cover design and paper thickness and arranged them along a narrow bench. While any would be suitable for Ava only one would be best. He stepped back and considered. The illuminated manuscript cover or the blue-green marbled design? A delicate Japanese garden or Venice's Grand Canal? He returned two of the books to the shelves and flipped through the pages of those still in contention. He weighed each in his hands, he compared size and thickness, he retrieved one of those he had replaced – a marbled cover in pinks and golds and far too lovely to discount. Now there were eight possible journals for Ava.

The air in the shop had thickened, sweat snaked beneath his shirt, he blotted his face with his handkerchief. The girl had finished her phone call. His back was turned to her but he was sure she was watching. Choose, he ordered himself, but if the books had magically reconfigured into a lavishly patterned vice he could not have been more paralysed. A minute more and he was defeated. He left the journals scattered across the bench and with gaze averted he rushed from the shop. Decisions about Ava had never been his forté.

He hurried from the lane into Flinders Street and made his way directly to the second-hand bookshop across from the railway station. He stepped through the doorway and immediately his stress dissipated under cover of the stacks. There were half a dozen people in the shop each silently browsing; the woman behind the counter was immersed in a book. He took down volumes at random, read blurbs, flipped through pages, checked for Ava's titles in the fiction area. He moved through philosophy, poetry, history, biography, military, self-help, car maintenance and only when he found himself leafing through a Mandrake comic, a favourite of his eight-year-old self, did he come to his senses. There was little point in lingering any longer.

It was a balmy spring day with a few puffs of cloud in a blue sky and he made his way down to the river. He had not been here since Harry's cocktail party months before. There was activity at the boat sheds on the opposite bank, and on the Yarra itself three coxed crews of eight. The voices of the coxes cut the air with authority, and the brawny rowers did exactly as they were told. If only life were so easy, Jack was thinking, someone to provide the instructions while you just listened and obeyed. Although a trade-off would be required. How many restrictions, for example, would one be willing to tolerate for the comfort of authority, or indeed the authority of an authority? His thoughts turned to his parents, whose belief in the socialist utopia was so strong that even when Tito was vilified and Yugoslavia expelled from the Cominform, even when government ministers in Bulgaria and Hungary were tried in the flimsiest of show-trials and subsequently executed, after so many events that showed the Soviet leadership to be brutal and corrupt, his parents still managed to produce explanations, increasingly far-fetched it must be said, that would preserve not only the communist struggle for a fairer world but Soviet authority as well. At what point, Jack wondered, did a belief in an ideology become so total, so intractable, that it transformed into an allegiance to the authority of the ideology?

It was an interesting idea, and of relevance, he realised, to radical Islam. Perhaps he might write an essay on the topic – and immediately he recoiled from the thought. He hurried away from the rowers and their unison stroking and strode back towards Federation Square. He paced himself hard, his stomach settled, the rabble in his brain quieted, he felt the familiar pull on his right hip as he stepped out strongly, and the stretch across his back as he swung his arms: thirty minutes of this, he thought, as he bounded up the steps to the square, and he would be ready to return to the office. When suddenly he saw her.

Ava.

Across the earthy stone, past workers on their lunch break and mothers with babies, past buskers and survey takers, charity collectors and tourists with cameras, he saw her, unmistakably Ava, in a waft of green and blue swirls, sitting alone at an outdoor café. Ava alone and waiting for him.

A thousand times in his imagination has he crafted just this scene: a city square, a busy street, a famous church, a gallery, and he comes upon Ava and she will turn and see him and show by her delight she has been waiting for him, that at last she is ready to pick up where they left off after their month together. He starts forward, zigzagging through the lunchtime crowd, seeing only Ava sitting at a café table now sixty metres away, now fifty, now forty, and if he hadn't tripped over a knapsack cast to the side of a kissing couple, what a fool he would have made of himself.

Of course Ava's not waiting for him.

A woman emerges from the indoor area of the café. She makes her way to Ava's table and takes the seat across from her. Her back is turned towards Jack. The two women are talking, then Ava laughs and points at something. The woman twists around and Jack sees her clearly. The cap of black hair, the dark skin, the kohl-rimmed eyes, the angular features. It's Fleur. Fleur Macleish, here in Australia. Fleur still with Ava nearly three years after she quit her life. *Forever*, Ava had written to Jack at the time. *Fleur has left me forever.* Ava swore she never wanted to see Fleur again.

Enough said of the determination of a lover injured before journey's end.

You can will anything in solitude. You can make the world stop on its axis, you can put life on Mars, you can even make someone fall in love with you. What a traitor real life can be. For it is Fleur. Who else but Fleur? Ava is talking with her and laughing, she's waving her hand at the buildings beyond the square. Let me show you my city, she is saying, drawing Fleur back into her life.

~

Twenty minutes later and Jack is back at the office, stunned and beaten. He doesn't bother to turn on his computer; whatever thoughts spluttered to life before he saw Ava are now well and truly extinguished.

Where to now Fleur is back?

He wants to leap forward to a time when this is all over or back to a time he knows well; he wants to be anywhere but here. But where is he to go? Some casual work down in Tasmania close to his parents? Teaching at a country school? Library work? He gazes around his grand office with its opulent space and spectacular views, and while he could be satisfied with far less, he also knows that after his last job there are limits to what he can tolerate.

Just a few months ago his office was a squat, nondescript cell with a meagre, non-opening window beyond which was a red-brick wall dribbled with pigeon droppings. Rather than plush-pile carpet and paintings by up-and-coming artists there was hard-wearing beige lino on the floor, beige plastic paint on the walls, beige acoustic tiles on the ceiling and harsh fluorescent lighting. His office was one of several boxes on a floor that comprised the entire humanities department of the university.

If a single factor were to highlight the sorry demise of the humanities in academe, it was in the allocation of university space; even twilight disciplines like his own comparative religion once occupied a significant strip of prime university real estate. But not any more. The New Zealand job put an end to any doubts: the modern university does not suit him, nor does he suit the modern university.

Down the corridor Harry Guerin is building his empire; a couple of kilometres away Ava is cavorting with Fleur on the russet stone of Federation Square; Jack finds himself clamped in the vice of his own conflicts. As the screws tighten, he feels the inescapable squeeze of a life gone wrong.

CHAPTER 6: Universal Fool

1.

Second novels have a bad reputation and deservedly so. After a positive reception to a first book, many writers cave in to an unjustifiable attachment to the novel they wrote prior to the first published one. Rejected several times over, this manuscript has been lying untouched but not forgotten in a dark corner of the house. As the clamour over the first novel subsides, the author, still warm from the experience and perhaps overly influenced by a good press, reaches for the earlier unpublished manuscript. That the lame novel of a writer's apprenticeship might suddenly in a new day find its legs, belongs in the realm of miracles or shady nostalgia. And while publishers should know better, given that the marketplace is crowded and new authors appear thick and fast, the chance to cement a reputation with a quick follow-up novel is hard to resist.

So there's the second novel which is really a first-novel apprenticeship, and sometimes there is no second novel at all. Through some perverse artistic alchemy, a highly successful first book transmogrifies into a straitjacket. Three, five, eight years pass and the author of the acclaimed *X of the Y* fails to produce the eagerly awaited follow-up work. With the expectation that the second novel will be better than the first, failure fattens and the straitjacket becomes a second skin.

Ava did not experience a second-novel problem of either type. As she completed the later drafts of her first novel, *Rock Father*, she was already jotting down ideas for the next one.

Rock Father itself had started in the way of wish fulfilment, a story of the father Ava would have chosen to fill the hole left by the father fate had assigned her. But ideal fathers, she quickly discovered, do not make for interesting writing nor, for that matter, interesting reading. The man who finally appeared in the pages of the novel was a walking disaster, whose good looks and easy charm attracted a ready supply of people to disappoint. He had not one, but two failed families, and a serious drinking problem; he also had an inexplicable and magical connection with owls. Ava had assumed owls to be a northern hemisphere phenomenon (all those hootings in the great nineteenth-century novels and quite a few in Enid Blyton's too). But she discovered that Australia – *Rock Father* is her only novel to be set wholly in Australia – has ten indigenous owls among which are some of the most handsome of the species. Harry, a relatively new arrival at this stage, immediately started an owl collection for her. But the figures he produced in glass, pottery, wood and textiles, sometimes as many as three a week, failed to captivate. What did appeal was Harry's motivation in buying them, and what kept her silent until they moved to a flat without display space was her gratitude for such love.

Rock Father entered the world, the owl collection grew, and Ava sifted through her ideas for her second novel. Eventually she settled on *The Universal Fool*, in which a woman, despite reason and common sense, follows her heart step by inexorable step to the final tragedy. The heart, Ava believed, had received a far too generous press; it was an unreliable judge and, as she would show in *The Universal Fool*, not to be trusted. The characters, the locations, the underlying themes and the general tone of the book were all different from those in *Rock Father*, but the idea for the new novel was spawned by the earlier one.

The Universal Fool was almost universally praised. 'Rare for a second novel'. 'Accomplished and mature'. 'Wise and sad'. One reviewer quoted Yeats: 'Bryant knows the "terrible gift of intimacy", another compared her favourably to Henry James. Ava was surprised and pleased, but also superstitious. So when the one killer review appeared, written by an embittered poet and fortunately published in an out-of-the-way corner of the world of letters, she felt the artistic scales were back in balance. Everything augured well for novel number three.

She read, she daydreamed, she made notes, she went for long walks and she was rushed with ideas, just as she had been following *Rock Father*. But the ideas fizzled out long before she found her stride. Not knowing what else to do she pressed on, cutting back on the walks and the daydreaming and forcing herself to turn her jottings into something more substantial. As drivel became not just her primary mode of expression but her only mode, and the search for words became a blind and desperate grabbing, the heart, so badly done by in her second novel became lethargic and sad.

Harry tried to smooth her anxieties with special meals and weekends away; he also offered advice. In the past he had stayed well clear of her work, regarding it as her special domain and well beyond his own expertise, so his sudden involvement actually exacerbated the situation.

Jack's intervention was more effective. 'You need to fill up,' he said. 'After two novels in quick succession you've emptied out.'

Jack had returned to Oxford for a six-month study leave. It was his first visit in ten years, since leaving soon after her marriage. He had a new book in mind – he had written to her about it – and hoped to complete the research in the period of his leave. But seeing the state she was in, he put his own work aside in order to ameliorate hers. He took her to the theatre, to galleries and a rally agitating for freedom in Chechnya. He took her to seminars and lectures and a forum on terror after the Tokyo sarin gas attack. Every day he proposed a new activity and she gratefully complied.

Pindar wrote that 'hope is the old man's muse'. With the bravado of youth and more than a touch of cynicism, Ava had stuck the quote on her study wall when she commenced university. The imagination was its own muse, she believed; high maintenance and addicted to its own surprises it fed off itself; as for hope, it was a branch of illusion she was determined to avoid. But after the barren months of working on the still non-existent third novel, she changed her mind: the thriving imagination, she decided, was a needy beast. And her own imagination, she was about to discover, needed Fleur Macleish.

Dr Fleur Macleish, a London-based specialist in Indian antiquities, was giving a lecture in Oxford as part of Somerville College's occasional lunchtime series. Jack had never heard of her, neither had Ava, but India was always interesting and hadn't Ava said she wanted to set a novel on the subcontinent?

India, Cuba or Kazakhstan, Ava would situate her novel anywhere if she could be assured of its gaining a head of steam.

'You need to be out and about,' Jack said. 'You need stimulation.'

When you feel like a nobody – and a writer who is not writing is definitely a nobody – you're tempted by any suggestion that is stamped with authority.

'I miss you.' She linked her arm through his as the two of them set off for the lecture. 'I really wish you'd come back to Oxford permanently.'

'Only while you're between books,' he replied, keeping his gaze hard ahead. 'Once you begin your next novel, you'll prefer our usual epistolary relationship.'

And she knew he was right, but when the next novel seemed as likely as a trip to the moon she was prepared to change even her most entrenched habits. She said nothing, just squeezed his arm and picked up her pace.

It was a perfect day in late spring and within minutes she stopped to slip off her jacket. With summer just a whisker away she would be complaining soon enough, but after the long winter it was bliss to be out of heavy clothes and feel the sun on her skin.

'I feel like I've been given a day pass from prison,' she said.

She had prepared a picnic and they stopped at the St Giles' churchyard for lunch. The garden was crowded, but eventually they found a spot on a low brick wall edging a flower bed. They sat close to each other to avoid the shadows from the trees.

She proceeded to tell Jack about a recent phone call with Helen. 'Most of it was about Luke,' she said. 'I think Helen's reinventing motherhood.'

'I think *she* thinks she's reinventing motherhood,' Jack said with a laugh, 'and given up sleep entirely. She must have written four papers already this year and attended half a dozen conferences.' Jack helped himself to a sandwich. 'It's lucky Connie lives close enough to look after Luke.'

'I have the impression Linda does most of the looking after.'

Connie had recently embarked on his third marriage. Ava had met Linda earlier in the year when she and Connie had visited Oxford. 'I liked her, I liked her a lot.' And added with a bemused smile, 'Connie says this one's forever. Rather a slippery concept in his lexicon.'

'And his work?' Jack asked. 'I expect he had a lot to say about the ongoing horrors in the former Yugoslavia.'

'Hardly a word, but then I'm convinced Connie's apolitical. He defends his lack of engagement by saying he's more interested in the essentials of being human.' (Connie could argue persuasively for practically any position, and both she and Jack knew it.) 'But the fact is, after his philosophy, his wives, his children and the stream of girlfriends, Connie has little time left for politics.'

She burrowed into the lunch bag and pulled out a block of chocolate. 'Do you want some?'

Jack shook his head, and helped himself to another sandwich.

'What about your parents?' Ava asked. 'How have they responded to the new Eastern Europe?'

'It's almost as if the collapse of the Soviet Union has vindicated communism for them – or what they refer to as *pure* communism.' Jack was smiling. 'With each new piece of evidence about Soviet brutality and corruption, my parents are vociferous in their condemnation of Soviet communism while holding fast to their old workers unite values.'

'And China? Cuba? North Korea? How do they explain them?'

'Ever the revolutionaries, they'd do away with nation states altogether. It's still the "Internationale" forever.'

Jack leaned forward and brushed an insect from her hair. 'Saved you from a midge,' he said, before returning to his parents. 'They're extremely wary of all these nation states that have popped up in Eastern Europe. They worry the new freedoms don't blend easily with old grievances. And "ethnic cleansing", such an appalling euphemism, they simply can't understand why more people aren't protesting.'

His parents had recently been appointed Australian representatives for an international group agitating for UN-controlled dismantling of ageing Soviet warheads. 'They'll be waving banners and signing petitions until the moment their hearts give out,' he said.

Jack's face bore that same warmth and pleasure you see whenever people speak about loved family. Ava envied him. She would never forget showing him Philip Larkin's 'They fuck you up, your mum and dad' – *High Windows* had not long been published, and Stephen had given her a copy. It was hard to know which had shocked him more, the sentiment or the obscenity.

'Do you think there are any words left with shock value,' she now asked as they started up the Woodstock Road.

Jack thought for a moment, then shook his head. 'No, not even cunt.'

She was quick to disagree. 'Responses to that word separate the girls from the boys, and probably one of the last remaining differences between us.'

Single words aside though, she believed that shock and

surprise were alive in language as much as ever. 'In the *creative* use of language,' she said, and let loose a stream of quotes from contemporary poetry – Thom Gunn's 'scheduled miracle', Ted Hughes' 'Letting time moan its amnesia/ Through telegraph wires', Bruce Beaver's 'creaking house, shrinking under/ the brute back-hander of the southerly/ buster.'

'This is language at its most astonishing,' she said.

Jack joined in – 'Gwen Harwood's palms "like feather dusters", Dorothy Porter's kisses "like smashed glass"' – rummaging his memory for startling language.

They were both still quoting when they reached Somerville.

'There's no equal to your poetic soul,' she said, as they entered the college grounds.

People like to think that significant loves will announce themselves, that the first glimpse, the first handshake, the first words will be life-changing experiences. In the case of Fleur's initial effect on Ava everything about it was ordinary. There were about thirty-five people gathered for the lecture. Ava greeted a couple of members of the college, but with the lecture about to begin she and Jack quickly found seats. Fleur Macleish, an old Somervillian and part of Somerville's Indian connection, was introduced with little ceremony.

'Dr Macleish's reputation speaks for itself,' the principal said.

Fleur Macleish cut a striking figure, pale dark skin of the northern rather than southern Indian kind, arched cheekbones, carved jaw, slender neck. The sculpted face was accentuated by the closely cropped black hair. She was dressed in Western clothes – trousers, shirt and blowsy scarf in a riot of pinks and reds and a startling contrast with the drab colours then in vogue. Fleur Macleish was an arresting figure, but Oxford was full of arresting figures. What was remarkable was the shock of the Scottish accent. Ava checked the biographical notes: Indian mother (herself an old Somervillian) and Scottish father, and settled back to listen.

It may have been the lyrical voice, it may have been the unaccustomed heat, it may have been the smooth comfort of Jack against her, but before long Ava lapsed into her own thoughts, nothing significant nor, she realised at the end of the lecture, enduring, for she could not say what had passed through her mind. As for Fleur Macleish's lecture, it had not even scraped the surface of consciousness. It was only when the applause had finished and people were preparing to leave that it suddenly came to her: Stephen, she had been thinking of Stephen, and a fillip of embarrassment, for it was not Stephen telling her about books or taking her to the theatre. While Fleur Macleish had been giving her lecture Ava had been back at Stephen's flat, in his bed and cradled against his naked body, the greying tufts of hair about his nipples, the rise of his stomach, and that crease where his abdomen ended just above the pubic hair. She now knew it as the shape of a mature man, but not all those years ago when his was the first male body she had seen. She had liked that quiet time after the sex, Stephen stroking the length of her back, and nothing required of her at all.

Where, she wondered, was he now? Had he replaced her? And because she was no fool she corrected herself: what was his new girl like? Very different from herself, she expected, for she truly believed he had loved her and wouldn't want his memories challenged. He'd still be sending her monthly cheques if she hadn't insisted he stop – with her marriage to Harry she didn't need his money. And while she would have liked to keep him as a friend, it was impossible to erase their sort of history and replace it with something more acceptable. So she had opened the door and let him out of her life. He slipped back when she wasn't attending – in dreams, in daydreams, but never before in this sexual way.

Jack was speaking to her. 'You didn't hear a word of the lecture, did you?'

She shrugged. 'But I enjoyed being here.'

They filed out. The sun was still strong, and whether it was the weather or being at Somerville, or whether it was Stephen or Jack or both, she realised there had been a lifting of her spirits. She looped her arm through Jack's and suggested they stop for a cider on the way back, 'At that pub we used to like, with the outdoor area.' She noted his pleasure, and while it was disturbing – it required so little to make him happy – she decided not to dwell.

They were passing by the Porter's Lodge when she heard a voice calling her name. It was Fleur Macleish, running to catch up with them.

'Ava,' she said in her Scottish lilt, 'Ava Bryant,' and extended her hand. The skin was cool, the grasp was firm, the smile was broad and blazing. 'I like your work,' she said. 'I like your work very much. Thanks for coming to my talk.' And before Ava could utter more than the briefest of courtesies, she had withdrawn her hand and turned back to the college.

'That was kind of her,' Ava said to Jack as they entered the road.

They paused at the corner to read a flyer advertising a series of lectures on Proust. 'Have you heard?' Jack said. 'There's another English translation of *A la recherche du temps perdu* in the pipeline.'

And Fleur Macleish was instantly forgotten as Ava condemned the project. The 1981 Kilmartin version had taken care of the English Proust for years to come, she said. Jack disagreed, but given her French was a good deal better than his, she insisted her opinion should have the greater sway. They were still arguing the issue as they started their second pints at the pub.

A month later Ava was in London for an evening of Australian women's writing at the Silver Moon bookshop in Charing Cross Road. It was a relief to leave her desk for a couple of days, for despite Jack's best efforts her work was still stalled. The shop, tiny by Waterstone's and Dillons standards, was a crush of women, and the air thick with chatter and bursts of delighted greetings as more people arrived. One could be forgiven for thinking that every Australian feminist in London had turned out for the evening.

There were four writers on the program with Ava slotted in third. After a short break to refresh drinks and accommodate the smokers, Ava took to the lectern. She began with a brief introduction to *The Universal Fool,* struggling against a mounting antipathy to this novel which, having sucked her dry, was now pointing to just one almighty fool. If her third novel did not start moving soon, she doubted there would ever be one. And then what would she do? Become the teacher she had never wanted to be? Or with her verbal facility and ease with people perhaps a job in public relations? Or one of those home duties women, given she did not need to work – need, in the sense of requiring money. Her need to write was something quite different. She'd only ever had one ambition, an ambition that rose to its feet early only to trip up long before the journey was finished. Was she permanently disabled? And how to live if she were?

She began her reading and at the same moment the door to the bookshop opened and the Indian antiquities woman, Fleur Macleish, entered. She eased her way through the crowd to a spot alongside a free-standing shelf of books. She was four or five metres away but it was as if a hot wire connected her to Ava. Ava could feel her listening, she could feel her soaking up the words, she could feel this stranger reaching out and pulling her close.

'You enjoy book readings then?' Ava said an hour later when the two of them had adjourned to a nearby café for supper.

Fleur put down her coffee. 'Readings have about the same attraction to me as an abattoir. I'm a vegetarian,' she added. 'The world's awash with bad books and even worse readers. But you,' and she reached across the table and lay the flat of her hand along Ava's left cheek, 'you demand to be heard.'

Ava had planned to stay two nights in London. She ended up staying ten.

'Research,' she explained to Harry. And when he suggested he might join her, she put him off: the novel was finally moving so best not to jinx it. She told him she was staying with a friend and gave him Fleur's phone number. Each evening Harry would telephone as was his custom whenever she was away from Oxford, to swap stories of the day just passed and exchange plans for the one to come. 'You don't have to stay with this Fleur Macleish,' he said. 'You don't have to stay with anyone. You could hole up in a hotel or even a serviced flat in Bloomsbury.' But she assured him she was quite comfortable and in the best place for her work.

New love is explosive, and first passion takes your breath away. Every night after Harry's phone call, she and Fleur went out to a concert or the theatre or just to walk together, and after a late meal they would fall to the bed, the couch, the bath, the floor in a furious feeding on each other. And later still there was more food, easy-eating food of crisps and cream biscuits, chocolate, cheese, roasted almonds and grapes. Night after night, so that late meals and wild love would forever be partnered. Then the quick sleep, the springing into the new day, breakfast together at a local café and leaning across the eggs, the croissants, the coffee to touch each other again and again and again. When Fleur left for work, Ava went to the library to write in the underwater blue of the Round Reading Room, rising from her desk only to use the toilet or slip out to the colonnade for a cigarette. Five days, that's all it took to fill the first notebook. And in another five days after the train pulled out of Euston, she was still writing and a second notebook was nearly finished.

She had never before worked liked this. The first draft of her third novel was completed in two months; the final draft of *The Glimmering Web* was ready to be delivered to her publisher in London four months after that.

'We'll celebrate when you return,' Harry said, as he handed her and the finished manuscript on to the train at Oxford.

As the train pulled out of the station, she saw him standing on the platform. He looked sad and strangely small. Harry knew about Fleur. How he knew, she could not say, but he had known from the beginning.

Fleur was not waiting to meet the train at Euston. There is a protocol to an affair – although already this felt far weightier than an affair – and it would not have been right to embrace her husband at one end of a journey and her lover at the other. Ava had come to London to deliver her new novel to her publisher and deliver it she did. The relationship with Fleur was extra to the trip, although no longer optional. Neither Harry nor Fleur was optional.

For the next seven years there was a reckless propulsion to each day. She knew she needed Harry's calm, reliable love as well as Fleur's unpredictable and fiery passions. And her novels needed the secure domestic space to be written and the turbulence of the affair for their inspiration. She had her safe harbour and she had her muse. The tranquillity and the energy. The earth and the fire. Beyond this she did not think.

2.

It was another spring day seven years later when Fleur left for good. She left in a trail of emails. She had met someone else, she wrote. And while she was always meeting someone else, this time was different, this time she had fallen in love. It was fortunate, she continued, that little was required in the way of housekeeping. No joint assets and any mementoes easily divided. All very tidy, she said.

Nothing provides consolation when you have been dumped, and certainly not tidiness. Ava rang Fleur, but Fleur wasn't answering her phone. She staked out Fleur's flat, but Fleur wasn't at home. She contacted the museum but Fleur had taken leave. Fleur was neither in Oxford nor London, or not the Oxford or London of her years with Ava. Ava was desperate to speak to her, to argue, persuade, cajole and reason with her. Fleur was not allowed to leave, and everything that filled her days was in service to this singular belief. It was a type of madness. But as it happened, madness was to prove far more effective than reason in providing the energy to keep going, for when Fleur returned to her job, her flat and her usual email address, Ava went a full fifteen rounds, fired by high-octane masochism and one-hundred-per-cent-proof stupidity.

Seven years jettisoned in a few sentences. Seven years recorded in letters, phone calls, emails and, in the last couple of years, texts as well, sometimes as many as a dozen contacts in a single day to spark the time between the afternoons and the occasional night when mindlessly hungry they would grab each other and not let go until the last minute had expired. So much feeling, always uncontainable and explosive – and always separate from her marriage. But in the chronic desperation of Fleur's leaving Ava could recall neither the substance nor the texture of those wild hours, she only knew they must not stop.

'We are each other's drug of choice,' Fleur used to say.

For seven tempestuous years even at a distance Fleur was pungent, heady, and stunningly intrusive; up to her neck in pure suffocating bliss, it was all rush and oblivion for Ava. And while the fact of Fleur infused her daily life, that they lived apart, in different cities, was essential. It was not simply that they ran the risk of burning each other up; there was Fleur's brigade of lovers. Ava would sense a rival in a new coffee mug, a theatre program, a different brand of biscuits, a spate of hushed-voice telephone calls. But rather than confront Fleur, Ava, who had no intention of ever leaving Harry, would take her jealousy home and transform it into emails and letters of such wit and artistry that Fleur would be persuaded to abandon the lover for her far more desirable self.

The distance was also essential to maintain her marriage, for Fleur was adamantly not Harry and never a viable alternative to him. Harry had always been wise to his wife's needs; as a preface to his marriage proposal he had actually said he recognised that marriage with him or indeed anyone would not give her all she required. So while Ava did not doubt the affair with Fleur hurt him deeply, at the same time if there was to be a lover, better she be a geographically distant one.

And the distance allowed the novels to be written. Affairs always operate at full throttle, and if barriers are not erected, an affair will ride roughshod over the solitary and time-hungry business of writing. If she and Fleur had lived in the same city, there would have been no novels after the first two. Although more fundamentally, if she had never met Fleur, Ava truly believed she was finished as a novelist.

The email announcing the end of their years together came without warning: one day the usual texts, emails and phone calls rolled in, and the next day Fleur was peeling Ava from her life – although not forever, she had been quick to add. She suggested a break for a few months so that when they met again it would be on 'an entirely new footing'. This plan, so Ava had written to Jack, reduced their relationship to one of Helen's microbes: *a blotch of bacteria, a period of quarantine.*

Fleur left, and it was not simply that Ava missed her, she hated the hours limp without expectation, the cool order of a life without secrets. If every second makes its presence felt, if every minute drags, if sleep has deserted you and alcohol makes you sick, a month can be a life sentence. If not for Harry making her tea and coffee and casseroles and comforting cheesy things, if not for Harry doing the shopping and washing and organising their return to Australia, if not for

Harry running both their lives until such time as she was ready to resume her own, Ava doubted she would have withstood the sustained assault of Fleur's absence.

The days dragged, the nights dragged more. The emails thinned out, life itself wore dangerously thin. It was in the week after Fleur's departure that the spider appeared. By day it lived under the eaves near the kitchen, but after dark it would emerge to weave a gorgeous web, a fluid polygon suspended by four fine filaments, a new web every night, stark and silvery in the light from the kitchen with the fattening black spider at its centre. And in the morning the web would be gone, rolled up was the way Ava thought of it, and the spider curled up again under the eaves.

Each night after Harry had gone to bed, she would go outside and with only the spider as witness, she would slough off all pretence. She wanted another chance with Fleur, to be a different lover, a better lover, she wanted Fleur to come back.

A bad love is very demanding. You'll twist yourself so out of character in an attempt to get it right that the misshapen scrap you present to friends and family is hardly recognisable. But you press on, never wavering in your belief that you know what you are doing. The obvious conclusion, that the relationship is harming you and you would do well to finish it, never presents as an option. Alone with the spider, Ava would address Fleur in the dark, every night a low barrage of words attacking, explaining, condemning, wailing, pleading. And every day rambling messages left on Fleur's phone and a stream of emails and long pathetic letters as well. Fleur responded half-heartedly at first, and by the end of the month not at all.

At last, reason began to stir. Fleur had left. Fleur was gone forever.

The spider remained throughout the long month of Fleur's leaving and for the first couple of months of bereavement. This little creature with no other motive than a good feed in a sheltered spot provided an easier and less guilt-ridden solace than Harry. When the spider eventually disappeared, the days and nights were still pitted with loss but Ava was aware of Fleur taking up less space. She stretched her limbs, she looked about. The short English summer had passed, the leaves on the trees were beginning to colour, the students were back in Oxford, and she and Harry were going home.

At first she had resisted the return to Australia. What would happen if Fleur changed her mind? She wouldn't change her mind, Harry said on one of the few occasions he referred to Fleur directly, and, besides, everything was arranged, a job for him, a university fellowship for her, too late to back out now. Ava packed up the flat, it was good to be occupied, she packed up their life in Oxford. She wrote lists in the evening and followed them religiously the following day. System took the place of suffering. The days and weeks passed, the flat was emptied out. There was a farewell party, she and Harry spent the last night staying with friends, and the following day they travelled up to London and caught the plane home.

Then, nearly three years later with life tripping along nicely, all the friends back in Melbourne, an ordinary Tuesday with the usual morning routine of breakfast, reading, shower, dressing, then to her email, an excellent alternative to the phone, Ava believed, but an extremely poor substitute for the romance of the post, and there it was, the familiar address.

Fleur.

Ava did not hesitate to open the message, one rarely does with email. Fleur was coming to Sydney to courier some treasures for an exhibition on Indian art and culture. Only a brief visit, but it would be wonderful to see her. Could Ava come up to Sydney? *I've so missed our times together,* she wrote. *We always had such fun.*

Riding the rapids of email, Ava hit reply and dashed off a 'what a surprise but what a shame' email citing long-standing work commitments in Melbourne. With only a short time in Australia, Fleur, never much interested in putting herself out, would not make the effort to come down to Melbourne.

Ava selected send, and then sat stunned in front of the screen, not seeing, not reading, not thinking, a minute or two and then rising out of the email those words: we always had such fun.

'We always had such fun,' Ava said the words aloud. There was plenty of fun in the early years, no question of that, but for the last four or five the fun was replaced by a good deal of distress. Had Fleur not noticed? Had she forgotten the betrayals and bitter arguments? Had she forgotten the barrage of criticism she aimed at Ava, the faults she found no matter how many changes Ava made? Was Fleur's fun at the expense of her own pain?

How easily, how surreptitiously can love become panic. That teetering at the edge of the chasm, that swimming endlessly against a swollen tide, that driving the wrong way up a one-way street. And you can't turn round and you can't go back. It makes a nonsense of happiness, it makes a nonsense of love too. And all it takes in this misery is one good time and the misery falls away (she loves me, I knew it, she loves me), one good hit and you're strengthened for the next several months of abuse. But never would you call it fun. Ava did not regret her rapid-fire response to Fleur's email: she had no desire to see her, not this woman with her fun and her forgetting.

There was no reason to expect a response from Fleur, nonetheless Ava checked her email a dozen times throughout the day. In between she potted lilies, she had coffee with her neighbour Minnie, she took Minnie's dog for a walk, she read Oscar Wilde's letters in an attempt to gatecrash other intimacies, and then more soberly a portion of *De Profundis*, she made vegetable soup, she tidied her desk, and finally at ten past five there was a response from Fleur. *Melbourne*, she wrote, *why not? May never have another chance*. She would tack a few days' holiday on to her trip.

There were so many escapes at this stage and Ava ignored the lot of them, for now a meeting with Fleur was possible it became, *ipso facto*, essential. By the time Harry came home, Ava had cancelled all engagements for the week of Fleur's visit with the exception of one reading on the morning of her arrival, just in case she required distraction. There was no question of telling Harry. If the visit turned out to be inconsequential he would never need know, and if not, with desire and disgust amassing in equal strength, she refused to consider that option.

During the weeks that followed, Ava applied herself to work. There were periods when she slipped smoothly into the new novel but mostly the narrative ran amok; sometimes her patience was so fractured that even reading was reduced to rubble. As she lay in bed on the Friday before Fleur's arrival, Ava wondered how she would make it through the next four days. The filming of Connie's pilot at the State Library the following Monday would swallow a few hours, but the weekend loomed endlessly.

From the kitchen she could hear the familiar sounds of Harry making his breakfast; it would be at least thirty minutes before he appeared with her coffee. She tried one more time to apply reason to the impending Fleur visit and yet again she failed. She was about to call Harry and suggest an earlier coffee when suddenly she remembered recitations from memory, the way they could moor attention in the most violent of currents. She began with the ice and albatross stanzas from 'The Rime of the Ancient Mariner' followed by the beginning of 'Prufrock'. Then Hardy's remarkable comment on modernity, 'We are getting to the end of visioning/ The impossible within this universe.' And finally, as if it were waiting for her, she seized on Auden's 'Musée des Beaux Arts'. She had recited it three times by the time Harry arrived with the coffee.

'I've been thinking of Auden's poem how "everything turns away quite leisurely from the disaster",' she said when he appeared in the doorway. 'Why is it, do you think, that in so many instances people go on with their business, despite a boy falling out of the sky, or war or famine or politicians lying in the name of democracy?'

Harry smiled and bent down to kiss her. 'I do enjoy our morning conversations.'

He settled himself on the bed, careful not to crush his trousers. 'It's a matter of self-interest I think. People turn away from a disaster because they're already consumed by events closer at hand, events that more directly involve them, events more important to them and considerably more pleasurable than war or famine or destruction of the planet.'

'But what about those occasions when the disaster has them in its sights, is hurtling towards them and about to swallow them up like a triffid? What then?' She was picking at a pulled thread on the quilt cover. 'And often the events that absorb them are not in the least bit pleasant.'

'Pleasant or unpleasant, the focus keeps the person at the centre of his or her universe – '

'But surely not everyone is that egocentric.'

' – and being so occupied provides the person with a sense of being in control.' He saw she was about to interrupt again and quickly continued. 'There's a deflection effect. Obsessing over something, being plagued by something, fills in time that might otherwise be used in grappling with more relevant issues. The prevaricating, no matter how uncomfortable, is delaying some difficult actions.'

Ava sipped her coffee and avoided his gaze. Harry knew about Fleur's visit, she did not know how he knew, but she was in no doubt he did know. She was wondering whether she should admit to it when he announced in quite a different tone of voice that he had a surprise.

'An early anniversary celebration,' – their anniversary was the following week – 'a holiday weekend.' He would go to the office for just a couple of hours, 'We could get away by midday.'

She leaned forward and pulled him towards her. It was exactly what she needed.

'We'll be eating freshly baked scones for afternoon tea,' Harry said, holding her close.

Ava passed the morning in preparation for their trip, including a visit to the Richmond Hill cheese shop for a selection of Harry's favourite cheeses, together with a loaf of the rosemary and walnut bread he said was the best accompaniment for blue cheese. By the time he returned from work she was ready to leave: for the coast, for the Grampians, for the lush farming country in East Gippsland, for the old gold rush country – neither had any preference, so they tossed a coin, and found themselves heading west to the Grampian mountains. They ate perfect scones at Dunkeld and reached the town of Halls Gap late in the afternoon.

They ignored the picturesque bed-and-breakfasts and searched instead for a motel where breakfast was delivered on a tray through a hatch and no one bothered you.

'Atmosphere can be so intrusive,' Harry said as he always did.

'– and so risky,' Ava added her usual reply.

They were still laughing when they turned into the driveway of a four-star motel which boasted grazing kangaroos at dusk. They were settled in their room, which looked and smelled exactly as a four-star motel room should, and were ticking off their desires on the breakfast menu when the first of the kangaroos appeared.

They sat together on the verandah watching the grazing animals, toasting each other with cider bought from the local pub and dipping into Ava's gift of bread and cheese. The Stilton, Harry said, was excellent, all the cheeses were.

Over the next two days Fleur was packed away while Ava and Harry walked bush tracks, climbed mountain paths and visited every shop in town that sold homemade jams and chutneys, places Harry found irresistible and which Ava tolerated only because of him. They saw galahs and crimson rosellas and rainbow lorikeets, and on one mountain slope a wombat waddling along. They walked arm in arm, breaking into favourite songs, Blake's 'Jerusalem', so at odds with this landscape, and the 'Hallelujah Chorus' for two voices. They talked about friends and Harry's family, they discussed home and abroad, they drew parallels between the present time and early last century, both periods of such rapid change and so few people concerned about where the world might be heading.

They talked about power and wondered if Joseph Conrad's *Heart of Darkness* were made compulsory reading for all fifteen-year-olds whether they would become more responsible citizens. Ava with her faith in the power of narrative believed they would, Harry disagreed as she knew he would. They talked about communication in the age of the computer – never been so efficient, according to Harry, never been so fragile, according to Ava. For two days they talked and laughed and sang and riffled their store of shared memories so well stocked after more than twenty years.

'Over twenty years,' Ava exclaimed, 'who would have thought it.'

On the way home, Harry pulled into a service station for petrol. He switched off the engine and turned to her. 'We're not doing too badly, Davey, we're really not.'

On Monday morning Fleur sent an email, not the cancellation Ava had both hoped and feared, but confirmation of time and place for their meeting and an excited, *See you tomorrow! Can't wait!*

The afternoon at the State Library passed quickly with hardly a thought of Fleur. Not just the bustle of TV, not just being with the others, but Connie in top form and fairly crackling with ideas. And Fleur stayed away during the evening with Harry, his potato pie for dinner and a DVD of *Charade*, 'For my own romantic,' he said. Ava took a sleeping pill and made it through the night.

The following day Harry left home early. He told her he had meetings in Canberra and was planning to stay overnight. Not knowing how long she would be with Fleur, Ava had invented an evening reading and overnight stay for herself, in Ballarat of all places – Ballarat simply popped into her head and she stuck to it. Harry left and Ava was saddled with three hours to fill before her reading – not in Ballarat but at the university a kilometre away, and the one engagement she had not cancelled when first she learned of Fleur's visit.

She fidgeted for an hour, and when she could bear the waiting no longer she grabbed her things and escaped the house. Soon she was wedged down the back of a tram crammed with workers on their way to the city. In the old days she had experienced none of this disquiet; there was an urgency to the whole Fleur business which, she now realised, must have diluted her usual moral responses. When you are compelled to see someone, compelled to contact them several times each day, compelled to love them, you do not think about the consequences to you or anyone else. How very different things were now.

Just before Harry left that morning, she had reassured him, or perhaps she was reassuring herself, that never would anyone come between them.

'I know,' he said. 'But I like to hear you say it.'

As the tram stopped and started and she was pressed harder into a corner, she instructed herself to put Harry aside: the next few hours belonged to the Ava connected to Fleur and quite a different Ava from the one married to Harry. By the time she arrived in the city centre the familiar churning was back: excitement, dread, and a determination to be sensible but in the presence of Fleur knowing she simply could not be trusted.

Once in the city she wandered across the river into the Botanic Gardens. She considered how best to present herself to Fleur, how much to disclose about their almost three-year separation, how much to reveal about her own anxieties now. She did not see the newly planted flower beds, nor the black swans on the ornamental lake, nor the scrub wrens rummaging in the leaf litter. She was, as she had been so many times before, simply filling the time with thoughts of Fleur until Fleur herself arrived.

She supposed she should eat something and made her way back to the city and the cafés along the river. She stopped at one of the less crowded places and ordered the house special-ity, a fisherman's catch breakfast. She fiddled with it until the hot portions were cold and unappetising and the cold parts were room temperature and suspect, before paying an astro-nomical price and re-entering the streets. She dawdled in bookshops, plodded through galleries, loitered in front of shop windows, sampled the samples at a Body Shop until it was time to catch the tram to the university for her reading.

The seminar room was already crowded when she arrived. Dotted among the traditional black-clad artistic students were quite a few in skimpy T-shirts and shorts suggesting a greater affinity with the sports centre than the sedentary life of the mind. Ava hoped that appearances would not prove too reli-able. She talked with academic staff and was introduced to several students, who were variously described as 'talented' or 'promising' or 'one to watch'.

At last it was time to begin. A serious young lecturer welcomed everyone – 'The largest turn-out so far for this series' – before providing an analysis of 'the Bryant oeuvre' in terms so abstract the novels might have been Hegelian philos-ophy. Then Ava stepped up to the podium, and after a brief introduction to her most recent book, *The Metropolitan*, she began the reading.

She had always enjoyed the performance aspect of public readings, so all her reading passages were well settled in memory and required only an occasional glance at the page. Today the audience was mostly comprised of creative-writing students. Five minutes into her reading she noticed two of the students playing the pads of their mobile phones. With another twenty minutes to go, it was anyone's guess how many more of the talented and promising would follow suit.

All these young men and women were enrolled in a course they believed would equip them to write the masterpieces for which they were destined. Although for many there was a greater sense of entitlement: they expected the course to grant them their masterpieces, and if the masterpieces failed to materialise it was the fault of the course and its teachers, and not any lack of ability on their part. Ava wanted to remind them that Woolf and Austen, Dickens and Henry James, the Brontës and the entire pantheon of Russians had not enrolled in a university program in order to write their novels. And despite earning a considerable portion of her own income through creative-writing courses, she wanted to tell them to quit their writing degrees and go home. Read, write, think, daydream. Writing is a slow and solitary learning, she wanted to say. Go home, all of you.

She glanced down at the page to pick up the start of the next paragraph. She couldn't find it. She couldn't find her place nor could she remember what came next. She scanned the open page. Where was she up to? Had she read that paragraph? She couldn't remember. She'd lost her place. She'd have to stop, she'd have to apologise. Never happened before. She felt faint – was she sick? – reached for her water glass and remembered just in time that the paragraph, the one she had just finished, ended on the next page. How could she have forgotten? Her heart was thudding, her stomach fumbling, she'd saved herself just in time. She left the water on the lectern and did not raise her head for the remainder of the reading. When it was over she answered the usual questions, she signed books. And all the while her thoughts jerked back to that moment of panic, and then jerked forward to its cause an hour ahead when she would be seeing Fleur again.

She looked just the same. The dark angular face, the athletic figure, the turquoise jacket they had bought together on a weekend trip to France soon after the Channel Tunnel was opened, the cropped hair bristly against her cheek as they embraced. And the scent of her. So much the same, but as they settled at an outdoor table of a café in Federation Square, ruggedly different. There was the old rush of seeing her, but the churning had stilled. And the usual excitement but without the dread of new revelations. And an easy pleasure, not the wild wind of old, something more sedate, kinder, and never before associated with Fleur. As Fleur chatted away, Ava found herself thinking of the blandness of skin you no longer love. Is there anything more poignant? Anything less ambiguous? And the confusion not to be feeling what you have long been accustomed to feeling. She looked at Fleur, she listened to Fleur, she touched Fleur's arm and she was perplexed.

They were just like any old friends catching up. They spoke of work, of mutual acquaintances, the situation in the Middle East. And Africa, they spoke of Africa where they had planned to visit. And sitting across the table from Fleur, Ava decided she and Harry would make the trip. She asked about the treasures Fleur had brought out, and whether Fleur would be the courier on the homeward journey in a few months' time. When told she would not, that these perks were shared around, Ava experienced nothing in the way of disappointment.

It was all very strange.

She asked about the woman Fleur had fallen in love with, the one who had resulted in her own dismissal, the woman whose name Ava realised with some surprise she had forgotten. Chris, Fleur said, her name was Chris, and then she laughed. It seemed her capacity to fall in love was more robust than reliable, for Chris had proved a disappointment. Fleur embarked on a synopsis of the end of that affair and the beginning and end of the one that followed. Ava listened with an oddly objective interest and, more curiously, only a modicum of unease. She was unsure exactly how to feel. Offended? Played for a fool? Amused? Put in her place? (Fleur had always excelled at putting her in her place.) And settled for amused.

As Fleur nattered on, Ava wondered about the passionate, irresistible woman who had colonised her heart, her mind, her work. Where was the woman who had supplied the spark, the vigour, the urgency that propelled her through seven breathless years? Might Fleur have always been this benign? And if so, how could Ava not have seen?

'It is so good to see you.' Fleur laced her fingers through Ava's. 'I really have missed you.'

Ava stared at their joined hands, aware of a weird numbness. The sharp edges had worn from her joy, the burn from her excitement; the longing had disappeared entirely. And along with the cravings, the adulation had disappeared too. Adulation: so essential to the type of relationship she had with Fleur, but – she had never before realised – only ever dished out by her. Once she would have done anything to earn Fleur's love. But while you can earn gratitude, loyalty, a car, a house, an overseas trip, you cannot earn love.

There's nothing to be picked from the rubble of a dead love, she told herself, and reeled off some unconvincing excuses before hurrying away.

She hailed a cab, she was desperate to be home, away from Fleur and the past. It was Harry she wanted. She'd ring him in Canberra. But there was a light on when the taxi pulled up outside the house. He was home! He must have changed his plans and come home. She ran up the path. And there he was, Harry, standing in the doorway, waiting for her.

He wrapped his arm about her shoulders and pressed his cheek against hers. She nuzzled into the familiar roughness, his familiar end-of-day smell, and the two of them entered the house together.

CHAPTER 7: **Bondage**

1.

It was ten o'clock in the morning and Jack was slumped across the couch in Helen's lounge. Sun plastered the room, the white walls glared. The night had disappeared in a bottle and a half of shiraz, a few glasses of ancient cooking sherry and a couple of stale joints. Jack couldn't remember walking to Helen's, he couldn't remember anything after finding the sherry.

His skull was tolling the seconds. A slab of meat was lodged in his throat. He lurched into the bathroom; vomiting made the pain worse.

He was cleaning himself up when Luke appeared in the doorway with aspirin.

'You sure got hammered last night,' he said.

The session had begun soon after he saw Ava with Fleur. Jack had returned to the office to collect his belongings and found Connie with time to fill. Minutes later, the two of them had headed across Princess Bridge to Young and Jackson's pub. They found a vacant table in the upstairs lounge far removed from the famed portrait of naked Chloe and her admirers, and plunged into an alcohol-laced raging at life. Connie was fed up with TV executives who were either unable to make decisions or lacked the authority – successful pilot notwithstanding, his TV series was far from being a certainty – and Jack mourned the attack on authentic love in an age of impermanence. By the time the second bottle of wine arrived, Connie was lambasting twenty-five-year-olds who showed no need for sleep and a great need of maturity. When Jack reminded him of Linda's maturity, Connie immediately switched to a sentimental riff on Sara's charms.

They were halfway through the second bottle when Jack reported his sighting of Fleur.

'She's here, in Melbourne. With Ava.'

'Whether Fleur or someone else, it doesn't make much difference,' Connie said. 'With the exception of Harry, Ava's never subscribed to fidelity.'

Jack found this ludicrous. 'Ava's been unfaithful to Harry numerous times.'

Connie stretched across the low table and gave Jack's shoulder a kindly squeeze. 'You never understood that of us all, all her lovers –' and seeing Jack's surprise, 'oh yes, I had my time with her too. Of us all, only Harry was permanent.'

Although Fleur was looking suspiciously permanent too, Jack was thinking as he swallowed the aspirin Luke had given him. As for Ava and Connie, he had known of their affair even while it was happening, but preferring not to know had pushed it to the very back of consciousness where it had slipped into the black forgotten.

He took his miserable body to the kitchen. Luke looked up from his laptop as Jack entered. 'Coffee's made,' he said, and jerked his head towards the cafetière.

Jack shot him a smile of gratitude and simultaneously Helen's voice, raised in irritation, soared into the kitchen.

'What's bothering your mother?' Jack asked.

'She wants to book a flight to America, but first she's trying to change the airline's scheduling policy.'

Jack laughed and clasped his head. He poured the coffee and joined Luke at the table.

'Working?' he asked, indicating the laptop.

Luke was home on a study day, but he was not studying. 'I'm learning self-hypnosis,' he said. 'To help my game.' And seeing Jack's incomprehension, 'Football. Aussie Rules. Linda's idea.' And responding to Jack's still-uncomprehending expression, 'Linda the anaesthetist, married to Connie. Knows about the mind.'

When he was Luke's age, Jack might have used hypnosis to crank up his memory or reduce his need for sleep; he would never have considered using it for sport. Perhaps if he had been more like Luke his life now would be more than a dusty pile of yesterdays. But with neither energy nor desire to deal with it, he pushed the thought aside.

Luke was prattling on about Linda, actually he was preaching Linda, so well did he think of her. She was honest and loyal, reliable and loving, and given what Connie was doing with Sara, far too good for him.

'Sara is far from being Connie's first indiscretion,' Jack said.

'Indiscretion? How pathetic is that, Jack? You mean Connie is cheating on Linda. You mean he's doing her in. You mean he's fucking her over.'

Fortunately Helen put an end to the conversation. She burst into the kitchen railing at airline scheduling that disregarded the schedules of working people. She had an important meeting near Atlanta at the end of the following week and she wanted to travel when she would normally be sleeping. 'I don't want to waste time,' she said. 'Is that so much to ask?'

'And if you lost twenty-four hours would it be so catastrophic?' Luke said.

Helen glared at her son. 'Some of us find every wasted minute unconscionable.'

'You need to get a life, Mom.'

Still muttering about the airline, Helen grabbed a packet of instant noodles and headed for the door.

Jack was horrified. 'You don't plan to eat that stuff. It's all chemicals and preservatives.'

Luke looked across at his mother. 'But very convenient.'

She smiled at her son. 'Exactly.' And then to Jack, 'Would love to talk, so curious to know what put you in your cups. Can't stop, got to run. We'll catch up soon.'

She kissed Jack, she kissed her son, she dashed from the kitchen. She rattled around in her study, ran down the hall, swore loudly, returned to her study to collect something she had forgotten, ran down the hall again and out of the house, leaving the door to slam behind her.

2.

By mid-afternoon Jack was recovered sufficiently to go into work. Not his first preference but he felt disoriented, nothing to do with the hangover, something far less tangible, a browning at the edges of the familiar, a fraying of the fabric of his life. He had forbidden all thoughts of Ava.

Within moments of his arrival, Harry appeared in the doorway. 'Great to see how busy you've been. And some very impressive engagements too.'

He proceeded to appraise Jack's recent calendar. The consultations with the Department of Trade were a real coup; the interview on public radio was a waste of time; the address to the shadow cabinet was politically smart. Harry had attended none of these occasions, but the newly omnipotent Harry made it his business to know everything that might be relevant to NOGA.

Jack was becoming increasingly wary of the Network. The fact was, Harry knew too much. He had his minions in the office, contemporary versions of the courtiers of old who willingly did his bidding. They turned up at selected meetings and briefings – one had accompanied Jack to the feedback session at the Department of Trade – and lurked in the corridors of NOGA. But a couple of sycophants couldn't account for the extent of Harry's knowledge.

Harry had passed comments, some of a highly personal nature, about NOGA members whom Jack knew Harry had never met. NOGA existed largely online; electronic surveillance of its ever-expanding web of members was, from a technical point of view, not difficult.

Jack had become so concerned he had confided in Connie.

Connie dismissed his suspicions. 'Harry's done us all a favour with these fellowships,' he said. 'And besides everyone should, as a matter of course, follow sensible web practice. Just be careful what you say on NOGA.com.' And with a kindly arm across Jack's shoulder, he wondered whether it was time to drop his 'personal vendetta against Harry'.

Harry was now checking through Jack's upcoming engagements. He seemed so friendly, so interested, so benign, and perhaps he was. But at the moment what Jack most wanted was for Harry to leave him alone. Finally he was finished and Jack closed the door behind him, aware of a reluctant sympathy for the poor sod given what Ava was probably doing at that very moment.

Jack stood in the centre of the room, absolutely still. He felt tense and raddled, and not just because of Ava; Harry was right, he had been busy. There had been consultations with lobbyists, bureaucrats and government advisers, and background briefings to business and export groups. Every few days the Department of Foreign Affairs contacted him, and he was the first port of call for a surprising number of foreign embassies and High Commissions. He had addressed think-tanks and university institutes, he had even been invited to speak at a literary festival. And every day brought a raft of phone calls and emails from the media requesting information, analysis, comment, preferably in a single quotable sentence. Sometimes he felt as if people hit on him instead of Google.

He tried to provide what everyone wanted – he would always feel obliged to give his best – but he was aware of a growing resistance from within. It could not be ascribed to his growing wariness of NOGA, nor the frustrating superficiality of the analysis required of him; rather it was the world events themselves which were increasingly repellent. The fact was he could hardly bring himself to study these events any more. It was not specifically terrorism and the never-ending Israeli–Palestinian quagmire, nor Iraq's disintegration and Iran's terrifying ego. It was men in a dozen different African countries displacing, starving, raping and butchering their own. It was communities reduced to rubble, fanatics waving guns, self-righteous politicians with blood on their Armanis, boys hurling stones in Gaza and wielding machetes in the Sudan, children across the globe whose lessons in hate were so masterful that the conflicts were assured for generations to come.

It surprised him how the Israeli–Palestinian horrors brought the Jew in him to the fore, although a different sort of Jewishness than he had previously known. Like a horsehair and silk undergarment, where the horsehair was contemporary Israeli policy and the silk was Judaism's traditions of liberal humanism and learning. He abhorred the rocket attacks on Israel, a country less than a third the size of Tasmania. At the same time he was appalled when Israel acted the brute and the bully. If force were the answer then the conflict would have been settled aeons ago. Not force but reason, he wanted to say to both sides. But with hatred blowing at gale-force, reason did not stand a chance.

Horsehair and silk, and he simply couldn't watch another Israeli incursion into Gaza, the tanks crushing the possibility of peace as they cracked open streets and mowed down houses, and in the dust so much hate fomented. And he couldn't watch another Palestinian suicide bomber kill ordinary Israelis – babies, children, teenagers, mums, dads, lovers, grandparents gathered in a restaurant or travelling by bus or just walking vaguely along. He couldn't bear the violence any more.

Everywhere he saw the ferocious inventiveness of injustice, and while he hated the simplicity of the media reports he found himself choking on the complexities. It was not simply a matter of disenfranchised Muslims having nothing to lose; these young people were being brainwashed to love death more than life. Goebbels was right: you can be taught to believe anything even if it destroys you. And it was not simply a matter of Islam's failure to modernise, radical Islam was filling a leadership and a values' vacuum in several parts of the world. Radical Islam was promising to restore to the Muslim people the power and confidence that used to be theirs.

So much of life was wonderful. Music, books, friendship, the natural world, the vast universe, the possibility of life elsewhere. Yet rather than these wonders, his own speciality was, increasingly, humanity's gangrenous underbelly. Every day he spoke about events that were causing him to rupture, events that had him doubting the essential human goodness to which he had subscribed all his life. He felt a responsibility to continue working in this field but a diminishing desire. That he lived in safety far from these conflicts and had no right to suffer them merely made him feel worse.

He went to the kitchen for a fresh cup of coffee. Through the open doors of offices he saw people working hard and, he assumed, with satisfaction. He wanted what they had, he wanted it in much the same way as a different sort of person would covet a Rolex or a Mercedes Benz or their own lap pool. To work, to be absorbed in a new book, that's what he wanted.

Back in his office he finished some briefing documents for the Department of Trade, then, with no particular plan, he wandered over to his bookshelves. Assuming a cool and distant curiosity – a less disinterested approach would have been too cruel given the prolonged sterility of his pen – he drew from the shelves a copy of his own first book, *Literatures of the Semites*. He wondered if Jacqueline du Pré ever listened to her own recordings after multiple sclerosis had swindled her of her gift. Not that he would put himself in her class, but still he wondered whether she ever visited her never-to-be-repeated joys and successes.

He turned to the title page, the dedication to his parents, scanned the contents – a great deal of ground had been covered for a first book – and then dipped into the body of the work. How unfamiliar it was, hardly recognisable as his own. He chose one of the shorter chapters and standing by the bookshelves read it in its entirety. It was good. He had been good.

Next he took down the original edition of *The Reinvention of Islam* and withdrew to his armchair. This was the book that had prompted his rehabilitation. He scanned every page from the dedication, *For AB*, to the end. By the time he finished, the city buildings were jutting brilliantly into the night sky, roads were glowing veins shooting into the suburbs. He closed the book and cradled it against his chest. He had been a good scholar: his analysis had been thorough, his approach original, and he had made creative and constructive use of his being Jewish.

What, he wondered, had happened to him?

There are Australian backblocks and American boondocks, but the back of beyond in New Zealand warrants its own category of end of the line, off the map, beyond consideration, beyond prospects, beyond hope. Whether it was lack of ambition or a self-defeating attachment to old-fashioned principles, the fact remained that if Jack had stretched the domain of comparative religion, if he had published a few papers or sought out some paying consultancies, he would never have had to resort to the New Zealand job. He had made one or two half-hearted attempts to offer his services on the open market, but in those days no one was interested in comparative religion, neither the non-religious, who saw all religious studies as anachronistic, nor the crowing packs of evangelicals and other fundamentalists who, already in possession of the truth, did not need Jack's interpretations. As for politicians and business people, in the absence of any efforts from Jack to promote his relevance, they showed no interest. Selling himself did not appeal, and selling himself for questionable means appealed even less. Jack's contract in Australia was not renewed and he took the New Zealand job.

Ava advised against it. *With such a huge teaching load, there'll be no time left for your own work*, she had written. *Your passions will starve.*

At the time he had taken little notice of what she actually said, so thrilled was he at her concern. But now her reference to passions in the plural returned. Once it had been true, but the diverse passions of his youth had coalesced into the one consuming passion for her. And all those years of cramming his mind with her had prevented it from wandering off on junkets of its own. No unfettered thoughts, no new ideas. If he had never met her, if he had never come to love her, how different his life might have been. Or perhaps there would have been someone else. An Ava substitute. Perhaps he was condemned always to love exclusively and hopelessly. Jack Adelson: fundamentalist in love.

He found a clean sheet of paper and jotted the phrase down. FUNDAMENTALIST IN LOVE. His love for Ava – singular, confined, obdurate, immutable and efficiently cannibalistic in the way it sought out only what nourished it. An intriguing thought, but disturbing.

He regularly intimated in his letters to her that he was working on a new project and she regularly requested to see chapters. When he felt he could stall her no longer, *The Reinvention of Islam* had been fortuitously discovered in the massive warehouse of minor scholarship, dusted off and relaunched.

Pundits, interviewers, academics and commentators praised his prescience. 'The world was such a different place when you wrote the book,' they said.

Even among the more intelligent observers there was an attitude that Islamic extremism had sprung up fully formed just a few years ago. Jack would point out that the signs were visible much earlier but it required a creative imagination to notice them. It's a quality of the future, he would say whenever he was given the chance, that no one can know it with any certainty, but one can and must imagine it.

Few interviewers would permit Jack to go beyond this point, and most had stopped him well before he reached it. But in lectures and symposia he could speak his mind, and he had plenty to say – about Western politicians in particular: that committed as they are to staying in power they have little need for creative imagination. That rather than inspired and visionary leadership, their ambitions are tethered to three- or four-year terms and played out in tangible temptations like tax rebates, affordable childcare and a plasma-screen television for every household. That if one were to listen only to politicians, one might conclude that the complex social, political, spiritual, ethical and intellectual fabric of human societies had been shrunk to a single economic dimension.

Islam, indeed any issue of complexity, simply could not compete.

Jack would speak his mind whenever he had the opportunity. And people were listening, for there had been offers of work when his NOGA fellowship finished. He was in demand, and all due to a book he had written years ago. As for anything new, the few ideas that came to him evaporated within days. Most did not survive beyond a page of notes.

How different it was for Ava. Nothing ever stopped her from working. She lived and worked with one hand grasped firmly to the safety rail of a speeding train. The risks were hair-raising, and when things went awry, as they often did, she was quick to shoulder the blame.

'Although it's human to make mistakes,' she used to say.

'Bad breath is human too,' Jack would reply, 'but that doesn't make me want it.'

Ava insisted that mistakes were a necessary corollary to taking risks. 'Life's an adventure. You never know what's around the next corner. And besides, who would want to?'

Throughout their friendship she had derided his desire for perfection. *Perfection is just a form of control,* she once wrote to him, *a means of reducing life in all its diversity to a few manageable absolutes.*

Ideals of perfection provided standards for behaviour, he wrote back. Far from exercising control, they undergirded a dynamic and progressive life. Perfection, he had argued, was justice without human jealousies, the oasis without the desert. But now he was having doubts. If he were to approach the issue differently, he could see that an overriding belief in perfection provided an immutable authority, which was – such a reluctant concession – characteristic of all types of funda-mentalism. He left his chair and paced the room, eventually returning to his desk and beneath the phrase FUNDAMENTALIST IN LOVE he wrote BELIEF IN PERFECTION PROVIDES OBDURATE AUTHORITY. He folded the sheet of paper and shoved it in his ideas' folder.

An ATM receipt fell out of the bulging file. Across the top in red ink he had written a line from George Steiner's *Errata*: 'Fundamentalism, that blind lunge towards simplification'.

Even chance, it seemed, was forcing him to think this idea through. He withdrew his sheet of paper from the folder, added the Steiner line to it, and left the page spread on his desk.

FUNDAMENTALIST IN LOVE.

BELIEF IN PERFECTION PROVIDES OBDURATE AUTHORITY.

FUNDAMENTALISM, THAT BLIND LUNGE TOWARDS SIMPLIFI-CATION.

Ava was an avid reader of biographies. Rather than absolutes, she searched for meaning in the often messy lives of writers and other artists. Creative people tend to behave badly, she said, they break boundaries both in their life and their work. It was how she lived herself, as Jack knew better than most, and yet there was a coherence to her existence, Helen's too, which he seemed to lack. Ava was compelled to write fiction (he had once heard her say she was 'helpless before fiction'), and in a similar fashion Helen was compelled to do science. As for him, he was compelled to love Ava Bryant. But when a great love is a compulsion, can it still be a great love? Compulsion in the emotional realm seemed to fit better with revenge and hatred and patriotism and religious fervour – not love, unless one were to include obsession. And obsession itself: just a nudge away from fanaticism.

Work. The imagination. Reality. Experience. All such distinct, even mutually exclusive categories for him, but not for Ava. He and Ava had discovered together Yeats's poem 'The Choice': 'The intellect of man is forced to choose/ Perfection of the life, or of the work.' They both regarded it as a false dichotomy but for very different reasons: Ava because life and art were inseparable, and Jack because it was a nonsense to compare two essentially different things.

'The dichotomy was dispelled by Yeats himself,' Ava said. 'He was involved in politics and the theatre, he had numerous friends and acquaintances, he loved well and he loved foolishly. Less life and there probably would have been less art.'

Perhaps life writ large was the mark of a true artist; if so, where did that leave him? His passion for Ava had become so deeply entrenched it had acquired the same sense of inevitability as God has for a believer, a taken-for-granted existence with its own rules and logic, its own *raison d'être*. His love for Ava, not Ava herself was, he realised, the most authoritative element in his life and his sole allegiance was to it. Like any form of fundamentalism.

What sort of life is driven by a single desire? Of yearning always for what one lacks. Never to be satisfied. What sort of life is this? Again he picked up his pen and wrote: PASSION AS DICTATOR.

He read through the odd list before switching off the desk lamp and crossing to the windows. There he gazed out at the strings of street lights, the towers of lights, the smoothly moving headlights, the illuminated boxes of trams, the flashing buy buy buy neon signs. And the patches of blackness: gardens, buildings, markets – places shut down until morning. As he stared through the glass, a strange night city rose out of the familiar day view, like those magic-eye drawings that separate from an easy-to-see pattern. And through the night and the lights, through all the years of forgetting, he thought he could discern the black patch of beachside parkland where he played cricket and football as a boy. And the St Kilda reserve where he had listened to the Salvos playing on Saturday mornings. And the black snake of the Elwood Canal where he had crouched in a putrid alcove to escape the neighbourhood bullies. And the cemetery on Alma Road where he had trespassed with friends and they'd deserted him as night was falling, leaving him to climb the gates and make his way home alone.

A whole forgotten life buried beneath his remembered life, and he found himself thinking how there is an exclusiveness to rehearsed memories and a literalness to a remembered past. He had always been wary of people who chained themselves to habit and routine, but memories were susceptible to habit too. Memories like a catechism carved into mind, the same memories revisited as days pass into months and years, the same regularly recalled scenes and events comprising an individual's personal history. And all the while the treasury of forgetting grows fuller – not seen, not noticed and certainly not questioned until someone produces a contradictory memory or one's own mind relaxes, and all of a sudden the habitual view is sabotaged.

Jack crossed to his desk and switched the lamp back on. He made a couple more notes, wavered over his computer, left it untouched. Again he found himself thinking of authority, not just its restrictions and demands but the safety it brings, whether it be the authority of a dictator, a god, of history, of memory, or one unquestionably perfect love. All those yearnings he had cut and polished so they shone like diamonds amid the unruly tumult of daily life. Grand passions make a pretence of shunning all restrictions but the passion itself is a restriction, for nothing must ever challenge it. And while you're flying fast and high on your grand passion, you don't realise you are confined to a single tight orbit and the rest of life is gathering dust. Not surprising his work had suffered.

Perhaps it was time for a new version of Jack Adelson. And immediately he registered a chill. To excise Ava from his life would render him a stranger to himself. Although something needed to change. He gazed around at the flash and glamour that was NOGA. He was not his parents' son for nothing, he knew that acronyms could camouflage a hornet's nest of intentions and practices, and that nothing ever came for free. NOGA was not the place for a scholar; but then neither was the university any more.

It was after ten. He unplugged his laptop, slipped it into his satchel, stood by his desk not moving. Fundamentalism, authority, love, memory, creativity: the concepts wanted to come together. He stood by his desk for another minute, then he pulled his computer from the bag and picked up his page of jottings. Slowly he walked towards the windows, slowly he settled in his chair: if ever he needed to take a risk it was now. Love, authority, fundamentalism, creativity, memory. This business of all-consuming desires and passions, that in his love for Ava he may have been as restricted as any fundamentalist. That in his singular focus, extending even to his storehouse of memories, he had relinquished his creative gaze.

He opens his computer, he creates a new document, he begins to write.

He writes a meditation on fundamentalism. He writes that where fundamentalist ideas, beliefs, attitudes or passions exist there can be no ambiguity, and where there is no ambiguity there is no impetus for original thought. That in a long and obsessive love, the lover is cut off from reason in much the same way as a religious fundamentalist, and both are locked in a world of fixed desires and singular passions where the imagination is either slaughtered or put in chains. That because of the authority accorded to certain ideas and beliefs, misguided lovers, like fundamentalists, feel entirely justified in their life's course and have no need to question it.

He writes that the appeal of absolutes today is their ability to supply bedrock at a time which is quite literally explosive; that absolutes – whether a belief in God or a perfect love or even the ultimate value of money – delude one into thinking one has some control over the events of one's life. And reason is the first casualty – after all, absolutes are absolutes, there are no shadings or gradings, no flaws or ambiguities – and an engagement with reality is another. Perfect love – fundamentalist love – immerses the lover in a cloud of agnosia in much the same way that religious fundamentalism renders its followers insensitive to everything outside the creed.

He writes through the night. Four and a half hours later he is finished. Nearly three thousand words. A whole essay. He is afraid to read it, has to force himself to stand by the printer as the pages slip into the tray. And when the job is complete he takes the stack still warm from the machine, fans the pages, *his* pages, the first for such a long time, and lets them cool against his chest.

He puts his essay on the side-table and turns off the lamp. He settles into his chair and falls asleep.

'BONDAGE. Musings on love, fundamentalism and authority' was published a week later in the online journal WEBster. In keeping with the journal's policy it appeared anonymously. Neither WEBster nor Jack's essay dominated conversation in universities or government offices nor indeed on the floor occupied by NOGA high above the city of Melbourne, but the essay was noticed. Conservatives saw it as an attack on smug liberals who were caught within the mould of old and inflexible ideologies, and liberals saw it as an attack on conservatives who had lost themselves to social extremism. Artists of all persuasions welcomed it as providing much-needed support for creative work.

Jack emailed Helen about it. *My first publication this millennium*, he wrote. A short time later she telephoned: it was worth the wait, she said.

Connie was so impressed he wished he'd written it himself.

By the time Jack contacted Ava, she had already read the piece and guessed he had written it – his old punchy style, the vocabulary familiar from his letters. Although the thoughts were new. 'It has the flavour of those articles you used to write back in Oxford,' she said in a phone call to him. And invited him for lunch.

She sounded tentative, but perhaps not surprising given he had knocked back so many of her invitations. Or perhaps it was Fleur and she was embarrassed at the rekindling of an affair she had insisted was over. But flush with energy and already toying with an idea for a second essay, he accepted her invitation. It was only when he was in the car and driving to her place that he realised something was amiss. He was not rehearsing the meeting which was about to take place, he was not nervous, he was not racked with yearning. He was excited to be seeing her, but his other usual responses were quiet.

3.

They settled in the courtyard with coffee, not green tea Jack was pleased to note, and talked in a way they had not for a long time, stepping off from his essay on to broader issues of political authority and control.

'How desperate we must be for security to relinquish so much in the way of responsibility and decision-making,' Ava said. 'It's not surprising politicians get away with blatant lies.'

'And blatant neglect of human rights,' Jack added.

Ava was thoughtful, often stopping to find just the right word. In fact, uncharacteristically she talked at his pace, which he found rather touching. Touching and nothing else, certainly not evidence that finally she was loving him.

They talked across a swathe of topics. But after an hour she seemed to be picking her way through the arguments with extra care.

'Are you all right?' Jack asked.

She blushed as if caught out.

But whatever had embarrassed her it was not Fleur. Ava spoke freely about Fleur's visit to Melbourne, about that vacant space when love has gone, her sense of incredulity that she had loved this woman for years and years, had suffered over her and made others suffer. She could still see Fleur's attractions, she said, but her flaws were now visible as well.

'Her self-concern, her vanity, her carelessness with people.' There was a long pause, almost as if she were redrafting the relationship as she talked. 'Even though I suffered as a result of these qualities, I never really saw them before. I expect I didn't want to.'

Might he have deluded himself in similar fashion? Jack wondered. After all – and it took an effort to acknowledge it – most of what had occurred between him and Ava had been produced in his own imagination.

It seemed that the protection, the deception, of years was shedding fast and there was nothing, nothing whatsoever he could do about it. Delusion? He had suffered it in bucketfuls.

Worse still, he had tethered his imagination to his love for Ava, and the imagination, knowing its master, had always placed him at the centre of its conceits. Not only deluded but narcissistic as well. Perhaps all romantic love is.

He looked at her, the love of his life. She sat slumped and pale against the red canvas of her chair – clearly the contact with Fleur had exacted a heavy toll. And for the first time he noticed the lines around her eyes and a faint staining of the skin on her cheeks. Her shirt in the gossamer material she had always favoured clung to her body; she looked as if she had lost weight. He was aware of feeling protective of her, as a parent might for a child.

She sighed. 'If only all days could be like this.'

And habit kicked in: they can, he wanted to say, I'm available, always available to you. And reason pulled him back. She's weary, she's relaxed, her statement has nothing to do with you.

He leaned back in his chair and he, too, relaxed.

'Could you kill someone you loved?'

The question so startled him he wondered if he had heard correctly.

'What I mean is: could you help someone end their life?'

Ava indicated a newspaper lying on the ground. There was a photograph of an elderly man flanked by police officers. The headline read, 'Husband to stand trial for wife's murder'. Ava related the story: a loving marriage of forty years; wife diagnosed with cancer; years of treatment; no hope; much pain; husband helps to end her life.

'Could you help someone you love die?' she asked again.

Jack looked at her, this woman he had loved all his adult life, and slowly shook his head. 'I don't believe so.'

She reached forward and took his hand. 'I thought as much.'

Jack had planned to put in an appearance at NOGA after leaving Ava's place, but instead he went home. He let himself into the flat and walked slowly through the rooms. This place, so full of memories, suddenly struck him as anonymous; with the exception of his old bedroom, a shrine to his eighteen-year-old self, he might not be living here at all.

Lytton Strachey in a letter to his brother James had referred to 'a one-place-at-a-table-laid-for-six life'. It described Jack's to perfection. Could he pick up his life now? Could he direct it differently? Or would he be like an alcoholic who remains an alcoholic even after he has stopped drinking? Would he always be addicted to Ava?

He had been flirting with a second essay. He planned to call it 'Starving for certainty'. It would connect the collapse of communism with the rise of religious fundamentalism in the developing world, and an increasing social fundamentalism with the collapse of liberalism in the West. The essay united the major points of his own past – his parents' beliefs and the values of his formative years as a student – as well as thrusting him deep into the contemporary world.

He made himself a coffee and went into his study. It took just a couple of minutes to remove the ancient flyers and posters from the walls. He wavered in front of the rubbish bin, then folded them in a neat pile and shoved them at the back of the filing cabinet. Before starting his new essay he sent an email to Ava, thanking her for a lovely day.

CHAPTER 8: Devotions

1.

Waiting, flying, more waiting, flying again, food, films, announcements, computer battery threateningly low and the man in the next seat threateningly large. The journey from Melbourne to Atlanta dragged on and on.

Helen tried to work but her mind ran on a different track. Might this be her last meeting? Might she be forced out of science? And how would she live if she were? The same questions plundered the endless hours. And when she did manage to sleep, it was a pseudo-sleep fractured by a series of microbe-related disasters. It began with the delivery of anthrax into a football stadium, with two sleeping Helens debating how many aerosol squirts of the bug would be required to infect all the spectators. She woke up long enough to drink a bottle of water and then was thrown into the thick of an APEC meeting brought to a halt by watermelon injected with contaminated water. It would be the work of an insider and easily traced, said one sleeping Helen, not so easily traced, argued another, given the army of personnel required to run the show. The APEC incident segued into an outbreak of food poisoning among the troops in Iraq – a disaster which had, in fact, already occurred, with one Helen arguing sabotage against the other's case for carelessness. From Melbourne to Los Angeles to Atlanta one terror scenario merged into another. When the aircraft finally touched down her brain had jammed.

She limped into the terminal. And then, to her relief, there was a shift in momentum. Her bag was the first to appear on the luggage carousel, security nodded her through, a driver was waiting to whisk her into the city. At the hotel she was welcomed as a returning guest and registered without delay. Her room was comfortable, the shower was vigorous, she changed into fresh clothes and went down to the hotel bar. Her colleagues were expecting her – Josh, originally from Israel but for many years at the Centers for Disease Control in Atlanta, Sam from the UK, Takeshi the shigella man from Japan, and Jeanne from Belgium, attending her first international meeting.

Greetings were brief, a drink appeared and soon she was immersed in the conversation. Two hours later and still talking, the group moved to the hotel restaurant. They ate while they talked and when the restaurant closed they returned to the bar to continue their discussion – including, to Helen's amusement, the science behind the food contamination affecting the troops in Iraq.

Josh and his group in Atlanta had coordinated the PFGE work on the outbreak. 'We eliminated sabotage as soon as the same contamination showed up in salad packs delivered to trainees on bivouac in Texas.'

'Same contractor do the salad packs?' Sam asked.

'You got it.'

PFGE, pulsed-field gel electrophoresis, a type of bacterial fingerprinting in which bacteria isolated in vastly different places could be shown to originate from the same source, had brought about a revolution in tracing techniques. And while tracking did not prevent outbreaks, PFGE had been extraordinarily effective in confining the damage. It also connected the scientists on a very regular basis: these days they counted one another as friends.

It was two o'clock when they called it a night. Helen could not say what she had eaten, she certainly could not describe the hotel decor, but the science was memorable and a fitting prelude to the coming days. She slept a deep and dreamless sleep.

The next day after breakfast, she and the other scientists, together with two minders, piled into a minibus. They were heading west to Aiken, South Carolina, a small city not far from the Georgia border. Here they would meet up with twenty-five more of their colleagues for the four-day meeting. The bus was brimming with conversation as it wended its way through the peach state's capital city, past Peachtree Plaza, along Peachtree Boulevard, over Peachtree Creek.

'What are all these peaches?' Jeanne from Belgium asked.

'Peaches have greater appeal than diseases,' Josh said in his languid throaty accent. And when Jeanne still looked perplexed he continued. 'Georgia is known both for its peaches and the Centers for Disease Control and Prevention – the CDC. But Ebola Plaza and Bubonic Boulevard wouldn't pull the tourists.'

As soon as they were out on the freeway one of the minders called for their attention. 'At Aiken you'll be staying at a boutique conference centre.' Her drawl reconfigured the French 'boutique' into the deep south's 'bo-wa-teek'. 'You'll find many excellent walking tracks nearby.'

The minder had been well-briefed. A few years earlier they had gathered near Como in Italy, the first time one of their meetings had been held in a rural location. The formal sessions occurred as usual, but outside of these, scientists discussed and argued as they walked by the lake and hiked into the surrounding hills, and solitary figures could be seen at all hours pounding the country paths rapt in thought. The formal sessions were nourished by these rambles – 'On a recent walk it occurred to me,' became a repeated refrain – and since then all their meetings had been held in rural settings.

Several well-documented discoveries in the early years of nuclear physics had occurred while scientists were out walking. Lise Meitner, one of Helen's favourite scientists, first identified nuclear fission while tramping through the Swedish snow with her nephew, Otto Robert Frisch. Meitner, an Austrian of Jewish ancestry, had worked for many years at the Kaiser Wilhelm Institute in Berlin. Following the Anschluss in March 1938, she had been forced into exile in Sweden, severed from her science, her laboratory and her colleagues. It was a sad and lonely time, and when she was invited by friends to spend the Christmas holiday in Kungälv on the west coast of the country, she was quick to accept. Frisch, also a physicist working in exile, at Niels Bohr's institute in Copenhagen, had also been invited for the Christmas holiday in Kungälv.

(It had always annoyed Helen that Frisch, half the physicist his aunt was, had found work with the great Niels Bohr while Meitner had been lucky to get a much lowlier position in Sweden. Meitner had been forced to put up with so many indignities simply because she was a woman. Fortunately she lived long enough to witness the start of a changing attitude towards women in science – she died in 1968 at the age of ninety – but how very different her career might have been if she had been born fifty years later, or a man.)

A few days before she left for the holiday, Meitner had received a letter from Otto Hahn, her long-time collaborator in Berlin, in which he described some puzzling experiments. Meitner suggested to her nephew that they take a walk in the countryside to ponder Hahn's results. Frisch donned his new cross-country skis, the tiny Meitner, barely 150 centimetres tall, relied on a pair of small wooden skis and off they went through the snow. Hours later, after much discussion and some crude diagrams – Meitner was a far better physicist than she was artist – Meitner hit on the solution: what Hahn had demonstrated but had been unable to interpret was nuclear fission. Nuclear fission, experimentally demonstrated by a German chemist working under the Nazi regime and interpreted by two exiled Jewish physicists as they pounded back and forth through the Swedish snow. The history of science is full of such wonders. And full of slights too: Hahn received the Nobel, Meitner did not.

'And horses,' the minder was still talking in her tour-guide fluency. 'The conference centre at Aiken has its own stables and the management is happy to provide horses for the guests.' Her tone of voice switched up a register. 'Aiken is regarded by many as the Florida for horses. Thoroughbreds from the northern states spend the winter there and horse training is one of the major local industries. Polo is popular in the region, and riding to hounds too.'

'Polo and fox hunting, I can't believe it.' Sam from England spoke so loudly he earned a suspicious glance from the non-speaking minder.

Ruggedly innocuous, this second minder was the sort of middle-sized, middle-aged, middle-of-the-road man who was born to be background. Helen assumed he was one of the 'observers' who attended all their meetings these days. They usually appeared in pairs (perhaps this man's mate was already at Aiken), had barber-shop groomed hair, were clean shaven (as far as Helen knew they had all been men), wore neither jewellery nor interesting neckties. To describe one was to describe them all. They attended every session, but made themselves so inconspicuous that you soon forgot they were there.

'Talking of major industries,' Josh said, 'the Savannah River Plant is – or was – another major employer in these parts.' He turned towards the speaking minder, 'Does it still produce plutonium?'

The speaking minder ignored the question and drew their attention to the highway turn-off to Augusta, home of the US Masters.

'I like a game of tennis,' Jeanne said.

Takeshi smiled. 'It's a golf tournament.'

'Hard to see the point of golf,' Helen said.

'Or any form of sport,' Sam added.

An hour later they arrived in Aiken. It was a surprisingly un-American city, pretty, with vast mansions set behind towering serpentine brick walls that unfurled along the roads in long, graceful waves. There were large and well-tended public gardens and a paucity of the usual chain stores; even aluminium siding was less abundant here. Helen had spent sufficient time in America to know there would be an other-side-of-the-tracks part of town and that as a visitor she would not be seeing it. Neither did it matter, for she was here for the science, four days of strenuous work, four days when she was determined to put her career worries aside, four days of willed myopia if need be.

As a result of her Austrian nationality together with the protection of Max Planck of quantum physics fame, Lise Meitner had kept her job at the Kaiser Wilhelm Institute long after other Jewish scientists had been barred from working in Germany. At the end of the war Meitner was critical of herself for not having left Germany earlier, but at the time – and what a time it had been for nuclear physics – she was prepared to keep a low profile and manage without several of the benefits enjoyed by her Aryan colleagues in order to do her science.

Helen believed Meitner had been too harsh on herself. Discrimination was one thing but mass murder quite another, and in the early 1930s when most German-Jewish scientists were forced from their positions, no one anticipated the systematic slaughter of Europe's Jews. Besides, where would Meitner have gone? When Hitler took power much of the world was still clawing its way out of the Depression. Jobs were scarce and often poorly paid, and while Einstein, the most famous scientist in the world, was welcomed everywhere, other immigrant scientists would be seen to be taking positions from local scientists.

(And where would she herself go, Helen wondered, if she took a stand on how her work was being used. None of the major laboratories would want her and, unlike Meitner, she had neither the patience nor tolerance to work in a minor one.)

Being born female in 1878 Meitner had struggled every step of the way. Forced by Austrian law to leave public school at fourteen, through private study she had eventually acquired her high school qualification and against much opposition from those who believed university was no place for a woman, she enrolled for her degree. She earned her doctorate at the age of twenty-eight but no university wanted to employ her. When first she started at the Kaiser Wilhelm Institute in Berlin, she was forced to work in a makeshift basement laboratory separate from the men – as if femaleness itself was not simply a distraction but an insult to serious work. For science, however, she was willing to tolerate the slights, the neglect, and certainly the lack of windows. Where other people had pride and envy and ambition, Meitner had only a passion for science.

Just like Helen. Too bright for her local state school, too outspoken for her conformist parents, too big for her rural city, if she had been any less strong-willed or any less passionate about science she would never have become a scientist. And such an exclusive and demanding passion it was. Whenever she returned from one of her scientific meetings, friends would ask about the Hermitage or the Louvre or the Taj Mahal or the Rockies or, as she stared through the window of the bus, Aiken's five-star stables. But in the hot-housing of ideas and argument she would never have voluntarily absented herself before the talking stopped. The tourist attractions, she would tell her friends, would be in the same place and the same form when next she visited. But science would have moved on and she was determined not to be left behind.

How could she give this up? And, more to the point, why should she? She was not living in Nazi Germany or Stalinist Russia, this was not the repressive 1930s or 1950s; the world had moved on. But had it? Had the world really changed? She stewed in the terrible question. She was not naïve, she knew of science's alliances with dictators and murderous regimes, but for most of her life she had been convinced the exceptions proved the rule: that science was essentially good and scientific progress desirable. But with science now moving so fast, and scientists comprising only a tiny element in enterprises far too large and complex for any one person to grasp, it seemed the exceptions had become the rule. She could no longer pretend that the purposes for which she was working shared much in common with the objectives of those who paid for her work or decided its applications. Well might she love her work, but at what cost?

Lise Meitner, whose research in nuclear fission had led directly to the bombs dropped on Hiroshima and Nagasaki, never worked on any weapons project. Like Einstein she was outspoken in her belief that the vast energy released in fission should be channelled into peaceful purposes. What makes one scientist speak out and others not? And for those who do not, what is this passion for science that it could so effectively mute ethical standards and beliefs? How can it happen that you find yourself behaving in ways that in a different context you would judge as indefensible?

How wily are beliefs, the way they insinuate themselves so completely into your existence that you would no more question them than you would your heartbeat. You know they are there, you know they are essential, you pay them little mind. Helen had long believed in the goodness of science and the goodness of her own motives as a scientist; she had tucked these beliefs away while she settled down to work. But you need to keep your beliefs active, you need to dust them off regularly, and most particularly you need to debate them and their allegiances. It seemed to her now that her beliefs had become like a comfy old couch she would notice only if it were removed. Her beliefs – there was no avoiding it any longer – had shielded her from some of science's more sinister happenings.

There was a crunch of gravel as the minibus turned into the driveway of the conference centre. At the entrance stood a welcoming committee of her colleagues, smiling and waving at the new arrivals. Helen gazed at these people, good scientists all of them, men and women with whom she had shared some of the best experiences of her life. These were her friends, she reminded herself, as she stepped out of the warm bus into the warmer embrace of her colleagues, not in the solid, unchanging, shared-past friendship of Jack, Ava and Connie, but with a more up-to-date, more immediate, more adaptable dynamic.

And despite her doubts, despite her fears, she was, she realised, exactly where she wanted to be.

She and the other newcomers were swept into the lobby. Soon they had separated into their usual groups – the cholera contingent, the salmonellas, the *E. colis*, her own shigella mob, and some general transgenic people, molecular free-floaters, who for the first time gravitated towards her group.

It was Heisenberg who said that 'science is rooted in conversations'. Many a marriage has disintegrated because a scientist prefers discussing research with colleagues rather than the children's schooling with a spouse. When scientists get together they start talking where they left off at the last meeting, the last paper, the last email communication. The shigella group comprised Dory from the CDC in Atlanta, Maarten from Holland, Takeshi and Helen. Katarina from Russia was absent as her son was getting married and, despite her pleading, the young couple had refused to change their wedding date when it clashed with the meeting.

They immediately started discussing a recent outbreak of *Shigella sonnei* which had occurred simultaneously in a number of observant Jewish communities in North America. The contamination had been traced to a particular kosher ice-cream.

'We did the typing at the CDC,' Dory said. 'As well as ice-cream, there was a problem with a particular batch of kosher cheese.'

'Same milk products obviously,' Helen said.

As it turned out, little was obvious about this outbreak.

'Given the restricted food choices of orthodox Jews, it took only a few interviews to trace the problem to ice-cream,' Dory said. 'We alerted the usual people, nothing out of the ordinary. And then just as we thought we were winding up, the security people arrived.'

'So was the contamination intentional?' Takeshi asked. 'Someone deliberately targeting Jews?'

'The security guys pounded us with questions, they insisted on more tests, but no other related organisms showed up on the system. The men stayed for two weeks then they disappeared.' Dory hesitated before adding, 'And we've heard nothing since.'

'You did the work,' Helen spoke slowly, 'but you've never been told whether the outbreaks were deliberate?'

Dory nodded. 'That's right.'

There was a long pause while everyone waited for someone else to raise the issue of the elephant in the room – or rather, the laboratory.

Finally Helen spoke up. 'How often does it happen that we do the science but are kept in the dark? And not just for outbreaks: there's also the issue of how our work is being used.'

There was a shifting of gaze, a shuffling of feet, a burrowing into a backpack, and in the silence Helen wondered how many of them had tossed in the ethical towel in order to do their science. How many even acknowledged what was happening to scientific research? Many of her colleagues were funded through groups that made no attempt to hide their military affiliation, but it was the rare scientist who owned up to any restrictions or compromises. Yet it had been clear to her for some time that the balance between research freedom and central direction had disappeared. And it was no gentle altering of the scales, more like a seesaw when one of the riders gets off.

The silence was finally broken with the approach of an organiser who herded them towards reception.

Helen moved slowly, letting the others go before her. For twenty years she had done the science of her dreams. She had presided over a fabulously equipped laboratory within an internationally recognised centre; she had been supplied with abundant funds and seemingly abundant research freedom; her team had made several significant contributions to diarrhoea control and prevention. She had been travelling the main highway, no doubt about it, but she could no longer ignore that while she might have been the driver she wasn't navigating, nor did she own the vehicle. Her laboratory was no more hers than Fritz Haber's had proved to be his when in 1933 Hitler 'Aryanised' the civil service, and Lenard and Stark, both Nobel Prize winners, had fostered 'Aryan physics' (and if ever there was a warning to be wary of the Nobel it resided in the awards to these two men). Or five years later when Lise Meitner had been forced from her laboratory, more home to her than her tiny apartment, and certainly more home than Austria or Germany. Helen habitually thought of *her* laboratory. But it wasn't hers, not when politics guarded the door.

Her relationship to her work these past many years now seemed rather like a marriage in which one of the partners stays purely for love while the other, in addition to love, has other more pragmatic reasons. And if now and then there is a vague hint of this, wouldn't you, the purely loving one be prepared to ignore or rationalise certain actions in order to maintain the marriage? In order to love in the way you have always wanted? Helen loved science. Whether working in her laboratory, writing up papers or gathered with the best scientists in the world she was – and this was no exaggeration – enraptured.

Some excellent scientists had already left research, including two from another division at her own centre, one for a community college, the other with more than forty publications to his credit to teach high school when no reputable laboratory or university would employ him – although what constituted reputable these days Helen no longer knew. These two scientists had cited political interference in their research and had lodged formal complaints. Within a short time they had found themselves frozen out of research funds and subsequently out of work.

Helen admired their stance, but at the same time she struggled with it. Never to enter a laboratory again, never to grapple with the mysteries of science, never again that blindingly beautiful moment of understanding. She had touched the very stuff of life; in moving genes around she actually changed life. And she found herself resenting those scientists who had taken a stand. No one wants to acknowledge they might be living in bad faith.

Back in their university days she, Jack and Ava had often debated the elements of a good and proper life, but back in those days there was little in their experience to test their beliefs. Now there was so much to lose. Helen wanted to do science and she wanted it to be the best science. But without acceptable ethical underpinnings, what exactly was the best science and was it possible any more? She suspected that if she could turn a blind eye to the current situation, if she could just ignore the shadowy presences that were working the cogs and pulleys of science, she would.

She had hoped Australia would provide her with the opportunity to work far from military policy and defence force funds. But everyone in the Western world was so closely connected these days and the reach of the funding bodies so extensive – the frontiers of space were nothing in this scheme of things – that Australia was no more outside the mainstream than the Virginia–Maryland–DC biotechnology hub where her own centre was located. As for research freedom, the same pressures were applied in Australian laboratories as in the US. An Australian scientist she knew, an expert in renewable energies, had recently been transferred to a huge government-funded project aimed at making coal cleaner – and you didn't need to be a scientist to detect that oxymoron. He had been told by the director of his institute that it was in the national interest, and when he had questioned whether it was in the planet's interest he had been given short shrift: coal was Australia's largest export so the government's decision made sound economic sense. And if he didn't like the work, the director added, he could find another job.

Helen did not want to find herself in a similar position.

As soon as she was checked in, Helen crossed the lobby and exited through the doors directly opposite the main entrance. She needed time alone to settle herself, to silence the doubts, otherwise she risked wrecking the next four days.

She stepped outside on to a broad terrace and paused in the crisp white air. Stretching before her was a vast sloping lawn;

plush and green even in early winter, it was a typical example of the perfect American lawn that makes its English progenitor look shabby. Leading down to the cabins was a gravel path. Helen had walked several metres pulling her suitcase behind her before she noticed the cross-hatch pattern raked into the gravel. It was a geometric wonder. She stopped and looked back at the mess she had made. Off to one side stood an elderly African-American man with a rake in his hand. With an apologetic gesture she picked up her suitcase, stepped on to the lawn and hurried down the slope towards her cabin. At the door she glanced back; the man was already restoring the path.

She entered a spacious motel-style room with off-white walls, tweedy carpet and good lighting. Adjacent to one of the windows was a pale laminated desk with ergonomic chair and internet access. Off the main room was a bathroom, and out the front a small verandah enclosed by insect screens. Helen unpacked the essentials, the rest could remain in her suitcase. She sent a text to Luke telling him she had arrived, then grabbed her gloves and coat and went outside.

The clouds were smoothly grey, the temperature low enough for snow. Helen had lived more than half her life in countries with huge winter falls, but still she maintained the Australian wonder of snow. The grounds were large, and except for the lawns and paths, attractively unkempt – perhaps intentionally or maybe just the normal roughing-up of winter. For about sixty or seventy metres in front of her cabin the vegetation was ragged and sparse, then at the bottom of the slope it thickened into an impressionistic forest of evergreen and deciduous trees. Some of the larger trees were draped in a climbing plant that looked like lengths of organza. The woodland stretched away to the horizon.

She settled in a deckchair on the verandah and rested her head against the canvas; she hoped she might sleep. All these suspicions and dissatisfactions disconnected her from her usual self. She did not know how to think her way out of the dilemmas, to sort through personal desire on the one hand and personal ethics on the other. Never had she felt so confused nor quite so alone.

She had thought Jack, Ava and Connie would help. But it was as if each of them had accumulated so much life in their own separate spheres that even with the desire to help, and she did not for a moment doubt their desire, it was not particularly effective. As for speaking with her colleagues as she thought she might at this meeting, now she was here she was afraid of revealing problems that might be exclusively hers.

There was a fat slimy slug squirming on the boards of the verandah. Too cold, too old or just plain lost, it was going nowhere. Helen watched its futile twists and turns, its clueless head raised weakly to the chill air. The slug might just as well be frozen stiff for all the gains it was making; the slug might just as well be her.

She had risen to go inside when her attention was caught by a solitary figure emerging from the woods at the bottom of the slope. It was a large man, wearing one of those old-fashioned dark blue woollen jackets she associated with revolutionaries and on his head a cap which, as he drew closer, sharpened into a beret. He carried a wad of pages in one hand, the other hand was pushed deep into his pocket. His pace was a stroll; she could hear a faint singing through the still thin air.

He continued up the slope, passing only a few metres from her cabin. It was Fabian Möller, the keynote speaker at this meeting, so close but not seeing her, his voice quite clear now in a bluesy riff that skittered over his tongue in a caramel-coloured tenor. Fabian Möller, a genius at moving genes around. Fabian Möller, the molecular scissors wizard and one of the giants in her field.

A great scientist, the blues, the possibility of snow: it was one of those perfect moments that only ever occur without planning. Helen was aware of being privileged to something private and special, enhanced by the voyeur's frisson of excitement. Enough of these seesawing moods, she told herself. She was at a professional meeting with the best in the world. For the next four days there would be only the rigours and pleasures of science.

2.

Möller's evening address was an exhilarating romp through recent advances in the manipulation of pathogen transmission and durability, followed by a more leisurely account of his own specific research in this area. He possessed that rare gift of showing how discoveries are made, of deconstructing both the inspirational connections and routine moves which produce new knowledge. He was, in short, the true *animateur des idées*. He would have been a riveting teacher, Helen found herself thinking, and such a shame he no longer taught in the classroom. Although none of them did any more.

By the time he was finished, Helen was firing with possibilities for her own work. She sailed through the pre-dinner socialising, but as the meal progressed and the effect of Möller's lecture wore off, it felt more and more as if she were playing the role of Helen Rankin, molecular biologist, and the spontaneous pleasure and energy the real Helen would have experienced passed her by. After dinner, when a number of the delegates produced musical instruments, rather than leave with the other non-musicians, she settled into an armchair in a poorly lit area of the room, grateful for time stripped of demands.

The concert began with a violin version of Mendelssohn's 'Venetian Gondola Song'. Insistent and rocking, the interpretation was quieter, nocturnal and altogether eerier than the usual piano version. Then the Chinese delegate played 'The Revolutionary' and another of Chopin's études with stunning technique and studied emotion. There followed a clarinet and oboe duo that produced the sounds of heaven, should heaven ever be shown to exist, and Josh played a vigorous jazz trumpet accompanied on guitar by one of his colleagues from the CDC. Helen might lack the musical gift of many scientists and mathematicians but she rarely failed to respond to music's power. She felt herself loosen and relax.

When Fabian Möller stood up and walked to the piano, she shifted her chair slightly so as to have a clearer view of him. She had heard he was an excellent musician, so good he might have made music his career. He began with Bach, the E minor prelude and fugue, 'My favourite of the Well-Tempered Clavier,' he said, and followed with selections from the G major Piano Suite. He sat erect at the keyboard, a tall substantial man, his head moving with the flow of notes, his face playing the mood of the music. After Bach, he travelled ahead a few centuries to Debussy and Gershwin, and when he was finished, his foot still pressed to the sustaining pedal, he looked up from the keyboard and asked for requests.

'How about some blues?' Helen said.

The words just slipped out.

Someone close by whispered, 'He's classically trained, he might not know the blues,' but Möller had already begun.

He started with a composer called Coleridge-Taylor. The piece sounded as if Mozart had spent a long and intimate summer with Billie Holiday. He then moved into a hard-edged barrelhouse number, followed by an easy-strolling syncopated jive, and from there to a more traditional lovesick blues freighted with weariness and pain. 'I love the blues,' he said, without lifting his gaze from the keyboard. 'I love the blues.'

He must have played for close on thirty minutes and stopped as abruptly as he had begun. He smiled at Helen before being swept up by the crowd. A pleasing moment that smile, she thought, as she crossed the room and headed towards the bar. She collected a coffee and settled on a couch in a corner, notebook open and a pen in her hand, happy to mull in the music. No one would disturb her if they thought she was working, her charred nerves cooling, her mind in a slow jive – towards an idea, she realised, an idea that had been flittering just out of reach, and soon she was improvising on it, a notion spinning out of a cluster of recent findings, writing and writing across the pages.

The coffee was cold when next she looked up. There were a few people gathered at a nearby table but no one was paying her any attention. She browsed her freshly written pages before closing the notebook and slipping it in her bag; she would study the jottings properly when she was back in her room but for now she was content to trace the shape of her thoughts from memory. There was, she decided, an idea to work on here, and was about to add the usual proviso – as long as she had a place to work – when Fabian Möller entered the bar and immediately crossed to where she was sitting.

He extended his hand. 'We've met before, at other meetings. I'm Fabian Möller.'

'I know,' she said, and wished she had not. 'And I'm –'

'Helen Rankin,' he said.

She was so pleased he remembered her.

He asked if he might join her. Of course, she said, making room for him on the couch.

She told him how much she had enjoyed his music, he told her how much he enjoyed her work. She was embarrassed he should acknowledge her work before she did his. Although it quickly emerged there was a reason: Möller had decided to split his time between Europe and America. He was considering three possible centres in the US, and hers was one. He listed the advantages and disadvantages of the other two centres; as for the third, the main attraction, he said, was her.

He laughed. 'Or rather, your work.'

As he talked about his own work in Germany, his future plans, why the move to America was warranted, where he thought precision genetic engineering was heading, Helen was trying to corral her excitement. If she could choose one person in the world she would most like to work with it would be Möller. But should she tell him of her doubts? Should she tell him how her centre was using her work? Should she tell him she had all but decided to resign? What should she tell him, this man who had done more in her field than any other?

He lowered his voice, speaking without any prompting from her. 'We think ours is a difficult area. That our work can be co-opted for purposes with which we may not agree. And perhaps this happens, how can a person know for sure? But that is no reason to stop you and me. We are scientists,' he leaned towards her but did not touch, 'and the good of our work and the natural good of humankind will, in the end, make sure that what we discover is applied well.'

It was as if he knew her struggles; perhaps he'd had similar experiences himself. This great man, the best in her field. And again he said how much he would like to work with her.

'What wonderful science we shall do.'

Throughout the next four days, Helen discussed and debated and problem-solved with her colleagues, all without a trace of the tension of the previous months. The snow did not eventuate, the clouds cleared and a weak sun shone; nothing on earth seemed troubled. As for Möller, with his humour and generosity and the brilliance of his mind, the prospect of working with him excited her beyond compare.

When the meeting concluded Helen travelled on the bus with him back to Atlanta. Möller overflowed his seat and for the two-hour journey, even though she pressed herself against the window, she was aware of his body against hers from shoulder to thigh.

'It's hard to believe it's taken so long for us to meet properly,' she said.

'But we have known each other for years,' he said. 'We have been reading the work of each other for – ' his shrug shot through her body, 'for ever. And soon, when I join your centre, every day we shall share our work.'

As to whether she wanted anything more from him, in a less imperfect world she would, no doubt about it. And twenty years ago she would have pursued him with little thought for the consequences. But now she would be sensible, now she would not forget that lovers were far easier to come by than congenial colleagues, and far easier to lose too.

She flew back to Australia in a vastly different state than how she had left. She had been offered a gift, a life-saver, a new beginning, a clutch of new opportunities. Fabian Möller at her own centre. As the plane descended into Melbourne, the flat brown land shimmering in the summer heat, she only hoped that Luke wouldn't mind having his Australian sojourn cut short.

CHAPTER 9: **Allegiances**

1.

Harry preferred to work with his office door open. His door was now shut. The NOGA board meeting was at five that afternoon. He had written his report a week ago, but because of Conrad and Jack the report now needed to be altered. There was ample time to make the revisions, that wasn't the problem; he was furious that Jack's hare-brained nonsense and Conrad's desperate libido required him to do it.

Harry always knew his wife's friends were a risky proposition, but given their prominence he believed they were a risk worth taking. Now as he rejigged his report, sifting through euphemisms and obfuscations in an attempt to disguise their stupidity, it was time, he decided, to remind everyone who was in charge here.

Jack had arrived at the office an hour ago. It was his first appearance in a week and what he thought NOGA was paying him for Harry could not begin to guess. Although there was a slothful side to Jack – or else he never was as bright as people believed. And of the two options, as unattractive as it was, Harry would opt for the former, providing as it did, at least in theory, for the quality of work NOGA expected of him. For the past month or two, in fact, ever since that article appeared – Bondage! What on earth was Jack thinking? – his work had gone to the dogs. He had provided little useful information to anyone, and if his calendar for the upcoming month was any guide he planned to keep it that way. Jack was a master at losing the plot: firstly, his pointless obsession with Ava, and now these navel-gazing ravings.

Then there was Conrad, nearly sixty years old and throwing away more opportunities than he realised with his ludicrous fling with a twenty-five-year-old. No one would approve vast amounts of money for a TV series fronted by a man of such tatty morals.

Of the three, only Helen was being sensible, having arrived home from the Aiken meeting renewed. She had decided to devote herself to the sort of work that had prompted NOGA's interest in her in the first place, and to advance that work in the most expedient manner, it was best, she said, that she return to America. While she would not be seeing out the full term of her fellowship, she promised to keep NOGA informed of any developments.

Helen was back on track and travelling with Fabian Möller – an unexpected bonus – and with his career so recently on the skids Jack could be pulled into line. Harry was less sure about Conrad; it was well-nigh impossible to prevent a grown man from making a fool of himself. But Harry had invested far more than just time in NOGA and he would solve these problems. More intractable and of far greater concern was Ava. She was not herself and had not been for months. His wife, who flew when others crept, who plunged where others paddled, seemed switched to low wattage. Several times he had come upon her slumped in a chair just staring at the wall. And she was vague, not with an out-of-step-with-the-moment vagueness which occurred whenever she was inside a new novel, rather a lagging-behind quality, as if she were unable to keep pace with the normal events of a day. His Davey was not herself at all.

His concern had been so great that this past weekend while she was out walking in the park he had slipped into her study and riffled through the manuscript of her new novel. Never before had he done such a thing but he had run out of options. The draft carried a date from six months earlier, the finished draft apart from some minor tinkering, so she had told him at the time. The pages were now heavily marked, no minor tinkering this, sometimes as many as four different inks on a single page. Some annotations were actually illegible, others were legible but made no sense; none as far as Harry could see improved on the original. The novel should have been in production by now, but it had gone backwards – staggered backwards.

He had left her study even more concerned. The sun was strong in the courtyard and he had adjusted the shade over the spa tub, picked a couple of leaves from the water, and then – why not? he could do with the relaxation – had switched on the spa, slipped out of his clothes and into the water. In the heat of a summer morning and rocked by the moving water he deliberated what to do. Was her work causing the malaise? Or was the malaise at the root of her work problems? He did not want to worry her, particularly as she did not herself seem concerned; and besides, if there was something physically wrong it would only be minor, the sort of problem for which his grandmother would produce a tonic. He warmed at the thought of his gran. How he longed for her common sense wisdom now.

As he lolled in the jostling water he applied logic to the problem. Ava had a strong constitution; in all the years they had been together she had never been seriously ill. It stood to reason, that whatever was bothering her was not serious, although no harm in ringing his sister for her opinion. It was possible that Ava in her mid-forties was suffering 'hormones' – his gran's diagnosis for most female complaints, and Wendy, a doctor, would know what to do.

Wendy was altogether reassuring. She was sure there was nothing to worry about but advised that Ava have a check-up. She talked diet and exercise, and yes, she mentioned hormones. That was a couple of days ago and in the intervening time Harry's anxieties had eased. It was only when his stress levels were raised, like having to rewrite his report, that the worries about Ava resurfaced. But his sister said there was nothing to be concerned about, and this morning Ava seemed to be back to her old self. As for those manuscript markings, what was havoc to him may not be to the author.

Harry returned to his report. He deleted a paragraph from his introductory remarks and pulled out some statements fairly bristling with possibility. Before attacking the specific fellowship items, he went to the kitchen for a hot chocolate and when he returned to his office he did not shut the door. An hour later he handed his secretary the revised edition for copying. He was pleased with the result.

2.

This is the life, Connie is thinking, as he lounges in a shaded alcove of the Prime Ministers' Memorial Garden at the Melbourne Cemetery.

Sara had assured him no one ever came here.

'Shows the parlous state of Australian history,' Connie said.

'More the parlous state of politicians,' Sara replied, pushing him against a wall and slamming her mouth against his.

'Isn't there a law against obscene acts in public?' he had asked.

She had responded by unbuttoning his jeans and guiding him to a bench. And he's barely seated before she's leaning over him and doing those extraordinary things she does with her mouth. He has known no one to compare.

This is the life. The private bower, the warm day, the gentle breeze, and this young and beautiful woman, all spontaneity and joie de vivre who cannot have too much of him. He runs his hand over her smooth dark hair. He has always been fortunate in the women who have loved him, and Sara is the best of them all. He should arrange a weekend away, a cottage with a view to the ocean, no phone, no demands, just the two of them together. But for now – he checks his watch – it wouldn't do to be late for the board meeting, and hooks his hands under her shoulders and raises her up to straddle him. At some point during the upward movement she does something with her knickers (how grateful he is for the return to skirts and dresses), and with a hand on his shoulder and the other positioning him she sinks down. There's no firm support for her knees so he cups her buttocks, lifting her up and slowly down, and with his arm muscles about to collapse he comes. A short time later she too is satisfied.

While they are tidying themselves, another couple enters the garden. She is olive-skinned and wearing a long kaftan over trousers. He, gingery and freckled, is dressed in shorts and T-shirt. They sit themselves on the solid bulk of Robert Menzies' grave – Dame Pattie is in there too – wrap themselves together and start kissing.

'Those two know where to go for Establishment approval,' Connie says, with a nod in their direction.

Sara loves cemeteries. 'Death's libraries,' she calls them with the flippancy only the very young can use with death.

'Sex and death,' she now says, looking at the couple. 'They know what works. Just like me.'

3.

Conrad Lyall was that intensely human individual, a flawed man. Gifted, hard-working, attractive, with the intellectual hunger that propels most high achievers, he was also driven by a desire for worldly success – although he would be reluctant to acknowledge this. He insisted that one must always stand up for one's beliefs, but his desire to be admired often undercut the courage of his convictions. Connie needed less vanity to be truly effective, yet a selfless Conrad Lyall would not have been a compelling figure. It was the mix of him which proved so seductive. He was a man who was easy to like.

Individuals like Connie tend to attract large and willing entourages – not of the paid sort, but more in the way of devoted followers. Look no further than Bertrand Russell and Jean-Paul Sartre, Nureyev, Ginsberg, Picasso, and men far more than women. People want to connect with them, merge their own world with that of the great man – who must of necessity be stingy with himself or else he would empty very quickly. Fortunately followers comply by being satisfied with tiny portions. Connie acquired his followers from among students and readers, autodidacts were particularly numerous, and women far outnumbered men. He acquired, too, a great many friends, more than the customary number of wives, and a slew of lovers.

While Connie totted up the years, his girlfriends all stayed much the same age. He believed that one's notion of attractiveness was formed early, that what appealed to the twenty-year-old self would appeal to the fifty-year-old. He also believed that one's sense of the age fifty was formed in youth, around the time when one's own parents reached that age. To be fifty then, remained extremely old and always a disturbing fit. When Connie turned fifty he refused to celebrate. The numbers were conveying him to the grave, he said to Linda, yet he felt he had hardly begun. He dreaded turning sixty. It was the lengthening distance from boyhood he hated, and the decreasing distance to death he hated even more.

Such intense self-interest as Connie's exacted an intellectual toll. Not that his work wasn't serious and challenging, but in order to satisfy his personal needs his imagination was all too often pulled away from those unchartered waters from which the most remarkable work emerges. Not for him the Socratic view that for the true philosopher the body was an irritating intrusion on the far more important workings of the mind. But then, as Connie was quick to point out, there was nothing Socratic about Bertrand Russell's way of life either, and even morose old Schopenhauer liked his food rich and his sex regular. What really set Connie apart was the sweep of his personality and it was this which brought his work to such a broad audience. When a reporter remarked on the difficulty of being the layperson's philosopher, Connie quipped it was easier than bricklaying and better for the skin. But in truth it came easily to him: he was a natural and beguiling communicator.

While the label – the layperson's philosopher – carried a certain lowbrow resonance, Connie enjoyed the recognition that came with being popular. After all, he would say, it's a short bridge between fame and forgotten, and who would doubt which was preferable? His skill lay in making original connections, of looking at a tree and seeing the sap, one of the many qualities he shared with Ava. But while he knew he had a masterful intellect, like all men and women of vast intelligence and unlike their mediocre counterparts, he was acutely aware of his limitations. Connie agreed with Browning's 'Andrea del Sarto' that 'a man's reach should exceed his grasp', so even when he overcame one set of limitations he expected a new set to appear.

What was indisputable about Connie was his verbal prowess. Cross a blowtorch with the OED and that was Connie in conversation. One former colleague who had fallen victim to it described Connie as a verbal terrorist and, with his own reputation to protect, refused ever again to exchange anything more than a quick social greeting with him. Connie didn't care. He agreed with Oscar Wilde that the worst a person can suffer is indifference and, like Wilde, he had never experienced that.

For all these qualities, his election first to the NOGA board and then its chairperson was passed unanimously. Connie's natural stance tended towards the maverick and he was not a good team member; however, he saw advantages in accepting the chair, not the least that it would add to his credentials when decisions about the TV series were being made. As it happened, he had misjudged. A couple of months earlier Harry had said the television series was just a nod away from signing, but despite the successful pilot nothing had been approved nor had any money appeared. Harry, so enthusiastic at the beginning of the campaign, now seemed a great deal more muted. And without knowing exactly why or how, Connie knew that in the issue of his TV series Harry was pivotal.

From his usual position at one end of the boardroom table, Connie looked down to Harry at the other. The meeting was drawing to a close and Harry was summarising the main actions: that NOGA appoint a full-time media officer – a proposal advanced by Connie, not that Harry had acknowledged this – and that it increase its penetration of the Asia–Pacific region. Seated at the table were the Minister for Science, an attractive woman around his own age far more interested in Helen's research than anything Connie had to offer; the director of the nation's largest fully privatised business school; Sir Richard Treat of North West Mining; the CEO of Pacific Media; the MD of Taylor Holdings, the construction company responsible for the NOGA building; Josie Stacie from the accounting firm of Stacie Palmer Ross, and the Pro Vice Chancellor for international studies, all of them high-flyers and all admirers of Harry. They asked his opinion, they valued his suggestions, they considered him the rarest of individuals, the wise yet practical man. Connie had made an effort to see Harry through their eyes, but it proved impossible even for his prodigious mind. Or perhaps he simply lacked the desire.

Not so long ago Harry had counselled patience about the TV series, that with so much money involved and producers in two different countries delays were to be expected. Patience, however, was not among Connie's qualities, nor for that matter did he regard it as a virtue in an intellectual. You need to be chafing at the unknown or the nearly known, you need to be filled with an urgency to propel you to the next idea, the next nugget of understanding. Patience, like satisfaction, is a poor achiever.

Linda berated him for his impatience, for while it might be crucial for new work it did not readily cement an enduring intimacy between two people, nor did it mesh well with children. In fact all three wives had at one time or another suggested he should have married a clone of himself. They were wrong of course, he would not care for the competition.

When Harry called the meeting to a close, he had said nothing about the TV series; more significantly, apart from a few general statements about the fellowships, he had not mentioned Connie at all. Nor had Harry involved him in the proceedings as he had in previous meetings. As much as he might not care for Harry, Connie would rather be on his side than in his sights. As the meeting broke up, Connie decided it was in his interests to make more of an effort with NOGA.

4.

It was after eight o'clock and a humid dusk when Connie turned the corner into his street. As he passed one particularly ragged place he inhaled the delicious reek of frying onions, that old smell of home-cooking. He missed cooking, he missed meals at home.

'What are cafés for?' Sara said, when he suggested they might eat at home more often.

Now the smell rushed into him, and to his surprise he felt the burn of tears. And loneliness. The notion popped into his mind, and just as quickly he popped it out again. He was never lonely, and he couldn't bear any sort of wallowing.

His own house was in darkness. He flipped on lights as he

walked from room to room in this still unfamiliar place, a large family dwelling organised through NOGA, close to the university, Federation style – he ticked off its attractions – owned by an academic currently on sabbatical, and exactly the type of house he, Connie, would covet if he were the sort of person for a settled life. He put his bag in the study, checked the phone for messages, and then to the kitchen – latest appliances, plenty of cupboards, easy-cleaning surfaces. On the bench was a note in Sara's large round writing: she was catching up with friends, she might be late, he was not to wait up. The note concluded with a row of X's and O's, but no signature. The dot of the 'i' of 'Connie' was heart-shaped.

He folded the note and put it in his pocket: that someone so exciting could also be so sweet was testimony to his good fortune. Although he welcomed an evening to himself, for there were problems to deal with, decisions to make, actions to take. Linda's work commitments and a long visit to America by her English parents had postponed her arrival in Australia, but there was no reason for her to delay any longer.

He poured himself a glass of wine and settled on the comfortable couch in the comfortable sitting room of this comfortable home. The owner had lived here for more than twenty-five years, Connie couldn't think of anything worse. He was a man of serial comforts, whether homes, countries, wives or girlfriends, and he was not ashamed to admit it. He worked hard and produced well, he was a scholar and an educator both within and outside the university, and while he may not be cut out for family life there were other weightier roles for which he was suited. And no man in his right mind would have turned his back on Sara. No reason for shame there either, though Linda would disagree. Yet Linda knew what she was getting into when they married; after all, she had been the girlfriend while he was still married to Susan.

The alcohol hit an empty stomach – he had worked through lunchtime in order to meet Sara at the cemetery – and he returned to the kitchen for a plate of antipasto, more cheese than anything else, couldn't find any crackers so made some toast, and with his wine replenished and a cup of fresh coffee he returned to the couch.

The Linda problem aside, he needed a night to himself. He was exhausted, not that he would ever admit this to Sara, and if he were to be entirely honest, her friends did not excite him in the same way as they did her. And suddenly he was alert, something she had said the previous night as he was dropping off to sleep: that now the wife and children were about to arrive the girlfriend would have to make herself scarce. She had mentioned friends who lived in a large house of numerous rooms, one of which was vacant. Were these the friends she was with now? Not a girl for patient deliberation, she may have already arranged to move. He grabbed his mobile and sent her an I-luv-u-&-c-u-soon text message.

He did not want Sara moving out, although the large house with numerous friends sounded temptingly bohemian. He had married so young he had never known the shared-living experience and he regretted it. Back when they were students and still living in communal houses, Ava and Helen had tried to disabuse him. All he had missed, they said, was dodgy wiring, stinking carpets, rising damp, ants and fleas, monthly fumigations, too many people using the decrepit plumbing, a roster that most people ignored, a kitty similarly treated, and strangers drunk in the lounge and high in the kitchen, strangers who came and went as they pleased in houses without locks. But no matter what they said, a lost experience was exactly that, and no amount of contriving or substitution could ever bring it back.

At the present time the experience he wanted was Sara, and she would not sit by patiently while he dithered about the future. Sara was across town with her friends, perhaps making plans to move out, and across the world Linda and the boys would soon be packing up their life to join him in Australia. Connie didn't want Sara to leave and he didn't want his family to arrive.

He was a man in his fifties, not old, but certainly old enough to know there was not another intelligent, beautiful, twenty-five-year-old waiting for him down the years. Although he was sensible enough to omit Sara from the end of his marriage. Several times before there had been other women and Linda had forgiven him. She loved him, she said, of course she didn't want him to leave.

In her position he would have been humiliated.

'You can't have humiliation without pride,' Linda said. 'And you have sufficient pride for us both.'

In the past Linda had persuaded him to change his mind. But not this time. His marriage was over.

The coffee was lukewarm and he poured himself more wine, just half a glass this time. He should check his email, after more than twenty-four hours his in-box would be bursting, but he could not face it. He should read through a soon-to-be-published article, but he couldn't face that either. He wandered into the room that would have been Linda's study, then the room which would have been Laurie's bedroom and the smaller one for Oscar. He felt sad, endings always had that effect on him, but it was the right decision and the sadness would pass. As soon as he had worked through the practical details he would ring Linda. He should encourage her to move back to England; it would be less lonely for her close to her family, and an English schooling for the boys would be less expensive than an American one.

He returned to the kitchen for the other half of his third glass, then decided he needed company. He really did hate endings. He would have walked around to Ava's but she had shut herself off recently, finishing her new novel he assumed. Instead he collected his keys, left the lights on for Sara, and drove across town to Helen's place.

She ushered him in without ceremony.

'I thought you might come over tonight,' she said. 'Luke decided to visit a friend.'

'Good of him to leave us to talk,' Connie said.

Helen snorted in that way she had. 'Sensible of him I would have thought.' She peered into the refrigerator. 'Have you eaten? I was about to prepare some food?'

He accepted crackers, lettuce and tinned sardines, and the two of them sat at the kitchen table as they had in so many kitchens around the world.

'So what do you plan to do?' she said.

Connie told her his thoughts about the divorce, including the benefits of Linda and the boys moving back to England. 'The NHS can always use a top anaesthetist, and there are plenty of good schools for the children.' He had been unhappy in the marriage for quite some time – 'But that's no surprise to you, and neither will it be to Linda.'

Helen attempted to interrupt, but Connie, in the process of talking himself out of his marriage, paused only for breath. Linda had known about his dalliances and was always threatening to leave with the next affair. 'But she never has. She can't possibly be happy,' he said. 'Someone has to make a move and it will never be her.'

Helen reached out and took his hand. 'Connie,' she said, and then more loudly, 'Connie, there's something you need to know.'

Linda had ended the marriage. She ended it in an email. She had sent a copy of the email to Helen. 'My marriage might be over,' she wrote to Helen, 'but not my friendship with you.'

In a follow-up email to Connie a couple of days later, Linda addressed all the practical details, including some that Connie thought rather heartless. There was no necessity for them to meet, she wrote, no phone calls – she had changed her cell-phone number – and no final goodbyes. Whatever needed to be discussed could occur by email or through their lawyers; her lawyer used to be their lawyer so Connie had the contact details. She included a draft financial settlement, which he could see was entirely fair. She was happy for him to have access to the boys whenever he liked (she knew she was safe with that one), and happy for them to spend half of their school vacations with him (she knew, too, there was little chance of that). She would be staying in Boston but moving house as she had never liked the house he had chosen. There was no 'have a good life', no 'thank you for our years together', and most of all there was no explanation. He went over and over the emails looking for clues.

His wife was divorcing him, although with his reputation everyone would assume he had left her. So no humiliation, although privately his pride was on its knees. He didn't like it, he didn't like it at all. But best to look on the positive side: Linda had saved him a great deal of trouble.

CHAPTER 10: Light in a Vacuum

Heat wave followed heat wave. In February alone there were eighteen days of thirty-five degrees or hotter and March promised no relief. Each predicted cool front imploded before it hit Melbourne, clogging the air with steamy, suffocating disappointment. Restaurants without air-conditioning struggled to meet the bills, families flocked to local pubs for the free cooling, department stores and chilled shopping malls posted record profits. Out in the streets children moaned, stressed mothers lugged bags and babies, red-faced workers wore suits with resignation.

Jack's office was equipped with the latest in climate control yet increasingly he worked at home. He had put aside all thoughts of a new book to concentrate on his essays, and while he knew this was not the work NOGA expected of him, he was enjoying himself as he had not for years. Like some omnipotent and omniscient headmaster, Harry seemed to be everywhere at NOGA. If Jack was at his desk, Harry would appear at the door; if he stepped into the passageway, Harry would be walking towards him; when he took coffee, so, too, did Harry. Even at the urinals he would find Harry still hard at work as he encouraged Jack to accept this speaking invitation or that consultancy. Harry took every opportunity to refer to Jack's remarkable change of fortune, how a specialty that just a short time ago had been politically irrelevant was now of vital importance to all free-thinking people.

Jack's time had come, Harry said, and NOGA prided itself on its association with him, 'Our *proactive* association.' His emphasis was unambiguous. 'So don't throw away this chance, Jack.'

It was best to avoid the office.

For the past several years it was as if the compulsion to work had been filleted out of him. And while Jack had learned to manage, much like an amputee adjusts to living without a limb, he could never forget that something vital was missing. But now, with his new essays he was thriving. Creativity feasts on creativity, he was rediscovering, and working well was the best way of continuing to work well. As he wrote and read, as he shopped and cooked, he was rushed with fresh ideas. The heat hardly bothered him at all.

There was a summer of his boyhood, another long hot summer like this one, accompanied by one of the worst droughts on record. Every few days clouds would gather, the air would bloat, and just as it seemed it was about to rain the wind would strengthen and the clouds would disperse and the never-ending blue sky would again glare down. Dams and lakes shrank to mud and then hardened to cracked clay, grass was as rare as gold; the heat sucked the marrow from every living thing. Finally when even skin was cracking with the terrible heat, it rained, real rain on a Sunday morning – Jack remembered because there was no school for him nor work for his parents, and the three of them stood on the balcony for an hour of glorious drenching. And exactly two weeks later there was more rain, clouds of it pelting down and his parents packed a picnic and the three of them drove through the rain into the country. On the wet, parched hills and along the sides of the road a green fuzz had already begun to sprout. Crimson rosellas darted between the trees and willy wagtails flapped their happy tails, and in the paddocks and on the slopes rain-soaked cows nuzzled the fresh new growth. There was even a wombat eating by the side of the road while the cars whooshed wetly past. The birds, the thirsting animals, the brown land with its spongy green fuzz and Jack remembered his mother saying how resilient was this land, how little it takes for it to repair itself. And now in this endless summer, after hours and hours of writing, Jack felt himself to be repairing, miraculously, just like the land after drought.

His parents had installed an air-conditioner in the living room of the flat, a single luxury in an existence not characterised by luxury for two Europeans who had never adjusted to the Australian heat. At the time Jack suggested they do the job properly and install a second unit in their bedroom, he even offered to pay for it; but they insisted that one unit was quite enough. Now Jack set up work on the dining table, pushing aside his papers to eat his meals, and made up a bed on the couch. On the hottest days he would douse his head with cold water; he noticed twists of grey in the black curls. And he had started playing the guitar again, his uneasy fingers becoming more familiar as he found his music again.

Thousands of people flocked to the beach during those blistering months and Jack would hear the whoops and cries long into the night. Every now and then he would go out to the balcony and watch the shadows moving across the sand, the white foam of late-night swimmers. Occasionally people strolling the street below would look up and shout a friendly greeting to him. Such rare camaraderie during those boiling days.

His second essay had been well received, and so too a third. He was now working on a new piece called 'The End of Originality', addressing the role of obsession in creative work. Obsession, that singular focus which holds a person at the desk, the canvas, the laboratory bench, the guitar, mindless of the leaking tap, the dirty clothes, the poor barking dog in the flat next door. Obsession, so crucial to a child's learning about a talent in the first place, yet these days more likely to be viewed as pathology and dissolved in medication. Although in the jostle of today's fabulous distractions, an obsession would have a hard job of getting off the blocks in the first place. So whither to originality?

Whenever he thought of originality, his mind automatically turned to Ava, Connie and Helen. But the obsessive drive they once had now seemed blurred, roughed up by other competing interests. For a time after the Aiken meeting Helen had been caught up in science's white water – the most exciting ride around, as she had often said. But a couple of months on and she seemed to be stranded again.

Connie, Ava and Helen, these three with their public achievements were also his intimate friends. He saw each of them regularly, even Ava, whose company now was mellowed by his own mellowing. He carried news from one to another, linking them together when other demands kept them apart. While the cool and unsentimental gaze of the future would sort through their achievements and garner a selection for the public record, originality looks very different rumpled and tired as Ava had been recently, or railing over a messed-up experiment as Helen was last week, or sprawled on a couch unshaven and drunk as Connie had been just a couple of nights ago. Jack witnessed all the personal upheavals as they occurred, and at this time, several months after they had all returned to Melbourne, he was seeing little in the way of new work and much in the way of lives unravelling. It is a difficult business analysing your own times before time itself has settled the silt of the inconsequential. Whether the changes he was observing in his friends would in the future be seen as smallish potholes in otherwise brilliant trajectories or prove to be the start of their winding down, Jack could not predict.

So much of their intellectual lives used to overlap. In fact, when they were students there was a canon for people their age – and the only people who mattered were their age, or dead. Perhaps their world was smaller then and their lives less complex making it easier to keep in step with one another. Now Jack had a sense that the group was leaving him, as if the ligaments connecting them had grown slack with age.

The extent to which the dynamic had changed was encapsulated one Saturday lunch at Ava's place when he overheard Ava and Connie discussing house-cleaning arrangements. The conversation must have lasted for nearly fifteen minutes, finishing only when Ava gave Connie the contact details of the person who cleaned for her and Harry. Such a conversation would have been unthinkable in the old days.

So trivial was their talk, on the rare occasions they did get together, and so biographically grounded Jack wondered if he had romanticised the old times, whether what he remembered as brilliant assaults on profound ideas were nothing more than the pompous and insubstantial rhetoric of impressionable youth. So one particularly steamy night when even the air-conditioner was straining he decided to test his memory. He unearthed his box of Laconics presentations, and seated in the direct line of the air-conditioner, he looked through the papers one by one. He could see the rooms where each had been presented, the speaker on a raised plinth, the rest of the group perched on chairs or cushions. He recalled the period when Connie sported a beard, the year Ava wore her hair in a hennaed Afro. And the changing fashions: bell-bottomed trousers, embroidered jeans, miniskirts, kaftans, long hair, short hair, sideburns or not. The seating was always uncomfortable and the room always too hot or cold, but he and the others would nonetheless turn up week after week. The formal presentation would last twenty to thirty minutes, followed by questions, discussion and argument. People would leap to their feet to drive a point home, others would insist on occupying the plinth for a more significant contribution. Always volatile and invigorating, some meetings lasted well past midnight.

He was sure his memory was correct, but to be absolutely certain he selected four papers at random: Allegiance and Ethics (Connie); Every Angel is Terrifying (Helen on microbes); The Turn of the Screw (Ava on children in the late twentieth century); and How Political was Henry James? – one of his own papers and surprising given James was a favourite of Ava's but never one of his. How much, he wondered, had he borrowed from her?

He settled in his armchair and read all four papers in their entirety, together with the annotations he had made. His memory had not deceived, their arguments and analyses were not always correct but they never failed to provoke. He leafed through a few more papers. All of them were witty and entertaining; indeed, the more trivial the topic the greater the wit employed. They would no more have spent time talking about house-cleaning as they would talking football or crocheting. It was not that practical or personal issues were shunned, when a relationship broke up or a refrigerator broke down the others would rally with comfort and advice, but there was a shared understanding that one had to move on. They believed that Pater was right, 'that to burn always with this hard, gemlike flame, to maintain this ecstasy, is success in life'. The days sparked with opportunity and it was their duty to exploit it. As for familiarity breeding contempt, it would have been a betrayal of the imagination to subscribe to such a view. But now it seemed the group had lost its way with nothing holding it together except that its members shared a common past. It was as if each of them was thickly swaddled in their own years apart and like fat Michelin people they simply did not fit the same space any more.

Jack piled the papers back in the box. When the box was full, a half-dozen papers still remained on the floor. For a moment he considered throwing them out in what would have been an act of punishing finality. Then he emptied the box and packed it again properly.

It was late. He gathered his pillow and sheets and was about to make up a bed on the couch when the doorbell rang. He guessed it was Connie – no one else would be visiting at this hour. And so it was, Connie unshaven and dishevelled, unsteady on his feet and stinking of alcohol.

Jack helped him into the flat. 'I hope you didn't drive over here.'

'Taxi,' he said, and flopped onto the couch. 'Couldn't bear the empty house.'

It was a repeat performance of a couple of nights earlier: Sara out, Connie tossing about in the empty house, the drinking, the taxi to Jack's place.

'Do you mind if I stay over?' And with Jack's 'Not at all' he pulled out his phone and with his surprisingly spoon-like fingers stitched together a text message to Sara.

'I need to let her know I won't be home,' he explained. 'I wouldn't want her to worry.'

It was a courtesy she did not return.

'Is this what you want?' Jack asked, when the phone was put away. 'Is she really what you want?'

And without hesitation Connie replied that she was.

Connie's opinion was sought on topics from community ethics to cyberspace; publicly he was colouring the stratosphere. Privately, however, his life was a disaster. Linda was divorcing him, and although she was doing so in a highly civilised manner, there were still ten years to pack up and the boys to consider. And the more Jack heard about young Sara, he guessed that she, like Linda, was also going her own way.

'I love Sara,' Connie said out of the blue.

'But she does nothing for you,' Jack replied.

'No one understands a relationship not their own.' Connie's words were slurred. 'Look at Ava and Harry.'

'All right then: Sara supplies nothing that you need.'

Slouched on the couch, the ballast emptied out of him and staring into the middle distance with a quizzical look on his face, Connie looked like a man who inexplicably finds himself on the wrong train. Jack was convinced it was not the flightiness and energy of Sara which was to blame but rather the absence of wise and competent Linda. Jack had raised the possibility of a reconciliation with Linda but Connie would not consider it. He'd been in a rut, he said. And he wasn't in love with Linda any more but he certainly was with Sara. When Jack suggested he was behaving like a teenager, Connie replied that Jack was no expert when it came to love. Jack wanted to protest that one can be a fool when it comes to one's own actions and wise with those of others, but decided to keep his silence.

Connie staggered to his feet and helped himself to more wine. Back on the couch he embarked on a long, convoluted account of how best to strengthen his relationship with Sara, what he could do to make her happy, how America would provide a more congenial backdrop to their relationship than Australia.

'I'm surprised Sara would consider leaving Australia. She's at an age when friends carry the highest currency.'

'You make too much of age,' Connie said.

Jack saw the broken blood vessels across Connie's cheeks, the skin slack on his bones, the tuft of grey hair poking out from his open-necked shirt and was in no doubt that age was relevant. Even a kinder woman than young Sara would be hard-pressed to find this Conrad Lyall attractive. Jack knew that his own credentials were suspect when it came to relation-ships, but nonetheless it was clear to him that Connie was struggling to make an affair into a marriage while throwing away a marriage that suited him well.

The following morning, a Saturday, after Connie had dragged himself off home, Jack walked around to Helen's place. It was not yet ten o'clock but the temperature was already in the thir-ties. There was a stillness to the air, heat haze shimmered above the bitumen. It was standing room only on the beach.

Helen's front door was open, he called out and let himself in. Her head appeared around the doorway of her bedroom.

'I was hoping you'd visit,' she said.

A short time later, dressed in polka-dot pants and lime-green singlet, Helen was ready to find some air-conditioning. Five minutes more and they were seated at a local café with efficient cooling.

Jack told her about Connie's latest visit. 'He's throwing away his marriage.'

Helen disagreed. 'Connie let go of the marriage a long time ago. And don't forget Linda's tossing him out. During the period they've been together, Connie's had a swathe of girlfriends from Boston to Dubrovnik. If Linda had known about even ten per cent of them, she'd have kicked him out years ago.'

Jack was tempted to add that on those particular criteria Harry should have done the same with Ava, but ever protective of Ava he kept the thought to himself.

'Much of what Connie needs to know will remain as incomprehensible to him as Linear A.' It was his own comment, yet it surprised him.

Helen smiled. 'What in particular?'

He took a moment to collect his thoughts. 'That it's easy to fall in love. That falling in love feels very good. For the feeling alone you're tempted to do it. And sex, new sex is even easier – you could be semi-comatose and still respond to lust.' He drained the last of his coffee before continuing. 'Connie speaks of his need for change, but he's living in exactly the same way as he did when he was thirty.' And paused again. 'The most difficult change is to keep the familiar refreshed.'

Helen stared at him – this did not sound like Jack at all. 'What's been happening to you?'

He shook his head slowly. 'I'm not at all sure.'

A moment later he stood up and went to the counter for more coffee.

'So have you booked your flight?' he asked, when he returned to the table.

Having made her decision to return to America, Helen seemed to be finding reason after reason to delay – primary among them that Luke wanted to stay in Australia.

'I'm going to have to act soon.' She looked miserable. 'Möller's already arrived. He keeps sending me ideas for future collaborations.'

'And they're clearly not projects to advance your shigella vaccine.'

She shook her head, 'I'm afraid not.' Suddenly she perked up. 'I've left a message on Ava's machine. I'm hoping to see her this afternoon – to help me decide what to do. You're welcome to join us.' And then added, 'Harry's in Sydney.'

Once he would have grabbed every opportunity to be with Ava but he had planned to work on his new essay, and despite a flicker of temptation he realised this was his preference.

It was not that he had ceased to love her, that would be as intolerable as a full blood transfusion with an incompatible blood type, but now that he could see her whenever he liked, see her beyond the hothouse of his own imagination, his desires had lost their urgency. In her company these days, he felt mostly calm and loving as he might with a wife of long standing. Or, indeed, an old friend. At long last reason had found a crack, slipped in and multiplied.

Such a fundamental change yet it had occurred seemingly unconsciously. One day towards the end of February, after a night when the temperature remained in the high twenties, a night of surprisingly calm and unbroken sleep, he had awoken and immediately knew something was different. He did not need to think of her. It was a new day, but he did not need to start it with thoughts of Ava. He knew – he didn't know how he knew – that the day would continue without her. He was no longer desperate for her. His desire had loosened. And no, he did not feel lighter or liberated, rather it was curiosity he felt, not simply at the change – when actually had it occurred? – but how he could have been in thrall for so long.

His love, it now seemed to him, had been like a perpetual transit lounge, always promising some place better. As for his fidelity, fidelity made sense to friends and family, to God, even to an idea, but not to an unrequited love. For years he had subscribed to the elaborate creations of his mind's eye, the lure of possibility, the ever-promising, never-exhausted 'perhaps'. He had been living in the abstract. Now, with his first tentative steps in the real world, he found himself inclined to linger.

CHAPTER 11: Lost Horizons

1.

Ava had wasted the entire morning fiddling with a chapter that six months ago she thought was finished. She pushed back from her desk: better to begin fresh tomorrow. But would it be better tomorrow? Yesterday was an improvement on today and most of last week was tolerably good, but the previous week had been full-strength frustration. And while every novel in the writing intermittently loses its way, what was happening now was of a totally different order. One part of her wanted to remain at work until the sludge cleared, another wanted to flee in terror, and a third, so logical and measured, assured her that novels in the making were intractable things and she would achieve considerably more if she stopped worrying.

The floor around her desk was littered with pages from the current chapter; she bent down to pick them up, then decided to leave them where they lay, ready for when she returned to work. She closed her laptop and turned away – sharp, decisive movements after the helpless fiddling at the keyboard; her shirt caught the arm of her chair and spun it against a side table. A vase of roses teetered, she lunged, but too late and the vase fell, showering the pages on the floor. The print in indelible laser survived, but her annotations in ink were collecting in coloured pools. She picked up a sheet, coloured water rolled down the paper: her words were literally running off the page. She lay the page gently back on the floor; it was all too much.

Outside it was stifling. A cool change had been forecast for late-afternoon.

'May the change come early.' Ava uttered the thought aloud and wondered at this new habit of hers.

Summer, all hot summers, put her in mind of Lily Bart from *The House of Mirth.* Lily was a favourite of hers, a fictional sister who had made many of the same choices she had made, although had been far less fortunate. Of all the slights Lily had suffered, that which best defined her social collapse was having to remain in New York City during the sweltering summer because none of her former friends had invited her to Newport or Long Island or some other breezy place by the sea. In those times and for that class, the summer exodus from the city was not simply an escape from the heat, it symbolised a civilised existence.

That morning over coffee Ava had suggested to Harry they should do as Edith Wharton's characters did and quit the city. 'We could move to the high country for the summer.'

Harry had smiled. 'Do you believe everything you read?'

'Only in fiction,' she said, returning his smile.

She wandered the courtyard beneath the ferocious sun, bending down every now and then to pull a weed; even the ants, scourge of her garden, had gone to ground. She was about to go inside when a spark of light near the fence caught her eye. It was a piece of apple-green glass. Neither she nor Harry had broken anything in the courtyard and she wondered where it had come from. It was a pretty little ornament with the clouded transparency of alabaster and edges worn smooth like sea glass; she rubbed it between her fingers and slipped it into her pocket. She crossed to the spa tub and dangled her fingers in the water. If only she had patience for the full-body relaxation touted by the manufacturers, but lolling around in warm electrified water had never appealed and certainly not as a means of making time pass more quickly.

What she needed was company, and Jack's company was her preference. Jack who would arrive with cakes and gossip and play his guitar for her, who was happy to sit or walk or do whatever she wanted, who these days seemed to require less of her than the others. The strain which had marred their early meetings had disappeared along with, so she believed, his all-consuming love. She smiled to herself: now this new Jack was a man to fall in love with.

How contrary life could be.

She went inside and dialled his home number. The phone rang through to the answering machine and she left a message. She tried his office phone and left another message. His mobile phone was switched off. No Jack today, and Harry was in meetings all afternoon, Helen was talking to some African politicians about shigella and Connie was in the process of ending his marriage. She went next door to see if Minnie was home. There was no answer to the doorbell; the dog barked from inside the house, otherwise all was quiet. No Minnie today either. If she were a gambler she would go to one of those gaming rooms that had infiltrated Melbourne's pubs and pass the time in reliable comfort while she lost her money. But it was that attitude, devoid as it was of the gambler's hope, which meant the pokies would never be an option for her.

She returned to her study, and avoiding the mess near her desk, dallied with a soon-to-be-released novel her publishers had sent her. Ten minutes later she swapped it for *Riders in the Chariot*, but while the familiarity of Patrick White was a comfort she lacked the concentration. Poetry so close she could recite it by heart was a better choice, but reading Coleridge primarily to pass the time does not sustain. She needed a practical task and seized upon her photographs, not the photos of her married life, Harry was in charge of those and they were mounted in albums within days of being taken. It was her Fleur photos that needed to be organised, seven years of pictures, and now that the burn was gone, a chore like any other.

She emptied the contents of the box on the floor. There must be two or three hundred photos here of Fleur, of Fleur with her friends, of Ava with Fleur's friends, of Fleur posing in front of palaces and cathedrals, of Ava posing in parks and gardens, of Fleur eating and drinking and shopping for clothes, of Ava reading and sleeping and walking through woods. Hundreds of photos and, no need to check, not a single shot of the two of them together. Here is Fleur with her friends Kristin and Diane on one of the many trips she and Ava made to Paris. Here is Fleur on their Italian holiday with Sarah and Paul. Here is Ava in Venice with Frances. Here is Ava on Capri holding a collection of Graham Greene's stories, the Mediterranean glistening behind.

'I'd like to go to Italy with you,' Harry had said, when Ava told him of the trip.

He uttered each word with careful emphasis so she would properly understand: he wanted her to change her plans, he wanted her to cancel this trip. And while she understood perfectly, she knew she must not hesitate.

'We'll go to Italy another time,' she said. 'Just the two of us, when your grandmother's not coming to visit.'

Each year Harry's grandmother made a month-long visit to England to see them. For two of those weeks Ava took a holiday – 'To give you time alone with your gran,' although they both knew the truth. While Harry and his grandmother travelled the British Isles, she and Fleur went to Portugal and Morocco, to Crete and Santorini, and yes, to Italy, a different location each year with different friends to visit and more photos to take. So many photos and not a single shot of the two of them alone together in the one frame. Never for them a quiet posing under a tranquil sun.

Mixed in with the photos were postcards bought at galleries and museums. Ava sifted through until she found a card of Picasso's Dora Maar as a weeping woman. In their last year together, on a weekend trip to Paris, she and Fleur had visited the Picasso Museum. As Ava had perused the exhibits, she was aware of a queer and disquieting recognition. Picasso painted Maar, he printed her, he photographed and engraved her, he wrote poems to her, he summoned her by incantatory writing – *DoraDoraDoraDora* covering sheets of paper. He created out of his Dora passion several series of women weeping, women sleeping, nude women, women being ravished by Picasso-like minotaurs, and all these women, all of them, were Dora Maar. And Maar in turn photographed Picasso, she photographed him at work, hundreds of photos as he created the great *Guernica*. She captured him asleep, she photographed him fooling around on the beach, she had him pose side on, front on, standing and seated, in shadow and full sun. So much art made of Picasso's Maar and so much of Maar's Picasso during ten fiery years, and while there were several photographs of them together with friends, there was only one image of the two of them alone. In this picture, Picasso and Maar, this man and this woman who had spent years in a frenzied feasting on each other, stood gravely facing the camera, not touching.

Most people can lay out their lives in photos: childhood, family shots, friends, travel, lovers, marriage, children, grand-children. What a distorted view Ava's photos would give. There was a plethora of public-life shots and Harry's beauti-fully mounted photographs of a long marriage. And dozens of photos of Helen, Jack and Connie. Of her early life there were just three pictures: one of her as a baby sitting alone on a bunny rug, another showing her on a swing alongside her brother, and the third was her parents' wedding portrait which she had rescued from a bonfire after one of her mother's vigor-ous spring-cleanings. If photos were an accurate depiction of a life, Ava was wife, author and friend. Childhood was little more than a time filler, Fleur would exist as a friend not a lover, and out of contention entirely was Stephen.

He had taken so many photos of her. 'Please,' she had asked again and again. 'Let me have just one picture of you.' But he never relented.

She shuffled through the photos on the floor, increasingly bemused. When Fleur left, these photos had been too radio-active to handle; when Fleur mattered, the photos mattered. Her fingers grazed the glossy pictures, touching what was lost or perhaps what never was. She paused, her hands briefly still, then she scooped the whole lot up and bundled them back in the box.

Ten minutes later she was locking the door and escaping the house; she would walk to Lygon Street to buy some pasta for dinner. It was hotter now and very humid, the clouds had rolled in and the sky was grey and heavy; she felt as if caught inside a pair of lungs. She slackened her usual brisk pace but by the time she reached the pasta shop she was soggy inside her clothes. It was already late March, but summer was still pumped up, all glistening muscle and bravado. How she hated it.

Of all the people she had cared about only Stephen had been, like her, a cold weather person – or that's what he used to say. It was possible he was just wanting to please her. He had always wanted to please her.

Stephen.

While she was in England he seldom entered her thoughts, but since her return to Melbourne so had he, in pleasant calming moments. It was, she supposed, being home, and Stephen was fused with home. Even this pasta shop was associated with him. She had been convinced with the certainty of a teenager that any pasta beyond macaroni cheese and spaghetti bolognaise was mere pretension. But once she had tasted linguine with pesto, and cheese tortellini, and mushroom ravioli (on that first occasion Stephen had bought small amounts of all three), she had changed her mind. Stephen taught her about pasta, Stephen taught her all about food beyond the roasts and takeaway chicken of her childhood. Stephen taught her most of what she needed to quit suburban Boronia forever.

Inside the shop Ava breathed in garlic and basil and that damp mellow smell of pasta, and any doubts over stopping work early were immediately dispelled. The bad patch would pass, and faster if she stopped chewing the end of her pen. Better to be in this cool shop inhaling the smells and admiring the variety, so much greater than when she first came here with Stephen. Agnolotti of goat's cheese with salmon, tortellini of mushroom and tarragon, roasted eggplant ravioli. How to decide? Salmon, mushroom or eggplant? Or perhaps the traditional ricotta and spinach? Salmon, mushroom, eggplant or ricotta? Her gaze glazes over the choices. Salmon? Mushroom? Eggplant? Ricotta? It's your turn. Salmon? Mushroom? Eggplant? Ricotta? The woman is waiting. Salmon? Mushroom? Eggplant? Ricotta? And Ava dashes from the shop, she's standing on the footpath, her face is burning, she's dripping with sweat – over pasta. Salmon, mushroom, eggplant, ricotta. She likes them all. So does Harry. She could have chosen any of them.

A man tells her to get the fuck out of the way; everyone looks hot and bothered. She collects herself and crosses Lygon Street. She resists the temptation of Readings bookshop and goes directly to the Italian food store at the corner. She'll find something here for dinner. As she enters, she instructs herself to buy the first thing that appeals.

She props in front of the delicatessen area with its patch-work of colours and its heady smells. But cheese, olives, capers and anchovies do not readily transmute into a proper meal. Parmegiano-Reggiano is on special and she buys a wedge, but with nothing to eat it with and reluctant to return to the pasta shop, she again finds herself stalled on the pavement outside.

People walk past alone and in pairs, some with shopping bags, others pushing strollers, some dressed for business, others for leisure, and plenty of students lugging laptops. Surrounded by so much purpose and none of it hers, the whole shopping expedition now seems a bad idea. A single meal for two people yet it might be a banquet for fifty for all the difficulty it presents.

She wants to blame the humidity, she wants to blame the restless nights, she wants to blame the crawling days. Most of all she wants to give herself a break. She shoves the cheese in her bag – not a day for work and not a day for shopping either – and sets off towards Swanston Street. She doesn't know where she's going and neither does she care.

The sky is darkening, the air is stiff and damp, she skirts around groups of students, negotiates her way past a building site which has spilled onto the footpath, and makes her way past the university towards the traffic lights. At the first drops of rain she steps into the intersection. She slips easily between the moving cars and hurries to the other side for cover.

The fat summery rain is pelting down now and making a huge ruckus. She dashes to the second-hand bookshop and takes shelter under the canopy. Her feet are drenched, her clothes are cool and clinging. She peers through the grimy glass to the array of books in the window. If not for some recent titles, it could be the same display from years ago.

It is the week after her fifteenth birthday, and Ava is on an expedition to the university, a place that since chancing on Frank Capra's *Lost Horizon* on TV she has created as her own Shangri-la. While she expects her journey to be less arduous than Ronald Colman's, given her background, the destination is in many respects just as exotic. No Bryant has ever travelled far – with the obvious exception of her father, whose absence from home is condemned as dereliction of duty and evidence of poor character. Indeed, the upward mobility of successive generations that has long contributed to the Australian dream is unknown in the Bryant family. The optimum trajectory for a girl in the Bryant scheme of things is to leave school, get a job, find a fellow and marry him.

Ava has quite a different future in mind and tertiary education is pivotal to it. She has been planning her excursion to the university for months; she needs to see this place where her destiny lies if only to give her strength for the journey ahead. The day is her own; school has broken up for the term holidays, her mother is at work, her brother is at a friend's place. Wearing jeans and a plain blouse, she hopes she can pass as a university student: she's a stranger here and unsure of the protocol and she doesn't want to arouse suspicion. With her hair pulled back and her eyes ringed with kohl she appears older than her years – although according to her mother, the blackened eyes just make her look like a tart.

She stops in front of a map at the entrance to the university then decides to ignore it, not simply through self-consciousness – what real student would need to consult a map of the campus? – but because maps flummox her. With no natural sense of direction either, she decides to follow her fancy, and crosses the threshold into a new world. The day is calm and gently warm, most people are carrying books, she smells freshly turned earth and the lingering ooze of hot chips; old shadows beckon and everywhere the mesmerising prickling of age. The usual edges of her life have melted away.

She strolls along corridors with greenish lino and yellowed walls. She is wrapped in herself and so content; no one stops her, no one interferes. She wanders from the law building with its must of age, into biology and the sour wince of organic matter. She browses the numerous pinboards, reads posters advertising film festivals, meetings and discussion groups – Kantians, Existentialists, Phenomenologists – labels which might be Greek for all she understands.

I will belong here one day, she tells herself, I will belong here.

She stops at a cylindrical bulletin board of a type she has only ever seen in pictures of Paris. It is thick with flyers. She walks slowly around, reading as she goes. A boy approaches and points to an advertisement for an anti-apartheid rally. This protest is not to be missed, he says. And Ava smiles and says she'll be there. But she won't; she'll be back at school where opposition to apartheid is definitely not on the curriculum, and at the end of the day she'll return to a mother who has never attended a political rally in her life.

'What if Tim had been old enough for conscription,' Ava had once asked. 'Would you have marched in the Vietnam moratoriums?' And her mother had simply assumed one of her 'How idiotic can you be?' looks, as she always did when confronted with a hypothetical situation. But without hypothetical situations Ava would not be exploring the university today. Without hypothetical situations she would have been unable to imagine an alternative future for herself.

After an hour of wandering the campus she follows the signs to the Union Building and the main cafeteria, where she buys coffee and chips and settles at a table. Most people are in groups, but those who are alone sit with food and a book, stretching into the space around them in a clear statement they are choosing to be alone. Ava puts her feet up on a vacant chair, spreads out her things and opens a book.

She sips the grey coffee and picks at the chips. She takes in the students with their conversation and laughter; she sees their friendships. There is an ease amongst these people which comes, she supposes, from their sense of belonging here. This is my future, she says to herself, my future.

She sits until self-consciousness makes further sitting imposs-ible, then gathers up her belongings and wanders outside again. Eventually she finds her way back to the campus entrance. She is reluctant to leave, but she'll return, she tells herself, as often as money allows, until she enters here as a proper student.

With the help of books from the library she has imagined herself in London and Paris, Oxford and Cambridge, and more recently, guided by Henry James, she has imagined herself in Venice and Rome. But in the next three years while she is finishing high school, it will be this university that will form the backdrop to the most satisfying of her dreams. This she determines.

She leaves the university and with no tram in sight she decides to walk down Swanston Street to the train station. A short time later she crosses with the traffic lights and immedi-ately sees the sign: Second-hand Books.

Wine lovers remember their first taste of good wine, orchid growers their first glimpse of an orchid, musicians the first time they heard Bach. Book lovers, too, have their firsts: the first book they read by themselves; their first visit to a library; the first book they bought with their own money; and for many, the discovery of second-hand bookshops.

Until that moment Ava had not known such places existed. Gordon Comstock worked in a 'used books' shop in *Keep the Aspidistra Flying* and she knows of other characters in fiction who have picked up bargains in shops that sell 'old books', but beyond the pages of a novel, a shop consisting entirely of second-hand books open to real people like her is a revelation. She should be heading to the station but she can't resist a quick look.

The man at the front desk glances up as she enters. With his shabby hair and beard, his baggy jacket and frayed cuffs, with the glasses held together with sticky tape and a wisp of cigarette attached to his lower lip, he fits exactly her image of an intellectual. A Gordon Comstock look-alike. And like Gordon, this man too is probably a writer, and one day he'll be famous, or perhaps he is already. And the book he is reading might be philosophy, or given its size perhaps an illustrated commentary on classical Greek literature. A second-hand bookshop, a writer at the front desk, the university just five minutes away. Life is extraordinary.

As much as she wants to explore every inch of this shop, she decides to forfeit this first area. She doesn't want the man looking too closely at her. He must be at least twenty-five and in his eyes she would be just a child, perhaps a runaway looking for a safe place to rest, even a common shoplifter. And besides, she doesn't want him watching her read. With books as a clearly signed short cut to the soul, you would have to be either very stupid or very careless to make your reading public. Although this doesn't stop her from sneaking a peep at his book as she passes.

It's a gardening book! This man, the guardian of this extraordinary place is reading a gardening book similar to those her mother borrows from the lending library. It couldn't be, Gordon Comstock would never read a gardening book, and with a flick of her mind she converts it to a volume on Versailles.

A sign on the wall advertises eleven more rooms beyond this one. Ava would rather starve than sell any of her books. Although another sign about deceased estates suggests that some of the former owners are dead bibliophiles whose heirs have dispatched their relative's books as if they were no more significant than crockery and cutlery. Passions are such personal things.

She is about to leave the front room when a tall, bearded man carrying a briefcase enters the shop. He is dressed in a dark suit and tie. A professorial type, Ava thinks, a man with a passing resemblance to the captain in *The Ghost and Mrs Muir*. He greets Gordon and hands him his briefcase for stowing behind the desk; meeting Ava's gaze he nods and smiles at her. Quickly she turns away, hurries up three steps which have all but disappeared under books and enters the next room. It is full of literature – hard covers, soft covers, literature from floor to ceiling. She takes a quick inventory before moving on.

The second-hand bookshop is not a normal shop but a two-storey terrace house with a series of small rooms flowing deep into the building. The walls of each room are crammed with books; there are more books on free-standing shelves, even the passageways are lined with books. And that distinctive tang of old paper – there was exactly the same smell when her class toured the State Library last year – here mingled with the smell of mice. There's dust on the floor, cobwebs streak the ceiling; in the rare places where skirting boards can be seen they are coated with grime. The lighting is buttery, the globes are old.

Room after room packed with books, and on such a variety of subjects – although why people would waste their time writing about trains she will never understand. And there's a whole wall devoted to flashy fantasy novels. Her fantasies plug the holes of this life, her fantasies are possible, her fantasies will happen; she has no interest in weird worlds with unpronounceable names where people speak a stilted English stitched together with antiquated courtesies. One less area to bother with, she tells herself, and moves on. She reads spines, she removes volumes from the shelves, she is aware of such longing, such frustration, just like Coleridge's mariners, water water everywhere and not a drop to drink. Volumes, volumes everywhere and not the brass to buy.

To know what you need, to know exactly what is required to move you on to the next stage of your life, to see it in front of you yet out of reach is a form of torture. Ava makes a pledge in an upstairs room of the second-hand bookshop that when she is grown up she will have the money and independence to own any book of her choosing. This is not mere desire, this is a decision: Ava Bryant will have freedom of movement and a full purse. The woman she plans to be could walk into a hundred different second-hand bookshops – she assumes this is not the only one – linger for hours if she so desires and walk out with as many books as she can carry.

Today, however, with two dollars eighty-five to spend, she might manage six, maybe seven, paperbacks and no treats for a month. She returns to the literature room. Modern literature, classical literature, hard covers and more orange-spined Penguins than she's ever seen. Some volumes are familiar, others beckon by covers or titles. She handles the books delicately, she turns pages, she reads paragraphs, she is gripped by old underlinings and margin scribblings, and wonders again how people can part with their books, particularly those that have hooked so deeply into their thoughts. Browsers come and go, Ava ignores them and they ignore her. She reads back-cover blurbs, she reads opening pages, she flips through chapters, she studies biographical notes to discover the age of authors when they published their first novel, she brushes a fragment of something from her face and smells old paper on her fingers. She takes down book after book; a few she replaces, the rest she adds to a pile on the floor.

The professor enters the room. He is carrying just two books – clearly he's more practised in resisting temptation than is she. The two of them move slowly around the tiny space, maintaining a distance like in a courtly dance. He does not disturb her, she does not disturb him. Each selects volumes, peruses them, replaces or adds them to their stacks. He is more presence than person, an extension of her own private experience and adding to the pleasure. Fifteen minutes, twenty minutes in this book minuet and she longs for more time, but unless she has the dinner in the oven before her mother returns from work there will be some explaining to do.

As if he knows she needs to be alone, the professor leaves the room. She glances at him out in the passageway; no longer an extension of herself, he is just a man old enough to be her father. Although if her father had possessed a fraction of the wisdom and sympathy of this stranger, he would not have deserted his family and she might have an ally at home. She shakes herself out of the thought: you don't choose your parents, you don't choose your family, but you can choose your future.

She has selected eleven books – far too many, and not just the money, it's carrying them home and hiding them in the tiny space of her bedroom. And suddenly she remembers: she's not finished. She dashes out of literature into foreign languages, and there on the French shelves she finds two copies of *Le Grand Meaulnes.* She selects the cheaper one with ink markings and a food stain that has penetrated a third of the book, is out in the passageway when she stops and turns – some compromises are simply not worth it – and swaps it for the other copy. She is about to return to the literature room when a book facing outwards catches her eye. She's heard of Jean-Paul Sartre but not this book. *Words*, that's all it is called. *Words*. A slender orange-spined Penguin in translation, and on the cover, instead of the usual picture there is a quote from the book: 'I loathe my childhood and all that remains of it ...'

This book has been written for her.

Back in the literature room now with thirteen books from which to choose, she begins by dividing them into two piles. *Le Grand Meaulnes* is a must. Madame says it is her favourite book, Madame who is small and dark and the main reason Ava has continued to study French; Madame who dresses always in black and wears heavy eye make-up; Madame who is said to have a past, and given that she lives with a man not her husband, a present too, Madame says this book changed her life. Ava puts *Le Grand Meaulnes* on the left, the definite pile. And Jean-Paul Sartre's *Words* – a risk, but worth it for the cover sentence alone. She adds *A Fairly Honourable Defeat*, one of two novels by Iris Murdoch she has chosen. The cover graphic is a close-up photograph of a woman's face. The eyes are daubed in black, a bit like Madame's eyes, the red lacquered lips are exhaling smoke. But is a cover picture enough? The back cover of the other Murdoch, *A Severed Head*, refers to the 'sombre themes' of the book: 'adultery, incest, castration, violence and suicide'; it is only forty cents. In the end she adds both to the left-hand pile.

With four books on the definite pile and enough money for two or three more, there are some difficult decisions to be made. She adds, she takes away, she makes three piles instead of two, she totes figures in her head, she counts her money. It's like playing patience with a short deck.

'Easier to choose between diamonds.'

Her head jerks up, the professor is standing a metre away. His accent is English, his utterance of a type she might read in a book. He is looking down at her, his face very serious. But with choices to be made and time running out, she just gives him a nod.

He does not move. He suggests she leave some for next time.

This man with his posh accent has no idea. 'It's not as simple as that,' she says, and doesn't care if she sounds rude. She glances at her watch, then returns to her three piles.

'How much do you need?'

She swallows the ache in her throat, she doesn't want him to see how much this matters. And then a slump like wet wool and her perfect day is in tatters. Her books are in piles before her. There's nothing more to lose.

'Six dollars twenty-five.' Each syllable is a tidy punch as if he, or anyone with money is somehow to blame. She will not look at him, she keeps her gaze on her books. Impossible to have all thirteen. She pushes the right-hand pile behind her, out of view and out of contention, and recalculates. 'Make that three dollars sixty-five.' She swallows hard, and now she looks up. She settles her face into a smile.

He opens his wallet and withdraws two two-dollar bills. 'Take the money,' he says. 'It delights me to see a girl your age so keen on books.'

Ava looks at the money, she looks at her books, *her* books, and then she looks at him. He is obviously rich and probably harmless. Being careful will only harden the cement of her current life. She stands up. Her heart is thumping. She takes his money. She tries to keep her voice steady as she thanks him.

'I'll pay you back,' she makes another quick calculation, 'in three months.'

He nods as if in thought. 'What I'd prefer is a note from you with your impressions of each book.'

'Like a book review?' The idea is so grown-up and so very writerly.

He smiles. 'Yes, like a book review.'

He writes down his name, Stephen Webb, his address and phone number.

'So you do work at the university,' she says.

He nods and gives another smile. And even though the beard makes him look old, it's a nice smile.

He is not finished. 'Perhaps one day you'd like to see my library.'

In her short life she has learned to be watchful for experiences and grab them when they present. Now she studies Stephen Webb with a different eye. He is tall, at least six feet, with lines around his eyes – not the crêpey collapsed skin of a truly old person, just clear smile lines, and across his forehead there are lines of thought. His hair is brown and thick and brushed to the side. The hair makes him look less old, perhaps even in his thirties – although thirty or forty makes no difference and she knows it. But he is not fat, and he doesn't look like a sleaze, and there's no hair on the backs of his fingers. And he has his own library.

I can do this, she thinks, as she pockets his money. I can do this.

'Nothing's free in this world,' her mother always said. The difficult part was arriving at a fair price. With Stephen, Ava believed she had. Over the next several years, like God with the Israelites, Stephen supplied her necessities in the desert – and, as far as she was concerned, for bargain prices.

He guided her through the classics, he taught her about poetry, he instilled in her the importance of memorising, he gave her old books, he gave her new books, he gave her the complete works of Shakespeare in a red leather-bound copy with tiny bible-sized print, and he gave her love. Stephen was worldly and he was wise and everything he had he was willing to share with her. Before she met him, every day was fretted with want, but Stephen made it clear that with him she would never want for anything. He had a wife, he had two sons, he had friends, perhaps he had parents and sisters and brothers as well, but she was convinced he put her first.

As they read and talked together she found a language for her life to come, a mysterious exciting future that grew ever clearer and ever more possible. She told him of her dream to write novels; he told her he had absolute faith she would. She told him she planned to live overseas; he said whatever she set her mind to do she could achieve. It was Stephen who taught her the importance of travelling, of knowing other places and other people, and so different from her mother for whom home was not only enough, it was unquestionably the best. It was Stephen who suggested Oxford and it was Stephen who supplied the money – for school, for Melbourne University, for Oxford too, a monthly deposit in an account he set up for her.

He told her his wife went her own way even more than he went his. Ava never pursued what he meant, not because of the wife's activities, rather she preferred not to know how Stephen viewed his own. He showed her photographs of his family because she asked to see them, but the images, like the people themselves, remained blurred.

She and Stephen usually met at his flat not far from the city centre, 'my private office' as he called it; only twice did she go to his home – a large old house in a leafy suburb. He denied he was rich but the big house, the sons at private school, his job at the university plus his private office, his Mercedes Benz, even his pen collection suggested great wealth to her. He was an administrator at the university, not an academic, a man who had come from the private sector and expected to return there.

She never coveted his money, only the freedom it afforded. Stephen could travel anywhere, he could buy any book he wanted, he could add to his pen collection according to his fancy. He collected Parker Duofolds, a classic workmanlike pen according to him, but with their round belly, the way they fit so snugly in the hand and their lovely weight Ava thought them lushly feminine. On the first anniversary of their meeting, he made her a gift from his own collection. It remained her favourite pen.

Stephen said he would always love her, and perhaps he would have but she never put him to the test. Six years after they met she was wrapping up her Melbourne life, she was going to Oxford, she was moving on. No false hopes for him and no Melbourne ties for her – although he had insisted on continuing his financial support, and nothing she said would make him change his mind. She hadn't seen her family for more than a year, her best friends were travelling with her, once she left Melbourne there would be no looking back. She did not talk about leaving him, and knowing how she abhorred dependence in others, he would never have raised the issue himself.

Some people treat their mistakes and regrets like bruises, prodding them every now and then to keep them tender. Ava was not the type to dwell on her mistakes: they happen, you learn, you make sure not to repeat them. But of all the mistakes she had made none involved Stephen Webb. He was the right person for those years and how she had missed him when she first left Australia. He still appeared in her dreams a quarter of a century on.

He would be well over seventy now, and rising up and taking her quite by surprise was an urge to contact him. But aside from satisfying some inexplicable nostalgia, what could possibly be achieved? Leave your memories alone, she told herself, for neither she nor Stephen had what the other wanted these days. He had loved her, loved her unconditionally as her parents had failed to do. He had loved her all those years ago like Harry did now. Contact Stephen? She was turning into one of those pitiful middle-aged people for whom the past acquired ever brighter and more varied hues while the present dissolved into a vale of tears. No purpose would be served by meeting Stephen now. Of course she wouldn't contact him.

She left the shelter of the second-hand bookshop. The rain had stopped, the humidity was worse than ever. She burrowed in her pocket for a tissue to wipe her face and pulled out a piece of green glass. She turned it over in her hand. How on earth did that get there? and tossed it into a rubbish bin. As she made her way back through the Carlton streets she felt a need for Harry. She picked up her pace, soon she would be home, and within a few hours he would be too. Perhaps he might leave work early. She rummaged in her bag for her mobile phone and turned it on, but the battery was flat. She would ring him as soon as she arrived home. It was not a day for being alone.

Helen Rankin was sitting on the front verandah of Ava's house. She had rung Ava's mobile but it was not turned on. She had dialled the landline and heard the phone ringing inside the house. She and Ava had arranged to meet at three, it was now a quarter to four. Ava had clearly forgotten.

Since the Aiken meeting Helen had been working flat out, not simply the demands of her current research, but there had been reports to write and grant applications for the laboratory back in the US, and almost daily communications with Möller. Her superiors in Maryland were haranguing her to return to America; NOGA had expected her to leave Australia months ago; but what seemed so sure and certain when she met Möller at Aiken was now blurred with doubt. After weeks of trying to see Ava, she and Ava had finally agreed on today. It was Ava who had suggested her place, Ava who had suggested three o'clock so as to have plenty of time to talk before Harry came home. 'And then,' she said, 'the three of us can toast your brilliant career.'

Helen couldn't help wondering if in the scheme of things friendship now received a lower priority than in the old days. And yet she really did want to talk to Ava – not to help in making a decision, for unless she had a kamikaze instinct as far as her career was concerned, the choice was clear, but to help settle the decision she had made. She wanted Ava to study the various issues, weigh up the ethical pros and cons and produce an inspired and original reason for the only sensible opton open to her. And if she was to be entirely honest, she also wanted Ava's approval.

Helen walked down the path to the gate. It was still humid, but with a misty rain falling it felt a little cooler. The drop in temperature had brought out some joggers on the cemetery track, and there was a group of boys kicking a football around. She checked her watch again, and was about to leave, when Ava appeared at the corner of the street.

Her floating clothes were easily recognisable, so too the shape of her as she walked along the footpath, but everything else about this unmasked Ava was strange. The drooping head, the slow inward shuffle, the arms immobile at her sides. Strange and infirm. Helen was about to step out and make herself known but something about this figure held her back. Halfway up the street Ava stopped. Now she seemed to be talking to herself, her arms were extended in front of her, palms turned upwards in a questioning gesture, or perhaps she was pleading. She appeared stripped bare. Helen continued to observe, undercover as it were and breaking the rules. You think you want to see your intimates without their public disguises, but confronted by this view of Ava, Helen decided there was too much to lose by such uninvited sightings.

Ava continued up the street, drawing closer to the house. Her arms were now wrapped tightly about her in an invisible straitjacket, her feet dragged against the asphalt. Helen's problems were bad enough, but if Ava's appearance was any guide, hers were a good deal worse.

Helen wanted to dash down the street and enfold her in her arms. But everything she knew about Ava suggested she would be embarrassed to be caught in this state. The Volvo was parked around the next corner. Helen grabbed her bag, slipped through the gateway and into the side lane. A minute or two later, when Ava entered the house, Helen walked the short distance to her car and quickly drove away.

'She seemed cut off from her surroundings,' Helen said to Jack. 'And blunted too, as if switched to one of those economy settings on air-conditioning units.'

It was the evening of the missed appointment and Helen, together with Luke and Jack, had packed a picnic dinner and joined the hordes at the beach. The earlier cool change had been no more than a tease. It was now after nine, the temperature was thirty degrees, and with their meal finished they had moved down the sand to sit in the shallows.

'I watched her walking up the street,' Helen said. 'She was hardly recognisable. And she forgot our appointment. Ava never forgets.'

And she was never sick, not that Helen believed there was anything physically wrong with her now. 'I think she's suffering some sort of psychological malaise. If she could just finish her novel, she'd be back to normal in no time.'

Jack was surprised Helen knew anything about the state of Ava's work.

'From the very first book,' Helen said, 'she's supplied me with regular updates. And for each new novel when the end is in sight she sends me a draft. She says I'm sensitive to the big picture – stumbling story, dull characters, that sort of thing.' Helen let out a laugh. 'What she really means is I have an extremely low threshold for boredom.'

Why had Ava not told him? Jack wondered. He had thought he alone read her work in draft. And might have said something he'd have regretted if Helen had not continued.

'Too bad I've been immune to the big picture in my own

work. Although,' and she slapped at a mosquito, 'now that I have the big picture, I wish I could forget it.'

And because Jack did not share Helen's concerns about Ava – far from being stressed or anxious, Ava seemed more relaxed with him than ever before – he stretched out in the shallows, propped himself on an elbow while Helen pursued her career dilemmas.

'Germany under Hitler had a policy called "*Gleichschaltung*" or "alignment",' she said. 'Organisations and institutes were required to "align" themselves with Nazi goals and methods. The policy determined what was acceptable in painting, sculpture, literature, music, architecture, journalism. And domestic schedules too: the composition of meals, exercise, friendship, the lot. And the policy shaped science. Subversive Jewish theoretical physics was outlawed in favour of "Aryan physics" – as if atoms wore little swastikas.' She slipped lower in the water and tipped her head backwards to wet her hair. 'So what's happening at the moment isn't new.'

Her hair was smooth against her skull. Water was dripping over her shoulders. She was not wearing her glasses. In the evening light she could pass for a young man, a quite beautiful young man, Jack was thinking. He looked across at Luke. The likeness between mother and son was at this moment quite startling, yet it was the mother who would make the more attractive male.

'And Möller?' Jack asked, turning away from his interesting thoughts.

'It was inconceivable to me he would knowingly work for the forces of evil.' She lashed out at another mosquito. 'And yes, it can be as dramatic as that. But when I consider how he is wanting our joint research to focus on producing new organisms, not specifically to further the shigella immunity issue but to customise the survival features of certain microbes, I can't help but have doubts about him. And if a man of his calibre could sell his soul to the military or the government – for good or ill, it really doesn't matter – anyone could.'

The issue now was what to do about the changing power in science, she said. There was a newly formed group of scientists who were devising a set of strategies to keep science honest – not the Union of Concerned Scientists but a more conservative group. 'If the plans of this group are implemented, scientific freedom will be obliterated.'

She could not understand why more of her colleagues were not outraged. 'The group itself is suspect; it's connected to government and big business, it's probably an arm of the CIA. But even if its credentials were more acceptable, it's absurd to curtail all of science because of the worst practices, to propose changes that will severely restrict the good ninety-nine point nine per cent of the scientific community because of the actions of a tiny minority.' She picked up speed. 'This sort of over-reaction to science's underside is as illogical and self-defeating as the developed world's response to terrorism. Our whole way of life has been altered because of unpredictable happenings far less frequent and not nearly as devastating as natural disasters. Terrorist attacks are unpredictable, that's the substance of their power. We're all running scared. We'd report our neighbour for using a crystal radio, we won't travel by air, we avoid crowds, we don't demonstrate in public places, we lock ourselves in our safe little houses and open our doors only to those like ourselves. And we call this taking precautions but it's snuffing the life out of life itself.'

Jack burst out laughing. It had always been Helen's way to start talking at one point and end up at quite another. However Luke, who had been largely silent to this point, looked grave. 'Surely you don't still believe in a self-enclosed, untouchable science existing independently of a corrupt world. With everything that's happened to your own work, how could you still believe this?'

'In the heat of doing science, there's only science. And when I discuss my work I talk biology not biological weapons, microbes not germ warfare. Of course I still believe in good science, ethical science.'

Soon afterwards they returned to Jack's flat. With a jug of iced water in reach, they arranged their chairs in the blast from the air-conditioner. Jack's mind was pleasantly empty, Helen was sifting through terror scenarios and Luke was playing a game on his phone. Several minutes passed before Luke broke the silence.

'Of you all,' he said in his surprisingly deep voice, 'you two, Connie and Ava, who will have the enduring reputation?'

His question came as a surprise. Jack had assumed the boy thought his mother and her friends all rather ordinary, having as he did the kitchen perspective of them all.

'Well?' Luke said. 'Whose work is most likely to last?'

A few months earlier Jack would have said Helen's; after all, her work was fundamental, her work would save lives. But he was no longer so sure, particularly if she ended up working on a bioweapons project. As for Connie, while he was a significant figure in analysing the current era, people seem to prefer their own contemporary versions of history and would more likely look to their own interpreters to make sense of this particular time. That left him and Ava and he was never in the running.

'Ava,' he said to Luke. 'Ava's work will endure, and if your mother ever finds a rich benefactor without strings,' he smiled in her direction, 'hers will too.'

'I'm pleased you didn't opt for Connie,' Luke said. His tone was not friendly.

'Tell him,' Helen said to her son.

'Tell me what?' Jack asked.

No longer the lovely ephebe in the shallows, Helen now looked exactly like a mother not pleased with her son. Luke's face was set stern and stubborn. His cheek muscles flickered.

'Connie is not Luke's favourite person at the moment,' Helen said to Jack.

'And why should he be?' Luke burst out. 'He's behaving like a shit. All of you,' and he looked accusingly at both his mother and Jack, 'all of you have let him get away with far too much for far too long.'

Jack was astonished at the attack. Connie and Linda had been like family to Luke. 'What's happened?' he asked.

Helen glared at her son. 'Well?'

'I told Linda about Connie's latest fuck.' And before Helen could protest at his language, 'Linda deserved to know. She's a good person. Connie was playing her for a fool.'

Jack looked to Helen. Helen merely shrugged. 'Anything you want to say I've already said. It was none of his business, he hardly knows Sara – '

Luke interrupted. 'Sara could be Keira Knightley crossed with Rosalind Franklin, she could be fluent in six languages and play concert piano, she could run a four-minute mile without breaking into a sweat and she could have a fashion sense as well, and I still would have thought Linda had a right to know.'

Helen's face relaxed into a smile. 'Moralists shouldn't have a sense of humour.'

'I'm happy to be a moralist if it means telling the truth.'

'And Linda,' Jack asked, 'how did she respond to your news?'

Luke shrugged. 'The truth can hurt. But that doesn't make it less right.'

CHAPTER 12: Behind Closed Doors

Connie stood by the stove browning onions for a curry. Sara was seated at the kitchen table threaded to various electronic paraphernalia. Her ability to do several things simultaneously via an array of different modalities was nothing short of Olympian – and Connie had studied some of multi-tasking's best. She phoned, she texted, she chatted, she downloaded, she emailed and she also appeared to be working on her PhD thesis. And because Connie was peripheral to all this activity and she did not want him to feel neglected, she provided him with an ongoing commentary.

Connie had learned to cook during his first marriage, in service to a more equitable division of domestic labour. Initially reluctant, within a short time he had appointed himself household chef and had carried over the role into his subsequent marriages. He liked the physicality of cooking, the chopping and slicing, the tossing and stirring; he would draw in the smells with the same appreciation as perfumery's most fastidious nose and he had always been an indulgent taster. Yet amid all this flamboyance, there was also a solitary, soothing side to cooking, as with musical improvisation or Linda's knit-ting. And with a headache now lurking, it provided exactly the right prescription.

Please let it not be a migraine, he intoned silently. For these days there never was a single migraine but rolling storms of them, and he not knowing when the cycle would stop until seven, eight, nine, sometimes as many as twelve days later there would be twenty-four hours without pain and then another twenty-four and he would know the headaches were finished – at least for now. Day after dreadful day, the morn-ings crushed by pain, analgesics useless, and the migraine pills so efficient at expelling today's pain but with a cruel tendency to bring on tomorrow's in 'an unfortunate rebound effect' according to the non-migraine-suffering neurologist. Connie would swallow a pill and by midday the pain would have stopped, but not that shadow, that thumbprint which is pain's reminder who is boss. By mid-afternoon the drug hangover would have lifted sufficiently for unchallenging reading or bill paying. By night, at least in the early days of a cycle, he would be feeling good, suspiciously good – fresh and flushed through with non-pain, a short-lived respite because come four or five o'clock the next morning the migraine would return triumphant. Then would follow more pills and more respite, but never from the threat of pain, which terrorised more than the pain itself.

Since his return to Australia the migraines had been as frequent as anything he had ever experienced. He could not explain it, although was tempted to blame tonight's on Sara. She had said she would be home at six but did not wander in until eight. The weather had finally broken and she and her friends had decided to celebrate with a special pagan thanksgiving. And where, he had asked, had these pagan revels taken place? And when she mentioned a pokey bar in a back lane with uncomfortable seating, poor ventilation and a clientele unlikely ever to have heard of paganism, he was rammed by an anger so powerful it actually silenced him. A moment later he was castigating himself: he should have eaten, he should have worked, he should have done anything other than fill the time by waiting for her. It wasn't her fault; she hadn't forced him to wait.

He touched his head. The pain had coagulated in his right temple and when he added the spices to the onions it flared. But like coffee, curries could be kind to migraines, so he threw in some more spices and put up with the pain. Please, he prayed to an unknown being as non-believers *in extremis* tend to do, please make this headache disappear.

Linda sometimes could. There would be a hefty dose of aspirin and strong coffee at the first signs of a migraine and she would stroke his head, bending the hairs close to the tender scalp and stepping her fingers up and down the back of his neck. His wife was a no-nonsense sort of person but often very effective.

Some women are head-strokers and some like Sara are not. Although it was Sara's difference from Linda, her difference from everyone he knew that underscored her attraction. He had always been drawn to the new. ('Everyone is,' Linda had said during one of their recent disagreements. 'Far more difficult is finding newness, new interest in what you see every day.' She had paused before adding, 'Definitely not your speciality.') Sara was turned up high in a way that in others would be overwrought but in her was exciting. He knew his friends disapproved, that they believed him to be mesmerised by her youth, but the problem, if indeed there was a problem had nothing to do with Sara; rather, when it came to loving attention he was a glutton. His mother's fault of course, who had given him far too much love when he was a child, burdening him with an impossibly large appetite.

His three wives, Rosalie, Linda, even Susan the brief disaster in the middle, had all tried to give him what he wanted, and for a time he made it appear as if it were enough. Rosalie would have eventually tossed it in if he had not pushed her first, and how much happier she had been with his replacement; he left Susan to a childcare worker at the crèche; but Linda was not the sort ever to admit defeat – although, as it turned out, neither was she fool enough to remain where she was not wanted. But it would be different with Sara. He twisted around to look at her. She was chatting online to her sister and talking on her mobile to a friend, she was lit up and laughing, all of her was laughing. Sara believed in plundering life for all it could give; she feasted on passion. And while today's passion could quickly turn into tomorrow's leftovers, it thrilled him that she was constantly on the move. Sara filled him to the brim, she gave him plenty.

He added stock to the curry paste and started up a smooth stirring. He was determined to make this relationship work. In the past he had loved well and to his mind enjoyably, but never steadily. His mother's generation, although not his mother, would say he lacked backbone. Linda accused him of shallowness. But if anything was to account for his changing partners it was his poor tolerance for boredom. He glanced at Sara with all her paraphernalia, it was a quality he shared with her generation.

He poured in the remainder of the stock, slowly brought it to the boil, then turned the gas back to simmer. The fish would go in once the spices had cooked through. He made himself another large coffee, and with Sara still on the phone, he went into the living room to lie down. He tried to organise the cushions so as not to aggravate his head, but the pain fisted inside his skull no matter what he did. In the end he sat up and switched on the mid-evening news. There followed reports from Burundi, Somalia, the Middle East, insurgents – again – in Chechnya, terrorists in half a dozen different hotspots, unstoppable fires, runaway floods.

'How can you watch that stuff?' Sara said from the doorway. 'It's so depressing.'

An extravagant user of rhetorical questions, he knew she didn't expect an answer – and besides politics provided little common ground for them. So he simply smiled in her direction and turned back to the TV; a moment later she returned to the kitchen.

The drugs began to kick in and he plunged into one of those deep, irresistible, fifteen-minute sleeps, more like passing out than normal sleep. When he awoke, Sara was sitting next to him still hooked up to her devices, watching a reality show in which people forced into embarrassing situations shouted abuse at one another. Sara had assured him it had a cult following, and while he had tried to see the attraction, as far as he was concerned the show was tripe.

Nothing is perfect, he told himself as he rose from the couch to check on the curry, and life would be the lesser if it were. He lifted the lid off the pot. He stirred, he sniffed, he risked a taste; just a burn in the throat from the drugs. With his spirits raised he went into the bedroom to change and freshen up. He was aware of that grateful sloughing off of deadness when a migraine is receding. He felt lighter, more spirited than he had for days; maybe he had beaten this one, the cycle finally exhausted, and then he caught sight of himself in the wardrobe mirror and was felled more efficiently than by the most determined migraine.

It was one of those glimpses of the unprepared self, when the gaze is brutally objective. The face that confronted him was not the face he saw each morning as he shaved and moisturised and combed his hair. This image was recognisably himself, yet foreign and horrifying. There were bruised pouches beneath the eyes, trenches joined the nose to the corners of the mouth, harsh lines cut through the cheeks, jowls souped towards the neck, the neck itself sagged, and there was something shrivelled about the entire figure which simply did not gel with his version of himself.

Connie was appalled to think others might see him like this, that Sara might see him like this. Inside his skin he felt as always. Not for him the tiny crepuscular world of the old, not ever for him that obliviousness to everything beyond the stifling familiarity of the old man's hearth.

He forced himself to stand in front of the mirror. He straightened himself up, he cocked his head slightly to the side, he coached the neck out of its sags, he arranged the mouth into a part-smile and the rest of the smile he put around the eyes. The lines softened, the face filled out, he looked altogether firmer. Now he concentrated on the feel of the arrangement, to imprint it over that ashen, ancient parasite of himself. Never again did he want to see that used-up old man.

When he returned to the lounge, the yelps and groans of the TV show were blaring into an empty room. He switched the television off. Sara's laptop was propped on the couch and playing across the screen was her Sara-as-mermaid screensaver replete with glistening tail and bare breasts. Her mobile phone was gone, but then Sara never separated from that.

From down the hall, past the bedroom he heard the slam of a cupboard door, a drawer opening, the squeak of floorboards in the hall outside the bathroom, the faint clatter of make-up containers – Sara never shut the bathroom door – and finally the flush of the toilet. Connie heard these noises with the same heightened but distant awareness he had to sounds in an audience when he was giving a lecture. A short time later she was standing in the doorway of the lounge room, smelling sweet, lips glossed, stretches of shiny skin around a silvery garment. She was clearly going out.

'I thought we were having dinner here,' he said. And after a hesitation, 'Together.'

'And we were. But Jimmy has just called and he's at No-Names and feeling miserable and he absolutely needs me, and of course you could come too, but I know it's not your scene.' And before Connie could do anything so embarrassing as to negotiate, she stepped forward, kissed him on the mouth, squeezed a buttock – 'I won't be late, and that's a promise' – and was gone.

There was an amplified silence whenever Sara quit a room. Connie immediately switched the TV back on, turned the sound to a murmur in deference to his head, and then realised the headache had completely disappeared. That at least was something. He turned off the heat under the curry, he wasn't hungry, and even though he knew it to be unwise poured himself a scotch. The TV was an irritation and he switched it off again and sat on the couch sipping his drink, wanting to metamorphose into Wallace Stevens's 'thinking stone'.

The scotch mixed with the drugs and he fell asleep again, another fifteen minutes, but this time one of those calm sleeps that feel so much longer and a dream about Linda in their early days before the boys arrived. It was winter and she was shovelling fresh snow from the path. On either side of her, the drifts were piled high and white, and a delicate white piping along the black branches of the trees. She was wearing the same red jacket she wore in the photo he used to keep on his desk and she was laughing. He was not visible in the dream but the perspective was his. The satisfaction of it rolled through him even while he slept.

When he awoke he no longer wanted to be alone. Briefly he considered joining Sara and her friends, but common sense kicked in and he walked around to Ava's place instead. The front of the house was in darkness and he went around the back expecting to find her in her study. The living room lights were blazing, the curtains were not drawn. Connie stopped and stared, a frozen moment before collecting himself and pulling back into the shadows. Harry and Ava were on the couch. Harry was cradling Ava like a baby, stroking her hair, bending over her and talking to her. Connie felt a physical revulsion. This was not how he wanted to see Ava, and certainly not how he wanted to see her with Harry.

He rushed from the courtyard and hurried home. Baby Ava and bovine Harry: had the marriage always been like this? Such ghastly possibilities he couldn't bear to think about it. He poured himself another scotch and drank it far too quickly. He was chafing in the empty house. He tried reading, he tried the TV, he doodled with the script for his TV series. Ava clinging to the gruesome Harry. Sara just walking out. Where exactly did he fit in her life? Was Sara tiring of him? He missed his boys. The script was rubbish. He was rubbish. In the end he took a Valium and went to bed.

At three o'clock he awoke. Sara was not yet home. The Sara-appropriate action would be to text her, but he lacked both the energy and the goodwill for such a ridiculous form of communication. At six o'clock he awoke again. No headache – and still alone in the house. He showered and dressed and went out for a slow breakfast. He hoped Sara would return while he was gone. She did not. But as he stood in his study wondering what to do, a text came through: Jimmy very upset, too many drinks, stayed with him, home later – in her own inimitable shorthand.

It was now after nine, and knowing Harry would have left for the office, Connie again walked around to Ava's. A multiplicity of reasons: he didn't want to be alone, Ava could always fast-track to the core of a problem, and he needed to replace the pathetic curled-up figure in Harry's arms with a more congenial image. She answered the door within moments of his knocking, smiling that whole-face smile of hers and a waft of her lily-of-the-valley perfume as they embraced. Ava was floating in sky-blue over faded jeans and bore no resemblance to the creature in Harry's arms last night. Although she did look pale, and as soon as they were settled on the couch he asked if she was quite well. She was so slow in answering there was time enough to worry.

She was a little tired, she finally said, and pulled herself straighter on the cushions.

'But nothing serious?' Connie returned, aware too late that the phrasing of his question was far more effective in revealing his fears than anything it might elicit about her health.

Of course it wasn't serious, she said. And sitting there an arm's length away, still with that radiance which was uniquely hers, he was sure he could believe her.

'So what's the latest on the TV series?' she asked. 'And Sara – still thriving with her?' She hesitated before adding, 'And Linda – are the two of you managing to sort things out?'

Connie held nothing back and Ava let him talk, prompting occasionally with a question or comment. He could not explain how Sara's differences nourished him but it was more than the easy pleasures of novelty. He was working steadily, although to be entirely honest it was without the same drive. Yes, he and Linda were managing the divorce quite amicably. And no, he didn't miss her, not really, although he did miss the way she challenged him.

'Sara is of the generation that believes everyone's entitled to an opinion and that all opinions are equal.' He forced a grimace into a smile. 'It's not an attitude to push the work along.'

He readily admitted to missing his boys. 'I miss their stories, their confidences, their – *dailiness*.' He paused. 'I miss their unconditional little-boy love.'

More difficult to acknowledge was how much he missed America. And, as if to excuse himself, he added, 'The un-American part of America – Boston and the north-east.' He shrugged. 'Embarrassing, isn't it?'

Ava understood exactly how he felt. She was happy to be back in Australia but it didn't stop her longing for Oxford. 'Its age, its weather, the whole dynamic of the place, and of course its proximity to London and Europe.'

Connie, however, knew his absence from America was far more profound than this. 'I feel like I've separated from my life.'

'Despite Sara? Despite your new book? Despite the TV series?'

He nodded and told her about the rolling headaches, the subdued work, his general unease. 'I feel disorientated, a rootlessness, even a sense of exile.' He hesitated. 'I think America has become home in a way Australia no longer is.'

It was a reluctant admission from a member of the generation whose suspicion of America was so entrenched it would have endured without top-ups from more recent fiascos.

He rose from the couch and wandered the room. His trousers pooled from his buttocks, the wild hair was thinning, skin drooped on his neck and arms; youth seemed to be draining from him.

'I can't believe it,' he said, turning to face her. 'I'm suffering separation pains from the United States of America.'

'Are you sure this new-found attachment to America mightn't be something more personal? Separation from your boys? Separation from Linda?'

Connie shook his head. 'I love the immensity of America, I love its excesses, the too-tall buildings, the loud-mouthed people, their unabashed confidence. I love life itself turned up high.' He looked helpless. 'I love the place.'

He felt himself to be America in miniature, but he did not admit this to Ava. In Australia and England he had experienced a sense of struggling against the current. But in America he *was* the current – he was the whole bloody river.

Connie talked through the morning, there was no stopping him. Ava ignored the phone and when the doorbell sounded she ignored that too. Around midday the phone rang again. As she had done earlier, she let the call pass to the answering machine, but a few words into the message – it was a man's voice, as to anything else, Connie could not say – she was out of her chair and dashing to the phone.

And probably just as well, Connie decided, as he checked his watch. Already he felt so much better. Although this new sense of home was worrying. What if it were not intrinsic to America? What if he were to spend the next ten years in Canada or Mexico? Would Canada then become home? Would Mexico? Was it possible that given sufficient time the substance and sensibility of any place would seep into him in a type of cultural osmosis. He remembered reading an article about Daniel Barenboim, how Barenboim spoke five languages fluently, all with an accent – so many languages but at home in none.

He would have asked Ava her opinion but there was no opportunity. When she returned she explained that something had come up. She looked rattled and he assumed it was a work emergency. She apologised, she hoped he understood.

'Of course I do,' he said from the doorstep, 'of course. And thanks, Ava. If ever I can return the favour.' But the door was already shut.

CHAPTER 13: The Real World

1.

There was a specific moment following months of moments when Ava knew she was seriously ill. It was not during an interminable hour with a huge roaring machine scanning her head, nor later that week when the neurologist outlined the numerous cerebral dysfunctions that could be causing her symptoms. Nor after hours of testing by a neuropsychologist in which her language functions were shown to fall within the average range – no consolation whatsoever to a woman accustomed to a thriving language universe. The moment came months earlier when she was seated at her desk, a site she knew better than any specialist could know her brain. At her desk, that euphemism for mind, for thought, for her very self, sifting through pages riddled with crossings-out. She skirted around the gaps and blotches as she read the flabby sentences, and even though these afforded no pleasure neither were they cause for concern: all writers are far more familiar with sentences that fail to make the grade than those which do. It was the misspellings that shocked her. She saw the misspellings in her own hand and she was terrified.

Occasionally she was unable to begin a word, sometimes she would trip up part way through, other times she would complete a word only to suspect it was wrong. The familiar had turned strange and the more she picked at a word the stranger it became. Simple words like 'pencil', 'mountain' and 'glue' were more susceptible to sabotage than more abstract ones. But then a pencil was simply a pencil and glue was only glue, while sadness could be loss, grief, bewilderment, failure, terror.

Her spelling had collapsed. And now she could no longer ignore all the other problems. Her speech would stagger and ultimately stop over words which flickered just out of reach. Thoughts would enter her mind clear and tantalising and a moment later dissolve. Other times the thoughts were solid enough but the words were occluded – like a stutterer, although unlike the stutterer she could not even hit on the first sound. Or she would begin an utterance and forget where she was planning to take it, and be left dangling mid-sentence, desperate to gather herself and her gaping mouth and flee the conversation, yet forced to remain exactly where she was, terrified at what was happening even while she tried to disguise it. She would intend to go to the shop but before she had reached the end of the street she would have forgotten where she was heading. Once she lost her way in the cemetery, a place she had walked hundreds of times, and one of the gardeners had to guide her to the exit.

For someone with a good memory, forgetting is simply not an issue. Ava had never kept a meticulous appointment diary and her shopping lists were unfinished affairs. But now she was hounded by forgetfulness, the threat of it most of all; for if you don't know the substance of your forgetting, the best you can hope for is to know you have forgotten something. She found herself stepping around holes and cracks in memory: a name, a place, a book title, even her own book titles would suddenly drop into the darkness. She set herself memory tasks – names of flowers, the novels of Charles Dickens, but as likely as not would lose the thread before she had completed the task.

With the benefit of hindsight she realised the problems had started soon after she and Harry had returned to Australia. It had been easy back then to attribute them to the stresses of the move rather than some recurring cerebral nightmare. Yet as time passed and she realised how happy she was to be home, the move back to Australia failed as an explanation. As for the sludge on the slaughterhouse floor post-Fleur, after Fleur's flying visit to Australia she had been packed away surprisingly neatly.

Then there was the plodding novel. After six books Ava was well-acquainted with the adolescent unreliability of a work in progress, so it seemed reasonable to blame her work. She simply drove herself harder. While some days passed with only an occasional lapse, these became increasingly rare. Indeed, there were times when as soon as she commenced writing – hand-writing or computer it seemed to make no difference – the problems were so insistent she could not continue, and she would crouch at her desk dazed with terror waiting for the morning to finish.

Finally she had confided in Harry – the memory lapses, the word-finding problems, the stalled novel, she told him every-thing.

'My mind is in ruins,' she said.

He insisted there was nothing wrong and reminded her she had always had an exaggerated fear of losing her mind. 'Some people have spider phobias, others have rodent phobias, you have a degenerative-brain-disease phobia. And besides,' he added, 'if anything were seriously wrong, I'd be the first to notice.'

But he wouldn't, and Ava knew this. Despite their travels, their homes, their laughter and domestic talk, despite all the time spent together, never had he shared the workings of her mind – not because she had blocked him out, although in truth, the situation had suited her, but he seemed unable to enter. Her mind, he said, was a mystery to him. Whenever she produced the completed manuscript of her latest novel he always reacted with the same mixture of surprise and delight as to a conjuror's trick. And in fact he did regard her artistic creation rather like a magical process, as if her novels sprang fully formed from some fundamental but unreachable part of her. It was a surprising and endearing response, she had always thought, from a man whose commitment to the observable and the measurable was in all other respects watertight.

Her interaction with Jack, however, was very different and given the years of their correspondence, extravagantly verbal. So a few months earlier, at the height of the long summer, before the doctors, before the brain scans, before the neuropsychologist and her language tests, Ava had written to him. She knew he would have sat with her while she explained her problems, but she was scared and bewildered and flagrantly raw. A letter was by far the best option.

She wrote at length as she always had with Jack, and across a range of issues. She began with their friendship, how pleased she was that the uneasiness which had occurred when first he returned to Melbourne had dissipated; how there were so many possibilities to explore now they were living in the same city. She moved on to torture, which was then being discussed in the media, what it meant that a society would be having such a discussion in the first place. Some commentators were citing the 'lesser evil' argument and she knew Jack would oppose this as she did herself. She composed an argument against malleable ethics, or what certain people were touting with approval as 'situational ethics', in which ethics were reduced to a form of pragmatism no different to that which coursed through commerce, politics and civic life. From there she moved on to capital punishment. Even her primary-school-aged self had argued against the notion of 'lawful killing': if it is wrong for a murderer to take a life deliberately, she had said in a schoolroom debate, then it is wrong for the law to do the same. She wrote to Jack about the idiocy of ethicists and law-makers in the US who were currently discussing 'the most humane means of execution'. *The killing itself is assumed to be acceptable and civilised,* she wrote, *but they must be sure to do it nicely – as if deliberately causing pain would be morally reprehensible in a way the actual killing is not.*

From current social issues she moved on to a discussion of the novel she was currently reading – at that time, despite all the other problems, her reading was still relatively unspoiled – and followed with an analysis of a remarkably good film she had recently revisited, the name of which she could not initially remember, although it resurfaced while she was writing about it. *Memento.* She gossiped about Connie and his women, and followed a critical remark about Sara with what she hoped was a humorous and astute observation about Luke being the default setting for the next generation. She wrote the first half of the letter on her laptop and the second by hand just in case there was a difference. She finished by asking if he noticed any change in her writing style or language.

She received his reply, also by letter, two days later. He could detect no change, no change at all. And so great was her anxiety she decided to believe him. Yet practically anyone could have told her that Jack was not to be trusted when it came to judgments about her. For all the words she had written to him, all the ideas, thoughts, observations and musings, jokes, gossip, opinions on books and films, all these originating from her became something quite different when in Jack's court. Even when he was forging a life beyond the confines of his old obsession as he was now, so deeply entrenched was his habit that Ava could begin to write in Sanskrit and Jack would have made sense of it, not with any reference to her desires and intentions – obsession is stubbornly incompatible with empathy – but within the ever-accommodating coffers of his own love. At the time of Ava's letter, Jack was still more in thrall than he realised to a love entirely of his own creation.

Ava put her questions to a well-informed friend, and he, ever the lover, replied that he noticed no change. So the problem must be with her current novel. She knuckled down with even greater determination, but dead-ends multiplied, thin ice everywhere, characters and situations kept deserting her, the words themselves failed to materialise. She went for her customary walks, but rather than the usual clarification – it was Nietzsche who wrote that 'all truly great thoughts are conceived by walking' – her own thoughts remained a scramble and she would return to her desk more defeated than ever.

The long summer lurched into a botched autumn. Oak trees were left with thick clusters of brown leaves clinging horribly to their branches and plane-tree leaves littered the ground like scraps of brown paper. Only the elms met the challenge with a brighter than usual yellow. The weather cooled, the days grew shorter and Ava's problems hardened. This was, she finally acknowledged, no passing stress nor the anarchic squealing of a novel in progress, something was fundamentally wrong. Tossing between terror and disbelief she searched the cerebral dysfunction sites on the internet, the semantic dementias, the familial brain disorders, CADASIL and a clutch of other tidy acronyms for a brain turning to compost. She listened to Harry tell her that nothing was wrong. And finally she consulted a neurologist and a neuropsychologist who sent her for scans and administered tests.

The scans were inconclusive but according to the neurologist this was no cause for celebration because the smallest elements of the brain were still beyond the reach of the medical gaze. The neurologist concluded in his matter-of-fact way that her clinical signs together with the tests indicated a degenerative brain disorder, 'probably some sort of dementia'. He did not hesitate over the dreadful word. As many degenerative brain disorders ran in families, he advised her to contact her brother and any other close relatives.

Numb and disbelieving she did as she was told, but her contact details for Tim were twenty years out of date and yielded no leads. She telephoned her mother's sister. Janet had neither seen nor heard from Tim in years.

A few days later she and her aunt met for lunch in a city café. Janet was so excited. She was a member of a book club, she said. 'We read each of your novels as soon as they come out, even in hardcover.' She paused to take a mouthful of calzone. 'Amazing what they can do with a pastie these days.' And returning to her book club, 'I don't like it when they're critical of your books.'

Ava laughed. 'If the author can take criticism from strangers in the media, then the author's aunt should manage to take it from friends in her book club.'

She had no intention of telling Janet she was sick. They chatted about old friends and relatives, they swapped tales of old times and at an opportune moment Ava asked about the family's health. There was little to learn.

'Your mother was never sick when we were growing up,' Janet said. 'And if she had taken better care of herself – I was always telling her to give up the fags – she would have lived to a ripe old age.'

Janet could provide even less information about her father. 'You look a lot like him,' she said. 'Such a handsome bloke, but a no-hoper as a father and husband.' There was a long thoughtful pause before she added, 'He's probably still knocking around the outback.'

Her father in the outback? Her mother's version had him as a womaniser who had dumped the family for a worthless floozy, then drunk himself into an early grave.

'It made your mother feel better to think that,' Janet said. 'Some men just aren't made for family life.' She paused as if unsure whether to continue. 'I expect your mother never told you he sent her money, regular as clockwork the first of every month.' Ava shook her head, she had not known. 'Your mother used to complain like blazes when a 31-day month finished just before the weekend. She wanted a postal delivery on Saturday and every month to be February.'

When they said their farewells they promised they would keep in touch. 'I have a mobile now,' Janet said. 'The children gave it to me for my seventieth birthday.' She wrote out the number. 'You ring me any time, dear.'

They hugged each other.

'I should have done more for you when you were young,' she said, before turning away.

Ava didn't really want to know if her father had bequeathed her a brain condition and made only a half-hearted attempt to find him. Neither of them it seemed were made for family life. Although she far preferred an irresponsible, renegade, anti-social father to the cold, duty-bound, blameless mother of her childhood. And while she knew an absent parent could claim a certain mystique denied a single woman encumbered by children and a stream of bills, she still opted for the father.

Ava had always steered her own way through life and she was not about to change now. Whenever she considered the progression of this thing – 'thing' rather than the neatly vague 'condition' and certainly not the blowtorch blast of 'dementia' – she would see a mechanical doll turning slower and slower as the motor wound down. It was not to be borne.

Considerations of God and afterlife were irrelevant to a life-long atheist, and while the feelings of those who loved her were not, she knew that Harry, her friends too, would not want a half-strength Ava. She had seen far too many elderly women with glazed stares led through public gardens by jolly smiling daugh-ters or long-suffering husbands – 'See the pretty flowers, dear. Aren't they lovely?' – or admiring the food at the market – 'Smell the heavenly smells, dear' – or oohing and aahing over a baby in a pram – 'Look at the tiny baby, dear' – or patting a dog in the street – 'Feel the soft puppy, dear' – demented women led by the arm, or worse, by the hand and always lagging a little behind, never quite sure where they were. For Ava the situation was glaringly simple: if she couldn't work, if she couldn't remember, if she couldn't reason or imagine, if she couldn't communicate, then she was in essence already dead.

Her face looked just the same, the hair that Harry sweetly if prosaically called her golden fleece looked just the same, she saw herself as she had always been, yet beneath the unchanged exterior she was rotting. She hated what was happening to her and she hated that she could do nothing to stop it. Harry would hold her face between his hands, 'My own lovely Davey,' he would say, as if nothing had changed.

If a disease were to attack only her face like this thing was destroying only her mind, she wondered if she'd be less terrified, less angry, less helpless, less not herself. She had always operated with the confidence of an attractive person and had carried herself through a multitude of publics knowingly supported by the benefits which accrue. So how would she cope if her face were to be wrecked? And she was sure, as sure as one can be with hypothetical disasters, that as much as she would despise the way she looked, as much as she would rage against the unfairness of it, as much as it would cause her to withdraw from public life, she, Ava Bryant, would still exist. She could still claim words and thoughts and imagination and memory sufficient enough to confirm her self as herself. She could still work, and she could still enjoy the company of her husband, her friends, film, music, even travel. And equally she was sure she would want to live.

A degenerative brain condition, she concluded, was the worst that could happen to her. And there was no real respite. She might be reading or listening to music and for a brief time she would not be aware of her disintegration. But when the music finished or the book was closed, the loss together with what she was in the process of losing overwhelmed. The good moments only reminded her of what she was becoming.

She knew exactly what she must do. But knowing did not stop her from resenting the situation, resenting the solution, resenting the loss of a future, resenting all that was left undone. If you know in advance you have only forty good years, then you live very differently than if you assume the usual eighty. She wasn't ready but circumstances had given her no choice. She and Harry would face this illness and its management together – management, what a pliable euphemism that was; with her competence no longer to be trusted, she needed him more than ever.

She waited for a Friday to broach the subject, giving them the whole weekend to make plans. She went to the market to buy food for a picnic dinner and was forced to take a taxi home when unsure of which tram to catch. She spread a picnic rug on the living-room floor, arranged cutlery and serviettes, put the food on platters and the platters on the rug. When Harry arrived home he found her dithering over the oysters and fresh prawns wondering whether she should put them back in the fridge. He off-loaded his work gear and came to admire the array. The cheese first, and such a delight to see his favourite ewe's milk blue, then the seafood selection – the South Australian oysters really took his fancy as she hoped they would; the antipasto platter with olives and roasted capsicum and dolmades was worthy of a Cézanne, he said, and the baguette with a chewy rather than crusty texture could be straight from Paris.

'This,' he said, 'is a perfect picnic.'

They settled on the floor. He poured the wine and they helped themselves to the food. Before he had tasted a thing

Harry turned to her and hugged her close. She heard his muffled, 'I'm so proud of you – although I've never doubted you. Never.' And a pause: 'We'll manage.'

That marked the end of the perfect picnic. She took his 'we'll manage' as her starting point: how pleased she was he had raised the topic, how he had always understood her so well, how fortunate she had been in her marriage, how much happiness they had enjoyed. And while they had assumed there would be a good many years more, with her brain turning to mush they would do what needed to be done, and do it together, and –

'Hush,' he said, 'hush. You're wrong. It's not over. Nothing's over. For better or for worse, and I meant it.' He put his hands on her shoulders and turned her towards him. 'I've stuck by you through some pretty bad times and I certainly don't plan to stop now.'

He surely couldn't be referring to Fleur. She didn't stop to ask, had to stay on the main track. But he fought all her arguments, he fielded all her objections. He was, and he could not have been more emphatic, utterly opposed to ending her life. And besides, he said, she was being precipitous. 'We don't even have a proper diagnosis yet.'

According to the neurologist, a diagnosis often could not be made until post-mortem examination of the brain. She was about to remind him of this when she ordered herself yet again to stick to the point. She moved away from him and perched on the edge of an armchair.

'Every week I'm worse.'

To help end her life, he said, would be a betrayal of the very love she had always relied on.

'But if you truly loved me then you'd want what's best for me.'

'I know what's best for you.' He was implacable. And before she could interrupt, he continued. 'I've never been one of those fools who kills the thing he loves, and I'm not about to start now. And I mean kill,' he spat the word out. 'Such acts are entirely self-defeating.'

'But this concerns me,' her voice was very quiet, 'not you.' She stood up and moved even further away. The smell of the food was making her sick. Something was.

He disagreed. 'You and I have been married half our lives. I've loved you and cherished you and cared for you all that time. And I'll continue to love you and cherish you and care for you. I don't see that anything essentially has changed.'

'Everything has changed. Already I'm not myself.' She grabbed a serviette and blew her nose. 'I can't believe you're doing this to me.'

'I loved you at your most unappealing.'

'An affair is not the same as a degenerative disease, Harry.'

He remained impervious. 'I loved you when you were revealing your worst. Whatever changes *may* occur as a result of this illness will be less unappealing than those I've already witnessed.'

She guessed what he meant without struggling through the negatives.

'You're not thinking of me, Harry. Of what I want.'

'I love you, Ava. You can't expect me to kill you.'

Briefly it occurred to her she might be better off without him, that he would sap her strength at a time when she most needed it. But she could not manage without him when she was well, so there was absolutely no question now she was ill. So, angry, resentful and hurt as she was, she told herself to move forward. With Harry continuing to love and care for her as he had always done, she should manage to take charge of this one area in which he had failed her.

2.

The following week Harry suggested Ava invite the friends around for a Sunday night meal.

'Just like in the old days at Oxford,' he said.

He was thinking of what would please her, for given the state of the NOGA fellowship program Connie, Jack and Helen were the last people Harry would choose to entertain. He made the suggestion and, with an entirely different agenda in mind, Ava arranged the evening. Now all of them were congregated in the kitchen with drinks and savouries and catching up on one another's news while Harry prepared a cheese and caramelised onion tart for their dinner.

Connie was finishing his second glass of wine and while he looked as haggard as Ava felt, his spirits had clearly lifted. Nothing to do with Sara, in fact since his arrival he had hardly mentioned her. His TV series was on the move again; a new pilot had been scheduled, with a new production team and a whole new approach. Harry, who must have been briefed on these developments, did not look up from rolling the pastry.

Helen seemed stripped of her usual spark; even her clothes, a scatter of browns, were uncharacteristically dull. Luke did not want to leave Australia, she said. And while he was old enough to make his own choices, she had decided to delay her own return to the States in the hope he would change his mind.

Of them all, only Jack seemed happy. He talked about his latest essay, 'The End of Originality' – 'The artists are giving it a wonderful reception,' he said. 'And a publisher has approached me about a collection.'

'And your new Islam book?' Harry did not sound pleased.

'That can wait,' Jack said.

Ava stood at one end of the kitchen propped against the bench, observing each of her friends as potential solutions to her problem. Jack was replenishing her drink and passing her food, clearly delighting in his role. But for all that he was easier in her company, she knew that for much the same reasons Harry couldn't help her neither could Jack. As for Connie, festooned with his own concerns – his boys, his divorce, Sara, the new pilot – and drinking far too much, he was not a reliable prospect. That left only distracted, anxious and working-eighteen-hour-days Helen.

Her friends chattered on. At first she tried to follow, but the effort required was too much. She let the words sink into meaningless noise, responding only to the rhythms of the conversation, smiling when the others smiled, looking concerned when they looked concerned, shaking her head, grimacing, raising eyebrows, shrugging shoulders in unison with them, folded into a sort of semi-conscious limbo space unknown to her before she became ill. Harry must have noticed, for as soon as the tart was in the oven he came and stood beside her, taking over from Jack in looking after her. She didn't mind, she understood his need. She only wished he understood hers.

The meal was finished, they were lingering at the table over coffee and chocolates. Ava looked at Jack, Helen and Connie in turn, she rehearsed her opening line, then she began. 'There's something I need to tell you.'

Harry leapt out of his chair and joined her down the other end of the table.

'There's something I need to tell you,' she said again. 'You may have noticed – '

'Ava's not well,' Harry cut in.

She looked at him and shook her head: this was her illness, these were her friends.

But he was determined. 'Nothing is certain,' he said, 'nothing is conclusive. Considerable mystery surrounds her symptoms – '

'But there is something wrong.' She gave each word a pronounced shove.

Harry met her gaze. 'Yes, there is probably something wrong – or rather it's unlikely that there is nothing wrong.'

Connie, Jack and Helen looked confused – not surprised and certainly not shocked, just confused.

'What is this illness?' Helen finally said. 'Is it serious?'

Ava silenced Harry with a firm hand to his arm. She had a job to do. 'The neurologist referred to a form of semantic dementia.'

They all looked horrified, exactly as she had been when the neurologist first uttered the terrible word.

'You're too young for dementia,' Connie said. 'Aren't you?'

Ava composed a wry smile. 'Apparently not.'

'No one knows the precise condition nor its cause,' Harry said quickly, 'nor any notion of its progression – '

'Or treatment,' Ava added.

'You mean this illness can't be fixed?' Jack looked to be in pain.

Ava shook her head.

'But what will happen to you?'

Again Harry went to respond and again Ava stopped him. 'There are many different types of dementia,' she said, as if reciting from a textbook. 'They begin with different symptoms, but all of them,' and she looked at Harry, 'all of them end up exactly the same way.'

'But Ava and I will manage,' Harry said. His eyes were wet and he reached for her hand. 'We will manage.'

Ava wanted to shake him off, not because she didn't feel sorry for him, not because she was unmoved by those rarely seen tears, but she needed to get on with the job. Although as she took in the stunned, distressed faces of her friends, she realised there was probably nothing more to be done now. In a few days, after the news had settled, she would approach Helen.

'You must have access to any number of lethal substances,' Ava said, as she and Helen strolled through the university on their way to lunch the following week.

'A smorgasbord of them,' Helen replied. 'Although more a well-stocked bank vault these days. The restricted stuff is kept under lock and key. It needs to be signed for in duplicate, in triplicate, in quadruplicate. It's time-consuming and a blasted nuisance.'

When you have only one issue on your mind and there's only one reason for making a statement or asking a question you assume your motives are transparent. Encouraged by Helen's tone and taking for granted she knew the point of this conversation, all that was required, so Ava thought, was for the two of them to plan the heist.

'So what would be the best way to get what we needed?' And after the briefest pause, 'I assume you know what would be the most effective?'

Helen stopped and turned to face Ava. She squinted behind her glasses. She spoke slowly, carefully. 'Let me get this straight. You want me to supply you with something from the lab? Something lethal?' She spoke as if the words themselves were poisonous.

Ava smiled and nodded.

Helen lowered her gaze and stood shaking her head through a long silence. 'I can't believe you're asking me this, Ava,' she said at last. 'I couldn't take – steal – materials from the lab.' There was neither sadness nor apology in her voice, if anything she sounded affronted. 'If I were discovered taking restricted substances, taking them illegally, my career would be finished. And even if I could get away with it, I wouldn't do it. It's entirely at odds with my professional ethics.'

With her comprehension not reliable these days, Ava did not at first trust what she was hearing. But Helen quickly dispelled any doubt.

'I couldn't steal poisons for you,' she said. 'It'd be professional suicide. I'm sorry, Ava,' and she put her arms around her. 'I hate what's happening to you and I'd do anything to help, but not this.'

Ava could understand Harry and Jack: they couldn't assist because they loved her too much. But Helen refused to help because she loved science too much. She shook herself out of Helen's embrace. She was alone, entirely alone.

3.

When winter finally arrived it did so with a fanfare from Antarctica. July was cold and August was freezing, but the crisp icy days Ava had always loved had come too late. Harry bought her pots of cyclamen bursting with bright, beautiful flowers. Too late, she thought, too late, and left them to die. Two weeks passed until she could bear it no longer, the long slender stems drooping over the sides of the pots, the flowers shrivelling into morbid stickiness. She watered the plants, she fed them, she hovered over them and protected them, and all the while she longed for someone to do the same for her.

She was making plans slowly, but then everything was slow these days. And while she made her plans she had her consolations. Several times a day she would slip into her semi-conscious limbo state, so safe and silent and trustworthy. And she gave herself over to Harry, who looked after her lovingly and efficiently. He was working at home a good deal more in order to care for her and his ministrations helped them both.

And art was another of her consolations.

'If I were to have collected anything,' she said to Jack at a recent exhibition of contemporary Australian art, 'it would have been paintings.'

They were standing in front of a small canvas, a shadowy cityscape of tall straight-edged buildings and what looked like a double-storey freeway ramp on one side. 'And look there,' she said, pointing to the window of one of the buildings. In the painted gloom was a human figure watching the scene beyond the window.

'That's me these days. Silently watching.'

And Jack was her final consolation. Three mornings a week he turned up just before ten as Harry was about to leave for the office. He relayed the latest gossip, he read to her from the newspaper, he told her stories she did not always remember from their shared past. When the weather was fine they would go for a walk, sometimes they went out for an early lunch; often they visited galleries and once a week he arrived with food and cooked the evening meal for her and Harry.

Jack these days had a future far more lavish than his past. As well as his essays, he was writing shorter articles on a range of topics: refugees and race riots, political leadership and personal expediency, the compromises of democracy, the threat to creativity in today's cultural climate. The pleasures of regular completions, he told Ava, were so much greater than the fanfare every few years that accompanied a book.

Even his Islam specialty had taken a new direction following a forum where he had shared the stage with a young Australian-born Muslim. This woman, a lawyer, had later contacted him with the suggestion of a series of public conversations. 'Not that you Western liberals have done much for us,' she had been quick to add. But a male and a female, a Muslim and a Jew, would, she believed, lend distinctive and interesting flavours to their intellectual positions. But it was what they shared, she said, their liberal, moderate stance, that would prove to be their greatest strength. 'Where we discuss and argue, where we employ reason and compromise, those with more extreme views would simply attack each other – if, that is, they were to talk at all.'

The first of the discussions had attracted a large and diverse audience – although not Harry, Jack told Ava. 'It seems I'm still not producing the work he and NOGA expect of me.' Ava ignored the comment as she had always ignored these asides about her husband. Two more discussions were planned with the woman lawyer and a follow-up series of articles under their joint authorship.

And Jack was playing his guitar again.

'I'm so pleased about your music,' Ava said one day as they sat at the kitchen bench eating a sandwich lunch.

He smiled. 'Words and music, two of my great loves.'

And welling up from goodness knows where in her brain: 'The two great imperishables.'

'You truly believe that the best of words and music endure?' Jack asked. And when she nodded, 'And you want that for your own work?'

She took her time to put the words together properly. 'It's what any writer would want,' she said finally. 'I'll be gone, but my books will live on.'

It was Ava's suggestion he bring his guitar when he came to visit. His playing and singing were restful, she said, but at the same time she felt her senses were exercised.

'When you play,' she said, 'I'm reminded there's still some of my old self left.'

Often she would toss off these references to what was happening to her, and Jack would never know how to respond. Not even in his private thoughts could he consider the course of this illness, although looking at her it was easy to forget she was sick. She was still the most beautiful woman he knew. She did not look particularly tired, she did not look particularly pale, she was thinner, but her loosely flowing clothes helped camouflage this. When he questioned her weight loss, she said it would be masochistic to feed what was fast being wrecked.

So much time the two of them spent alone, and with all the sharp yearnings soft now like an old comforter, Jack found himself properly enjoying her company. She called herself a half-strength person and would refer to the old Ava as the real Ava – 'not this ruin', yet he was seeing her more fully than ever before. It was as if the two of them had finally settled into each other. And yet he knew how much she was suffering. She hated what she was becoming, she hated what was left. Even when she spoke like Ava of old she felt no pleasure.

'A sentence or two in the old mould just grinds in the losses more harshly,' she said. 'I'm taunted by my used-to-be self.'

For him it was all too easy to forget what was happening to her, and then something would wrench him back.

'Read me your latest article,' she said one morning.

What she really meant was: Read it to me, Jack, because I can't manage it myself.

He recalled her question of several months ago, whether he could help a sick friend end her life. He tried not to think how he would answer now. He hoped she would not ask.

CHAPTER 14: Into the Silence

1.

Ava had always been attached to weather, not simply as background to the movements of a day but as connective tissue to mood, and today was perfect – early spring, cool with a white sun and a crisp wind. Standing at the long window of her study she gazed down at the courtyard, observing it as one might a masterpiece. Leaves still yellow from last autumn lay in an impressionistic spotting on the dark garden beds. Along the shady boundary her azaleas all in flower were soft like a Renoir. Scattered across the paving were pots of colour, polyanthus and cinerarias just starting to bloom, and Harry's cyclamens still going strong. She observed the scene with a pleasing appreciation as if she had all the time in the world. Rituals seemed appropriate at a time like this.

For some inexplicable reason it had to be done right, inexplicable because she was an atheist, although an increasingly shoddy one. With the passage of years she had found it impossible to ignore those unheralded blood-flushing intrusions of a presence or presences beyond earshot of rationality. That she was about to discover the truth brought her no satisfaction: it was a ridiculously high price to prove a belief. Yet the conviction it had to be done right remained, not in the sense of pulling it off, she was sure she would, but observing a certain form, a certain reverence for the life that had been filched from her. The right room, her desk and papers, her books, the cool weather, her old cashmere jumper, even the right view. The last view of life – it sounded so melodramatic, but perhaps everything about death has a touch of melodrama, even the fading of a nonagenarian in bed, the shutting down of ancient organs, the lengthening pauses between breaths, the tiny splutters, the sudden stillness, the absolute end.

Through the years and several different Oxford dwellings Ava had always set up home in her study, each study arranged identically despite the rooms being larger or smaller, flanked by many windows or few, hot rooms, cold rooms, silent or noisy. Always there was her desk and chair, the stack of three drawers, her books installed in their usual configuration, the filing cabinet, the chipped mug she used as a pen holder, the same photos on display, the corkboard muffled with old notes, the mask from Venice, a stone frog the origin of which she had now forgotten.

And in a similar way she experienced home in her garden. Sometimes the garden had been just a cluster of pots or a window box, once there was the full regalia including a lawn, and these past few years this small courtyard garden. She wondered what would happen here after she was gone. Harry was no gardener, and besides, the house was too big for one person. Who might live here next? And would they preserve her garden? As a legacy there would be her books, yet the garden as an expression of self was a legacy too, an inexorably pleasurable one.

'Inexorably pleasurable.' She repeated the phrase aloud. How odd it sounded. And repeated it again and again until all she heard was a collection of sounds divorced from any meaning.

She turned away from the window as if that would remove the confusion, her poor brain struggling in the disease's oily spill. For years she had pondered the notion of meaning without language; now she knew all about it but lacked the words to explain it.

There were times when she really could not believe what was happening and it would take a doctor's appointment or the withered stump of a once-thriving recollection, or a book open but making no sense to confront her with the hard facts: she was losing her mind, there would be no repeal, she had a job to do. But mostly she had stayed on track, driven by a robust and unmerciful terror. She'd had to labour through each stage alone, making lists to fill in for her crippled memory and discarding them when each item had been crossed off. She laboured secretly and to be honest, resentfully, for she should not have to do this alone. But the major resentment was always of the thing itself: she should not have to do this at all.

The disease had invaded her like termites; she touched, tasted and smelled the useless dust of decaying cortex. And while she was more scared than she had ever been in her life, scared of killing herself, scared she might bungle it, she was adamantly not afraid of death itself. She had always believed that death was as fundamental to being human as birth and maturation. It should have made the act of killing herself easier, but nothing made it any easier.

She sat down at her desk and checked her last list. All the items were ticked off, she tore the paper up and threw it in the bin. She had been nagged by those common sayings, the need 'to settle your affairs', 'to put your house in order'; she expected she had used such expressions herself. But death fills the whole screen, or rather the act of ending life does. Such intervention into the natural course of things demands all your logic, all your attention; suddenly she was required to sky-dive, she who had never cared for heights. It was too much to expect she would put her affairs in order as well.

She cleared a space on her desk and lined up her three pens parallel but not touching, her three fountain pens marking the three major journeys of her life. On the left, the full-bodied, red-orange Parker Duofold from Stephen, nearly eighty years old and still her favourite – a graduation gift, Harry believed, from one of her high school teachers; in the middle, the silver modernity of Fleur's Lamy; and on the right, the elegant black and gold Waterman from Harry.

He had been so happy when she asked him for a fountain pen. It was her first birthday back in Australia, Fleur was in England; the past, so he believed, had finally been relegated to the past. And how hard she had tried to work with his pen. But despite its elegance it was never as smooth nor as comfortable as Stephen's Big Red. As for Fleur's Lamy, like Fleur herself, it had never been a good fit. Eventually she returned to Stephen's pen, although she kept the truth from Harry.

Gifts come bursting with attachments. Harry's Waterman was bigger with hopes and expectations than ever could be squeezed inside the cap and barrel of a pen. Yet when she settled on Stephen's pen she was choosing an object not a person. A writer's tools are few, you use whatever helps the work. With Stephen's pen there was an ease of flow, a lovely stretch of sinew as she wrote, the wrist seamless with hand and arm and not the stiffened pivot it became with Harry's pen.

And there was the weight of history in Stephen's Duofold, the engraving on the barrel, JES 1928, in Old English lettering and a queer privilege to use this pen that had belonged to John Edgar Smith or Jane Elizabeth Scott or the more exotic Jacqueline Eve Slonim. A writer uses whatever works best and it is quite separate from the character of the giver. For Stephen was never more comfortable than Harry, although, like the pen, his advantages had endured. Her life would have been very different without him.

Ms Bryant could put passion into growing potatoes.

The sentence fell into her mind. A reviewer? A publisher's grab? Where on earth had it come from? And why now?

Ava put the Lamy in a drawer. Stephen's pen she slipped into its felt pouch and placed on the shelf containing her favourite books. She took a sheet of paper and using his Waterman she wrote to Harry. It took just a moment – no noble world-worn insights, no humorous asides putting death in its place; she had finished her deliberations long ago and now just wanted it over.

She shuffled through the stack of envelopes she and Harry had collected from hotels around the world and settled on one from Paris, the small family-owned hotel on the Left Bank where they had spent their honeymoon and to which they had returned many times since. One of their special places, it was off the tourist track but so perfectly located that with a precarious leaning from the tiny wrought-iron balcony of their room they could see the flying buttresses of Notre Dame.

She propped the letter against her computer where Harry couldn't miss it. She had cleaned out her email and computer files weeks ago just in case she lost the ability. As it happened it had not been necessary, but the disease was so sly, so well-armed with dirty tricks, she felt she had to be prepared. She had always rejected anthropomorphism but it didn't matter now. This disease was a terrorist, a monster, a psychopath. This disease was a murderer.

She checked her watch, half past ten, still plenty of time for a leisurely amble to the end and no possibility Harry would return early. He had a day of meetings following his ten o'clock session with the therapist – the same man who had been assigned to them when the disease had first been recognised. 'To help you get through this,' he had said at the first and only session Ava attended.

'Seems to me the disease will take me through with or without your help,' Ava had remarked.

The counsellor had countered with a speech about adjustment issues. But Ava was still functioning well enough to argue that adjustment to a degenerative condition seemed to be an exercise in futility. 'You make your adjustment only to discover the horse has bolted, or the drama has shifted, or the whole bloody landscape has changed.' She paused to swallow her distress before adding, 'Choose your own metaphor.'

The counsellor had then moved on to grief and anger issues, but Ava had never unpicked herself in front of a stranger and was not about to start. In fact she didn't want to unburden herself to anyone, all she wanted at that particular time was knowledge. So after the first meeting she opted for the library and the internet and left the counsellor to Harry.

After she was gone, Ava suspected Harry would continue his sessions, he and the therapist passing a weekly hour together in the rich swirl of life's offerings. And how it irked her. The future was like fiction, so she had always thought, a ream of blank pages waiting to be filled. The books changed, the scenery changed, the characters in life and fiction changed, but whether teetering on the brink of a new novel or a new city or a new relationship she would experience wonder. Not to have a future. It was the greatest of her resentments.

She left her study and crossed the courtyard to the house. She tucked her hair into a clasp, applied fresh lipstick and went to the toilet. For the last wash of her hands she used a small tablet of pure lavender soap, there was no point in saving it any longer. Finally she dabbed on some Je Reviens, not out of any macabre irony but because she liked the scent. Then she took a last walk through the house.

For weeks she had been rehearsing this last hour, for not knowing what else the disease would destroy she had to be sure she could do what was required. And again she was struck by how unfair it was that of all the wounds to shut her down this disease had fed on her words. If there was a God, he was a cruel bastard, or given the play of her life, a vengeful one. But then happiness is always part angel and part debt-collector.

Had she faced death courageously? Not particularly, although courage did not really figure in this. But anger did, and an envy sharp as thorns, and a sense of deprivation that caught like a vice. And she would find herself arguing with something or someone: What have I done, to deserve this? What right have you to mete this out to me? Bloody death and far too soon, bloody disease without a cure. For if the lesions, now quite clear on the scans, had occurred in her breast or uterus or lung or liver, if they had occurred practically anywhere but in her brain, she would have fought and won and lived for years to come.

She was told by one expert, who seemed to know every-thing except how to cure her, that anger was bad for her. These doctors with all their advice were useless. And the one thing they can do they refuse. 'I'm trained to save lives,' the neurologist said when she asked him to save her from a long and protracted dying. And how could she lecture him about the invisible seam connecting life to death, how life is more than a simple drawing of breath, how life without the capacity to remember is no life at all? How could she explain this with her language in tatters and the doctor so self-righteous in all his damned ignorance?

She collects Valium, water, a glass and her favourite single malt and returns to the study. She takes from the bottom drawer of her filing cabinet a plastic bag with an elastic collar – not her choice, but what else is available when barbiturates are not? She positions herself on the carpet near the window and swallows fifty milligrams of Valium with a glass of well-diluted Cardhu, enough of both to put her out but not so much to make her sick. She takes in a last view of her garden. It shimmers through the glass. Her head is light her whole body is levitating. She opens her collected Eliot to *Prufrock* and reads or recites or remembers – whatever she is doing it is sweetly comforting – and nestles into the yellow fog. What will her life be measured in? Why did Eliot choose coffee spoons not teaspoons? And pulls the plastic bag over her head. She checks the pillow – no time, eyelids closing, impossible to stay awake, such relief to sink back, the sound of her own breathing, and rustling, a rustling of trees, trees in her study and sinking into the pillow down and down.

And suddenly she's awake. She's tearing at the plastic, she's tearing it from her face. She defies the Valium, she defies the scotch, she defies the desire to die. She's tearing at the plastic. Can't help herself. Her body rears up, it's fighting carbon dioxide. The bag is in her hands, she shoves it in the drawer, she grabs the note and shoves that in the drawer too. No one must know, no one must suspect. She drags herself to her feet, she drags herself down the stairs, she drags herself across the courtyard into the house. She staggers past the couch, she staggers past Harry's room, at last she reaches her own bedroom. And even as she is falling asleep she is furious at being reduced to a plastic bag over her head, furious at her failure to bring it off, furious at having to cover her tracks. There's no privacy when you're ill. And there's no bloody justice.

2.

There's a mysterious, not-quite-conscious dynamic that develops between people in a close and long marriage. Exaggerated gestures, twitchy eye contact, a particular choice of words that would be irrelevant to other people are significant to a partner. And there was something about Ava this morning that is haunting Harry, just a scraping at the edge of consciousness while he was at his counselling session but far stronger now.

He tries to shake it off with a cup of peppermint tea and the morning papers, but it will not be ignored. A shuffling of guilt for leaving Ava alone all day? General anxiety about her diminishing abilities? And suddenly he neither knows nor cares but he has to go home, he has to see she is safe, the phone will not do. He grabs his coat, gives instructions to his secretary and rushes out of the office. The way Ava looked at him this morning, her farewell hug, he cannot put his finger on it but something was not right.

Both lifts are at the ground floor. He pounds the call button. At last they begin to climb. Come on, he says through gritted teeth, come on. The lifts are rising in tandem. They stop, they start, they stop, they start. Closer they come to the twenty-seventh floor, closer and closer then both soar past. Both of them are heading to the penthouse suite. How many people could possibly be up there? At last one descends. The doors open, the lift is empty. Express to the ground, and he keeps his finger pressed on the 'door closed' button. But the system overrides him. The lift stops at nine different floors. The screeching inside him threatens to burst. When the lift reaches the ground he pushes out first, dashes across the lobby and into the street. There's a line of cabs. The fellow in the first car looks like he just got off the boat, but the driver behind has the appearance of a man who hasn't left his cab for a couple of decades.

The driver protests: Ya gotta take the first one, mate.

Harry ignores him and jumps into the passenger seat. He gives the address.

The cabby shrugs and pulls into the traffic.

It's a quagmire.

Harry is desperate. 'I need to get home.' He raises his voice. 'Matter of life and death.'

And suddenly the cabby perks up. He pulls down on the steering wheel, whips out of the traffic, clips a wedge of foot-path, enters a narrow lane. A right turn into a bluestone alley and the car jolts and rocks over the clotted stone. He dashes up slender alleys, he cuts across a vacant lot, he weaves through a building site, he negotiates lanes built for bikes and hand-carts. No danger, he says, everyone will get out of the way. No worries, he says, he'll have Harry home in a jiffy. He runs a set of lights. He overtakes a car on the inside. What about the police? Harry asks. Better things to do, says the cabby. He turns into Lygon Street at the southern end of the cemetery. He plants his foot. They're doing eighty kilometres an hour along the tram tracks.

Ten minutes later the cab pulls up outside his house. Harry shoves a fifty at the driver and is out of the car, calling Ava's name even before he opens the front door. Down the hall and into the living room. Ava, Ava, where are you? Then to the kitchen – where is she? He opens the back door, is about to cross to her study when he stops and turns back into the house. He enters her bedroom.

And there she is. She's slung across the bed on her back, a pillow under her head. From the doorway he notices the rise and fall of her breathing. She's asleep – odd for her to be sleeping on her back – but undoubtedly asleep. Her colour is good, she's breathing normally, she's all right. And hasn't he told her to rest? Take naps during the day, he has said to her, conserve your energy.

He sits gently on the edge of the bed, careful not to wake her. He watches the rise and fall of her chest; her breaths draw slow and deep. She's wearing the cashmere jumper he gave her for her thirty-first birthday. He reaches out and lays his hand over her heart. Her chest rises and falls, his hand rises and falls. If only he were able to channel his life into her. Down his arm out of his hand into her skin through her ribcage into her heart into her blood, his life pumping life into her body and making her well. He focuses on his arm and hand, wills something – heat? energy? life? – to flow from him to her. But it won't work, the exercise is far too contrived for a man like him. But he wants to believe, he wants to believe he can save her.

She snuffles in her sleep, her eyes move behind the lids, there are her usual purrings and murmurings. He catches a whiff of alcohol, her perfume or cleanser. His girl, his Davey, still so beautiful. He will never be ready to lose her.

He sits on the edge of her bed. His hand rises and falls on her breast, while she sleeps on.

CHAPTER 15: The Ghost of Youth

1.

There were several trams lined up in the street outside Flinders Street Station. Ava boarded one with a number more familiar than the others on the assumption she must have taken this route as a girl. In the late morning lull the tram was almost empty yet she was still vacillating in the aisle when it started to move. This is not a major life decision, she told herself, and took the nearest seat. She jammed herself against the window and stared through the glass.

The tram passed Federation Square and crossed over the Yarra River into St Kilda Road. This broad boulevard lined with great knobbly plane trees had been known as the golden mile back in the 1970s, an allusion, Ava had believed with youthful idealism, to the art and beauty of the period homes and not the prime real estate. At that time most of the mansions had already been converted into offices, but the original blue-stone and red-brick façades had been preserved along with the wrought-iron lacework and the leisurely English gardens. Entrances were via tessellated tile verandahs and heavy timber doors, and there was a plethora of brilliant leadlight windows.

Art and beauty had now succumbed. The plane trees remained, but the splendid old places and their glorious gardens had all disappeared. And while the Botanic Gardens and the Shrine of Remembrance had postponed the glass-clad towers on the eastern side of the boulevard, a kilometre or two beyond the city centre, the road was wedged between skyscrapers on both sides.

Ava was sorry for the loss. Place supplies the scaffolding to memory, and given her memory's wear and tear it needed all the support it could get. She travelled down this boulevard and looked out on a landscape that was largely foreign. She knew she had walked here many times by herself, also with Stephen. And Helen too, a vague memory, early one morning – had they been up all night studying? – the two of them leaving the city after breakfast with the night workers and crossing the river into the Botanic Gardens. Dew on the grass, the new blue sky and she and Helen dancing over the lawns.

The days of dancing at dawn with Helen in the Botanic Gardens might have happened in another life. And while she expected friendships to change, to stroke with the current of the times as her friendship with Jack had done, these days the familiar Helen was almost entirely absent. Ava understood the time-consuming passions for a son, and she had always understood work passions, but the allegiances Helen's science now required were in a different league altogether. Her old friend Helen would sell her soul out of misguided loyalty and a warped integrity, but she would not help her best friend.

It was in the wake of Helen's refusal that the surprising idea had started to form. At first she shoved it aside along with all the other bizarre thoughts this illness threw at her. But it kept nudging her. Finally she took it on and considered it properly. Stephen Webb. The only person who had never refused her.

The block of flats where they used to meet was located further down St Kilda Road. Twenty-five years ago it had been a building with neither style nor distinction and always a disappointment in this grand thoroughfare; it would, she was sure, have been ripped down. As the tram glided through the Toorak Road intersection she kept a close watch. Closer and closer they came to where she thought the block had been. And there it was! Brinsley Close. She recognised it immediately. Brinsley Close, still standing. She could not believe her luck.

She disembarked at the next stop and as she walked back she was filled with hope. The block had survived, her fortunes had turned, she would find Stephen and he would help her. A new entrance had been installed with a board of buzzers and a list of tenants. She propped herself in front of the names and looked down the list for Stephen Webb. She started again at the top saying the name of each tenant aloud. She zoned in on the number of his old flat. There was no Stephen Webb here.

All of the tenants appeared to be companies; perhaps no one lived in these flats any more – although given her experience with Stephen, perhaps no one lived here twenty-five years ago either. And how foolish to think he would still be here, her mind on a fantasy rampage and not to be trusted. And because she realised how stupid she had been, she could not feel much in the way of disappointment.

She smoothed herself down – even a solitary woman nicely if a little flamboyantly dressed was sufficient to arouse suspicion these days – and walked outside. The car access was an open drive with a boom gate; whatever Brinsley Close had become it was not security conscious. She hesitated just a moment, and then she entered.

She was standing in the centre of a rectangle. Bushes, a bit of grass, a tidy but uninteresting garden. And exactly the same sense she'd had more than a quarter of a century ago of being enclosed by the flats, three storeys high on all four sides, enclosed and exposed. Who is looking at me? she was thinking now. Who is looking at me? she had wondered then.

Four weeks had passed since Ava had met Stephen Webb in the second-hand bookshop. She had read all her new books and written the reviews he had requested. She kept changing her mind about ringing him but, in the end, taunted by a future that was still out of reach, she collected her courage and called.

He seemed so pleased to hear from her. 'Come and see my library,' he said again.

He offered to meet her in the city and accompany her to the flat, but she refused: she wanted to appear independent, she wanted to feel independent too. And yet her nervousness was so great as she boarded the tram, she could hardly draw breath. She felt in her pocket for the reviews. She'd worked hard on them, and what if he didn't ask to read them? What if she had misjudged this entirely?

It was a Sunday, the traffic was light, the tram sped along St Kilda Road and less than ten minutes later passed his block of flats. She deliberately missed the stop. During the walk back she reminded herself that no one was forcing her to come here and nothing was stopping her from turning back. And she did hesitate at the entrance, just a moment before walking through to the patchy garden. She gazed at the flats on all four sides; his unit was located on the first level, he had said, on the northern side. And again she wavered: she could guess what she was letting herself in for, and while that was far from reassuring, the man might be crazy or violent as well. She waited just long enough to recite what had become her motto: if you risk nothing, you'll gain nothing. She was not here in all innocence; innocence would not be here at all. She found the stairs and made her way along the walkway to his door.

There was no doorbell, she knocked on the door and stepped back to wait. He took his time, sufficient for her to rehearse her fears, sufficient for her to run back along the passage, down the stairs, across the garden and into St Kilda Road. But she stayed exactly where she was, breathing down her jitters and feeling her pocket yet again for the reviews.

At last the door opened and there he was, large and smiling. He seemed to fill the doorway. He was not wearing a jacket and tie; his shirt, white with a dark blue stripe and causing a shuddering in her eyes, was open at the neck. So pleased you could come, he said with fastidious courtesy – adult courtesy was how it seemed to her – and invited her in.

Three years would pass before she learned how Stephen had prepared for that first visit, how in the days since her phone call he had moved bookcases and a couple of hundred books into the flat, sufficient to cover an entire wall. Over the next few years he would bring in hundreds more. But on that first day a wall of books more than satisfied as a private library.

He offered her a Coke, he offered lemonade, but she asked for black coffee; it was important, she believed, to appear grown up – that he did not want her grown up was only a later learning. As for the black coffee, what she had assumed to be a sophisticated choice turned out to be almost undrinkable. The biscuits he offered were of a type she had never seen before; with a tiny pattern of two-tone checks each looked like a miniature draughtboard. If it had been possible she would have nibbled with geometric precision, eating the chocolate squares separately from the vanilla ones – not simply for the different tastes, but an appealing neatness in the messy situation in which she now found herself. (Years later when she saw Jack eating cherries as if each were significantly different from the others, eating in such a way to provoke a false sense of order in his jumbled world, she recalled Stephen's biscuits. As if food could reduce disorder in her life, or indeed anywhere in the well-fed world.)

She had missed lunch in order to cover her fares so she was hungry, nonetheless she took just two of the biscuits, an acceptably adult number she thought. As she ate she looked about her. The kitchen benches were bare, there were no mugs on the hooks nor utensils in the wall brackets. The bathroom door was ajar, no bottles on the shelf and a single towel over the rail; there was a double bed, a side-table and a solitary lamp in the bedroom; and in the living room, just the two chairs, a fold-up table, a desk and the wall of books. There was none of the clutter of a lived-in home, none of the activity of a busy office either, the place seemed to be waiting for something. The curtains were the only oddity: stiff and new with bright splashy colours they were like neon signs in a desert.

He saw her looking at them,

'Ersatz Marimekko,' he said.

She had no idea what he meant but pretended to understand. Later she would never pretend, later she learned she could ask him anything. But for the first few months it was as if she were walking blindfolded, and she moved forward only very cautiously.

They drank the terrible coffee and ate the patterned biscuits, he in his chair on one side of the small table and she in hers on the other. She had dressed in jeans and a crimson and black zippered jacket. The jacket had been a find – literally – in a tram shelter. It was the right size and the height of fashion and she had wavered only briefly, for if she hadn't taken it some-one else would have. Now under his barrage of questions and despite the coolness of the flat she was hot. But with a scrappy shirt beneath the jacket she was stuck with the discomfort.

He began with questions about school, then moved on to her interests. When he asked about her family, she told him very little apart from presenting her long-absent father as the prototype of the actively involved dad. She seemed to know how to be careful and how to control and that both were required. She was more forthcoming about her studies, but generally she never liked talking about herself.

When he moved on to her ambitions, she stood up and took the reviews from her pocket,

'You can read these now.'

'Of course, of course,' he said. It was the only time he appeared flustered.

He took his time over her reviews, and while she realised from his comments there was much she had failed to notice, he seemed genuinely impressed. But it was when he turned to his own library, his own books, that she knew she had been right to come. He would select a book and start with a personal statement. 'This book,' – *The Secret Garden* – 'taught me about loneliness, about friendship too. And this,' – *The Catcher in the*

Rye – 'made me feel better about being the odd sort of child I was.' *The Longest Journey* 'convinced me never to compromise my dreams'. *A Tale of Two Cities* 'showed the power of books to take me anywhere at any time in history, and into the hearts and minds of people I would never meet in a lifetime'.

With each book he would provide a brief description of the characters and the story, situate the novel within the context of the author's career and the prevailing times, mention the main themes and then place the book in her hands for her to browse.

On that first visit she selected Patrick White's *Riders in the Chariot* – it became one of her favourite books, and *Wuthering Heights* because Stephen said it was one of the best novels ever written. She also took home the *Penguin Book of English Verse* because Stephen pressed it on her, despite her confident 'I don't like poetry.' He was sure, he said, there would be a few poems in this anthology that would appeal. And he was right, as he invariably was, although it worried her that of all the authors in the collection only a handful were women and most of these had received very short entries.

'It's up to you to change that,' he said, as if he already knew she wanted to be a writer.

She refused to let him drive her home. She knew it must appear that she came and went as she pleased. He walked her to the door and rather than be at the mercy of how he was planning to say goodbye, she put out her hand like in the movies.

'Thank you for the books,' she said. And before turning away, she added, 'I'll ring you when I've finished them.'

From the beginning she set the limits and he obeyed. And for the first year it was innocent enough. There was always the lavish attention, his sweetness, and so much affection, more in a single year than in the fifteen that had gone before. And he was always polite and always gentle. 'I'd never hurt you,' he said, 'never.' While they talked he might stroke her hair which felt very nice, her back too, and even though there were things she didn't much like, neither were they so bad that she couldn't manage.

'I can do this,' she told herself. 'I can do this.'

She thought of it as a friendship, an unusual and secret friendship. It never seemed wrong to her. She liked him and he loved her – and that made all the difference. And the sex was bound to happen with someone, and how much better with a man who was kind and gentle rather than a clumsy boy her own age.

And so generous. He gave her scores of books, he bought her clothes and jewellery, he gave her the leather satchel she still used today and the fountain pen from his own collection. He only collected Parker Duofolds, nothing else. He stressed 'nothing else' as if he were embarrassed by the idea of collecting, and though he tried to explain his unease, how issues of power and control often fuelled collecting, she failed to see his point. In the end he gave her John Fowles's *The Collector* to read. With Stephen there was always a book to explain, even if like *The Collector* it raised an entirely different set of questions.

During the last two years of high school she and Stephen met every couple of weeks. However, once she started university they saw each other far more frequently. She would leave her friends at the pub or a café to meet him, mostly at his flat but also at galleries and theatres and interesting restaurants. He taught her about art from Rubens to Rothko and music from Bach to Glass; he told her about the absurdists and modern minimalism in the theatre, and he guided her through the European film classics. He took her to Canberra – it was the first time she had travelled in a plane; they visited Sydney several times, and Adelaide and Brisbane too. They always stayed in good hotels; she checked in as his daughter and no one ever questioned it.

One time in Adelaide she quipped that Humbert Humbert would have fared better if he had stayed in posher places. Stephen was appalled. This, he said, you and me, can't possibly be compared with Humbert and Lolita.

Ava was convinced he would have been less affronted if there had been less truth to her words.

And when she asked whether he had other girls like her: 'Why is it so hard for you to understand,' he said. 'I love you.'

'But will you still love me when I'm twenty-one? When I'm twenty-five?'

Stephen had said he would always love her. But would he love a woman in her middle years with a rare form of dementia? She looked up at the flat that had once been his and down at the woman she had become. He might not even recognise her. She hardly recognised herself.

She walked back into St Kilda Road and, lacking the energy to get herself on to the right tram, she hailed a taxi. With the prospect of an afternoon alone suddenly intolerable, she gave the address of NOGA. Thirty minutes later she was sitting with Harry in his office, sharing his sandwiches. He was so pleased with her surprise visit that after lunch he collected his things and together they left the building. They made their way across the river to the aquarium, and once inside went immediately to their favourite area, an open space surrounded on all sides by floor-to-ceiling pools full of flamboyant, floating sea creatures. There were fish large and small here, even sharks and stingrays, and swaying underwater plants among vast rocky shelves. They sat on a bench in the centre of the space holding hands, she leaning lightly against him.

'We should come here more often,' Harry said.

And even as she agreed, she ticked off yet another experience she would never have again.

2.

It was not so difficult to find Stephen via the web, even for Ava who had clung to the dust and clamour of the real world long after most people had migrated to cyberspace.

'The web's no different from libraries,' Harry had insisted years ago, 'and far more convenient.'

Ava had disagreed and still did. For a start, there was that plural – libraries – each with its own distinctions, its own delights. And the issue of cataloguing, finite and reliable for libraries, but liable to propel you in entirely the wrong direction on the web. While writing her last novel, Ava had done a search on hermaphrodites and afterwards had been inundated with email advertisements about 'shemales'. It was all very interesting at first, but soon she realised that having entered the world of cybersex nothing short of changing her cyber-identity would stop the web's fetishists and erotomaniacs from pestering her. As she pointed out to Harry, no librarian had ever stalked her because of catalogues she had browsed or books she had borrowed. And there was the surprise of libraries. You're wandering the stacks, a book catches your eye, a must-read book which no amount of refined searching could have led you to.

Ava far preferred libraries – unless she knew exactly what she wanted. And what she wanted now was to find Stephen Webb.

The afternoon stretched ahead with at least four hours before Harry returned from work. But with nothing easy or routine any more, a task that might once have taken thirty minutes could now occupy a whole day. You have to manage it, she told herself as she collected the thermos of coffee Harry had left for her and crossed the courtyard into her study. You have to manage.

It was not simply that Harry was spending more time at home, she had no privacy any more. She would leave the bathroom and he would be waiting for her in the hall; she would be reading in the courtyard and look up to see him watching from the living room; and worst of all he would slip into her study without her noticing and stand behind her, the computer screen in clear view. There was no malice in his actions, he loved her far too much for that. He was determined to watch over her and guard her from all harm.

'But it won't be me,' she had protested over and over again. 'It's not me already.'

From the moment he knew she was seriously ill, his love kicked into overdrive. And while it appeared as if it were devoted to her, it was, as love so often is, primarily in service to his own interests. She quite clearly wanted to die, he quite clearly did not want her to. His hovering, his thermos of coffee, his neat luncheon sandwiches, his neck rubs served his desires far more than hers.

Several weeks ago he had arrived home to find one of the elements on the stove alight. Ava could not say how long it had been burning, she could not even remember turning it on. Within twenty-four hours Harry had fitted the stove with a childproof safety feature, he had emptied the spa tub of water and he had organised a weekly care schedule.

'I don't want you to be alone,' he said, sticking the schedule on the door of the fridge.

She glanced at it. 'No shortage of people to baby-sit me.' And then reaching in deep and pulling hard on the person she used to be, she waved her hand at the timetable. 'I don't want these people.' And pointing to Jack's name, 'Even Jack's no attraction if he's just one of the guards.'

'Do it for me,' Harry said, knowing how hard it would be for her to refuse him. 'Otherwise I'll worry. I'll feel unable to go to the office.'

She would not give in. 'You're leaving home late most mornings, and Jack's already here three mornings a week. So give me the remainder of the mornings.'

She argued, she pleaded and in the end he gave her the mornings.

Then she asked for the afternoons, she begged for the afternoons. She challenged Harry's exclusive provenance over emotional persuasion by arguing she was tired after lunch and more likely to rest if there was no one around.

It took all her ingenuity, but Harry finally gave her a part of each afternoon.

Helen insisted on being involved. 'Put me down for the late-afternoon shift,' she said to Harry.

'How late?' asked Ava, for having fought so hard for her afternoon hours she was loath to give up a minute, and would not have considered it for anyone other than one of her old friends. And no, she did not forgive Helen, she did not forgive any of them. But she had always believed too much is made of forgiveness, that one unforgivable act is rarely enough to toss away an essential relationship.

It was in the spirit of the friendship they used to have that Helen asked for three late-afternoon slots and it was in the same spirit that Ava agreed to Mondays, Wednesdays and Thursdays from four to six. But the friendship which was now theirs meant that three times a week quickly became two, twice a week became once, and the last two weeks had seen Helen cancelling altogether.

'You do understand?' she said to Ava over the phone. 'It's my work.'

Ava let her off lightly, not because she believed her cancelling to be slight – she didn't – but she did not want Helen to know that seeing her mattered, and that not seeing her mattered even more. She already felt worthless and Helen's actions merely added to the dust.

She had always thought that to refer to death in the present continuous was an oxymoron. I am dying. You are dying. He, she or it is dying. There was life and there was the winding down of life that would eventually lead to the split-second finality of death. But she had been wrong. This gradual erosion of ability, this slow-motion wreckage of everything that made her life worth living – she was dying, no doubt about it, this disease with its sinister navigations was killing her.

She had no intention of going gently into the dark night. Although she had discovered how punishingly difficult it was to kill yourself. Heroin was a possibility but injecting it posed a problem. She had considered hiring a car and driving it over a cliff but was afraid of being left alive and physically disabled. Her courage failed at the hair-dryer-in-the-bath method, if indeed it still worked with modern electrical circuitry. She had never been able to tie a good knot so hanging was out of the question, and the logistics of robbing a vet's surgery for Nembutal, the drug of choice, defeated her. Without a garage, carbon monoxide was not an option; paracetamol was too inexact; household cleansers were painfully cruel, and having failed once on the Valium-plus-plastic-bag approach, even with the addition of helium which she had learned would neutralise the carbon dioxide build-up, she was not inclined to try it again. She discounted option after option – the situation was laughable in a tragic sort of way – before settling on drugs. Barbiturates. Fast-acting and one hundred per cent lethal. And Nembutal the best drug of all. The only problem: where to get it.

One afternoon when Helen had cancelled, Ava slipped out to an internet café to investigate pharmacies on the web. There were many online pharmacies but none had a listing for Nembutal. There were pages on Nembutal but not how to buy it. A search on barbiturates yielded abundant results, but despite reading the side-effects, precautions and overdose information for several of them, it was not clear which would reliably lead to death. She suspected there was something wrong with her search technique, but when you're looking for a drug to end your life you are not inclined to ask for assistance.

The future stretched before her as unremitting horror. Ava Bryant would disappear and demented Ava would take her place, demented Ava who couldn't read or write or speak or understand, who needed to be bathed, toileted, dressed and fed. Demented Ava at home in the passive voice, a despoiled creature in a despoiled existence. Ava could not understand how people in her situation would see it to the end – not that there was anything wrong with the actual end, blessed relief as they say, it was the getting there that was so horrible. In the absence of depraved predilections – and given the more shocking outposts of human desire Ava assumed there were dementia fetishists – there were no winners in this game.

She needed someone to do the research she could no longer do. And she needed someone to obtain the drugs for her.

Ava sat in front of her computer staring at the still-familiar screen with its screensaver of a snowy owl in flight.

'You,' she now said to the bird, 'be my guiding angel.'

It seemed she would be sliding around in her fraying atheism right to the end. Although it occurred to her that dementia might just be the non-believer's trump card, that dementia, incontrovertible proof of human fallibility, might provide sufficient proof against an infallible deity. For if there were a God, she reasoned, he would allow dementia only as the worst of punishments. Yet an appraisal of her own life, although it revealed many actions of which she was not proud, produced none so reprehensible to justify dementia.

Dementia, the ultimate proof against God. Yes, she liked that. And yet she longed for faith. Faith would mean that instead of plumbing the depths of her crumbling mind to organise her death, she could pass without anxiety into passive voice oblivion, confident of leaving everything to a capable, all-loving God with an eternity plan for her. But without faith and saddled with diminishing faculties, it was up to her.

Stephen Webb had saved her once, to satisfy his own desires to be sure; now she wanted him to do it again – this time for her benefit alone. She had never harboured ill-will against him, how could she when he had provided her with her life? It would, however, have been different for him. He had been in his forties, she had been a teenager; that sort of imbalance makes for a hefty debt.

She clicked onto the internet and googled Stephen Webb. There were nearly two hundred thousand matches from which to choose. She read the top twenty before linking her search with fountain pens: she had no doubt that if he were alive he'd still be collecting. Still more than ten thousand matches, so she limited her search to Parker pens, and finally to the Parker Duofold. Forty minutes later she was left with four possibilities. She allowed herself a sweet moment of triumph: she was not immobilised in the passive voice yet.

She emailed all four with an innocuous but nonetheless painfully difficult to compose 'If you are the collector whom I knew years ago in Melbourne, Australia, please contact your old friend Ava.' And set about to erase her search tracks as best she knew how.

That afternoon while she waited for replies she took up smoking again. Not in the way of a restrained indulgence, but a cigarette whenever the fancy took her, and a second unopened pack in the drawer. She lit up and embraced the light-headed-ness, the familiar foul taste, the slow leisurely waft of time. Such a pity smoking wouldn't kill her, yet so much pleasure in guilt-free smoking. When Harry returned home, he saw the cigar-ettes and watched her light up but made no comment.

After dinner he had work to do, a dozen phone calls, he said, from Tokyo to London. And while he would far prefer to spend an unbroken evening with her, it shouldn't take too long. He left the room and soon afterwards she followed him across the courtyard. She could hear his telephone voice rising through the floor of her study; when it stopped, so must she.

She settled at her desk and opened her email. She couldn't

believe it! There were three replies and her email sent only a few hours ago. She forced herself to calm down, for with her brain silting up, she'd learned that any heightened emotion made it harder to think.

She opened the first email, glimpsed a long message – a good sign – lit a cigarette, read the warm greetings, an offer of friendship, an outline of the sender's interests and significant life events. He offered her a 1960 Parker 21 forest green with lustraloy cap as evidence of his good intentions, and, if all went well, marriage was an option, even children should she want them. He was a Pisces and open to all other star signs except Aries. His name was Steve, Steve Webb, and he lived in Nevada – although he was willing to relocate.

She was about to delete the message when she found herself caught by his circumstances, poor sad creature he was. She hit reply and wrote: I'm an Aries, sorry, and sent it off.

The second email was very short: It's not me. Have never been to Australia. Hope you find him. She deleted it and clicked on the last email. It was laid out like a proper letter. There were four short paragraphs, each indented. The letter finished with 'Toujours – S'. The very first words, 'Dearest Girl', she recognised immediately.

She had found Stephen, she had found her Stephen Webb.

Harry was fond of saying that email was as secure as a door sealed with sticky tape and about as private as a peep show. Ava used email only to establish that Stephen was in good health, long divorced, no partner, lived an hour south of London in Kent, was retired and travelled widely.

Two days after the initial contact during another of Helen's cancelled visits, Ava slipped cigarettes and mobile phone into her pocket and left the house. Once in the park she went straight to a seat out of sight of the main path and laid out cigarettes, phone and the piece of paper on which she had written Stephen's telephone number. She settled herself down and dialled. She had hardly begun when she lost her way in the string of digits. She cursed herself for not having stored the number, started again, was nearly finished when a breeze lifted the paper and blew it across the grass. Bloody bloody thing, she said as she grabbed it, bloody bloody everything. She didn't want to make this phone call, she didn't want to manage the practicalities, she didn't want to be Ava Bryant with dementia, she didn't want to die, she didn't want to live.

And that was the nub of it.

She calmed herself through the duration of a cigarette and then used the pack to hold down the paper. She picked up the phone and said each digit aloud as she pressed the tiny keys. When she was finished she stored the number, then waited a moment before selecting it. She heard the play of the numbers, then a long pause, followed by a ringing tone. Silently she counted the rings. Four, five, six and then an answering machine. His name, his voice, that still-familiar voice. She hadn't planned on a machine. No words came, not even her own name, and suddenly a click, someone picking up, a voice, his voice, 'Hold on while I turn off the machine,' and she immediately disconnected.

It took another fifteen minutes and a circuit of the oval to collect herself. She created an opening sentence and rehearsed it as she walked. She returned to the seat, waited a couple more minutes, then she called again. There was no answering machine this time. As soon as he said hello she spoke her opening line – rather too quickly, but it would have to do.

In the pause that followed she heard the scrape of a chair, a fiddling with the receiver.

'You sound exactly the same,' he said at last.

'If only.'

And suddenly her nerves settled. With nothing to lose and no reason to delay she told him she was sick, that she was dying of an old person's disease.

'I have a rare form of dementia,' she said.

There was a long silence, more fumbling with the phone, then a rush of questions: Was she sure? Did she have the best specialists? Could nothing be done? She answered his questions, he sounded so distressed, the girl he remembered was now dying of dementia.

She found herself calming him: There, there, she said, don't worry. I've a good husband, the best doctors. I'm all right, she heard herself say. It's not so bad. But she wasn't all right and it couldn't be any worse, and she tossed aside her niceties and told him exactly what she wanted.

'Nembutal,' she said. 'From an online pharmacy or anywhere you can get it and send it to me.'

Too blunt, too direct, more demand than request but desperation surely brokers some licence. He said he needed to think, he needed to do some research, he would call back in a couple of days.

It was safer, she said, that she ring him, and asked for his mobile number. He laughed, the only time during the call. He did not use a mobile, one stationary phone was more than sufficient for him. They arranged a time for her to ring him again.

On their second phone call he agreed to do as she wished.

'But I won't send the drug,' he said. 'I'll bring it myself.'

3.

Time slid by. Late in the afternoons while Harry was still at the office, Ava would go to the park and telephone Stephen. They spoke every day, sometimes two or three times. They were making plans together. Stephen would fly from London to New York then to San Diego, the best stepping-off point for Mexico where Nembutal was readily available. Ava bought him a mobile phone, prepaid and anonymous, and mailed it to him for his use in Australia. She told him to throw it away when it was all over. She told him he would need to change his home phone number.

'Don't worry,' he said. 'I've already thought of that.'

Don't worry, he said. And she allowed him to take over more and more of the planning.

Despite her public life, she thought it unlikely he had upgraded his memories of her. What would have been the point? And she was aware of feeling sorry for him, that seeing her as she was now would be as profound a death of his long-ago love than her actual death would be.

She felt sorry for him but she needed him. Illness seizes far more than health and ability. Purloins far more. *Purloins*, the word fell into her mouth. She riffled her desk mess for an unused Post-it note, tried writing the word but couldn't decide on the second letter. *Purloins.* Already the word was losing recognition. *Purloins.* Already losing sense. No time to yourself when you are sick. No solitary time. No privacy. Not that it mattered any more. Stephen was on his way, soon everything would be all right.

The following morning when Jack arrived, Ava greeted him more warmly than usual, or so Jack thought when he looked back on those last days.

'If only more people were like you,' she said, as they walked down the hall together. 'You know the difference between care and company.'

He put his arm around her and felt her lean into him. At last he was giving her what she wanted.

He had brought chocolate éclairs for their morning tea, and the two of them settled in the lounge room with the cakes and coffee. Jack began with the latest news about Connie. He was nervous but optimistic about the second pilot, he was still drinking too much, and while paradise with Sara seemed a chaotic and treacherous place from Jack's perspective, Connie was still insisting he was happy. By the time the éclairs had been reduced to a streak of cream, they had both agreed that Connie would be far better off if he returned to America and Linda – 'If she would have him,' Ava added. They then moved on to the Australian Wheat Board scandal and the Howard government's denial of knowledge of three hundred million dollars worth of kickbacks to Saddam Hussein's regime. 'Clearly the government has decided that gross financial incompetence is more acceptable to the electorate than illegal and unethical trade practices,' Jack said.

Ava nestled into the corner of the couch and lit a cigarette. Jack was about to launch into a diatribe over the government's slaughter of the Australian heart, when she asked him to play for her.

'The blues,' she said. 'Play me the blues.'

Jack made no attempt to hide his pleasure; he had always loved playing for her. He began with 'Cross Road Blues', a rugged melancholic number, then moved on to T-Bone Walker's 'Mean old World Blues', followed by Blind Willie Johnson's 'Dark was the Night'.

'This selection goes back a long way,' Ava said with a smile. 'Almost as long as we do.'

Her memory for recent events was frail, and there were numerous holes in her long-term storage, yet she could remember that night, the first of many, when she listened to him play the blues. It was the night their love affair began and, if Jack was to be honest, when it should have ended.

'You forgave me, didn't you?' Her voice was low, the words came slowly.

She had never before asked; in fact, she never referred to their brief time together. He walked over to her and knelt down by the couch.

'Of course I forgave you,' he said, taking her hand. And wanting to give her something in return added, 'We found a different intimacy in our letters.'

She looked hard at him, she was so close, and laid her other hand lightly against his cheek. 'You've always been special to me,' she said, with a vague smile and was about to continue when a voice sounded from the passage.

'Oh dear. Bad time. Sorry. Should have knocked.'

A tall woman dressed entirely in red stepped into the room carrying a baking dish. Her face was a gesture of helplessness. 'The front door was open,' she said.

A large dog pushed past her and headed straight to Ava. The animal nudged Jack aside, plopped down next to the couch and nuzzled Ava's lap.

'This is Bertha,' Ava said, patting the dog.

The woman put the dish down and stepped forward, hand outstretched. 'And I'm Minnie.' Nodding at the guitar on the couch, 'You must be Jack.'

Minnie was a good deal taller than Jack. Later she would tell him she was named after her very short grandmother who died just before she was born – one of those failures of attribution that families commonly make.

Ava looked up at Minnie and smiled. 'Did you think you were interrupting a …' she hesitated a moment, 'a secret assignation?'

Jack kept his face steady. Poor Ava. Often she was reduced to simple words or hackneyed sayings, other times she would alight on an absurdity like 'secret assignation'. Not wanting to embarrass her he tried not to react. But she did.

'Wasn't that awful?' she said laughing. 'I mean the secret assignation bit.' Her laughter was not convincing.

Minnie laughed too. 'Half your luck,' she said. 'Not even a whiff of an assignation in my life.' She put the casserole in the fridge together with written instructions for heating it up and returned to the living room. 'Won't stay now,' she said to Ava, bending down to kiss her on the cheek. And to Jack, 'Good to meet you at last.'

Minnie lived next door with her two school-aged children. Jack was surprised he had never met her before. 'In fact, I don't think you've even mentioned her.'

Ava shrugged, whether she had mentioned her neighbour or not didn't seem important to her. 'I see a lot of her. She works from home, a graphic artist. Designs art and craft materials for children. Stickers and glittery things.' And as if it had suddenly occurred to her: 'She's Jewish. Like you.'

'Husband?' Jack asked.

Ava shook her head. 'Apparently he was overwhelmed by the responsibility of children and headed north some years ago with a twenty-year-old. When his new love started to make noises about having children, he swapped her for another twenty-year-old.'

'He and Connie would have a lot to talk about.'

Jack chatted on about Connie while he put his guitar away, and was about to join Ava on the couch when she stood up.

'I want to give you something.'

He followed her across the courtyard and up to her study.

'This,' she said pointing to a sealed carton. 'I'd be grateful if you'd store it at your place.' And just in case she had not made herself clear, 'I'd like you to look after it.'

He asked what it contained.

'Your letters. A few old papers.' And as an afterthought she added, 'Harry, of course, is my executor, but I want you to have your letters back.'

Jack had preserved every single one of her communications, every single letter, every single note, even her emails. And while he had always wanted to believe she had kept his letters, he had thought it best to assume otherwise. So moved, so very satisfied was he, he didn't think to ask why she had decided to return his letters now.

The box was heavy. He carried it down the stairs, through the house and out to the car. He was about to settle again in the living room when she said she was tired. In the doorway she put her arms around him.

'I've always loved you,' she said. And with a nod to Dowson's 'Anatomy of a Poet', one of their favourite poems, she added, '"In my fashion."'

He was at the front gate when she called out to him. 'Tomorrow,' she said, 'don't come tomorrow.' She told him she had a medical appointment.

'I'll see you Monday then,' he said.

But already Ava had turned back into the house.

4.

While Jack was driving home with Ava's box of papers, Connie was in his bedroom preparing for the second pilot, which, being second, was even more important than the first. He had been told there would be hairdressing and make-up at the studio but he wanted to arrive looking his best. He played through a scene in which he would be greeted by the make-up person with a warm smile and a 'not much to do here' sort of comment. It helped calm his nerves.

Connie possessed the confidence of a man who had always been attractive alongside an exaggerated fear of ageing and decrepitude. The fear might not have plagued so vigorously if not for the TV series, a circumstance he would admit to, or his preference for girlfriends more than half his age, which he insisted was irrelevant. Then there were the facts of this second pilot. A new production team had been brought in, 'young, hip and funky', a team whose stated purpose was to open up the public broadcaster to a more youthful audience. This team had viewed the first pilot and insisted on a whole new approach. And no, they did not want Connie's friends as extras. Connie would have to do this one alone.

He peered into the magnifying mirror: shaved, plucked and moisturised he thought he looked urbane and contemporary, youthful yet wise. Only the eyes disappointed. He willingly confessed to physical dissatisfactions like his claw-like toes and narrow shoulders, but he had never told anyone, not even his various wives, that his eyes were a cooler blue than he would have liked. It was a colour too readily aligned with 'chilling', 'suspicious' and 'transparent' rather than the 'remarkable', 'mesmerising' and 'oceanic' of his preference. Unlike toes and shoulders, eyes were burdened with such significance. Although it could be worse: Harry Guerin's poached-egg eyes, for example, were a worrying indicator of the state of his soul.

Sara had selected his outfit, a woven cotton shirt in a smudged blue-grey pattern worn loose over jeans. Connie had thought his polo-neck jumpers and corduroy trousers to be timelessly stylish, but Sara had pronounced them dated and ageing. He did not argue; like all young people Sara was media savvy.

He could hear her taking a shower. She had arrived home very late after what she described as a rave with friends, and had tossed and turned through a drug-sprung sleep, only settling around the time he got up. She assured him she would be as good as new after a shower. He hoped she was right; he was relying on her today.

He had tried to give the impression he welcomed this second pilot but in truth he had been shocked. The books did not come so easily these days, and he needed, or rather his career needed, the series to go ahead. And despite the prejudices of some of his colleagues, as the person who first proposed cyberspace as the contemporary transcendent realm replete with a world wide web of devotees, a TV series could be seen as a more fitting launching pad than conventional print for the next phase of his career. Already he was drafting an online version of the series, teeming with interactive tangents, video, music and games, stimulation of such variety that even twenty-something cyberspace aficionados might feel overloaded.

Connie had never been an appendix to another person's life. But he was beginning to feel as if he might be an appendix to his own: what he once was, what he hoped he now was, and what he expected still to be. He needed this series to go ahead; he had staked his future on it.

A suspicious person like Jack would have known as soon as he walked on to the set that there was some serious white water ahead for Connie. The filming had been moved from the State Library to a TV studio. There was a backdrop of three huge plasma screens to create the impression of changing web pages.

'For the target audience,' the director, Tamara, said. 'The twenty- to forty-year-old group.'

'Why the upper cut-off point?' Connie knew his usual demographic was in the forty-plus range.

'The ABC has already captured the grannies and grandpas.' Director Tamara looked as if she should still be in high school. 'We want this show to reveal the cool side of public broadcasting. We aim to be *au courant*.' And for his benefit added, 'Cutting edge.'

For a moment Connie took some pleasure in being the focus of a cool and cutting-edge program and overlooked both her appalling French accent and that she thought he required a translation. But the pleasure disappeared when Tamara handed him to her assistant who handed him to Lexi in make-up. The pleasure disappeared and it did not return.

Lexi shredded his fantasy script before he even sat down. 'I'll need at least forty-five minutes for this job,' she said to the director's assistant. 'And you'd better alert wardrobe. This,' she picked at his shirt, 'won't work with this,' she clapped a hand under his chin and tipped his face towards the light.

She draped him in a smock and sat him down in a glare of lights and mirrors. She made it quite clear she was too busy to talk, in fact she behaved as if it were not quite fair she'd been given this job in the first place. Her touch as she laid foundation was firm to punishing. She slathered his face in a cover-all beige and then repositioned one of the lights on his neck. She touched the loose skin as if it were rotting lettuce. She shook her head slowly – the situation was clearly impossible – and sent the assistant out for the director.

Wordlessly she pointed to his neck.

Tamara looked and nodded. 'Best we just cover it with a polo-neck sweater,' and returned to the set.

If Connie were not so humiliated he might have enjoyed a small moment of triumph.

Lexi settled into the job. The forehead, the cheeks, the dark rings beneath his eyes. She leaned in close, he could smell her spicy perfume, he could see her fine unblemished skin. Her manner might be abrupt, but she was quite an attractive girl.

She stepped back to check progress. He heard her mutter something about 'a mature gig', and wanted to protest, to enumerate his youthful credentials, but instead he sat in silence while Lexi, who according to the birthday cards on display had recently celebrated her twenty-first birthday, set about putting cosmetic filler in his wrinkles and camouflaging sun damage with cosmetic paint. It was as if this girl had seized him in her smooth white hands and held him up to scrutiny like a tatty old jacket. But rather than throwing him out as she believed he deserved, she had accepted the challenge of getting a bit more wear out of him.

Finally she was finished. She looked him over and merely shrugged, and when she packed him off to wardrobe failed to acknowledge his 'I expect we'll see each other again', making it quite clear she thought the pilot had no future.

Wardrobe was similarly unhappy. The shirts and long-sleeved T-shirts of their preference would not be kind to his neck. A tie was out of the question for their demographic. They tried a kerchief scarf but he looked like a 'pirate preparing to meet the mother-in-law' according to one wit. The solid colour of a polo-neck jumper against the changing plasma screens made him look like 'an escapee from Pentridge' according to someone else. In the end they opted for his own shirt: it would fight some of the screens, but it had less against it than the other options.

'And I'll see what the lighting people can do about the neck,' Tamara said.

Throughout the exercise the wardrobe people and the director talked as if he did not exist. In service to self-preservation Connie had taken his attention elsewhere, so when Tamara did finally address him he did not hear. Tamara raised her voice to deaf-old-man level and leaning in very close asked if there was a hearing problem. Connie shook his head; he did not trust himself to speak.

Two hours after he arrived they were ready to begin filming. Sara, perched on a high stool beyond the cameras, blew him a kiss and gave him a thumbs-up as he walked on to the set. He was desperate for a minute alone with her, a restorative of sorts, but with so much time spent in preparation the director insisted they begin immediately. She took him by the arm and positioned him on the left of the set. She wanted him moving through cyberspace, and moving with authority. 'Like God,' she said, with neither humour nor irony.

'God would choose a different outfit,' a lark called from the darkness.

The director was grim. 'We'll manage.'

During the filming of the first pilot, Connie had been treated with the respect due a man important enough for his own TV series. How quickly are the mighty fallen, he was thinking, as he was shoved here, pushed there, told how to stand, how to hold his head, how to speak. In a matter of minutes he knew his good side – actually he lacked a good side, there was a bad side and a worse side; he learned about the asymmetry of his posture; his walk, he was told, was more of a slouch. He was wondering just how much more demeaning this could become when the director slapped a script into his hands.

'What's this?' he asked, knowing exactly what it was.

It appears Connie will not be writing the script to his TV series based on his work. Although director Tamara assures him he will have major input.

'We need the writer to be someone in touch with our target demographic.' She mentions a name familiar to Connie as the brains behind several reality shows.

'I must be missing something.' Connie's voice is louder than he intended. 'What does this tosser know about philosophy?'

Tamara is suddenly all smiles – Connie's question is right on the money. For reality-TV writer knows nothing about philosophy, that's Connie's area. Reality-man's job is to make sure Connie's ideas reach a young audience.

Dispossessed of his appearance, dispossessed of his sense of self, and now dispossessed of his work, Connie is desperate to find Sara. For a moment he is afraid she has deserted him, but then he finds her off to one side speaking with some of the crew. She must feel his gaze because suddenly she turns her brilliant smile on him and immediately he feels better; she's the only person here on his team.

The script for the second pilot is, in fact, much as he wrote it, although it has been cut through with 'entertainment'. There are kaleidoscopes of kids at computers, concertinas of laptops, figures of people fractured and reconfiguring as animals, trees, buildings – the impermanence of the present, Tamara explains. And a Q and A segment has been added in which Connie interacts with viewers via computer-cam. At this point, the director invites Sara to take part. Having her involved repairs his confidence and his own performance improves. By the time the filming is finished he is feeling much better.

As he and Sara prepare to leave, a number of the production team, including the director, gather round. Everyone is buoyant.

'I think it'll get the go-ahead,' he says to Sara once they are outside.

She gives him a hug, she thinks so too. And yes, she thinks he did an excellent job. Yes, she says, he looked great on camera. Yes, yes, she says, he was very *au courant*.

He suggests a cautiously optimistic celebration and they arrange to meet up later at their favourite bistro. He watches her in his rear-vision mirror as he drives off. She's still standing near the studio entrance, waving and blowing him kisses.

Chapter 16: Utterly Changed

1.

It was an ordinary evening in late spring with a fading sun and a few smears of cloud. The deciduous trees were fleshed out with new leaves, the jacarandas in the college gardens were in bloom. There were the usual fumes as Harry walked home from work, the usual cars parked in the street, the usual joggers on the track alongside the cemetery. It was just an ordinary evening.

Harry had spent the morning on the NOGA fellowship problem. Fortunately he alone knew there was a problem and he intended to keep it that way. He would not be extending any of the current fellowships. In fact, he was prepared to dump the entire program – a drastic solution, but as none of the inaugural fellows had produced the work expected of them, it was better to kill the project than let it tarnish NOGA's otherwise impressive slate.

Conrad was beyond saving. Anyone could have told him an affair with a twenty-five-year-old would end in disaster, although not even Harry could have predicted this particular disaster. In less than a month Sara had swapped Conrad for a

TV career – Conrad's TV career. *Travels in Cyberspace* had been put on hold while a four-part 'post-modern frolic through post-colonialism' fronted by Sara was already in pre-production. Conrad was drinking himself into oblivion; he was also making a fool of himself on email with his wife. Of them all, the self-designated web expert should know better than to try and sort out his personal life online.

Not that Harry had any intention of giving advice, for it was clear that Conrad Lyall drunk or sober was more concerned with his personal life than the broad cultural issues that used to occupy him. Charm, reputation, style, all those qualities which feed reputation need a solid undercarriage of ability. But whatever ability Conrad might still possess had remained hidden during his NOGA appointment. Last year's celebrity philosopher will only make it to this year's list if he produces this year's goods. And Conrad had not.

Jack was in a different category altogether. His kindness to Ava mattered to Harry far more than his absurd essays and misjudged public conversations. For all the help he gave Ava, and no matter what happened with the fellowship program, Harry would find Jack some sort of job at NOGA.

Which left Helen. After a year of indecision, an entirely wasted year from NOGA's point of view, she was finally returning to America. She had promised to keep NOGA in the loop regarding her research, and with her son remaining in Australia she would be a regular visitor home. Whatever benefits flowed from Helen would happen irrespective of the fellowship program.

At the usual monthly board meeting that afternoon – just an ordinary day – Harry had signposted the possibility of the fellowship program being forfeited for more high-yield

NOGA projects. He would, he said, be providing a comprehensive report at the next meeting. He had proceeded to table several member reports, including some interesting information out of the former Yugoslovakia regarding natural gas – there was a surprising number of Australians now working in Serbia and Croatia – followed by discussion of his future directions paper. As Harry had expected, the board welcomed an expanded role for the Network and was happy to approve all but a couple of the minor recommendations. Conrad had sensibly phoned in his apologies. Harry had left the meeting greatly satisfied.

On the way home he detoured via the market. Most traders had closed for the day and with the shutters drawn, the bare shelves and the wan cry of a solitary spruiker, the place seemed strangely derelict. It unnerved him, but still nothing so significant to topple the day from its perch. He stood at the top of the delicatessen aisle. Only two stalls remained open. He bought smoked mussels for Ava and a wedge of a nicely ripened Livarot, and as he was leaving he spotted a single *bâtard* on the near-empty shelves of a bread stall and he bought that too.

He caught a tram back to College Crescent and walked home via his usual route alongside the park. There was a group of boys playing cricket and a cluster of dog owners on the oval. Everything was ordinary. Perhaps now was the time to get the dog he and Ava had always promised themselves, not the border collie of their discussions but a smaller dog to sit with Ava and keep her company.

He turned into their street; there was the familiar squawk of rainbow lorikeets on their evening rout, and in the distance the growl of home-going traffic. He reached their gate; Minnie from next door waved, he waved back. On the verandah the deckchairs were in place; in the front window the cedar blinds were set for maximum light with minimum intrusion; the mail had been collected. Everything was as it should be.

He opened the front door, the house was comfortably warm. 'Ava,' he called. And when there was no response, he called again, 'Ava.'

Still nothing out of the ordinary. He removed his jacket, put his briefcase on the bed, then entered the kitchen. He paused in front of the wine rack and settled on a middle-aged Coonawarra cabernet sauvignon that he knew Ava would enjoy. Four coffee mugs perched unwashed on the draining board – Ava had never seen the point of washing dishes several times a day. Her lunch dishes were stacked in the sink, again unwashed. He noticed traces of one of her favourite meals, grilled processed cheese on a crumpet. What in others would be an unacceptable failure of good taste was an endearing eccentricity in Ava. Her preferred cheese resembled a block of yellow plasticine that blistered and burned when grilled. 'It's for comfort,' she explained, 'not for taste,' – and not a distinction he would make himself.

He opened the wine, and with the bottle and two glasses went into the living room. She wasn't there nor in the garden beyond, but neither was that unusual. He crossed to the stables and called up the stairs; no response from her study. Back in the house and to her bedroom just in case she was lying down, but the room was empty. He carried the wine and glasses through the house to the front verandah and settled himself in one of the chairs; she often took a walk in the early evening, he would wait for her return.

At twenty past six he checked the house phone and his mobile. No messages on either. He took both phones outside to the verandah and poured himself a glass of wine. At six thirty-five he was surprised to find his glass empty; at six thirty-seven he began to worry. At quarter to seven he couldn't stop himself and dialled her mobile. There was a faint delayed ringing, which he traced to the living room. Wherever she had gone it was without her phone.

It was just before seven when he crossed the courtyard and climbed the stairs to her study. He was looking for clues, he told Jack later, to indicate where she might have gone. What struck him first was the tidiness of the room. Papers were stacked in neat piles, pens were in their jar, her desk was clear, and she'd removed her working notes from the wall. Ava tidied up at most once a year, but he had suggested recently that less clutter in her study might clear away some of what she called her 'cerebral debris', so what might have been odd in other circumstances could be easily explained.

'I kept staring at the tidy desk, the bare wall,' Harry said to Jack, 'taking in the strangeness of it.'

And then he saw her. On the floor, on her back, her head resting on a cushion, lying motionless, her eyes closed but – a glance was sufficient to reveal – not asleep. And in that moment when everything was blatantly not normal he found himself thinking about the lies perpetrated about the dead. For dead people do not look as if they are sleeping peacefully. Dead people look lifeless. Dead people are changed, changed utterly. No peace to that pallor, no peace to that stillness. His wife overlaid by death, death-wrapped. It was horrible, it was fantastic. His wife dead on her study floor, wearing a shirt he had never seen before, her feet bare, her hands spread on the rug, her face utterly lifeless. His lovely, lively wife. He had promised to be with her at the end. 'Please don't let me die alone,' she had said.

He knelt on the floor and touched her breast, an automatic reaching for the heart which had failed her. There's no predicting these things, the neurologist had said recently. Her body was in a weakened state, anything might take her. But not yet, not yet.

He pulled in the air and expelled it forcefully in a brutal resuscitation of his own arrested life. He couldn't look at her, it was too brazenly real – her death – and a sense that if he didn't see, if he refused to cooperate, this unnatural turn of events might be reversed. Seconds later and he had to look at her, this woman he had loved for most of his life, had to take her in before she disappeared entirely. She had a fearful uniform bloodlessness. The lines, the flaws, the tics, her idiosyncrasies had all disappeared from her face. Sheared of expression it was as if the life, all of Ava's big brilliant life had been fleeced from her. The face on the cushion was perfect.

He touched her arm just above the wrist, plastic skin just like her favourite cheese. And cold, already cold. How quickly does it happen, this settling of the blood? And how long has she been lying alone? He hated the thought of her being here without him. And if she had died in distress, he would never know, this awful death mask would have removed all signs. Only her hair was unchanged, her beautiful golden hair, and he sat there stroking it as she had always liked him to do, stroking the hair of his wife.

Outside night fell, and a chill breeze eased through the open door and up the stairs. On the floor in her study Harry sat quietly stroking his wife, as if that might hold triumphant death at bay. But it was a struggle; he needed the sort of imagination Ava had possessed to survive this no-man's-land between a normal past and an incomprehensible future. He opened his eyes and felt for the desk lamp, knocked something to the floor, winced in the tight hard glare, looked down and picked up a bottle. Pentobarbital was clearly written in black block letters; the rest of the label was in Spanish.

He knew exactly what it was. Pentobarbital was Nembutal. He knew exactly what it meant.

He held the bottle to the light. There was a lick of fluid left, the last unnecessary drop. Her heart hadn't failed, her brain hadn't haemorrhaged, she had done this to herself, she had done this to him. How could she have left him like this? And lying flat and white on the desk surface, an envelope, her handwriting, his name on the front. Nembutal and a note. And despite the incontrovertible evidence, he couldn't believe she would have killed herself. He couldn't believe she would have killed herself without letting him know. He couldn't believe she would kill herself knowing he would find her. He couldn't believe she would leave him before it was time.

2.

Thirty-eight days had passed since her death and the house reeked of her absence. Each new day loomed with a frightening twenty-four hours, each new hour threatened with sixty impossible minutes. Harry felt as if normal life had been stuffed into a pipe lined with glass shards. Grief in others with its self-indulgent drear had always made him impatient. Get over it, he had wanted to say, just get over it. But it wasn't self-indulgent and he had no idea how to get over it.

He wanted to throttle those idiot commiserators with their inane 'better it happened now'– publicly the cause of death had been given as heart failure; 'it was time'; 'she was saved from the worst'; and the one he hated most of all: '*you* were saved from the worst'. Because it wasn't time and he hadn't been saved, he wanted more, much more of Ava. She was wrong not to have waited, she was wrong not to have told him what she planned. If she had been so desperate, so determined, why hadn't she begged him, forced him to change his mind and help her?

Several times a day he would cross the courtyard and enter her study as if he might find her reading or tapping the keyboard or just staring through the window. The condemning patch of floor he had excised from his field of vision. At four o'clock the morning after her death he had leapt out of bed. If anything should ever happen to me, she had always said, check the shelf of my favourite books. Her Parker pen lay in its felt pouch in front of the books; he put it in the pocket of his pyjamas. He removed her Proust, her collected Milosz, her cloth-covered *Portrait of a Lady.* Nothing. Behind *Mrs Dalloway* was a flashdrive marked as a copy of her latest novel, behind *Wuthering Heights* was a wad of Euros. Nervous, expectant, desperate for something, anything, he had continued along the shelf. But there was nothing. No letter, no proper explanation of why she had acted as she did.

Thirty-eight days after her death, her desk drawers, the filing cabinet, the stacks of paper still remained exactly as she had left them. Such finality, unbearable it seemed, if he were to move any of her things. Yet he had found her dead in her study along with an empty bottle of Nembutal – how much more final does it get? He had seen her coffin, he had buried her ashes and now he was rattling around in the life they once shared. How much more brutally blatant could it be? None of this was logical, but logic played no role here.

His loneliness grew large in their kitchen, at a table set for one, in front of their collection of CDs. Her garden was a hell of loneliness. He would dash outside when he could no longer tolerate being indoors, and dash inside when her bushes, her pot-plants, even the mottled sky threatened to crush. From house to garden to her study and back again, always on the move, always slamming against the walls of his own loss.

His eldest brother, Miles, flew in from Adelaide as soon as he heard the news. It helped to have someone in the house. But the day before the funeral, when the rest of the Guerins arrived, Miles moved with them into a city hotel. Harry would have been happy for the entire family to have stayed with him, anything to drown out the roar of Ava's absence. But the Guerins had never been the sort to press their needs, so he remained in the house alone.

During the first two weeks Helen had phoned every day, but it was her loss not his that prompted the calls. Each day her gushing tears and the same questions: Why so soon? Surely there were signs her heart was failing? Surely you noticed something? And his unspoken accusation: if you'd turned up when you promised, perhaps Ava would be alive today. He loathed Helen's outpourings and in the last days before she left for America he screened his calls to avoid speaking with her.

Conrad had called in regularly with a bottle of wine and, as they drank, they would talk about Ava. But Conrad's Ava was not his Ava and the conversation did nothing to let the steam off his own grief. By the second glass the talk would have shifted to Connie's problems, all, as far as Harry was concerned, as a result of his own stupidity. The last time Connie visited he was so full of guilt and so wrapped up in self-pity – 'Linda will never take me back', 'I'll never see my boys again' – that Harry snapped.

'Guilt is nothing more than an excuse for inaction,' he said. 'Linda should have tossed you out years ago. But if you're so keen for her to take you back, then you need to show her that despite your appalling behaviour and despite what her common sense directs, you're worth another chance.' And as if he had not said enough, he added, 'You're just an old sleaze, Conrad.'

He had not seen Connie since.

Various acquaintances from the literary community had put in an appearance and talked for the duration of a coffee or a glass of wine. These visits inevitably left him vexed and angry. In life everyone had wanted their bit of Ava Bryant and in death they boasted they'd had it. Even some of the obituaries oozing with insider warmth had been written by people who had never met her. Harry, forced to share his wife while she was alive to a degree that was never fair, would be a fool to give an inch of ground now she was dead.

Jack Adelson was the one exception. He came round to the house several evenings a week, happy to listen to Harry for hours on end. And when Jack talked about Ava, when Jack shared stories of her life, it was the Ava Harry knew.

'She wrote to you about that?' Harry said, when Jack reminded him of the barbecue he, Harry, had built in the window box of one of their Oxford homes and the subsequent fire. 'She wrote about that?' when Jack recalled 'Bryant's Back Lane Tour' which Ava had designed especially for Harry when they settled back in Melbourne. Other people flaunted what were essentially very flimsy relationships with Ava, but next to himself, Jack knew Ava best.

Each day brought an avalanche of condolence cards. The phone, now left permanently on the answering machine, hadn't stopped ringing, and if Harry hadn't switched off Ava's mobile that would be bleating away too. It had rung on the second day, just twenty-four hours after he had found her. He had called out to her in an all-too-brief moment when he forgot she was gone. And then a shock so violent it winded him, and rage at her phone ringing when she was dead.

Her favourite rug, her mask from Venice, her watering can, the flowers drooping in their pots ransacked his empty self. He doused himself in her perfume and bought a back-up bottle for future losses. He washed her cashmere jumper in her shampoo and used it as an antimacassar on the couch. He opened a can of smoked mussels and with the first fumes began to cry reluctant unpractised tears over one of her favourite foods. He slept in her bed on her pillow until his smell replaced hers and returned to his own bedroom furious over what he had wrecked.

He went to bed late and after a couple of hours in the fake solace of sleeping pills he would read, doze, listen to music, tune into the BBC World Service, wrestle his wakefulness until six o'clock when he would allow himself to get up. Today on the thirty-eighth morning he had capitulated at five. It had been a disaster of a night with not much more than an hour of continuous sleep. His head was throbbing and there was a jangling in his ears as he pulled on clothes, made coffee and crossed the courtyard to his office. He searched for work to distract him and found some figures to organise. When the task was finished and he sat holding several spreadsheets of newly printed tables he realised with relief that four hours had passed. A whole four hours without a single thought of her.

He crossed the courtyard back into the house. He would be all right, of course he would be all right, and paused in the living room: he may as well move his office in here, the mess wouldn't matter and it would help put some distance between their old life and a future without her. No hurry, but plans helped. He made some fresh coffee and with the first mouthful felt a gripping in his stomach. He had not eaten properly since a meal with Jack two nights earlier. He rummaged in the fridge and found the last of the Livarot he had bought the day he found her. This cheese was thirty-eight days old. He had bought it for him and Ava. It was these things that straddled life with her and life alone which cut the deepest.

He made some toast and covered it with the cheese. It wasn't the same without her, but then nothing was. The food lodged in his throat, he forced it down. And when he was finished he stood at the kitchen bench, an ugly croaking crawling from his mouth and the tears rolling down his face. Five, ten, fifteen minutes later, he tried the coffee, it tasted rusted and sour, all of him was rusted and sour. He heaved his body to the bathroom, had just finished shaving and was about to shower when the phone rang. He heard Jack's voice, ran naked to the living room and picked up: yes, dinner tonight … six-thirty here … then one of the local cafés.

Nine hours to fill. He showered and dressed.

Eight and a half hours to fill. He went for a walk through Princes Park.

Eight hours to fill. He left the house again and caught a tram to the city. In the past thirty-eight days spring had moved into summer – not that it would be a reliable passage given Melbourne's jittery weather. But today had one of those warm buttery suns softened by a cool breeze, the sort of day Ava would have liked. The mall was crowded with the usual shoppers, idlers, buskers, shouters, coughers, beggars, kids on the wire, kids on the nod. Harry felt in his pocket for change – Ava's doing: no one would beg if they didn't have to, she used to say, and would always have change at the ready. But no one approached him for money. Perhaps there was something about him that warned people off. Perhaps he appeared as desperate and mad as some of the beggars.

The funeral home – what a contradiction in terms – had provided him with a list of bereavement groups, strangers who met regularly to grieve together. But he wasn't interested in other people's grief, and he certainly wasn't interested in diluting his own in order to communicate it to others. And no, he could not say why he was so angry.

He wandered up Bourke Street to check out the cinema complexes, but of the dozen films screening, there was not one of even the slightest interest to use up a couple of hours. The cafés were filling with lunchtime eaters, the shops were full with lunchtime shoppers. He decided to walk to the tram stop at the top end of the street and was settling into his stride when he found himself face to face with Ava in the window of The Hill of Content bookshop. There was a notice carrying her name and dates in large blue letters and a display of her books.

Harry stared through the glass at the over-sized figure of his wife, a familiar photograph taken in the gateway of Somerville. His throat began to swell, and a moment later with the tears again falling he hurried to the nearest tram stop and headed home.

Five hours to fill. He collected the mail from the box. The bundle was as large as yesterday's and bigger than the same time last week. There had been hundreds of cards from friends and acquaintances, and hundreds more from readers whose lives, they said, had been changed by Ava Bryant. How he hated their homemade intimacies. They still had her books – it was all they ever had; his Ava was gone.

He was tempted to swallow a couple of pills and sleep through the hours until Jack arrived, but he didn't trust this person he had become and couldn't be sure that if he forfeited one afternoon to oblivion he might not start a pattern. He put the cards in a box with all the other cards and took the remaining letters, mainly bills, out to his office. Gas, water, telephone, credit card, Ava's Amnesty membership. He decided to pay the accounts the old-fashioned way, and for the next half-hour he wrote cheques, addressed envelopes, balanced bank statements. The phone bill he left for last as he liked to check it.

He opened the envelope; it was not for the house phone but Ava's mobile. He looked at the amount, he stared at the amount. It was an extraordinary $779 – obviously a mistake. Ava was a reluctant mobile-phone user; several days could pass without her turning it on. He checked the dates: a twelve-week billing period finishing exactly four weeks after her death. And again that sense of unfairness that life continues even though the centre has dropped out of it. He was left with Ava's telephone bill to pay, her dry-cleaning to collect, her Amnesty membership to cancel, but not Ava herself. He looked at the bill again. He couldn't make it out. He scanned the pages of calls and found his own mobile number several times, all for short calls and typical of her mobile usage. Nothing like these other calls for forty-three minutes, fifty-nine minutes, one for a huge seventy-seven minutes. It must be a mistake. He checked the account details, it was definitely her phone. And the phone hadn't been stolen, he knew exactly where it was. He looked more closely at the dates of the calls; one or two long calls every day for six weeks and then during the last week of her life several short calls every day. Three of these were to his own number – the last call had been made to him the morning of the day she died – two were to Jack, and the rest to a mobile number he did not recognise. Without stopping to think, he rang the unknown number. There was a recorded message: the number was out of service. He did not understand. The number was similar to his own, a variation of Ava's birth date. Was Ava trying to phone him? He did not understand.

It was as if his mind had slipped into a certain gear and there was no changing it. He returned to the earlier weeks of the billing period. Such long calls. Very few made in the morning, many in the late afternoon and some in the middle of the night. She had been phoning someone while he was asleep! He simply did not understand. And most calls were to international numbers. For five weeks of the billing period they were to a British number; he recognised the code as the outer London area. Then in the next week there were several different overseas' numbers, and in the last week the majority of calls were to the unknown mobile – and judging by the low cost they were local. Nearly all the calls on the bill had been made from inner Melbourne, their home he assumed; it was the receiver numbers that kept changing.

He crossed the courtyard into the house and to her bedroom; her mobile was where he had left it on her bedside table. He plugged it into the charger and turned it on; the phonebook was empty, the file of recently received calls was also empty, text messages in and out, empty. She had stripped her phone of information, or rather someone had; if it had been left to Ava she would have simply thrown out the SIM card. Maybe she needed to have her phone working until the very end? Back he went to her study for her telephone directory. It took less than fifteen minutes to check: none of the unknown numbers was listed.

He went online for a list of country and city codes. He confirmed that for a period of five weeks Ava had phoned someone living in outer London forty-one times. During the first three days of the sixth week of the billing period, she phoned someone in New York City and Los Angeles. Over the next two days, she made two calls to Tijuana in Mexico, three to San Diego and two more to Los Angeles. On the sixth day in the morning, a brief phone call to Sydney – he felt this unknown person drawing closer – and then in the afternoon, rather than phoning from her home region, Ava made three short calls from a place called Bulla – the first two calls were to the unknown mobile number, the third was to his own phone.

Where on earth was Bulla? He ran outside to his car for the street directory. Bulla. Bulla. Bulla. He'd never heard of Bulla. He scanned the map and there it was – the region for Melbourne Airport. She must have travelled out to the airport that day. He ran back into the house for his organiser. He scrolled back: it was a Friday and the start of the three-day 'Energy in the Asia–Pacific' forum. He had been at meetings all day and had attended the dinner in the evening. In all the months of her illness it was the only time he had left her alone so long. And she had gone to the airport to meet a person who had travelled from outer London, via the US coasts and Mexico to be with her in Melbourne.

There was someone else. There must have been someone else. Someone else at the end as there had always been someone else. Even when she was dying she could only love him if there was someone else. He cannot believe this is happening. He goes to her computer and turns it on. He enters her email files, he does not hesitate. The mail folder labelled Fleur contains just nine emails, and what sad, innocuous communications they are. In Fleur's last email sent months ago, she says she has settled well in Geneva and is renting a flat in a building where George Steiner once lived. The last email from Ava wishes Fleur well in her new job. Nowhere in her communications does Ava mention she is sick.

It isn't Fleur, not this time, but there was someone else. What a fool he has been, what a fool she must have thought him to be. This is worse than Fleur, this unknown person. And suddenly he is hit with the naked, unsparing truth. The tidy computer, the empty phone, her body lying so peacefully on the floor. And he knows with absolute certainty that this other person was with her. Someone else, not him, was with her at the end.

Despoiled. That's the right word – his wife was mistress of the right word. Despoiled. She has despoiled his love. She has despoiled their marriage. She has despoiled his memories. She has despoiled his future. At the end there was someone else. But wasn't there always someone else?

He scrolls down the email folders. Each name is known to him. He almost doesn't open the one labelled SW, assuming it is her US agent Stephen Weinberg, but Steve's is labelled with his nickname, Berks. This is another SW, an unknown SW. Harry pauses, he feels sick. There will be answers here. How quickly does a life unravel. He doesn't want to know. He wants to know. He clicks on the folder.

It is empty. The folder labelled SW is empty. Like the mobile phone, it is blatantly and significantly empty. But the erased emails will have left traces and Harry will track them down. He'll find this SW. This SW will not escape.

CHAPTER 17: The Waiting Page

1.

On the thirty-eighth day after Ava's death, Jack was seated at his computer dressed in pyjamas. He had been at his desk since dawn, finishing the introduction to Ava's first novel. He scrolled down the screen reading the fresh sentences. What a godsend this work had turned out to be.

It was the day of the funeral when Ava's Australian publisher had first approached him. Hundreds of people had crammed into a Carlton bar after the service; hushed, stunned and sombre they huddled close over their drinks. Death is always short on supporters but this death seemed particularly wrongful. The publisher – 'Call me Victor' – had cornered Jack. He had plans for Ava's work, he said. 'New editions of all her novels. Small format, like Penguin classics but much more hip, each with its own introduction.' Victor's face all doleful sympathy a moment before had perked up. 'And who better than you to write an introduction to her first novel.'

'But we've only just buried her!' Jack's voice was shrill in the muted air and several people glanced in his direction. 'We've only just buried her,' Jack said again more quietly.

The publisher took him by the arm and guided him through the throng to an alcove at the end of the room; Jack, with insufficient energy to resist, allowed himself to be led. The publisher sat him in a chair, put a drink in his hand and settled beside him.

'Given this tragedy,' he said, 'what would Ava want?'

In her various workrooms over the years, Ava had pinned to her noticeboard quotes in her own handwriting. Eliot, Shakespeare, Rilke, Woolf, all her favourites, and some lines from Milton: *A good book is the precious life-blood of a master spirit, embalmed and treasured up on purpose to a life beyond life.* Ava would want what all writers want, and had said as much to Jack not so long ago. Victor's timing might be crass, but his plan was right.

Victor had already spoken with Harry. 'He's well aware of Ava's views and he's right behind our proposal. But we need to act now.' Victor looked concerned. 'We need to bring out all her novels quickly before the public has moved on.'

Jack wanted to protest. The unseemly haste. The bereft heart. But Victor spoke first. 'I know the reading public, and believe me, the window of opportunity is very small.'

Again Jack tried to speak, and again Victor prevailed. 'We propose to market the new editions in such a way as to remind her usual readers how much they've always enjoyed her work while simultaneously attracting a new and younger audience. By the time we publish her last novel – our aim is to release it on the first anniversary of her death – we hope to have a best-seller on our hands.' Only now did Victor pause, and with a nonchalant cocking of his head, 'Have you read it?' And when Jack failed to respond, 'Have you read her new novel?'

Choking on a cocktail of the publisher's opportunism and the fact there would be nothing new from Ava ever again, Jack could not speak.

Victor was not deterred. 'We have one opening in our current publishing schedule for the reissue of the old novels,' he continued. 'If we miss the spot then the whole Bryant project is finished.'

Jack was desperate to get away. He said he would think about the introduction – although he knew he had no choice – and before Victor could stop him, plunged back into the crowd. The mourners, fortified by alcohol and an avalanche of memories, were gaining voice. Jack found Helen and the two of them got drunk together.

Victor contacted him a few days later and after discussion with Harry, Jack agreed to write introductions to Ava's first and sixth novels. Connie would do the second and fifth, although exactly when was anyone's guess given Connie had embarked on a full-time campaign to persuade his wife to take him back. Each of the other two novels had been given to 'the best in the business', according to Victor.

With the first of the introductions finished, it was a relief to know there was another, and possibly more given Connie's parlous state. It was the only work Jack wanted at the moment, for as long as he was focused on Ava, she was not so adamantly gone. There would come a time, so he had been told, when she would fade, and while he longed for the terrible ache to subside he dreaded any diminishing of Ava herself. He struggled to erase her absence – deny her death – by keeping her close. At the same time the very fact of his efforts reminded him she was gone forever. Not departed. Not absent. Not passed away nor passed on. But the unpoetic, unlovely, defiantly unchallengeable gone.

He worked, he spent time with Helen, he visited Harry and he ran. Penned in by grief there was hope in movement. He ran during the day and in the early morning, he ran at night. He ran through the streets near his place and those near hers, and although you can't trample down pain the movement made time pass. But it was touch, physical comfort, he most wanted. Helen understood, perhaps because she needed the same herself, and the two of them would hold each other, not saying a word, just holding on while the evenings drifted away.

Then Helen left. Two weeks after Ava's death, she flew back to America and Jack missed her ferociously. He found himself in an absurd searching of passers-by for anyone familiar from whom he might engineer an embrace. He would admire dogs on leads, admire them in order to have an excuse to touch them. In truth he wanted to gather the animals in his arms and bury his face in their fur. He considered a visit to his parents in Tasmania, but the comfort of family was not the raw comfort he craved.

One evening the previous week as he was leaving Harry's place, Minnie, Ava's friend from next door, called out to him. She was watering pot-plants on her front verandah.

'These were hers – Ava's,' she said, indicating the plants. 'Harry couldn't be bothered with them and I couldn't bear to watch them die.'

Jack heard tears in her voice. What right did this woman have to be so upset, as if grief had a pecking order. She met him at the gate and rested her hand on his shoulder. 'I've only known Ava three years and I miss her terribly. I can't imagine how bad it is for you.'

And he burst into tears. He had cried over Ava's photo, he had cried into a scarf she had sent him from India, he had cried over a fox and hedgehog figurine she had given him one birthday. As for the box containing her cards and letters, just looking at it started the tears. And now with a woman he hardly knew he cried uncontrollably, they both did, holding on to each other as if they were not strangers. And Jack found himself sinking into a sweet quilted state in which grief had shut down for a moment and his mind was soothed and silent.

He went inside with her. The dog settled on a rug in the living room and fell asleep. They talked about Ava until it was very late, then they moved to the bedroom. They took off their clothes, little was said, they had perfunctory sex and fell asleep in each other's arms; they did not lose hold of each other all night long. The following morning there was neither embarrassment nor explanation. Jack showered and dressed, he declined Minnie's offer of breakfast, he took a last embrace, he drove home. And for the first time he understood why a man or woman who has lost a beloved spouse often remarries so quickly and disastrously. Comfort, that's what you want when you're grieving, and whoever supplies it is the person you need most. Hard sometimes to tease out gratitude from love, impossible when you are clogged with grief.

Jack had not contacted Minnie since that night. Now he wrote a note to slip into her letterbox when he went around to Harry's for dinner. The action energised him and he showered and dressed. At midday he made a sandwich and took it into the lounge. He opened the doors to the balcony, a breeze floated in from the bay. It was cool for a summer's day, Ava would have approved. Any warmer than twenty-five degrees she considered uncivilised: 'You can't think, you can't work, and you certainly can't be kind to others,' she would say. She firmly believed in heat rage, a meteorological version of road rage. She used to joke she had been born at the wrong latitude and proposed a particular recycling of the soul (it was an atheist's prerogative, she said, to play around with an afterlife), which would have her again enter the world as a human being, but one born and raised in Iceland. And no, she had never been there, but she had checked its weather patterns and they were entirely to her liking.

Jack gazed up at the sky. 'Here's to you in Iceland.'

2.

It was early evening when Jack arrived at Harry's place. The traffic had been unusually light and he had made good time across the city. He parked outside Minnie's house and was about to slip the note into her letterbox when she appeared at her front door. She was dressed all in red as she had been the first time they met. Her black hair stretched straight and smooth past her shoulders and, as she stepped on to the verandah, her face relaxed into a smile. He walked up the garden path, she met him halfway; they stood there facing each other, both smiling, before she leaned forward and kissed him lightly on the cheek. He gave her the note.

She read it quickly and laughed. 'I was worried you might have had the wrong idea about the other night. While I,' and she paused a moment, 'I was more concerned about the right ideas – *all* the possible outcomes, some of them very beneficial, very satisfying and very short term.'

He laughed too, more from relief than anything else. 'You mean you don't want me to move in with you?'

'Not just yet. But dinner,' she said, indicating his note, 'would be lovely.' She suggested the following weekend. 'The children can stay at my parents' place.' And anticipating his next question, 'You'll meet them in good time – if you're still visiting. And if you're not, then they're saved any unnecessary emotional rides.'

It was the hour before dusk and the evening gently cool. The two of them sat on the edge of Minnie's verandah their feet propped on the steps. The shadows in the street were long and soft-edged, the muted shouts of children playing in the park floated on the air. Jack was struggling to think of something to say when Minnie broke the silence.

'Ava and I spent hours in exactly this spot. When she and Harry moved in, I wasn't at my best. My husband had tossed me over for a woman half my age, I was under assault from toddlers being toddlers, and reeling from knock-backs by advertising executives who've perfected the art of the knock-back. It was a difficult time for Ava too. Harry was establishing NOGA seven days a week,' – Ava had never told him she was spending so much time alone – 'and she would come over here with a plate of home-baked biscuits,' – Ava baking? Never in Jack's experience – 'and we'd sit here on the verandah and talk. If the children were at kindergarten it would just be the two of us, otherwise we'd sit up here while the children played in the garden.' Minnie had that glazed concentration of someone who was seeing exactly what she was describing. 'Ava liked children. She never talked down to them and children always respond to that.' Jack realised he had never seen Ava with children. 'We'd talk for hours,' Minnie continued. 'Ava talked about Harry, she talked about their return to Melbourne, she talked about her childhood in the suburbs,' – with this stranger she had talked about her mysterious, untouchable past? – 'she talked about you,' she smiled at Jack, 'and of course she talked about Fleur.'

Jack was aware of a weird sensation as a result of this almost incidental information about Ava, as if he were being jemmied from his long-time relationship. Or perhaps the relationship itself was being moved. He picked at a splinter of wood on the step, it came away in his fingers; the timber beneath was pale and fresh, like new skin under a wound.

'Did she talk about being ill?'

There was a long silence before Minnie answered. 'Not much. I assumed she was talking with you and Helen.'

Jack shook his head.

'I know how much she hated what was happening to her.' Minnie twisted around to look into his face. 'She really hated it. I was sure she'd never stay the distance.'

It took a moment for Jack to realise what Minnie was implying. 'Ava died of heart failure,' he said.

Minnie let out a disbelieving snort. 'I think that's highly unlikely. Whenever we went out walking, I struggled to keep up with her. Heart failure? I don't think so.'

'You're wrong,' he spoke louder than he intended. 'Ava loved life.'

Minnie shook her head. '"It won't be me," she kept saying.'

Jack's brain was shovelling loose ends. 'What you're suggesting doesn't help any of us.'

But it helped Ava, Minnie was thinking, and perhaps it helped the stranger too. Ever since Ava's death, Minnie had wondered about the elderly man who had appeared in those last days, wondered if his presence was known to any of the friends. Given Jack's response now she was sure it was not.

The man had appeared a week before Ava died. A hire car had pulled up in the street, the name of the company scrawled across the rear window. Ava was in the passenger seat, the stranger was driving. They had entered the house together and about thirty minutes later they reappeared and drove away. Early in the afternoon they had returned. The man had changed out of his suit, and perhaps it was the more casual clothes, but he and Ava seemed easier together, in fact so comfortable he might have been a close relative. As it turned out, he was an old friend on a visit to Melbourne, or so Ava had said when they met Minnie in the street a short time later.

He stood erect and tall, taller than Minnie herself, a man who clearly looked after himself. His face was kind, with leisurely smile lines about the eyes. His jaw and neck were firm, and about him wafted a pleasant eau de cologne.

As they shook hands she had remarked how fortunate Ava was in her friends.

'Stephen was the first,' Ava said, smiling up at him.

Minnie asked how long he planned to stay in Melbourne.

'Just a short time.' His accent was English, his expression grim. This, Minnie decided, was no holiday visit.

That evening Ava had knocked on her door. She would prefer, she said, to keep her friend's visit private. 'I would prefer you not to mention him to anyone. Ever.'

The urgency of the request was unmistakable. Minnie quickly reassured her: she would tell no one.

'Who is he?' she had asked.

And Ava, who had talked freely about secret lovers and unsatisfactory parents, would say no more about the stranger than he was her oldest friend.

That evening was the last time Minnie saw Ava alone, but it was different for the Englishman. Minnie observed him with Ava several times during that last week, including the day she died. She saw how solicitous he was, taking her elbow as they crossed the street, putting his arm around her as they stopped to admire some flowers. And once in the park she glimpsed the two of them sitting on a seat holding hands.

Minnie had searched the crowds at the funeral but this man, the first among her friends, was not there. Nor was he at the pub afterwards. Jack was squirming with the idea of Ava's suicide, yet surely he was grateful she had been saved from what would have been a prolonged and obscene dying.

She turned towards Jack. His face was overlaid with anguish and without thinking she moved closer and put her arm about his shoulders. She felt immediately his sinking against her.

They both smelled the smoke at the same time.

'I think it's coming from Ava's place,' Jack said, standing up.

They ran down the garden path, turning briefly at the gate to look next door. Smoke was billowing into the sky from behind the house.

A terrible premonition of disaster struck Jack: poor Harry who wasn't managing, who hadn't been managing ever since Ava died. 'I can't imagine a future without her,' Harry had said over and over again.

Jack banged on the front door and when there was no answer he threw himself against it. The lock was solid. He and Minnie ran round to the lane. The courtyard gate was bolted. Smoke was thick in the air.

'Harry,' shouted Jack. 'Harry, are you there?'

He heaved against the gate, and just as Minnie was about to hoist herself over the fence, the gate opened and Harry stood before them. His feet were bare, his arms akimbo, he was clad only in filthy singlet and underpants, he reeked of sweat. The hairless skull, the face and neck, his arms and legs, all were streaked with ash; a lick of soot had extended one side of his moustache. His face was off balance, all of him was off balance.

He looked at Jack. 'Is it six-thirty already?' And glanced at his watch. 'I quite lost track of time.'

3.

There was someone else, but then there had always been someone else. Harry scrunches up the telephone bill and shoves it into his pocket. He slams down the lid of Ava's laptop and flees her study. She has poisoned everything; every one of their homes, every holiday they've taken, every special weekend, their picnic meals, their private jokes, their holding hands at the movies, all their rituals. She has poisoned their marriage. Even if it were possible he would not give her a chance to explain. The loving husband who tolerated the string of affairs, who stepped aside for publishers and journalists, who stood in line behind readers and besotted fans, who waited patiently for her to emerge from her latest novel, this loving husband would give her an opportunity to explain. But not Harry Guerin whom she has hurt so convincingly that every breath has become strange.

He strides into her bedroom to the smoothly made bed where he has spent so much time these past thirty-eight days, the bed where she did not kill herself – thinking of him, he believed, she killed herself outside the house. Thinking of him, what a laugh! His wife never thought of him. Perhaps it was this person, this unknown man who considered Harry's feelings when helping Ava decide where to die. And why is he so sure it was a man? Because except for Fleur it always was a man. And how does he know the man was with her? He just knows he was there, holding her hand and stroking her face, 'I'm here, I'm here,' uttered over and over in a voice not Harry's own.

The telephone bill is hard against his thigh, he rams it deeper into his pocket, and not realising what he is driven to do until he has already begun he grabs bottles and creams from her dressing table, ornaments from the chest, knick-knacks from the side table and hurls them at the bed. Perfumes scatter and rise in an unbearably sweet swill. He goes to the laundry, riffles the cupboards, returns with a full bottle of methylated spirits. He tips it in a tidy stream up and down the bed. Foul and pungent it swallows her scents but not the stench of her wrongdoing. He runs to the shed and returns with a small bag of blood and bone and a bottle of liquid plant food. The plant food stinks of rotten fish, he drips it over the bed, drip drip drip, he is as determined and delicate as a painter. He punctures the bag of blood and bone. The dry plastic bursts, the contents splatter his shoes, manure catches in the weave of his trousers; he swears as he tosses the useless bag on the bed. He removes his shoes and trousers and throws them on the stinking mess too.

She made him do this, she who always had someone else.

He walks to her clothes chest, steadies himself before opening the top drawer. A gust of her lily-of-the-valley perfume is quickly swallowed by the stench from the bed. He yanks on the drawer, carries it through the living room to the courtyard. He tips bras, knickers, socks and singlets onto the paving. He nudges the pile with his bare foot. This last man of hers, he knew these private clothes. And at the end did he lift her jumper, did he lay his trespassing hand on her breast? Did this stranger do what her husband did not, a man she never put first?

He returns to her bedroom for the second drawer. It lurches against the door-frame and grazes his hand. Out in the court-yard he tips jumpers to the ground, comes back inside for the third and fourth drawers. Then to her cupboard. He tears clothes from hangers and flings them onto the pile, makes several trips back and forth until the cupboard is empty. The paving has disappeared beneath his wife's clothes, all her pretty colours twisting in the dust.

Up the stairs to her study. And now he stares at the patch of floor, now he sees her lying there with someone else alongside, someone touching her, murmuring last words of comfort and love – her husband's words if she had given him the chance. He walks across the room, he takes three smallish steps from her head to her feet. He turns around. Three small steps from her feet to her head. He marches the length of her body. He tramples her from head to toe.

Next her papers. Letters, notes, cards, jottings, short stories, beginnings of novels, essay drafts, newspaper articles, all the personal papers destined for the Bryant archive at the State Library he hurls out her study window. The breeze has dropped and the papers fall tidily to the courtyard below. In bundle after bundle, his wife's paper life falls without sound onto the cushion of clothes. He grabs her laptop and yanks it free from its extensions. Why should he waste any more of his life on his wife's betrayals? He doesn't want to track this SW down; he just wants to destroy the bastard. He tucks the laptop under one arm and the manuscript of her final novel under the other – Ava's last betrayal along with her last novel, it's a tidy symmetry – and descends to the courtyard. He puts the computer to one side and walks over to the empty spa tub. He fans the pages of the novel and then lets go. The manuscript falls with a resounding slap. He stands on the rim looking down at his wife's last work, the familiar typescript riddled with the familiar handwriting.

Into the kitchen he goes for her special tapers from the Bloomsbury whisky shop. There are seventeen left and he intends to use the lot. Back outside he grabs the garden rake, scrapes aside some papers and rummages among her clothes until he finds two of her filmy shirts. He picks them up with the tines of the rake and shakes them into the tub. He selects some underwear and summery trousers in the same way. Carefully, he doesn't want to injure himself, he steps down to the bench inside the tub and reaches for a page of her last novel. He twists it into a candle and lights it. The paper flares and he touches it to other pages in the tub. The paper burns, the shirts curl and shrivel, he watches them disintegrate in the flames. To and from the tub he walks, adding clothes and paper in an easy rhythm, and when there is a thick bed of ashes he tosses in her computer. He adds more paper, he adds more clothes. The breeze strengthens, it lifts the smoke from the courtyard. Harry breathes easily, he feeds the flames. He burns all he has left of his wife.

'Is it six-thirty already?' And turning to Minnie, 'Are you join-ing us for dinner?' It was not an invitation. Minnie leaned in close to Jack as if to speak, then gave his hand a squeeze and left them alone.

Jack stared beyond Harry to the courtyard matted with paper and Ava's clothes. Flames reared in the hot tub.

'Have you gone quite mad?'

Harry shook his head. 'Not at all. Just tidying up. Moving on.'

There was no reading his face, not a flicker of emotion. Wary and watchful, Jack followed him into the house. Harry pointed to a bottle of wine on the sideboard. 'Help yourself while I clean up.'

When Harry reappeared he had returned to his old self, dressed in his usual dark trousers, pale blue shirt and lace-up brogues; the fringe of hair below the shining pate was wet and smooth; he had shaved. He poured himself a drink and sat in one of the armchairs. He was absolutely calm. But Jack knew this was a mood not to be trusted. He had traced the terrible smell to Ava's bedroom. Poor Harry had descended into a grief-fuelled vandalism.

The photographs of Ava were missing from the mantelpiece, all her ornaments were gone, even the Tiki he had sent her from New Zealand was no longer hanging on the wall. Harry had worked hard to clear his wife out. The poor man must be mad with grief.

'Did you know?' Harry's accusing voice entered the silence.

'Know what?'

'There was someone else.' Harry spoke in the same soft accusing voice. 'At the end there was someone else.'

Of all Harry might have said, Jack would never have anticipated this. He did not hesitate. 'There wasn't, Harry, there was no one else.' And then remembering, 'You don't mean Fleur? That visit she made months ago?'

Harry was dismissive: of course he didn't mean Fleur. 'No, this someone else was a man.' He looked hard at Jack. 'You really didn't know?'

Jack shook his head. And if there had been, he was sure Ava would have told him. 'You're upset Harry. It's been terrible for you, but there was no one else.'

Harry remained silent. It was immaterial now whether Jack knew. It was immaterial who this last man was; they could all choke on their secrets for all he cared.

'I finished the introduction to her first novel today,' Jack said, in an attempt to change the subject.

Harry snorted. 'You've wasted your time.'

There was no meal that night. Jack fought Harry, he fought him on every front. But Harry was intransigent: there would be no new editions, no seventh novel, no sifting though her unpublished writings for a posthumous collection of shorter pieces. There would be no profiles on Ava, no documentaries, and when the outstanding film options on her novels expired they would not be renewed.

Over the next several weeks Jack tried to change Harry's mind. He tried reason, he tried pleading, he absolutely refused to countenance that Ava had someone else at the end.

'You were the centre of her life, Harry. Others came and went, but the only love that lasted was for you.'

Harry would not be persuaded. 'Her future for my past. It's a fair deal.'

Jack sought Connie's help, but Connie accused him of over-reacting – 'Your habitual response, incidentally, when it concerns Ava,' he said. 'Harry's upset, he's grieving. He'll come to his senses.'

Connie hadn't seen Harry wild and filthy and burning up Ava's life. Jack ignored Connie's needling of him and begged him to speak to Harry. But Connie refused.

'I have to get my priorities straight,' he said to Jack about a month after the fire. As they talked, Connie was walking through his house gathering up clothes, books and other para-phernalia and dropping them into open cartons.

Connie was returning to America. Linda still insisted their marriage was over, but he had detected a softening in her atti-tude, or so he had told Jack. Jack was sceptical, but Connie hoped with a desire that surprised him that his marriage was salvageable. He had changed – nothing he wanted to discuss with Jack, he doubted that he could, it was a change that rendered him strange to himself. He had tried to attach it to the specific case of Sara. But while her theft of his TV show counted among the worst of betrayals he was not unhappy to see her go.

The woman he wanted was Linda. And even more surpris-ing, he wanted to be settled. He wanted to know he and Linda would be together next year and the year after and the year after that. And if he projected himself a decade ahead, as much as it shocked him, he still wanted to be with Linda. In truth he would also like to maintain the girlfriends, but he realised it was either Linda or the girlfriends. And even if both had been possible, there had been another disturbing change: his spirit was as willing as ever for the affairs, his body too, but a certain lightness of temperament was required to live as he had lived. Now his old temperament felt stretched and threadbare. It simply did not satisfy any more.

Two weeks ago he had written to Linda. He had written by hand, not just for the added pith of a proper letter, but emails were too easy to skim and delete. He acknowledged all she had put up with over the years. And he apologised. It was not just a generalised 'I'm sorry'; he apologised for his neglect, for his affairs, for demeaning her and their marriage, for taking advantage of her, for not being a more reliable and responsible father and a half a dozen more transgressions. He finished the letter with a statement of his love, *a declaration of my love* was how he expressed it. And when he returned home from the post office he booked his flight to the US – not because he was so confident Linda would take him back, but to allow for face-to-face persuasion should his letter fail. A few days ago she had sent a brief email acknowledging receipt of his letter. By return email he told her he was coming home. Last night he received another email: she was prepared to talk. He immediately arranged to see her at the end of the week.

He admitted none of this to Jack. He just wanted to go home – yes, home – to see Linda, talk with her, eat meals with her, sleep with her. And the boys, he wanted his boys too.

'I'm leaving, Jack. I'm sorry about how Harry is behaving. Remember, I loved Ava too. But I've my own future to think about.'

Jack glanced at the mess of half-filled boxes, the clothes, the books, the pots and pans littering the house and was about to offer to help, but pulled back: it was Connie's mess, all of it was Connie's mess.

Helen was even less helpful. She was either travelling the US from one high-powered meeting to another and assiduously not answering her cell phone, or working so hard she slept on a fold-up bed in the laboratory. This was an established habit of hers. 'All scientists do it,' she said. 'Experiments don't conform to circadian rhythms and you have to keep an eye on things.'

'She just can't bear the separation anxiety,' Luke said.

Helen dashed off a single line in response to Jack's many and detailed emails: *Don't have time to deal with this over email. I'll call you.* She didn't call and she didn't answer his calls. In the end Jack borrowed Luke's phone and on his first attempt

Helen answered. As soon as she ascertained that Luke was safe and well, she made short work of Jack's concerns.

'What Harry does as Ava's executor is not your business, it's not any of our business.' And when Jack reminded her she was talking about her oldest friend, she cut him off, 'Things change, Jack. Perhaps not for you, but for the rest of us things change. Yes, I was Ava's best friend, but Harry's her husband. Any decisions about her work are his.'

'Ava was not just a wife. She had a huge public presence – '

Helen interrupted. 'Harry will come to his senses. There's too much in it for him.' She promised to give the situation more thought and ring back in a few days.

Jack waited a week before calling her again. Helen made it quite clear she did not want to be involved. 'I've my own work, Jack. The sort of work that affects millions and millions of people. It's work I struggle with. It's serious work.' She paused, Jack thought he heard her sigh. 'It's only fiction, Jack,' she said. 'Ava's work is only fiction – none of it is true.'

Jack turned to Ava's publisher. 'Bryant was an attractive ready-made package,' Victor said. 'But our hands are tied without Harry's permission.'

Only Minnie shared his concerns.

'Don't you have a draft of her last unfinished novel?' she asked over dinner one evening.

Jack nodded.

'And you've read all her novels?'

'Several times, both in draft and published form.'

'Seems you're better placed than most to pull Ava's last novel into shape,' Minnie said. 'Perhaps in a few months time when Harry's calmed down, if he were confronted with the finished product he'd change his mind.'

Over the next six months Jack laboured over Ava's final work. He persevered out of loyalty to her and an ingrained sense of justice, for it was clear almost from the beginning he was not the man for the job. Finally he sought help from the English department of their old university only to be told that while there were plenty of scholars available, including a Bryant expert within the department, monographs simply couldn't be justified in today's academic climate.

'In the time it takes to write one book,' an Australian literature expert told him, 'you could have written a dozen papers and earned far more in the way of publishing credits.'

Jack pointed out this was not a monograph, rather a unique chance to study and edit the last work of a major novelist, and was told that editing was even more of a fool's enterprise than monographs.

He contacted the Literature Council but unless he was a publisher or the author of the work he could not apply for an editing grant. He was about to put the novel aside until he had sufficient funds to pay for the editing himself when Harry emailed requesting a meeting with him. They had not spoken since Jack's NOGA fellowship ended and with nothing left in common except Ava, at last Jack had reason to hope.

Harry named a fashionable Japanese restaurant more notable for its flare than its food, but with the possibility of Ava's work back on the agenda Jack was not about to argue. The restaurant was empty at six o'clock but gearing up for a busy Friday night. Jack settled at a table and was about to order a glass of wine when Harry arrived.

Harry appeared to have discarded most of what was previously Harry. He wore a black three-quarter-length coat with the sleeves turned back to reveal an exquisite, pale green satin lining. His shirt was white with hidden buttons and a small mandarin collar, the slacks were black and smooth, the shoes were slip-ons. The moustache had disappeared as had the clammy stippled skin. Chemical peel? Cosmetics? Plastic surgery? Jack supposed anything was possible given the radical turn of his transformation.

Jack stood up to greet him. 'You look great.'

'Never felt better.'

Harry chose the wine and as the waiter poured, Jack asked about NOGA. The Harry of old had liked nothing better than to talk about himself and in this he had not changed. He began with the fellowship program; not only had he rescued it, it was proving to be the rich repository of information and connections he had always foreseen. Among the current fellows were an economist, a coal and gas expert and a Sinologist. 'A solid, untemperamental lot,' Harry said.

NOGA had surpassed all his hopes. 'We're a think-tank, a lobby group, an information hub for research. We're linked into business and government agencies internationally. Where there's influence, you can be sure we're connected.' Harry looked so satisfied. 'Not too many major decisions happen in this country without our involvement.'

Harry had moved out of the house next door to Minnie months ago. 'I've bought an apartment. St Kilda Road. Twelfth floor. Magnificent views.'

Harry's new apartment sounded like the NOGA offices with its 'swathes of space', floor-to-ceiling glass and minimalist furnishings. Ava and Harry had always preferred bolt holes – cubby-houses for grown-ups was the way Ava described their serial rentals. And the houses they chose were always old; Ava said she and Harry liked to be surrounded by other people's history.

Ava had been dead less than a year, but time enough for her husband to reinvent himself. And the woman to complete the picture was exactly as Jack would have expected, if it had occurred to him there would be a woman. He and Harry were settling into their second glass when she joined them. Her name was Victoria. She was short and slender and like Harry she was dressed in slacks and a three-quarter-length black coat. Nothing about her bore any resemblance to Ava.

Harry and Victoria sat on one side of the table and Jack on the other. A waiter distributed menus and Harry suggested they leave the ordering to Victoria. Without consulting the menu she reeled off half a dozen dishes. With the meal organised she moved closer to Harry and put her hand on top of his. Jack watched with fascination as Harry twisted his hand so it was now palm to palm with hers, and then neatly flipped the hands over so his was on top.

At last Harry was ready for business.

'As you can see, Jack, I've moved on. But there remains the matter of the Bryant literary estate.'

'You mean Ava's work.'

Harry shrugged. 'Call it what you like. As her executor I'm inundated with inquiries and I simply don't have time to deal with them.' There was a movement alongside him and he added, 'Nor do I have the inclination. But if people want to use her work, or if there are to be films of the novels, or new editions – ' Jack sat forward. '*If*,' Harry continued, 'there are to be new Bryant projects, as literary executor I'll always need to have some involvement but I want it to be minimal.' He saw Jack was about to interrupt and held up his hand. 'I'll be reasonable about any proposals, but the less I have to do with her work the better.

'And here's where you come in, Jack. I need someone to handle the day-to-day requests and inquiries as well as monitor the various projects that receive the go-ahead. I need someone who will manage her affairs and keep them away from me.' He paused, there was a superior smile playing across his face. 'Now's your chance, Jack. You can have her at last.'

'You want me to do the work of an executor?'

Harry nodded. 'Of course you'll be paid and we can negotiate that. Just keep me informed – email will be fine. You'll have free rein except that I'll retain right of veto, and of course I'll remain the only signatory.'

He looked so satisfied. His new lady looked so satisfied. If it were not so important to gather as much information as possible Jack would have left immediately. Instead he sat through the entrée of sashimi – his stomach churning, the raw fish impossible – and picked his way through the main course.

'What about the royalties from her work?' Jack asked, once the food was cleared away.

'They'll continue to come to me as Ava wanted.'

Ava had wanted a lot more than that, Jack was thinking, including Harry's happiness – Harry and Victoria planned to marry in the new year – but not at the expense of her own memory. As for the royalties, of course Harry would want them. Ava's death had sparked new interest in her work. Most of the novels had gone into new printings under the terms of existing contracts. Harry had made a packet out of Ava's work in the time since she had died, and he stood to make a good deal more in the years to come.

Jack did not stay for coffee. He said he would consider Harry's proposal and contact him in a few days.

Friday-night revellers fill the streets. The lights of the restaurants flash and flicker. Jack hurries down to the tram stop, and then on a whim turns in the other direction towards the university district. A few blocks further on and the footpaths are crowded with students. How familiar they look with their shaggy hair and tight jeans. All these young people in a paradise that once belonged to him. Him, Connie, Ava and Helen.

Everything, it seems, comes full circle.

The day he met Ava the future opened up as an endless brilliance. They travelled together through the days and years; even when oceans separated them Jack would reach out convinced it was Ava he touched. He will never understand what happened to Harry who truly had Ava in reach. There wasn't someone else. Ava was sick, she was dying. An affair was no more likely than the break-up of her marriage.

He makes his way along the footpath, past outdoor tables packed with laughing drinking youths; so much noise and bustle that Harry's presence soon loosens and fades. He strolls into Readings bookstore. It is crowded here too, but there's the hush of books and people reading, and in the background a recording of a woman singing in a worn and weary alto. Jack walks the length of the shop to the philosophy section. He finds several copies of Connie's most recent book and two of his signature *God and the Webmaster*. Across in history and ideas there are two copies of his own *The Reinvention of Islam*, to be joined soon, he hopes, by his new book of essays. And last to fiction, and an entire shelf of Ava's novels, a shelf of Ava Bryant. The books and the author have merged – and not mere semantic convention. For when he reads her novels, he finds percolating through them her beliefs and ideas, her pleasures and peccadillos, her yearnings and losses – all, of course, couched in fiction. But then Ava always said there was no better vehicle for the truth.

He stands back to allow two young women access to the Ava Bryants.

'Start with her first novel,' the taller woman says, taking *Rock Father* from the shelf. 'It's one of my favourites.'

Her friend flips through. 'I wonder who these people are,' she says, pointing to the dedication to Jack, Helen and Conrad.

The Ava Bryant devotee doesn't know. 'But I envy them, whoever they are.'

Jack leaves the women with Ava's books and soon after he exits the bookshop. He walks to the corner where he turns and makes his way towards the university. The footpaths are less crowded here; students are strolling arm in arm, three and four across, heading down to the main action. They don't move aside for him, and twice he is forced to step off the pavement into the gutter.

He, Ava, Helen and Connie used to talk as if they would change the world. Perhaps all young people do. They felt bound by the wonder of having found one another, and the wonder of what was possible – not just singly but together. Not surprising that during the period they were reunited back in Melbourne the friendships had felt so strange.

Helen is changing the world but not in the way she planned. And if she has any moral qualms about her work, she is now keeping them to herself. Occasionally she mentions Möller, and Jack will hear in her voice the excitement and, yes, the wonder of working with him. She does, however, talk frequently about Ava. Jack will be eating his breakfast, or working, or preparing for bed and the phone will ring and it will be Helen in Boston or Washington or Atlanta or Dallas, Helen with a few minutes to spare and a sudden memory of Ava. And she will regale Jack with the trip to Sydney and her first taste of mango, or the breakfasts with the night workers after she and Ava had been studying all night, phone call after phone call filled with her rich store of exploits. As for those difficult months prior to Ava's death when Ava figured so low in her priorities, Helen appears to have buried them.

Helen will be in Melbourne within the month, a quick visit to see Luke. She says she wants a ceremony for Ava, what she calls 'a remembrance'. She doesn't yet know what form it will take but she promises to work out the details before she arrives. 'Just you, me and Luke – and the Ava we know.'

Jack finds the whole idea abhorrent and he is sure Ava would too, but where once he would have tried to persuade Helen to change her mind, he won't bother now. Friendship is no longer the complete and coherent package it once was; both more clear-sighted and more browned about the edges it requires far greater understanding than its youthful progenitor.

Come and visit me, Jack, Connie had written in a recent email.

Poor Connie, every moment's genius until the inevitable future seized him by the neck and began to squeeze.

I miss you, I miss us as a group. And: *When did our friendship become old times?*

Connie wrote of a gap where Ava used to be. *I'm aware of it even more than I was aware of her presence.* This was not lost opportunity, he insisted, but lost possibilities. Jack detected a flatness in these communications, a resignation, but Connie was adamant: he had made the right choice in returning to his family.

How different they all had been at the reunion. Jack can still feel the texture of that evening: the terror of seeing Ava mingled with his desire, her easy duet with Harry, the carefree conversation of his oldest friends, and a sense of being locked in a scene in which he had no role. Looking back on that night and all the nights preceding it, it was as if, for him, love and friendship were a one-way ticket not to the next stop, nor even the next suburb, but right to the end of the line.

He had always assumed he loved Ava best. Loved her better than did Connie or Helen, loved her better than Harry. But he had just loved her more exclusively.

He crosses the road and enters the grounds of the university, the place of their beginning. What now? he wonders. What now with Ava? After decades of wanting nothing other than to devote himself to her, the answer to Harry's proposal is no longer so clear. He has read about the strange neurological tricks of a damaged brain that cause people to know that one side of their body is paralysed but have no real sense of the existence of that side. It is how he feels about Ava. He knows she is dead but he cannot quite believe it. When the bewilderment overwhelms, he reaches for her fictions, but then he has always felt more at home in her work than he ever felt with her — until those last months when finally he shaped his love to something she truly wanted. He came to their friendship too late. But there are the books. The only life remaining.

He has no photographs of those last days. None of them do. Yet he pictures her easily: Ava perched on the verandah of her house, Ava stretched on the couch in all her lovely lushness, Ava in her courtyard, Ava strolling through the cemetery, Ava listening while he played his guitar. And Ava asking whether he could help a loved one end their life. Did he let her down? Jack has posed the question so many times and still he is not convinced that if she wanted to die (and, unlike Minnie, he will never be sure she did), she understood why he could not help her. Although he knows she valued his visits those last months, that they gave her life when the rest of life was wearing thin.

It is quiet here in the grounds of the university. The library is lit up and through the glass he sees the night students at work. There are people walking the paths, shadowy figures and solitary like him. The wind has freshened, life itself rushes into his face. He picks up his speed, he begins to run. He feels his heart racing, the knots fall away. He passes familiar buildings, he moves swiftly through this landscape of his past.

And now he leaves the campus, a lone man in his middle years streaming through the streets, back to the city centre, across the river and into St Kilda Road. He passes the Botanic Gardens where he spent so much time with Ava; he is skimming the asphalt, like skating or flying. He runs and runs, pulling away from the past. Finally he slows down, finally he stops. He waits at a tram stop outside a block of flats he has never before noticed, a tatty oddity amongst the glassy towers. His head is so clear he sees everything tonight.

The tram picks him up and carries him through the darkness to the terminus. He disembarks and walks the short distance home. The flat is still warm after a day of sunshine. He switches on lamps and shuts the blinds, then he collects Ava's novels and settles on the couch. He has no regrets. He rests one hand outstretched on her books, and the other curls in that vulnerable human hollow above the heart. Early friendships are cemented with the hardest glue, Ava used to say. But time has the hardest grip of all. Jack closes his eyes and sees himself as he once saw Ava, one hand grasped to the rail of a speeding train as it hurtles into the future.

Endnote

My partner, Dorothy Porter, died on 10 December 2008 after a brief illness. She was healthy all through the writing of *Reunion*, she was healthy when the novel went into production in late 2007. We looked forward to celebrating together the publication of *Reunion* in 2009.

Both Dorothy and I believe in the power of fiction to take one into the hearts and minds of characters who owe their existence to the author's imagination. *Reunion* is a work of fiction. None of the happenings in the novel are drawn from my own personal loss of late 2008.